# The Mundane and the Arcane

Danielle Cerrone

NINTH HOUSE
PUBLISHING

Second Edition, 2025

ISBN (Paperback): 979-8-9990615-0-8

ISBN (eBook): 979-8-9990615-1-5

ISBN (Hardcover): 979-8-9990615-2-2

Published by Ninth House Publishing

Printed in the United States of America

www.daniellecerrone.com

For those who have ever lived more fully in the pages of a book than in the world around them—may you live happily ever after.

# Contents

THE GREAT BEYOND

ANIMA SEA

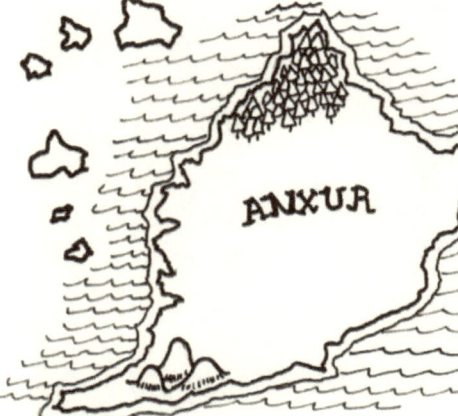

ANXUR

# Prologue

T HE SKY HAD BURNED crimson that morning—an ill omen. Every sailor knew that a red sky at dawn meant a storm was on its way.

Serafina stared at the open sea, pondering how a symbol of freedom for so many had become her prison. The ocean mocked her, its green the precise shade of the eyes she was desperate to outrun.

Jaw set, she nodded, her decision made. She shouted orders to her crew and disappeared into her quarters. The wooden chair groaned as she pulled it from the desk and sat down, thoughts racing. She laid fresh parchment in front of her.

Inspiration struck. A crooked grin broke across her face as she laughed, wild and unrestrained. She unscrewed the ink pot, quill ready in her hand.

The irony of her situation wasn't lost on her. The storm had arrived, yet they were still two days from land, where she would be executed anyway. At least she would die at sea as a free woman.

Her hand flew across the page, writing feverishly with furious purpose. Her laughter dissolved into a sob, salt tears streaking down her sun-worn face. She didn't cry out of fear or regret. It was the poetry of it that undid her.

She let the ink dry, then rolled the parchment and slid it into a dark glass bottle. From her pocket came a small, shimmering purple stone. She pressed it to her lips, whispered a quiet plea, and dropped it in. With the wax sealed and the bottle tucked safely in her coat, she stepped back onto the deck.

Waves hammered the ship as lightning split the black sky. The crew fought to run before the wind, but the stern took relentless, punishing blows from the sea.

"Tie yourselves down!" Serafina shouted.

Overhead, Jupiter's star blinked through the clouds. Pulling the bottle from her coat, she kissed it and hurled it toward Jupiter's light. She prayed to the Ancient Gods that the current would carry it to shore.

Mid-prayer, she laughed again. Of course the message would find its way. It already had; fate had written it so. She marveled at the order of the heavens and their exquisite cruelty.

A towering wave tilted the ship violently. Lightning flashed just in time for her to see the oars from the longboat hurtling through the air toward her. But before they could strike, a colossal wave embraced the ship with a swift and strangely tender finality.

# Chapter One

R EMO RENATO TRUDGED HIS way up a steep, mountainous hill to his family's small farmhouse, a bone-deep weariness emanating from him that had nothing to do with his hike.

Glass bottles clinked together within his leather work bag as he hoisted himself atop the stone wall surrounding the farm, his preferred place to brood. The vantage point afforded him a bird's-eye view of his village and the distant islands scattered across the Anima Sea.

He rubbed his weary grey eyes, wondering how he'd survived another lesson in the healing arts on so little sleep. He supposed there was humor in brewing tea for insomnia while half-asleep, but he was too tired to find it.

Remo loved his work as a healer, yet his passion for the craft had dimmed in recent months. His fatigue wasn't from overexertion but a creeping dissatisfaction, a quiet question that echoed through his mind: *Is this all there is?*

At nineteen, Remo told himself he should've outgrown the fairy tales he still devoured, perhaps to make up for how lackluster his life felt. He was haunted by the feeling that his soul longed for something completely unattainable, that home would always feel elsewhere, tucked within the pages of his fantasy books.

He watched merchant ships drifting in and out of the port below, indifferent. It was a shame, Remo thought, that he didn't have loftier material ambitions. However out of reach ostentatious wealth may have seemed compared to his humble upbringing, he knew nothing material was ever impossible to obtain. But how could you attain something that didn't exist?

Remo stretched himself taut and then relaxed, breathing in the sweet dusk air heavy with the scent of lilacs. Twilight was his favorite time of day. The light of the gloaming hour made it easier to believe in impossible things.

Stories told that the veil between worlds was thinnest at this time, and when Remo was fully present in nature, listening and not thinking, he fancied that he could get a fleeting glimpse of something faintly magical: Movement spotted from the corner of his eye, or a trick of the light could send his imagination wild. But the feeling always slipped away from him, as surely as books always had endings.

As the periwinkle sky's gradient darkened along with his thoughts, Remo gathered himself from his pensive state and entered his family's home. He had barely set a foot over the kitchen's terracotta tiles before his mother called for help to reach a bottle atop a high shelf.

Remo obliged; his height was the only part of his appearance he liked, if only for how useful it was to others. He handed her the bottle with a greeting and sat for dinner: two thick slices of bread slathered in butter, a wedge of hard cheese, and a handful of olives.

"How was your day?" his mother asked as she poured the bottle's contents into a bubbling broth and stirred.

"Alright. Same as every day," he said around a mouthful of bread.

He couldn't muster his usual effort to put up a cheerful pretense. His discontent was visible, though unspoken. No one would understand it anyway. He stifled a mirthless laugh, imagining what his father would've said if he'd voiced his depression. Most likely, he would've made Remo's internal pain external.

"How are things around here?" Remo asked.

She clucked her tongue. "Your brother was in the caves again. Slipped, nearly broke his neck. Now he's limping. Too proud to admit he's hurt. That boy gives me no rest. At least *he's* sleeping now."

"I'll check on him tomorrow."

"I worry enough for his own sake, but if he gets injured and can't pull his weight around here..." his mother trailed off. She didn't need to finish. Remo heard the implication clearly.

Remo remembered how hard his mother had worked to maintain their farm after his father had passed. She depended heavily upon her eldest son to share her burden. When Remo's younger brother Aemilian became old enough to shoulder some of the more physically demanding tasks, it freed Remo to begin the four years of required, intensive training to become a healer. He was grateful Aemilian embraced the responsibility because Remo wasn't certain he could bear to spend the rest of his life toiling on the property that held a bad memory in every corner.

The pieces of his mother's broken heart never fit back together again after being shattered by his father's death. Whichever half—or quarter—had belonged to her children had become too chipped, too fractured to restore. He knew, more than felt, that she must care for her children the best she was able, though they never received much in the way of affection from her to confirm this notion. She had certainly never stepped in to soften the blows their father dealt.

Remo's eyes glossed over as he recalled the most distinct memory he had of his father, a gruff, no-nonsense man with a quick temper. One afternoon, Remo had forgotten to do one of his chores and sat reading a novel when his father spotted him, tore the book from his son's hands, and beat him with it. Remo had no clue what he'd done to invoke his father's wrath until he growled, *"You sit there with your nose buried in silly books as usual while there's a man's work to be done around here."*

After completing his forgotten chore, Remo hid in his room and clutched his bloodstained book, muffling his sobs. His father would only hit him more if he heard him sniveling. Remo made the mistake of crying in front of his father once before, whose reaction was to slap the instinct out of him. His father's severity only pushed him further into his beloved fantasy worlds.

His mother's voice pulled him back to the present as she poured hot broth into the clay bowl in front of him. "Your hair's getting too long, Remo. People will think you're a girl."

He forced a wry smile, hoping it hid the resentment he felt as he ran a hand through his shoulder-length dark brown hair. "I like it this way. Honestly, I'd probably pass for a decent woman. Certainly better than I pass for a man, with this excuse for a beard."

Her scandalized look was softened by laughter. He'd mastered the art of hiding behind humor, keeping things light so no one saw how deeply he felt. He downed the broth and excused himself.

In his room, Remo sat at his desk, where his pharmacopeia lay open. Dipping a quill into blue ink, he recorded the properties of the plant he'd studied earlier. Then his gaze moved to the wide window ledge, large enough to sit with a book. Moonbeams touched the smooth surface, beckoning him.

Giving in despite his tiredness, he grabbed the book he'd been rereading, *Tales of Alden the Scarred Sorcerer*. Returning to his favorite books gave him a nostalgia for people and places that never were.

He had never been in love but imagined that pining for an uninterested lover could not be half as miserable as pining for a world you could never inhabit, a person that never lived.

With a sigh, he closed his book and settled into bed, willing his dreams to take him where he belonged—not as a bystander in Alden's story, but as the one defeating the evil wizard himself.

At Trota's cottage the next afternoon, Remo prepared an astragalus root tincture for a patient suffering from fatigue.

Part of what drew him to the healing arts were the tools of his trade; the oddly shaped glass flasks, siphons, small amber bottles, and distillation apparatus. He relished the methodical process of mixing tinctures and elixirs, which lined the shelves in the back room where they were prepared. While he was in the flow of such tasks, he secretly liked to pretend he was preparing a magical potion instead of medicine.

Earlier, he had weighed the powdered astragalus root and added his mixture of alcohol and water to get it to the correct texture. Then, he packed the material into a glass on a lab stand, placing a cloth on top and pouring his solvent into it.

Now, it was a matter of waiting. He would wait around a day for the tincture to percolate, a short amount of time compared to the elixirs that would sometimes macerate for up to three moon cycles.

As he tidied his workstation, Remo considered that much of his life was spent waiting. Waiting for change. Waiting for something interesting. He wondered, without much hope, whether his own transformation was quietly percolating just out of sight.

Trota entered the room, her grey and white hair swept into a neat bun. Though in her sixties, she radiated vitality and was revered across Anxur. Elsewhere in the continent of Terramundi, Trota's accomplishments might've been dismissed despite her formal medical education (a rarity for women), but in Anxur, she was a renowned physician and midwife.

"Excellent job with those stitches earlier. Poor lad, it was only his first day on the job," Trota said ruefully. Remo had sewn up an apprentice stonemason's hand who was unlikely to continue training until his wound healed.

"Thanks," Remo said with a modest smile.

"Come, have some tea."

He followed her into the sun-strewn room with dried herbs hanging from the ceiling's wooden beams. She poured burnt orange tea into two chipped cups—turmeric, he guessed. Not his favorite, but he drank out of politeness.

Offering him a tray of almond biscuits, she fixed him with a knowing look. "Now, tell me what's troubling you. And don't insult my powers of observation by pretending everything's fine. You look like you haven't been sleeping well."

He hesitated. Lying to her was impossible. Her piercing blue eyes surveyed him too closely for his comfort, and her analytic gaze honed by her profession would see through his act immediately.

"I've just been feeling... down," he admitted. Her silence urged him to continue. "I feel as though there must be more to life than this. Not *this,*" he said quickly, waving his hands to indicate the room at large. "What I mean is..."

Trota remained silent, waiting for him to continue. Her silence encouraged his honesty, and the rest spilled out. He confessed how he'd been feeling, embarrassed but relieved to speak it aloud.

"There's no real potions, only medicines. No princesses need saving;

only patients need seeing. There's no dragons or unicorns, only goats and chickens. I know I sound ridiculous; I have a good life, and my basic needs are met. I should be happy," he concluded guiltily.

While he braced for judgment, Trota remained impassive. He expected her to scoff, to tell him to grow up. But she only smiled.

"There's no shame in what you feel," she said gently. "You're young. You crave adventure and stories of your own. I think you should leave Anxur—see the world. Live a little before you declare it uninteresting."

He had often wished to visit the islands that surrounded Anxur and more distant lands. But his longing to travel to unknown lands was also mingled with a fear he didn't understand, and in recent months, this longing was eclipsed by his desire to live in a fantasy world instead.

There was no more magic on the nearby islands than there was in Anxur. But perhaps the change in scenery would do him some good—*just like this disgusting tea*, he thought to himself.

"Perhaps I should take my talents on the road," he said, only half-joking. "Does the world need a mediocre traveling healer?"

"You'll do fine," she said, lips twitching into a smile. "And if you return, there'll be a place for you here. But I'll manage well enough without you. I think traveling would lift your spirits."

Remo was surprised by her support and slightly stung by how easily she could do without him.

She studied him carefully as if deciding whether to tell him something. "Sleep on the idea. In the meantime, I'll brew you something stronger to help you get a good night's rest. We still have purple lotus leaves left over from yesterday's patient. I need to add a few more ingredients to it, though, so it won't be ready until the Moon's day." It was currently Saturn's day, and he did not work on the Sun's day.

Remo thanked her for the present tea, future tea, and advice. As he returned to his work, his thoughts wandered not just toward his usual daydreams, but toward real places he might go and things he might do.

When he returned home, he looked over Aemilian's ankle, which would heal without issue. By the next day, the swelling had gone down, and Aemilian, ever restless, was ready to head back into the caves. Their mother objected, but relented when Aemilian insisted Remo would accompany him. She did have one request; they were to buy a new candlestick at the market on their return.

The village square was bustling with activity. Booths lined either side of the cobbled street, merchants calling out their wares. The scent of fish from the mongers' stalls mixed with the din of voices and clinking coins.

As they walked, Aemilian chattered about a stone he'd found in the caves. "Might fetch a good price," he said. "The fair's coming next week. I want new hides for a sling."

Remo smiled at his brother's excitement. Aemilian had always been light-hearted and adventurous, content with small pleasures. Remo often envied that simplicity.

Since their father's death, Remo had been more than a brother; he was a protector. Even as a child, he had stood between Aemilian and their father's rage, shielding him as best he could. And now, he tried to give him the care he never received. Aemilian in turn brightened some of Remo's darkest days with his carefree attitude.

As Remo watched his brother gaze after a ship sailing out of the port, his short hair whipping in the breeze, he was struck by how little had changed. Aemilian's fascination with the sea was the same as it had been when they were boys playing pirates in the fields. Remo had always let his little brother be the fearless sea commander, victorious every time.

"Remo!"

He whirled around to find Ninfa, a girl his age with whom he was on more than friendly terms. They agreed to keep their relationship purely physical. When Remo suspected that she began to want more from him, he guiltily put an end to that aspect of their friendship. She took it well, but Remo had the sense she thought it was just a temporary pause, that he would change his mind. He knew he wouldn't.

"Hi, Remo. Hi, Aemilian," Ninfa said. "Are you both heading down to the caves?"

"Yes, would you like to join us?" Remo asked.

"I'm sorry, I can't," Ninfa answered, and she indeed looked sorry to miss out. "Maybe I'll see you sometime next week? There's a fair that's arriving then," she said, expectant.

"Aemilian was just telling me about it. I'm sure we'll see each other there."

Ninfa looked crestfallen. "Right... Sure. I'd better get going. See you." She hurried away before Remo could say goodbye.

Frowning, he turned to his brother. "Did she seem upset to you?"

Aemilian looked at his elder brother with something akin to pity. "She was hoping you'd invite her to go to the fair *with* you."

Remo blinked. "What?"

"For a clever boy, you're a fool," Aemilian chuckled, shaking his head at his brother's folly. "What she sees in you, though, I have no idea. Maybe it's the brooding air? You wear it like a poet's cloak."

Remo snorted at his brother's teasing, but his laughter died in his throat at the thought of accidentally hurting Ninfa. He thought briefly of his tentative plans to leave Anxur and how typical of him it would be to leave town purely to avoid an uncomfortable situation.

Sunlight streamed through the cave, causing the water to glow a luminescent blue. Remo stripped his clothing, tucking his money pouch safely beneath the discarded bundle. He and Aemilian inched into the water, getting used to the temperature before plunging themselves wholly into its depths.

Remo dove underneath the surface, searching for some object that may have been washed in from the last high tide. He kicked hard off the side of the cave, propelling himself downward toward the bottom of the pool. Being underwater was oddly peaceful; he'd always felt an innate respect for the sea.

"Find anything?" Aemilian asked half an hour later, perched on the lip of the cave's pool.

"No," Remo conceded as he pressed against his eyes, squeezing the salt water out of them. Neither had much luck, finding only some petrified wood, sea glass, and a rusted iron key.

Aemilian was ready to return home, unsatisfied with his haul. Normally, Remo was the one ready to leave first from their pilfering sessions, but he found himself bobbing in the water, reluctant to leave. The shimmering sea splashed against his chest as if coaxing him to take one last dive before returning home. Remo lingered, drawn by a sense that something remained hidden.

He dove under the water for a final time, heading for a section of the cave he hadn't yet searched. With a hard kick off the cave wall, he descended to the bottom of the pool, spotting a vague form through his blurry vision: A glass bottle sealed with wax. Grasping it, he forced the air out of his lungs and propelled to the surface. His heart leaped as he inspected the dark brown bottle and saw a scroll of paper within.

"Aemilian, I've found something!" he exclaimed, swimming to the edge and pulling himself over it.

"What is it?" his brother asked eagerly, pulling his clothes back on. Aemilian's eyes lit up as Remo handed him the bottle and something rattled inside it.

"Let's open it at home," Remo said. "After we get mother's candle." He wanted to hold onto the feeling of anticipation for as long as possible.

Aemilian groaned but agreed. Remo suspected his brother held back out of respect for their unspoken pilfering rule of finder's rights.

The market was eerily silent as they approached the candlemaker's stall. People whispered to one another, the source of their unease unclear until Remo spotted a man in full knight's gear. The townsfolk gave him a wide berth. Remo recognized the crest emblazoned on his gold armor. He was a Knight of Saffiro, one of the imperial guards of the Sun Kingdom.

Knights of Saffiro were dispersed throughout the Saffiran Empire, enforcing the emperor's will and laws across the land—but Anxur wasn't part of the empire.

The continent of Terramundi consisted of seven kingdoms, each connected to an ancient god and planet once said to rule over them. Hundreds of years ago, the six mainland kingdoms fell to the burgeoning Saffiran Empire, which dominated them ever since. Only the island of Anxur, Kingdom of Jupiter, remained unconquered.

Remo handed the candlemaker denarii and ushered his brother out of the marketplace. Aemilian continued to ogle the knight, strutting about the market in his full suit of armor, sending a tangible ripple of fear through the crowd by his presence alone.

Aemilian wondered aloud what the knight might've been there for, but his attention soon drifted back to their treasure as he began musing instead about what the message might say. His best guess was that it was a distress message from a sinking ship, though he hoped it might be a treasure map leading to a hoard of gold somewhere. Remo was silent, venturing no guesses of his own. Eager as he was to open his newfound loot, he also felt an inexplicable sense of reverence for the object.

Once home, Aemilian could hardly contain himself. Remo felt he'd rather have read the message in privacy. The notion struck him as odd, considering the contents wouldn't be personal to him. Knowing it was futile to delay it any longer, Remo perched on the wall and pried open the wax seal and cork.

Gently, he pulled out the piece of brittle parchment, careful not to tear it. A purple crystal poured out, the stone etched with a strange glyph like the number four.

Finally, with the utmost care, Remo unrolled the parchment and read written in tiny, hasty penmanship:

*You have done this many times*
*You've mastered these lessons*
*You've served for your crimes*
*But at the opposite, you'll always fail*
*If you chase the dragon's tail*

*The opposite does not come easily to you*
*You may even fear it*
*It is completely new*
*Now you're where you've never tread*
*If you chase the dragon's head*

*The dragon's head*
*The dragon's tail*
*Chase the former in this life*
*And lest you fail*
*You must not in the next*
*May you prevail on the eternal quest*

# Chapter Two

THE BROTHERS SPENT HOURS trying to decipher the message's cryptic meaning, ultimately concluding, rather unsatisfyingly, that its only purpose might have been to confuse whoever found it, in which case, it had succeeded.

Aemilian quickly dismissed it as nonsense. He was more captivated by the amethyst that accompanied it, though he refused to keep the stone when Remo offered.

Remo, on the other hand, was convinced the poem held meaning. It stirred something in him, equal parts excitement and unease. An intensely curious person, he was determined to uncover the message's deeper purpose.

After finishing his work at Trota's cottage on the Moon's day, Remo decided to seek her counsel. He shared the story of the bottle's discovery and handed her the parchment and the amethyst. Trota read it several times, a knowing smile teasing the edge of her mouth.

"My, my," she murmured, sinking into her chair. "You couldn't ask for a clearer sign that destiny is calling you."

He raised an eyebrow. "You know what it means?"

"Oh, I do. I know quite a few things you don't," she replied mysteriously. "I think the time has come to reveal something to you. Sit down."

He frowned but complied, suspecting she was planning some elaborate joke.

"Well, you see, Remo," she continued, her manner businesslike. "I'm a physician. I'm an herbalist. I'm a midwife. But first and foremost, I am an astrologer."

His frown deepened. Now he was certain she was having a joke at his expense. "Please be serious, Trota."

"I'm as serious as a Satrian," she replied, her stoic delivery drawing a reluctant laugh from him.

Not only was astrology ancient, unscientific hogwash, but it was also illegal. If Trota was surprised or disappointed by his laughter, she didn't show it, which made him laugh more.

"If you're quite done," she said calmly, "I'll explain—assuming you're still interested in solving the riddle."

"You're just joking, aren't you? I mean, you're an educated woman. The most brilliant person in Anxur! You can't believe in astrology," he said, wondering just how far she would take this prank.

"Thank you for that appraisal, Remo. Now, since you seem to equate intelligence with education, let me remind you, I've had far more of it than you. And I've seen far more of the world."

Remo's face heated in his shame. "I'm sorry. I didn't—I would like to understand."

Trota's expression softened. "I know. But you must learn not to dismiss what you don't understand. And to answer your concern, I don't just believe astrology works. I know it works. I studied it under Professor Cosimo, one of the greatest astrologers of our age."

He gaped at her. "But astrology is illegal."

"Is it?" she asked dryly, her brows raised in mock surprise. "Tell me, Remo, if it's nonsense, why outlaw it? What threat could it possibly pose?"

"Well, lots of ridiculous laws exist. Like the old rule against commoners wearing purple."

"Which had a purpose," she countered. "Purple dye was rare and costly. It marked nobility and controlled who could visibly wield power. The ban on astrology does something similar. It keeps knowledge from the people. Keeps power in the hands of the few."

She paused, then added, "Do you know the real story of King Septimus and the Banishment?"

"The king's astrologer betrayed him," Remo said. "She helped his enemies and was exiled. That's why astrology was outlawed."

"That's the official version," Trota said. "Now let me tell you the truth."

She launched into the tale: King Septimus of Saffiro, a cold and calculating ruler, had appointed Serafina, a brilliant astrologer and former Vestal Virgin, as his court advisor. Serafina's knowledge of celestial patterns helped him time laws, treaties—even executions.

But Septimus abused her gifts. Without her knowledge, he used her predictions to eliminate rivals. When he demanded she select the ideal date to invade the Satrian kingdom, she refused, realizing at last the full measure of his cruelty.

He exiled her, perhaps as a final gesture of lingering affection. But Serafina warned Satria of the coming war. Though Satria prepared, it was not enough. The Corvi royal family was presumably killed; no trace of them was ever found. Satria fell, thus becoming the kingless kingdom.

Septimus, now fashioning himself as emperor, conquered each of the other kingdoms soon after, aside from Anxur. Most of the kingdoms bent the knee to Septimus out of fear, seeking to protect their people from bloodshed, while others put up a fight and lost. Serafina was chased at sea by Septimus' men, this time on orders to have her killed.

Soon after the Calamity of Satria, Saffiro pursued Anxur. Septimus was overconfident, and his armies were exhausted. After many casualties on both sides, a negotiation was made: Saffiro would retreat and Anxur was to banish astrology. If Serafina sought refuge in the kingdom, she'd be sent back to Saffiro for execution.

He outlawed astrology elsewhere to prevent anyone from using it against him. He turned public opinion against it, branding astrologers as charlatans. Serafina, cast out from every shore, lived her final days at sea. She founded a secret school with her teacher before she died, preserving the knowledge they'd fought to protect.

Remo sat in stunned silence. "But how do *you* know all this? If it's true, why isn't it widely known?"

"Because history is written by those in power," she said simply. "But this version was preserved, passed down by Serafina's teacher and the astrologers who came after."

It was a lot to take in. Remo ran a hand through his hair. "So... What does any of this have to do with me?"

Trota's eyes gleamed. "Everything. Far more than I expected, especially after reading that message."

He stared. "What do you mean?"

"You have indicators in your natal chart, signs that you're a natural astrologer. And now, this message appears, full of astrological symbolism..."

Remo sighed, frustrated with her riddling talk. "Trota, please. What does the message mean?"

She studied him, then smiled gently. "I've given you enough to digest for one night. Tomorrow, I'll answer your questions."

He understood he was being dismissed. Curiosity burned in his chest, but he didn't want to push. He bid her goodnight and made his way home, mind spinning with thoughts he couldn't organize, wondering ceaselessly why the story she told should matter to him.

Back in his bedroom, he was absorbed in his thoughts, hardly noticing the hoot of a nearby owl or the spider on his window. As intrigued as he was by all that Trota had told him, he felt apprehensive about her insistence on astrology's validity and her belief in its significance to him personally.

He glanced at the worn stack of books on his desk and gave a soft, wry smile. *At least*, he thought, *I've finally found a story I haven't read a hundred times before.*

# Chapter Three

A PINK AND BLUE dawn lightened the sky as Remo hurried through a breakfast of blueberry bread and tea too hot to drink, though he swallowed it anyway, more scald than flavor. His only concern was reaching Trota's cottage as quickly as possible.

The sun had barely crested the horizon when he arrived nearly half an hour early. Trota sighed as she opened the door, looking not the least bit surprised to see him.

He stepped inside and hung his cloak. "I was hoping we could continue our conversation now," he said, making no attempt to disguise his eagerness.

"As I thought you might," she said with mild amusement, gesturing for him to sit in the same spot as the night before. "Where were we? What would you like to know first?"

"How did you come to know the story you told me about King Septimus and Serafina?"

Trota nodded in approval of his question. "I was told it by my teacher, Cosimo, who learned it from his teacher, and so on. After astrology was banned, naturally, a school formed. As I said, Serafina and her teacher established the Academy of the Arcane Arts before her untimely death. It's an underground school where the study of astrology continues in secret. That's where I trained. Cosimo is now the headmaster."

Remo shifted in his seat. "What exactly is astrology? Why would people risk breaking the law for it?"

Trota studied him for a moment, as if weighing his readiness. "Astrology is the study of planetary motions and their effect on us. Through recorded cycles, we recognize patterns that reflect both the world around us and our inner lives. *As above, so below. As within, so without.* We are not separate from the universe; we are part of it. The idea that humans are somehow exempt from that interconnection is a fantasy of its own.

"And while astrology may lack scientific validation by current standards, that doesn't mean it's without truth. Correlations between planetary movements and human behavior are undeniable to those who've studied them deeply."

Remo listened, uncertain but intrigued. Trota, sensing his struggle, stood. "I don't expect you to believe just because I've explained it. You need evidence. Give me a moment."

As she disappeared into the back room, he thought he heard her mutter, *"Damn Geminis."* He blinked. That wasn't even his sign. He was born in Pisces season.

Trota returned with a yellowed parchment, a circular chart inscribed with arcane symbols. "This is your natal chart. One of the perks of being a midwife—I knew your exact birth time."

He leaned in. "Do you draw one for everyone?"

"I try. A natal chart shows an individual's temperament, strengths, challenges. The planets' positions influence different areas of life, reflected in the twelve houses. For example, with the woman we treated for insomnia, Mars is currently transiting her twelfth house of sleep."

"You can use astrology to diagnose illness?"

"Certainly. To diagnose, treat, and even choose ideal surgery dates. Once upon a time, physicians *had* to study astrology."

Remo was stunned. "What can you tell me about my chart?"

"I could tell you a lot. But since we know each other so well, you'd probably think I was just echoing what I already know. No, I think you should meet with a stranger. Let Professor Cosimo read for you."

His frustration mounted. After all the buildup, she'd only give him fragments? His disappointment must have been palpable because Trota then made a concession.

"Very well. I'll tell you this much: Your moon is in Sagittarius, ruled by Jupiter. The moon represents our emotions and what we need to feel secure. This means you crave adventure, freedom, new ideas, and far-off places. Your sun sign, Pisces, reflects your imaginative, intuitive, compassionate self. Fantasy books let you escape and explore. That's the influence of your sun and moon combined. As for your current transits, well, there's certain powerful forces at play."

The insight rang strangely true. He wanted more—*needed* it—but her expression stilled him.

"Have you thought more about traveling?" she asked. "Given your chart, I hope you do. If you go, visit Cosimo. I can't write a letter; it's too dangerous. But if you find him, he'll help you. Perhaps he'll even explain that poem you found. Bring the crystal, too."

He'd nearly forgotten the poem. "It really does have to do with astrology?"

"Oh, yes—and the amethyst bears Jupiter's glyph. But where's the fun in me just handing you the answer? You must *earn* it."

That familiar twinge of annoyance surfaced. "What forces are you talking about, then?"

She smiled brightly. "Why, fate itself, my dear boy!"

Twenty minutes ago, he would've rolled his eyes. Now, he wasn't so sure.

"But what if I'm caught talking about astrology?" he asked. "I could be arrested, or worse. I could endanger Cosimo and the school."

Trota's smile faded. "Yes. And yet, here we are, speaking openly. I've done so for years. I won't push you, Remo. If you choose not to go, then choose something else. Just *choose*. Find something that makes you want to get out of bed."

Remo nodded. And he realized, for the first time in a long while, he *had* leapt from bed this morning. He wondered if that was all the justification he needed to pursue this path.

After the last patient left, Remo cleaned the cottage while Trota stood at the window, eyes narrowed toward the square below.

Two Knights of Saffiro, clad in their golden armor, moved silently through the streets. She frowned.

"What are they doing here?" Remo asked, joining her.

"Nothing innocent," she murmured. "A solar eclipse just passed. And already the winds are shifting. Eclipses bring transformation. As within, so without." She turned and pressed an amber container into his hand. "Time for home. Drink the tea. And don't forget: if you *don't* want me burned at the stake, keep our conversations secret."

Remo chuckled. "You have my word. Besides, who knows what other witchcraft you're hiding?"

She folded her arms, grinning. "How very wise of you."

That night, Remo knew sleep would be elusive.

His father's fists had taught him to fear authority, and the empire ruled with the same brutal hand. Those who challenged the empire's rule or broke the law were imprisoned without trial or killed. Could he really risk everything for something he barely believed in?

He sat by the dying embers of the kitchen hearth, carefully pouring still-hot water from a pot hanging within it into a clay cup filled with purple lotus tea leaves. With each sip of the floral, slightly nutty brew, he doubted there was a tea in Terramundi strong enough to still his rampant mind.

By the time he took his final, ineffective gulp, he knew sleep would not come and pulled on his cloak, took a lantern, and stepped out into the indigo night.

He exited the front garden with no plan. His feet moved of their own accord as he breathed in the balmy night air and marched along the grassy clifftop path that led to the ancient temple dedicated to Jupiter, one of the Ancient Gods long since forgotten by most in Terramundi.

He had been to the ancient ruin on top of the hill a handful of times, drawn to the extraordinary sensation he felt there, though afraid that if he visited it too often, he'd find the sensation finite, lost to him forever.

The old structure loomed, roofless and vine-covered, moonlight pouring through it like water. As expected, he was alone in the ruin, walking through the time-worn archway. The crumbling structure was one large chamber, overtaken by nature as moss grew thick across the stone walls. He approached the enormous wisteria tree at its center.

As he sat beneath its drooping blossoms, something small and uncomfortable poked at his side. He dug his hand into his pocket to search for the culprit, finding the amethyst crystal. The stone was warm against his palm; his eyelids grew heavy, and then everything stilled.

Though his eyes were closed, Remo could *see*. His body slept beneath the tree, but his mind drifted freely. A being stepped into view, robed in gold and violet, crowned with a star-shaped amethyst. Though aged, his bearing was regal. He radiated calm and joy.

By all accounts, the being looked like a human man, though Remo instinctively knew it was not. The stranger glowed with soft violet light.

"Who are you?" Remo asked.

The being smiled. "You visit my temple, and yet you do not recognize me?"

Remo hesitated. "You look human. Aren't you a god?"

"Yes and no," the figure replied. "I am what humans made me—Jupiter. I take this form for your sake. My true form would turn your hair as white as mine." He laughed, the sound shaking the stones.

"Is this fate?" Remo asked. "Am I meant to go?"

Jupiter studied him. "Fate doesn't exist as you believe it. What you call fate is often the echo of choices made long ago. Free will shapes it. So long as one can master themselves, fate is never fixed."

Remo felt the words settle into his soul like seeds in soil. But the more he tried to grasp the meaning, the more it slipped away.

The dream faded. He awoke beneath the tree, the stars bright above. The temple was silent, unchanged, and yet, he wasn't the same.

By the time he reached home, the first light of dawn touched the sky. He didn't know if what he'd seen was a dream, a vision, or the effect of Trota's tea. But he knew one thing for certain—tomorrow, he would begin planning his journey.

# Chapter Four

A WELL-WORN MAP OF Terramundi crinkled under Trota's hands as she spread it across the table.

She had been pleasantly surprised by Remo's sudden determination to travel to Mavortis in search of answers. Remo hadn't mentioned his vision at the temple, still uncertain what to make of it himself.

"From Anxur, you'll travel to Juno by boat"—she traced her finger across the blue sea to a small, crescent-shaped island between Anxur and the mainland—"then wait for a ship to Lunaria. From there, you'll walk through the Forest of Numa to Mavortis' gates. Avoid Knights of Saffiro at all costs, stay alert, and join other travelers if possible. It's safer in numbers."

Remo stared at the map. He felt a prickle of fear, mingled with the thrill of knowing he was finally stepping into an adventure outside the pages of his books. "Understood. But how will I find Cosimo? A secret school doesn't exactly advertise itself."

"Be sure to address him as *Professor* Cosimo. Once in Mavortis, find the inn called The Crooked Cupola—"

"The Crooked Cupola? Does he own it?"

"No, they simply make delicious pies," Trota deadpanned. "Would you allow me to finish before interrupting, Mr. Renato?"

He smiled apologetically and she continued. "The innkeeper is a former student of the Academy. Cosimo visits daily, it's a safe place to meet him. He's a respected man, formerly an astronomy professor in Merucia. Austere, but fair. You'll need to be polite, discreet, and adaptable. Use your Gemini Rising charm."

"My what now?"

"Gemini Rising," she said, sighing as she bustled out of the room. "It means you're curious, clever, and incapable of shutting up."

She returned a moment later with a polished blue and gold lapis lazuli in her palm, engraved at its center with a golden crescent moon and sun, joined beneath a star to form a rough triangle. The stone shimmered gently in the fading sunlight.

"Anyone who wishes to study at the Academy of the Arcane Arts must be given a token bearing its sigil, bestowed only by someone the school trusts. Even then, Cosimo reserves the right to turn you away. And even if you *don't* wish to study, he'll need to see the stone before you speak a word about astrology.

"Keep it hidden. And this, too." She handed him a scrap of parchment with his birth time. "Memorize it. Burn it. The fewer questions you attract, the better. I'd write you a letter of introduction, but if it were discovered at a border checkpoint..."

"Understood. I'll keep these safe."

Trota dipped her quill into red ink and marked Remo's intended path on the map. "Have you told your family yet?"

"No, but I'm speaking to them tonight. I'll tell them I'm spending the required year on the mainland to become a traveling healer—half-true, anyway. I'll omit the astrology part."

Trotta nodded. "When do you leave?"

"As soon as Anxur permits my travel. I'll need boarding papers for Juno and Lunaria."

Trota gave him a sly smile and shuffled through the stack of papers on her table. "The best thing about being a healer—aside from helping people, of course—is earning favors from high places."

She handed over official-looking travel papers bearing Anxur's royal purple seal. "Now you won't be delayed."

Remo blinked. "You already arranged this?"

"I had a feeling," she said. "And here. Your final wages."

The pouch was heavier than usual. Remo suspected it had been padded. She also handed him certified healer credentials, required for working in other kingdoms.

Remo took it all, then hesitated in the doorway. "What if this is a mistake? What if something goes wrong?"

Trota's expression softened. "Bad things can happen anywhere, at home or abroad. Locking yourself away prevents the good, too. You must live life, Remo—not just read about it."

Predictably, Remo's mother disliked the idea of him leaving indefinitely but accepted it, along with the denarii he insisted she keep in case of an emergency.

He packed up a small bag, cramming his medical kit and other essentials, somehow finding room for his favorite book, *Milena and Devlan*, which he could not imagine parting with.

Aemilian hugged his older brother tightly. "Don't bother coming back without a gift."

Remo ruffled his hair. "Stay out of trouble."

"You get into some for once," Aemilian replied.

Descending toward the sea, Remo glanced back at his village, purple jacaranda trees lining familiar paths. His heart leapt at the sight of the waiting boat, ready to carry him toward places he'd never seen.

Sea air stung his cheeks as the boat neared Juno, its white cliffs gleaming above the aquamarine waves.

The crescent-shaped island was carved with grottoes, the setting sun's rays dancing on the water as Remo disembarked at the western dock. He learned the next boat to Lunaria wouldn't arrive until the Moon's day, giving him a full day to explore.

He found a small inn run by a cheerful, plump woman who promised a hot meal. His room was cramped but cozy, its whitewashed walls encrusted with seashells. Dinner was seafood stew, rosemary bread, and honeyed wine. It wasn't the stuff of fantasy novels, but it was, he decided, a damn good start to an adventure.

The next morning, Remo followed a winding path down to the beach and stripped down to swim. He reached the cave at the tip of the island and explored several alcoves, one leading to a sunlit pool with a circular opening above. Something moved in the shadows, and a flicker of unease sent him back the way he came.

After drying off, he lay on the sand, eyes half-closed. Gentle splashing drew his attention. A beautiful woman stood in the shallow water, her wavy brown hair cascading down her back like a sea siren. She lifted her dress with one hand, dragging a boat ashore with the other. A stocky young man his age helped her. Suddenly self-conscious of his undressed state, Remo quickly dressed as the woman approached.

"Hello," she greeted Remo warmly, green eyes bright. The man looked wary.

"Hello," Remo replied nervously.

"Did you know this is a private beach?" the young man asked pointedly.

Remo felt stupid far earlier into the conversation than anticipated. "No. I'm sorry."

The girl chuckled. "You're not the first to trespass. The villa up there?"—she pointed to the hilltop—"Belongs to a senator of the Saffiran Empire."

Remo paled. "Then I'm doubly grateful to have met you before the guards did."

"But you don't mind trespassing on *less* important people's land?" she teased.

Remo's lips curled upwards at her playful challenge. "I'd rather avoid anyone with pointy weapons."

She smirked. The boy relaxed, clearly re-evaluating Remo's threat level. "We're heading to the port. Want a ride back?"

"I'd appreciate it. I'm Remo."

"Cecco Fattura," the boy said. "This is my sister, Sabelle."

As Remo's eyes met Sabelle's vivid green ones, his heart quickened. Her full lips curled into a confident smile, unsettling him far more profoundly than the shadows of the cave ever could.

As they paddled, Cecco asked, "Where are you visiting from?"

"Anxur. I'm leaving for Lunaria tomorrow."

"How come?" Sabelle asked.

Remo met her intense gaze, his nervousness having nothing to do with her question. "I'm a healer. I'm hoping to work on the mainland for a while so that I might eventually travel freely across kingdoms."

"You should stay here," Cecco said. "Healers are scarce. I got sick last month, and Quirinus at the apothecary told me to tie garlic to my feet and pray three times. Charged me six denarii."

Remo laughed politely. "Garlic does have restorative properties, but is better consumed than worn."

When they finally reached the port, Remo thanked them.

"Good luck on your journey," Sabelle called. "May we meet again."

Remo lingered on thoughts of her long after they parted, struck by her resemblance to the fictional Milena from his beloved novel's description. After walking for what felt like hours and exploring many levels of the island, he decided nothing about Juno captured his attention as much as Sabelle had.

He visited the apothecary to replenish his supply of medicinal herbs and, to his amusement, recognized the old man behind the counter as Quirinus from Cecco's story. He bought laurel and borage, then returned to the inn.

Not in the mood for further exploration, Remo wandered back into the inn's tavern and ordered a mead. He was debating whether to study the map Trota had given him when a commotion outside drew his attention. He leaned toward the window and saw two men locked in a violent scuffle, bystanders shouting and scrambling to pull them apart.

Remo rushed outside, instincts taking over. Shards of glass from a shattered perfume stall glittered across the cobbled street, and the air was thick with the sharp tang of spilled scent. The vendor hovered nearby, not angry, but frightened.

Bystanders finally pried the men apart. One of them, bleeding and limping, stumbled off down the road. The other lay dazed and bruised amid the debris. Remo dropped to his knees beside him, and recognition jolted through him.

"Cecco?"

The boy's eye was already swelling shut, his shirt torn and streaked with glass cuts. Remo offered his hand. "Come inside. I'll clean you up."

Cecco grunted something unintelligible, attempting to get to his feet. Before he could follow after the limping man, Sabelle sprinted into view, her eyes wide with alarm. She caught her brother by the arm and steered him toward the inn without a word. Cecco grumbled his thanks to Remo and allowed himself to be ushered inside. The bar woman gasped when she saw them enter. Remo requested a cold, wet rag, which she hurried to fetch.

"I'll be right back with my kit," he told Cecco, who was settling stiffly onto a bench. "Stay here."

He darted upstairs and returned moments later, case in hand. Taking the rag from the innkeeper, he pressed it into Cecco's hand. "Hold this against your eye. It'll help with the swelling."

Still fuming, Cecco obeyed.

Remo turned to Sabelle. "Are you hurt?"

"I'm fine. It's my brother who needs your attention," she replied quickly, though Remo noted several fine cuts on her face and forearms.

"I'm alright," Cecco muttered, jaw clenched. "Just look after her."

Remo dampened a clean cloth with alcohol and gently dabbed at Sabelle's injuries. They weren't serious, but they did need cleaning. As he worked, he tried not to stare at her too long, though her green eyes, flecked with brown, made that difficult.

He glanced back at Cecco. "Anything else hurting?"

"No. Though honestly, I wouldn't care if there were. It would've been worth it to land one more punch on Franco."

Remo returned his attention to Sabelle, who allowed him to tilt her chin with a finger so he could reach a small nick near her neck. He deliberately avoided meeting her gaze this time.

"What happened?" he asked.

Cecco answered before Sabelle could speak. "The bastard made another comment about her. It's not the first time."

"I know he's vile," Sabelle said dryly, "but don't you think you overreacted a little?"

"No. He had it coming," Cecco snapped.

Remo finished tending her wounds and turned back to Cecco, retrieving his forceps. He had only begun to remove a small piece of glass from the boy's forearm when Cecco waved him off.

"I don't have time for this. I'm already late meeting someone on behalf of my father."

Remo paused, watching as Cecco seemed to weigh something behind his bruised eye. Then, reluctantly, he said, "Would you walk my sister home? I don't want her running into Franco again."

Sabelle shot her brother an exasperated look before turning to Remo with a small, sheepish smile. "You really don't have to," she said.

"I'd be happy to," Remo said. He glanced at Cecco. "Are you sure I can't finish patching you up?"

"I'll live," Cecco grunted. "Thanks for the help. I'll see you at home later, Sabelle." He gave his sister a significant look—one that clearly held more than a simple goodbye.

"Is that a threat?" Sabelle muttered as he limped away, rolling her eyes.

Remo and Sabelle exchanged an uncertain glance. He couldn't help wondering what kind of meeting was so urgent that Cecco would entrust his sister to a near stranger. She didn't seem like someone who needed guarding, yet Cecco clearly thought otherwise.

Remo cleaned his tools, carefully disposing of the waste. "I'll just be a moment to put these away."

"Take your time," Sabelle said, watching the light outside the tavern window.

He hurried upstairs to stow his case. But when he returned, Sabelle was gone.

# Chapter Five

A WAVE OF DISAPPOINTMENT struck Remo, not just because he'd lost track of Sabelle under his watch, but because he was looking forward to the excuse to be near her.

He told himself he chased after her for Cecco's sake, though he knew she was perfectly capable of taking care of herself. He spotted her walking ahead and caught up quickly. She glanced at him from beneath her lashes, smiling like someone pleased to have been followed.

"Why did you leave?" he asked.

"It's not necessary to walk me home. I'm eighteen, I'm not a child. My brother's far too overprotective, as I'm sure you've already figured out."

"I get it," he said. "And if you'd rather I leave, I can. But for my own safety, I'd better not let Cecco find out I let you walk alone."

Sabelle chuckled, eyeing him with amused interest. "Fair point. Alright, you can walk with me. But it's a long journey, so consider yourself warned."

"I can think of worse ways to spend my time," he said, trying to sound casual. She tossed him a flirtatious smile, and he silently thanked Jupiter for his luck.

He didn't know what emboldened him. Maybe it was because he was leaving tomorrow and wouldn't see her again. But missing this chance was scarier than the idea of speaking up. When she wasn't looking, he studied her as if he might be tested on every line of her face later, as though understanding it might explain the strange pull he felt toward her.

"So," she said, eyes glinting with mischief, "how are you enjoying

Juno?"

"It's been refreshing," he said. "I've never left Anxur before. The change of scenery is nice. Have you ever been to the mainland?"

"I have," she said. "My father works in Saffiro, so I've visited a few times. But he made his fortune here, so he travels back and forth."

She said it simply, but Remo noticed the brief falter in her ever-present smirk. Her family was wealthy, then. He wasn't sure why that should matter, but it stung anyway.

They moved off the main road, climbing a rockier path toward the upper levels of the island.

"And do you like Saffiro?" he asked.

"Not really."

"Why not?"

She scrunched her nose. "Because I have even *less* freedom there. At least here, I can outrun Cecco half the time."

He sensed the frustration under her words. "I'm sorry," he said. "I can see he's protective."

Her tone softened. "He means well. And I don't let him stop me. I take my freedom by force, since no one's willing to give it to me." She hesitated, then added, "Like this morning."

He glanced at her. "What happened this morning?"

Her smile returned. "I went into the caves again. Cecco hates that."

"I was there this morning too," Remo said. "Easy place to get lost."

"I know them well. I saw you, actually. I hid until you left."

Remo realized she'd been the source of the noise he'd heard, and silently prayed to whichever god would listen that he hadn't looked as cowardly as he'd felt hurrying out.

"What do you do in the caves?"

She studied him for a moment. "I use my tarocchi cards. I ask questions. I interpret their meanings."

He blinked. "Tarocchi?"

They were illegal cards used for divination and considered witchcraft. Even owning a deck was punishable by law.

"Should you be telling me this?" he asked, voice low. "You could get in serious trouble."

Sabelle didn't flinch. "Will you tell on me?" she asked, voice sultry.

His gaze dropped briefly to her lips. "No. But is trusting strangers with dangerous secrets a habit of yours?"

She smirked. "Only the handsome ones."

He fought back a smile, keeping his face neutral to draw the truth from her.

Sabelle sighed. "No. It's not a habit. But you seem trustworthy. And you made a good impression on Cecco, too—he wouldn't have let you walk me home otherwise." She paused, then added, "Besides, I knew I'd meet a strange man today."

Remo arched a brow. "Did the cards tell you so?"

Her answering look, intense and intimate, sent a jolt through him. He wasn't sure how a glance could feel like a secret.

"If you'd like, I could read your cards," she offered. "Will you let me?"

He hesitated. He didn't believe in tarocchi, and yet, Jupiter's temple had made him question more than he cared to admit.

But there were other risks. "No," he said firmly. "Thank you, but I wouldn't risk getting you in trouble."

He didn't explain that his own caution wasn't only for her sake. Knights of Saffiro didn't need a reason to arrest someone, especially a traveler. He fell silent, letting her lead.

"What does freedom mean to you?" he asked after a while, her earlier words lingering in his mind.

Sabelle gazed up at the sky. "It's doing whatever I want, whenever I want, wherever I want. Choosing what I wear, who I speak with, who I marry. These freedoms aren't promised to me. Maybe that's why I do rebellious little things like read cards and swim naked in caves."

Remo blushed so violently he looked away, his imagination betraying him. She burst out laughing, and Remo risked a glance at her, feeling his awkwardness fade as he realized she was joking. He laughed with her, easily shaking off his embarrassment.

"You didn't say hello because you were playing tarocchi, then?" he asked, recovering.

Sabelle shrugged. "I'll let you believe whichever story you like better."

She was wildly inappropriate and unabashedly bold, but somehow, that made her easier to talk to.

They reached a wide stretch of land dotted with foxgloves and tall grasses. She knelt to pick a few. Remo watched her, partly afraid of her unpredictability and partly hoping he'd get more time to see where it led.

Sabelle glanced around. "You know... it's rather secluded here. And I happen to have my tarocchi cards with me."

Remo began to doubt this was truly the path to her home. Had she deliberately led him somewhere private just to give him a reading? He wouldn't have put it past her. Everything about Sabelle suggested she took what she wanted willfully, and without apology.

He tried to hide his uncertainty behind a disapproving look. "Sabelle," he said, savoring the sound of her name. "I don't think that's a good idea."

She tilted her head, not mocking, but curious. "What are you afraid of?"

He didn't answer. Truthfully, it was the loss of control that frightened him, the idea of being caught doing something illegal, of attracting the wrong kind of attention before even reaching the mainland. But her open question stirred something deeper in him. He had left home searching for adventure. If he kept letting fear dictate his steps, he'd never experience anything for himself, only ever through books.

Remo made his choice, and maybe a sizable part of that choice was made in an attempt to impress the attractive, daring woman in front of him. He sat down in the grass beside her.

Sabelle grinned, radiant, and pulled the deck of cards from her dress. She held them to her lips, whispering a silent prayer before shuffling. Then she handed the deck to Remo.

"Cut them into three stacks with your left hand," she instructed. "Then reorder them however you like."

He did as she asked. Her fingers moved over the cards with practiced ease.

"Now choose three groups of three cards and flip them over."

He followed her guidance, revealing nine cards painted in red, gold, and blue. The imagery meant nothing to him.

"The first row shows the situation at hand," Sabelle murmured, eyes glinting.

A horseman with a club. Seven of swords. Five of clubs.

"An attractive, intelligent young man goes on a journey," she said with a mischievous smile. "It could be a vacation, or a new courtship..."

Remo arched a brow, half-skeptical, half-amused.

"There's a parting, perhaps from a person or an old version of himself. There's fear. Uncertainty. Secrets, maybe. Clandestine meetings."

She bit her lip, gaze flicking over the cards. Remo thought of Cosimo, and almost laughed. Nothing about meeting an old man at a pie-serving inn felt romantic or sensual. But her look suggested she was imagining something else entirely, and now, so was he.

Sabelle turned the next set. "The second row represents agents influencing the situation."

A king holding an ace. A lady with a cup. Two of coins.

"You'll meet a person of authority, and a good woman. There's a union or an agreement, perhaps a partnership. Something that will change your direction."

Remo frowned slightly, wondering how much of this was true interpretation and how much was her invention. Then again, even if she *was* embellishing, something in her voice gave him pause.

The last three cards turned over. "This row is about the effort you must make and what will come of it."

An ace of clubs. A six of swords. An ace of swords.

"You'll have to triumph over something. An initiation of sorts. You may experience a mystical event, but it will come with a cost. A challenge. The last card is a powerful one. It could mean good news, victory. Or betrayal. Either way, something significant lies ahead."

They sat in silence. Remo traced blades of grass between his fingers, absorbing her words. For the first time, he didn't think she was playing a game. There was a sincerity in her tone he hadn't heard before.

Sabelle tucked the cards away, her playful mask slipping. "Did any of that feel right to you?" she asked.

Remo looked up from the grass. "Yes," he said simply.

Something shifted in her expression; it may have been uncertainty, maybe even self-consciousness. He felt the urge to ease it.

"I don't know much about cartomancy," he added, "but I think you have a talent for it."

Sabelle's smile bloomed, warm and real. He stood and offered her his hand. She took it, and neither let go right away. When they finally did, they walked in silence, but the silence wasn't empty. It carried all the unspoken tension between them, a mingling of shared attraction, curiosity, and the ache of inevitability.

The walk after felt longer than the one before. At last, Sabelle stopped. "This is close enough to my home," she said, voice softer now.

It caught him off guard how much he didn't want to say goodbye. They'd only met that morning, and yet the thought of parting stung more than he cared to admit.

"I know I'm leaving tomorrow," he said, "but, if it'd be pleasing to you, I'd like to see you again someday."

"Yes," she said. "I'd like that very much."

He interpreted her silence as a sign that his declaration had been well-received. They walked a little farther. At last, they reached the edge of a grand estate with whitewashed walls, a curved stone fountain, and intricate mosaics made of turquoise, coral, and white pebbles. Guards stood watch in the distance.

Remo froze. "So the villa I trespassed on earlier..."

Sabelle giggled. "It's my family's. My father is a merchant. And a senator of the Saffiran Empire."

He took in the marble garden paths, the towering cypress trees, the perfectly manicured blooms. "Why didn't you or Cecco say so?"

She frowned. "Why does it matter?"

He opened his mouth, but no words came. It *shouldn't* matter. But it did. He was leaving, and any possibility between them had always been fleeting; her status just underlined the point.

"I suppose it doesn't," he said finally.

"I asked Cecco not to say anything," she replied. "People treat me differently when they know who my father is. I'm expected to act like a good little senator's daughter."

"And... you're not?"

"Thought you would've figured that out," she teased. "Cecco's scared of me, you know."

"Why ever would that be?" he played along.

"I'm afraid we won't have enough time together for you to find out," she answered, the gleam in her eye fading.

There it was again, that ache. The weight of an ending. They stood in silence, not wanting to move.

At last, Sabelle cleared her throat. "Well, I suppose this is goodbye. Perhaps if we're lucky, our paths will cross again."

"May we meet again," Remo said.

She smiled at the echo of her earlier words. He bowed slightly and turned to go, forcing himself not to look back. By the time he reached the inn, twilight was falling. As he ate, he found himself thinking not of fictional heroines, but of Sabelle.

The card reading lingered in his thoughts, but he stopped trying to decipher it. Whatever fate meant, he decided, it wasn't his job to guess. His role was to choose what felt right in each moment and let time reveal the rest.

# Chapter Six

THE JUNO SEAPORT WAS already buzzing with activity despite the early hour. Remo presented his boarding papers to a surly dockhand who barely glanced at them before waving him aboard the ship bound for Lunaria.

He took one last look at the island, exhaling a long breath of salty sea air. Nothing could solidify Sabelle's place in his mind quite like the finality of departure, the impossibility of any potential future with her.

Screeching gulls soared overhead as the boat pulled away from the shore. He leaned over the starboard side, narrowing his thoughts toward the path ahead: he'd find Cosimo, have his natal chart read, and unravel the message in the bottle. That was all that mattered now.

Once he reached Celeste City, a helpful local directed him north toward the Forest of Numa, the route winding from the luminous city into the shaded green wilds that bordered the Kingdom of Mavortis.

Lunaria was beautiful but subdued, masked in a quiet tension. Most passersby avoided prolonged eye contact. Knights of Saffiro, clad in radiant golden armor, patrolled the streets like sharks in shallow water. Their presence cast a long, silent shadow over the city.

The Moon Kingdom shimmered in hues of silver and pearlescent white. Round buildings with conical roofs, frosted windows, and clean stone streets glimmered beneath the pale, descending sun. The Veil River weaved its way through the silver city, birthing tranquil ponds dotted with water lilies. Remo followed the path toward a tall tower to orient himself before turning toward the forest.

Twilight wrapped around him like a velvet cloak as he stepped beneath the trees. The road ahead narrowed between towering trunks and thick underbrush. Magenta skies deepened into purple, and the last rays of sunlight gave way to the faint glow of a waning moon filtering through the canopy, allowing some illumination along the path.

With no fellow travelers in sight, Trota's advice to seek companions proved impossible to follow. And even if there had been others on the road, Remo doubted he would have found the nerve to approach them.

He decided to camp within the Forest of Numa rather than waste his remaining coin on an inn. The remainder of the bread and cheese he purchased earlier would have to do. If his visit with Cosimo extended longer than expected, he would support himself with healing work to meet the twelvemonth requirement for guild certification.

When the darkness became too dense to continue, he stepped off the path to a patch of mossy ground and settled beneath a tree. His pack under his arm, his cloak drawn over his head, he leaned back against the trunk and closed his eyes. Sleep came quickly despite his alertness. His body, worn from travel, had no interest in further protest.

Remo woke to hushed voices and the thud of approaching footsteps. His heart leapt to his throat, already cursing his decision not to stay at an inn.

"...and after all that, the stupid cow still tried to nick my purse," one voice muttered, followed by a crude laugh. "Hold up, Scapino, I've got to piss."

Remo didn't dare breathe. Lanternlight flickered through the branches. One of them was urinating only feet away.

"Ay, what's that, Zanni?" the man with the lantern called.

"What's what?" came the reply.

Remo's pulse thundered in his ears, frozen in place. He had no weapon handy to defend himself and fumbling within his bag for a knife would only attract attention.

"Well, well. Look what I've found." The lantern shifted toward him, its light illuminating the edge of his cloak.

Remo tensed as the two men stepped into view. Scapino, the thinner one, grinned wide enough to display a mouthful of missing teeth. Zanni, built like a brick wall, stepped closer.

"Lower your hood," Scapino snapped.

Remo complied.

"What's a pretty boy like you doing out here all alone?" Zanni sneered, reaching for him.

"I'm a healer," Remo replied evenly. "On my way to Mavortis."

Scapino snorted. "A healer? Then you can patch yourself up after we've finished with you."

Remo stood, slowly.

Zanni stepped closer. "Going somewhere? Urgent house call?"

Then Zanni lunged.

The back of Remo's head forcibly met the tree behind him. Recovering quickly, he grabbed his bag, and swung it upward. It collided with Zanni's head, exploding open and sending vials, herbs, and tools scattering across the forest floor.

Zanni bellowed in pain but wasn't down for long. Remo didn't have time to grab a weapon before Zanni was back on his feet. Remo narrowly ducked another blow, circling fast, desperate to find his shears, or anything sharp, amidst the mess.

The next punch landed squarely in Remo's gut, knocking the wind from his lungs. He collapsed to the ground, barely aware of the blade pressed against his throat.

"I'm gonna cut you up so fine, even you won't be able to sew the pieces back together," Zanni growled, breath foul and hot. Behind him, Scapino was looking through Remo's dropped belongings.

The keen sting of irony rivaled the cold bite of Zanni's blade, warmed by drops of Remo's blood as he realized he would die so soon after he'd decided to start living. Although a feeling of not belonging had made him feel an indifference towards his life, he now knew that he did not want to die.

Maybe the glimpse he had over the past few days of what life could be like if he'd lived it more was all he would be given. Maybe in his next life, he could remember to live it sooner.

Then Zanni screamed.

Remo barely registered the blur of motion before a third figure tore Zanni away and slammed him to the ground. The newcomer straddled him, blade poised.

"Please! Please don't—" Zanni whimpered, shrinking away.

"Run," the stranger said. His voice was deep and calm, its cadence unshakeable.

Scapino didn't wait for a second invitation. He took off into the woods, abandoning Remo's items and Zanni, who limped far behind him.

Remo blinked, wiping blood from his neck. He quickly assessed himself; thankfully, it was only a superficial cut. His body ached, but no ribs felt broken. The worst injury he suffered was to his pride.

The stranger turned and lifted the lantern. He had brown skin, intense dark eyes, and a closely trimmed black beard. His cloak was rumpled from travel, his presence radiating control.

"You alright?" the man asked.

Remo sat up slowly, wincing. "I think so."

The stranger extended a hand, which Remo gratefully accepted.

"Name's Andrea," the man said, lowering his hood to reveal close-cropped black curls.

"Remo. Thank you. I'm in your debt."

Andrea gave him a short nod. "Don't mention it. I left my horse a little ways back when I heard voices. Figured there'd be trouble."

"Well, you figured right," Remo said, forcing a tight, sheepish smile.

Andrea tilted his head. "Perhaps we can travel the rest of the road together for our safety?"

Remo knew Andrea was being excessively kind by suggesting so; his muscular frame suggested he required no protection his own body couldn't offer. Nevertheless, Remo figured he didn't have much in the way of pride left to refuse.

"I'd like that. Although, I fear I'd offer you as much protection as the skinny one provided his large friend."

Andrea's mouth widened to reveal a dazzling smile that even Remo could recognize held the ability to melt many a maiden's heart.

"Safety in numbers is still wise," Andrea said before he disappeared briefly to retrieve his horse.

Remo used the opportunity to collect the scattered remnants of his medicine kit. A few bottles had shattered; the sharp scent of astragalus and dried myrrh clung to the earth. He cursed softly, stuffing what remained of his salves and tinctures back into the pack. His fingers trembled slightly, either from residual nerves or the pain beginning to set in.

He was nearly done when he realized with dread that the lapis lazuli was missing. Panic rose in his throat as he dropped to his knees and swept through the fallen leaves and grass. It had to be nearby.

"Looking for this?" came Andrea's voice behind him.

Remo turned. Andrea held the stone in his palm, the golden sigil glinting in the lanternlight.

Remo's mind scrambled. He forced a blank expression, willing his voice into calm neutrality. "I don't know what that is. Maybe one of the thieves dropped it."

Andrea studied him in silence for a moment, then pocketed the stone. "Spoils of my victory, then."

Remo's stomach dropped. He couldn't ask for it back without drawing attention. But without it, Cosimo might never agree to see him. Trota's warning echoed in his mind: *he'll need to see the stone before you speak a word about astrology.*

Andrea gestured toward the road. "Come. Dawn's still a ways off, and we've got ground to cover."

Remo hoisted his bag onto his shoulder, trying to ignore the ache in his side. "Thank you again. For what you did back there."

Andrea smiled modestly. "Like I said, safety in numbers."

They walked side by side through the forest, Andrea leading his sleek black mare by the reins. The predawn hush surrounded them, broken only by the crunch of earth beneath their boots and the occasional rustle of wind in the trees.

Remo couldn't stop glancing at the pocket where Andrea had stowed the stone. He wondered if he'd ever get it back or if Andrea had already guessed the truth.

"So," Andrea asked, "Where are you from?"

"Anxur," Remo answered.

"What takes a healer from Anxur all the way to Mavortis?"

Remo stuck to his practiced lie. "I'm hoping to join the Healer's Guild. Eventually, I'd like to work anywhere on the mainland. That means spending a year here first."

Andrea raised a brow. "Ambitious. Not many from Anxur stray far from home."

Remo offered a noncommittal smile, then quickly deflected. "And what about you? What brings you this way?"

"I live in Mavortis," Andrea said. "Just returning from an errand down south."

"What kind of errand?" Remo asked, then cursed himself for the boldness.

Andrea shot him a sidelong look. "Nothing of interest, I assure you."

Remo chuckled, letting it go. Andrea's evasiveness only made him more curious, but he sensed pushing would get him nowhere.

"What made you want to leave Anxur?" Andrea asked, intent on steering the conversation away from himself.

Remo rubbed his temples, his head still aching from being smashed against the tree. "Nothing of interest, I assure you."

Andrea barked a laugh. "Fair enough."

They walked for hours, their rhythm settling into something companionable. By midday, they stopped in a shaded glen where a stream babbled through clusters of daisies. Andrea tethered his horse and shared his provisions of plums and almond biscuits with Remo, who offered what remained of his bread and cheese in return.

Remo felt comfortable around Andrea, whom he learned was 25 years old and originally from Saffiro. He had a disarming manner that made him instantly likable. In the daylight, Andrea's features stood out more clearly: the strong jaw, the golden earring glinting in one ear, the quiet confidence in the way he carried himself. He was undeniably charming, and yet, there was something carefully guarded in his expression, a layer of restraint that suggested a life far more complicated than his easy smile let on.

"When do you think we'll reach Mavortis?" Remo asked, licking plum juice from his thumb.

"By nightfall, if we keep pace."

"What's it like?" Remo leaned back on his elbows, genuinely curious.

Andrea's gaze drifted skyward. "Overwhelming, at first. It's all stone walls and winding streets. Crowded. Loud. But alive. You'll find everything there—priests and prostitutes, drunkards and scholars. Chaos and brilliance in equal measure. It's easy to blend in there if you'd like to go unnoticed."

He paused, jaw tightening slightly. "But the guards... they're particularly ruthless in Mavortis. They've got their own soldiers too, called the Salian Order, led by the kingdom's Crown Prick Marcellus."

"You mean Crown *Prince?*" Remo laughed.

Andrea shrugged. "Same difference. But the Knights of Saffiro don't just patrol there, they dominate. There's corruption. Some are little more than thugs with fancy armor and imperial sanction."

Andrea's voice had changed, his usual levity stripped away. "They rob and kill without consequence. But the ones who truly believe in the empire's mission are the ones to fear."

Remo sat up straighter. "Why?"

Andrea glanced at him. "Because they're the ones who'll follow orders to the letter. Even when those orders involve conquering kingdoms and crushing dissent."

Remo frowned, turning the words over. He knew what the empire had done to the other kingdoms, how each had fallen in turn, bending the knee to avoid bloodshed. Only one remained untouched. A chill passed through him. "You think... they might try to take Anxur?"

"I've heard rumors," Andrea said darkly. "More than rumors, really. Knights showing up in peaceful towns. It's what they did before the fall of Satria."

Remo recalled the guard he saw at the market in Anxur. Their presence in his relatively small province validated the whispers.

"I've seen what they left behind in Satria," Andrea went on. "Cities stripped bare. People impoverished and broken."

His fists clenched at his sides. "The scars haven't healed, even now. The Knights of Saffiro ensure rebel groups get snuffed out before they gain any momentum. Satrian men are practically enslaved in the mines and quarries, yet all of the riches of their kingdom line the pockets of Saffirans."

Satria's Calamity had never felt very real to him, living in Anxur, so far removed in time and space from the reality of the event. But hearing it from Andrea, who had *seen* the ruins... it made everything feel immediate and terrifying.

They resumed walking, the sun sinking slowly behind the trees. As dusk painted the forest in golden tones, Remo turned to Andrea.

"A friend of mine who's been to Mavortis told me of an inn called The Crooked Cupola. Have you heard of it?"

There was a knowing sparkle in Andrea's eyes as he said, "Yes, I'm familiar with it."

"Is it far from the gate?"

"No. I'll take you there," Andrea offered easily. "It's not far from my home."

They walked in silence for a few minutes before Andrea slowed, reaching into his pocket. He held out the lapis lazuli stone.

"Are you *sure* you don't recognize this?"

Remo hesitated.

Andrea watched him carefully. "Because I do."

Remo sighed. He could lie again, but something in Andrea's expression told him it would be useless. Besides, Andrea saved Remo's life. He almost couldn't help trusting him.

"My mentor gave it to me," Remo admitted. "She told me to show it to someone named Cosimo at the inn."

Andrea gave a short nod, then handed it back. "Then it seems our paths are more entangled than either of us realized."

Remo blinked. "Wait—what do you mean?"

"I mean," Andrea said quietly, "you've got nothing to worry about at the gate. Just let me do the talking."

They continued on through the thinning trees as twilight deepened. The gate loomed before them, iron and red stone interwoven like the bones of some ancient beast, fitting for Mars' kingdom. It was flanked by two guards. Each held a lantern and a lance, their stances alert despite the late hour.

Remo's nerves churned. His palm brushed the secret compartment in his bag, now once again housing the lapis lazuli, but only barely; it was hanging by a thread after the fight.

One of the guards, a stocky man with a bushy mustache, stepped forward. "State your business in Mavortis."

Andrea answered smoothly, with practiced ease. "I'm returning home from a brief visit to Lunaria."

Remo wore what he hoped was a convincingly blasé expression. "I'm a healer looking for work in Mavortis."

The guard gave Remo a long, cold stare. "And what papers do you have?"

"I have a healer's license," Remo offered quickly, reaching for it, but the second guard stepped forward and gruffly snatched the bag from his hands before he could present it.

"And you," the first guard said, turning his attention back to Andrea. "Got a letter from a noble permitting travel between regions?"

Andrea didn't flinch. Instead, he raised his hand and extended his middle finger.

The guard's mouth opened to retort, but then he saw the golden signet ring gleaming on Andrea's finger.

Remo, watching silently, noticed the subtle change in the air. The guard's face paled.

"I—my lord," he stammered, stumbling back a step. "Please accept my apologies. We weren't expecting—"

Andrea cut him off with a flat stare. "Just don't let it happen again. The healer is with me."

The taller guard, who had begun rifling through Remo's bag, froze. He looked over at his companion, clearly confused.

The first guard hissed under his breath. "Let them pass."

"But—"

"Let. Them. Pass."

The silent guard returned the bag to Remo without a word. Remo muttered his thanks, shouldering it once more. He followed Andrea through the now-open gates, heart pounding as they passed beneath the archway.

# Chapter Seven

THEY EMERGED FROM THE gates into the sprawling outer district of Mavortis. Remo didn't dare ask what was burning on his tongue to know until they were well out of earshot of the guards.

Even at night, the kingdom teemed with life. Torchlit market stalls guided their path, and the scent of roasted chestnuts hung in the air around them. A beggar strummed a lyre near a well; laughter echoed from a nearby tavern.

Remo couldn't help himself any longer. "You're—You're royalty, then? Sir," he added awkwardly.

Andrea laughed darkly. "If I knew you'd start calling me 'sir,' I'd have let the bandits lay one more good punch on you." His voice softened. "There's no need for that. But yes, I am of noble birth."

Something bitter flickered in his expression that Remo didn't understand.

"Well," Remo said, wishing to lighten the mood, "it seems to me the bandits would've made off better stealing from you instead."

Andrea's laughter came easier this time. "The inn's not far now. I'll be staying there too tonight; I'm too tired to walk home. It'll likely be quiet at this hour, though. You'll have to wait until tomorrow if you're hoping to strike up conversations with strangers."

Remo studied him sidelong, wondering if Andrea himself was a student of Cosimo's. It would explain how he knew about the lapis lazuli's significance.

They walked on, The Crooked Cupola soon coming into view. A crooked turret stood silhouetted against the dark sky, its windows glowing with buttery yellow light.

"Aptly named," Remo murmured as Andrea went to stable his horse.

Inside, the inn was larger than it appeared from without. Timber-framed walls cradled simple iron sconces with dripping candles. Lanterns bathed the wide room in a gentle light. Toward the back, a large burgundy curtain shielded a more private seating area, where a roaring fire flickered behind shadows of cozy chairs.

Behind the bar, an ample-bellied innkeeper wiped down the counter, casting a disapproving look at the dust their boots trailed across his freshly polished floor. "Welcome—and Andrea! Good to see you back."

"Hello, Sevo," Andrea said, smiling.

Sevo poured Andrea a measure of amber liquid without asking. Then he turned to Remo. "What can I get you?"

"Ale, please."

"Food?" Andrea asked hopefully.

"Of course. You think I'm running an empty inn?" Sevo barked. He vanished through an archway and returned minutes later with steaming bowls of mushroom risotto.

They ate quickly. When Remo finished, he caught Sevo casting a questioning glance at Andrea.

Andrea wiped his mouth. "How rude of me. Sevo, this is Remo, a new friend I met on the road. Remo, meet Sevo—an old friend I met here. He was ancient then, too."

"Charming," Sevo said humorlessly. "Room tonight?"

"Yes, please," Remo said. He paid for both of them before Andrea could protest, tossing fourteen denarii onto the counter.

Andrea tried pushing half back toward him, but Remo waved him off. "You saved my life. Let me at least buy you dinner."

Sevo chuckled, pocketing the coins, and showed them upstairs. Remo's room was simple but inviting. It had a medium bed with a crimson quilt, a glowing hearth, a basin for bathing, and a window looking down onto the cobbled street.

The moment his head hit the pillow, sleep claimed him.

The next morning, after a quick bath using the basin and jugs provided, Remo dressed and went downstairs for a breakfast of milky tea and a flaky pastry.

Andrea was nowhere to be seen among the other guests. Remo wondered if Andrea was avoiding him, wary of more questions about his royal status. Remo couldn't blame him. Curiosity gnawed at him, but he resolved to respect Andrea's privacy.

The truth was, Remo hardly ever met people he liked enough to wish to see again. Wanting someone's continued company made him feel vulnerable. It was easier to guard his heart behind loneliness than to risk the sting of rejection.

When Remo inquired about Andrea's whereabouts, Sevo informed him he left earlier that morning. "But he asked me to pass along a message: the man you wish to speak with will be visiting the inn after dusk," Sevo added.

Rather than wait nervously at the inn all day, he decided to use the time to inquire about establishing himself with the region's Healer's Guild. Whether or not he stayed long-term in Mavortis, it was prudent to keep his alibi intact.

In daylight, Mavortis, the Kingdom of Mars, revealed itself fully as a kingdom of terracotta rooftops rolling in waves under an endless blue sky. Angular cobblestone streets crisscrossed the Iron District, leading into winding alleyways and hidden corners.

It would be easy to lose oneself here—or to hide, as Andrea had hinted.

Sticking to the main thoroughfares, Remo crossed a bridge over the Veil River. In the square beyond, a fountain bore the likeness of a man and woman riding atop a fierce-looking wolf, their stone faces fierce with triumph.

Following the advice of a street vendor, he found a local apothecary. Since apothecaries, herbalists, and healers often worked together, he could find out more about one through the others. The balding shopkeeper eyed him suspiciously but, after questioning, directed him to the head of the Healer's Guild.

Two streets down, Remo reached the hospital, a towering edifice with an endless facade of red stone and arched windows. Inside, it was orderly and immaculate. He asked the clerk at the front desk for the guild's head physician, Arlo Acerbi.

The man huffed. "He's busy."

Before Remo could reply, a voice from behind interrupted.

"That I am."

Remo turned. A tall, broad-shouldered man with white-blond hair and sharp blue eyes approached, dressed in a spotless white robe. His skin was slightly pockmarked, his gaze glacial.

"State your name and business."

"Remo Renato," Remo said, feeling the weight of the man's assessing stare. "I'm seeking to join the guild."

The physician studied him, then snapped, "Follow me."

They entered a well-appointed office. Acerbi sat behind a heavy oak desk and gestured for Remo to sit across from him. Without ceremony, he rifled through Remo's papers.

"Anxur, is it?" Acerbi said, lips curling faintly. "And why Mavortis? Why not a larger city's guild in Anxur?"

Remo forced himself to keep his voice even. "I seek broader experience. Mavortis has the finest medical universities in Terramundi."

Acerbi leaned back in his chair, cold amusement glittering in his eyes.

"You are young. Barely a year's worth of real experience, from what I see here." He tossed the papers back across the desk with disdain. "Normally, I'd dismiss you outright. We are not some village clinic desperate for bodies. We are a distinguished establishment."

Remo bit down on his anger. He thought of Trota, of her wisdom and her training, and swallowed his pride. Let the man underestimate him.

"But as it happens," Acerbi continued, "I find myself in need of healers. A pestilence outbreak on the Merucian border has depleted my staff." He stood abruptly, signaling the end of the interview. "Return in two days at this hour. You'll undergo a practical examination. If you prove competent, you'll be allowed to work here under supervision."

Remo rose, bowing his head slightly. "Thank you, Physician Acerbi."

Acerbi gave him one last withering glance. "Don't waste my time."

Remo left the hospital with clenched fists and a tight jaw. He wandered the city for a while longer, trying to calm the knot of frustration growing in his chest. He couldn't help but feel as though he had been weighed and found wanting.

Main squares with hectic markets gave way to residential streets with balconies covered in flowering vines. Hidden courtyards held crumbling statues of forgotten gods, their stillness contrasting with the lively din of people trying to survive and pursue their ambitions within Mars' kingdom.

He returned to The Crooked Cupola in the late afternoon, feeling battered in ways that had nothing to do with bandits. Sevo served him a hearty dinner of Venus' hair pasta served with cheese and black pepper, charred bread with olive oil and garlic, and a cup of strong, bittersweet wine.

Remo ate sparingly, his appetite dulled by the prospect of his meeting with Cosimo. The lapis lazuli stone weighed heavily in his pocket, a silent reminder of everything riding on tonight. He caught himself scanning the tavern every few minutes. When Andrea appeared, casually shouldering his way through the evening crowd, Remo exhaled in relief he hadn't realized he was holding.

"Sorry I wasn't around this morning," Andrea said, sliding into the seat next to him. "Had a few things to take care of. Did you have a look around?"

"I did," Remo said. "I found a hospital. I'll be taking my practical exam in two days."

"Will you be staying here permanently if all goes well, then?"

"I don't know. I suppose it depends on how my conversation with Cosimo goes."

Andrea picked up on Remo's apprehension, perhaps mislabeling it as nervousness for the practical exam alone. "You'll pass your practical. We'll be toasting your success here after, I'm sure of it."

Remo managed a smile, grateful for the encouragement more than he could say.

A few minutes later, the tavern's door swung open. An old man entered, robed in green and gold, a bronze walking stick tapping against the floor. His beard was neatly trimmed, and his black eyes glittered with tempered power.

Andrea grinned and leaned close. "That's your man," he said. "Would you like an introduction?"

Remo nodded, swallowing his nerves.

Andrea stood, weaving through the crowd with casual grace, and Remo followed.

"Good evening, Professor Cosimo," Andrea said.

The old man looked up, black eyes sharp and alert. "Good evening."

Andrea gestured to Remo. "This is my friend, Remo Renato."

Remo bowed his head. "A pleasure to meet you, sir."

"Well met, Remo," Cosimo said, his voice surprisingly gentle.

They sat together at the bar, Sevo discreetly watching from the corner of his eye.

"I understand you traveled together?" Cosimo asked, sipping from his cup.

"Yes," Remo said, assuming Sevo must've filled him in. "And if not for Andrea, I might not have survived the journey through the forest."

Cosimo smiled faintly, a glimmer of amusement in his eyes. "Fortunate, then, that fate placed him in your path."

Remo took a breath. He hated small talk. He needed to move the conversation forward toward why he had come all this way.

"I've been looking forward to this meeting," Remo said. "My mentor spoke very highly of you."

Cosimo tilted his head. "And who is your mentor?"

Remo glanced around to ensure no one was paying them close attention. Then he leaned in and produced the lapis lazuli stone from his pocket, shielding it from view. "Trota," he said.

Cosimo's eyes sharpened as he caught sight of the sigil. Remo tucked it away again swiftly.

Behind them, Andrea shifted subtly, placing himself between any prying eyes.

Cosimo nodded, a slight motion, but it carried immense weight. "Come," he said, rising carefully from his stool. "Let's speak somewhere more private."

They followed him through a curtained archway into a secluded back room where a fire crackled merrily in the hearth. Andrea pulled the heavy curtain closed behind them, sealing out the noise of the tavern.

Despite Andrea's clear familiarity with Cosimo, Remo found it surprising that another student, if that indeed was Andrea's relationship to Cosimo, would be granted access to their continued conversation.

The room was cozy but simple; a few chairs, a worn rug, a round table cluttered with old books and parchments filled the space.

Cosimo seated himself by the fire, motioning for them to do the same. "May I see the stone again?" he asked.

Without hesitation, Remo handed it over to him.

Cosimo turned it over in his hand, his sharp eyes softening slightly. "Yes. Trota's mark is unmistakable. She was one of my brightest students."

Remo smiled. "She spoke of you with great respect, sir."

Cosimo looked at him thoughtfully. "And what brings you here with her token?"

"Trota believed I would benefit from a natal chart reading. She thought it might help me... find my path."

Cosimo's brows lifted. "And do you believe that?"

Remo hesitated. He didn't want to offend the man, but honesty seemed the better course. "I'm not sure what I believe yet. But I'm willing to learn."

"You traveled a long way for uncertainty." Cosimo's face was inscrutable.

"Uncertainty seems to be the only thing I can claim with any confidence these days," Remo said ruefully.

Cosimo chuckled. "You are wise enough to admit it," he said. "That's more than most can say."

"There's another thing, sir. I found these in a bottle washed up at sea. Trota thought you might help me understand their meaning."

He leaned back in his chair, steepling his fingers. "Very well. Let's see them."

Remo handed the items over. Cosimo's eyes widened at the sight of the delicate scroll of parchment, his fingers gently unfurling it as his lined eyes absorbed the words. His mouth curled slightly at the edges as he read it over as if he and the poem shared a secret.

There was an inexplicable expression of tenderness on Cosimo's face as he admired the amethyst and handed both objects back to Remo, his eyes returning to their former unreadable, tolerant gaze.

Cosimo tapped his fingers against the armrest thoughtfully. "The poem is rich in astrological symbolism. But its meaning would be lost on you without proper study."

Remo fought to keep his frustration in check. "I understand. But... respectfully, sir, I don't know if I'm ready to dedicate myself to something I don't yet fully believe in."

Cosimo's dark eyes glittered. "No one will force you. It is your choice. But consider whether you can live peacefully without knowing."

Remo sat still, the words sinking deep into his chest.

No, he realized. He couldn't. The questions would haunt him.

He thought of the vision in Jupiter's temple. He thought of the ache for something more that had never quite left him.

Remo lifted his chin. "I would like to study astrology at your school."

A small smile curved Cosimo's lips. "Good."

Andrea clapped Remo lightly on the shoulder, beaming.

Cosimo's gaze sharpened again. "You know your birth time?"

"I do." Remo handed him the small scrap of paper with the information. "Trota told me to memorize it."

"Wise of her," Cosimo said. "I will dispose of this once your chart is drawn." He tucked the paper into his robes. "You'll also need a place to stay. The Academy doesn't provide housing."

Before Remo could respond, Andrea chimed in, "He'll stay with me for now."

Remo turned, startled. "I don't want to impose—"

"You're not," Andrea said firmly. "It'll be good fun, having a roommate."

Remo's life had already been in safe keeping yesterday in Andrea's hands, so he was quite certain Andrea wouldn't slit his throat in his sleep. But the offer was too generous.

Before he could stammer another refusal, Cosimo clapped his wizened hands. "So it's settled. We'll discuss tuition after you're settled. Welcome to the Academy, Remo Renato."

"Sir—er, Professor," Remo said, standing up as the headmaster made to leave. "Where *is* the school?"

Cosimo chuckled, his austere features breaking. "Above... and below." He tapped his walking stick once to the floor, then escorted himself out of the room. Remo bid him goodnight, looking at Andrea in a wordless plea for an explanation.

Andrea merely shook his head in sympathy, apparently used to Cosimo's cryptic remarks. "I'll tell you in a minute. Grab your things and meet me outside."

Remo and Andrea walked along the dark streets. Drunken laughter spilled from taverns and hooded figures hurried past on unseen errands.

Before Remo could ask again, Andrea said quietly, "The Academy is literally beneath The Crooked Cupola. There are also a few hidden entrances throughout Mavortis, including a dovecote nearby where Cosimo holds astrology lessons under the open sky, masked as astronomy lessons."

Remo cracked a smile. "Above... and below."

Andrea chuckled. "Exactly."

They turned down a narrower lane, lined with modest, well-kept buildings. They entered Andrea's home, the top story of a sand-colored building. Andrea lit a series of lanterns, bathing the room in a faint orange glow.

It was humble but charming. A well-loved settee faced a hearth stacked with wood. A large oak desk cluttered with strange instruments dominated one side, and near the bed, a screen provided privacy for a basin and washstand.

"Welcome to my palace," Andrea said with mock grandeur, sweeping his arms wide.

Remo grinned, setting his bag down near the settee. "It's perfect."

Andrea flung open the balcony doors, and they stepped outside into the cool night.

The Iron District sprawled before them, a sea of red-tiled roofs glinting under the moonlight. Beyond the city walls, the faint outline of distant hills loomed like sleeping giants.

After a moment, Remo asked, "Can I ask you something else?"

Andrea raised an eyebrow. "You can try."

"You're a student at the Academy, right?"

"Correct," Andrea said easily. "I study Alchemy."

Remo's interest piqued immediately. "Alchemy? As in turning lead into gold?"

Andrea laughed. "That's one very tiny part of it. Real alchemy is about transformation—of materials, of the mind, even of the soul. Learning the properties of substances, sure, but also learning the properties of yourself."

Remo leaned against the rail, intrigued. "What other subjects are taught at the Academy?"

"Just one more called Awareness."

"What's that?"

"That one's harder to explain. Think of it like learning to clear your mind so completely that you can feel things most people miss. Sensing the currents beneath reality. You'll meet my best friend Lyra soon," Andrea added. "Awareness is her specialty. She's better at explaining it than I am, although I still don't pretend to understand it."

The wind stirred their hair, carrying the distant smell of roasting meats and the salty tang of the river.

After a moment, Remo said hesitantly, "Thanks for letting me stay here. But... why?"

Andrea looked genuinely puzzled. "Why what?"

"Why you would bother?" Remo asked, the clarification coming out more blunt than he meant it. "Why did you bother saving me, and being kind to me since? I'm afraid I don't have anything to offer you in repayment."

The amusement on Andrea's face disappeared as a pitying look replaced it. "It saddens me if you think that saving your life wasn't worth the bother. As for being kind to you, well... This world is cruel enough. Someone was once kind to me in a similar way when I didn't deserve it, and I believe in paying it forward. Besides, this is what friends do for one another."

"Friends inconvenience each other?" Remo questioned, only half-joking.

Andrea breathed out a laugh. "You're not inconveniencing me. But yes, I suppose friends *do* go out of their way for one another and inconvenience themselves from time to time. But you find that you don't mind doing so for some people."

Remo was silent as he processed Andrea's words. "I wouldn't really know. I don't have many friends," he said, looking over the balcony at the sea of roofs ahead.

*It would have been more correct to say I don't have any,* Remo thought self-consciously. He wasn't sure why he felt he had to admit so to Andrea, to warn him that perhaps he wasn't worth the effort.

"Well, you have me now," Andrea said cheerily as he flashed his winning smile, and Remo couldn't help but return it.

# Chapter Eight

THERE WERE FOUR DIFFERENT entrances to the underground tunnels that made up the Academy of the Arcane Arts.

Predictably, one was accessed through a private room within The Crooked Cupola. Two others were hidden within blind alleys tucked deep inside the Iron District, their entrances so well concealed they escaped public notice. The fourth was located inside a crumbling dovecote on the far eastern edge of the kingdom's walls.

Most students favored the two hidden alleyways, but Andrea preferred the one at the inn. Tavern-goers were typically too distracted to notice whether anyone disappeared through the back. At this early hour, the inn was quiet, save for Sevo preparing breakfast. He unlocked the door to let Andrea and Remo inside, barely sparing them a glance as he kneaded dough for the morning's bread.

In the storage room, Andrea knelt and revealed a cleverly concealed trap door. He climbed down a ladder leading to a stone platform below. Remo followed, glancing around with cautious wonder.

"I'm surprised Cosimo can manage a ladder at his age," Remo muttered.

Andrea waited for him to descend before moving forward. "He's surprisingly nimble for an old man. I think confusing his students with riddles keeps him young."

Remo exhaled a short laugh. "Is he really that bad?"

"He's brilliant," Andrea said, torchlight catching the easy grin on his face, "but he likes to push you to figure things out yourself. You'll see."

The passageway twisted ahead of them, its stone walls lit by flickering torches set in iron sconces. Above, Remo could still faintly hear the patter of Sevo's footsteps.

"What did Sevo study?" Remo asked, curiosity getting the better of him.

"Alchemy," Andrea answered. "Specifically, spagyrics—herbal alchemy. Handy skill for a tavern owner. He can brew bitters, syrups, tonics; that sort of thing. I'm studying it too, alongside metalworking."

The path eventually opened into a large stone chamber with three archways. Each doorway bore a different carving: a crescent moon to the left, a diamond-shaped star ahead, and a circle with a dot in its center, the ancient symbol for the sun, etched above the rightmost entrance. Remo recognized the symbols from the lapis lazuli stone Trota had given him.

Andrea pointed as he explained, "Moon for Astrology. Star for Alchemy. Sun for Awareness. Classes rotate times and days each week, just in case anyone ever tried to follow us."

"Thanks, Andrea. See you after class," Remo said.

Andrea clapped his shoulder lightly and headed for the star-marked doorway, disappearing into the Alchemy wing.

Remo steeled himself and entered the left passage.

The Astrology classroom was stately. Shelves lined the far wall, stuffed with leather-bound books. Rich blue tapestries depicting the zodiac hung behind Cosimo's desk. A luminous globe-shaped lantern, suspended from a painted ceiling medallion, cast a soft glow over a map of golden constellations. The combination of scholarly order and artistic grandeur filled Remo with awe and intimidation. This was no charlatan's tent; this was a true university.

Six students already occupied desks arranged in a semicircle. Remo took a seat toward the corner, acutely aware of the curious stares of the others, including a wide-eyed girl with a mop of brown curls, a brooding pale man, a solemn monk, a dignified dark-skinned woman, a plump older woman with merry eyes, and a scrawny teenage boy who looked as nervous as Remo felt.

Cosimo surveyed them all with serene satisfaction. "Ah, and here is the last of you. Good morning, Remo. Welcome."

Remo bowed his head politely, tucking his hands into his lap to hide his nerves.

"Each of you, in one way or another," Cosimo began, "has unearthed knowledge of the noble art of astrology. It must have been enough to whet your desire to learn more, for all of you have sought me out and chosen to be here today. As you know, I am Professor Cosimo. I will be your Astrology teacher and guide in navigating the language of the heavens."

He walked slowly between the desks as he spoke, his voice firm but kind. "Astrology is the ancient study of how planetary movements shape life on Earth. It is a language, a precise, structured art, built on thousands of years of human observation. Today, you will begin learning that language, starting with the signs, planets, aspects, and houses. These are the building blocks of understanding the heavens."

He gestured to a large chart behind him, filled with unfamiliar symbols. "Through the planets' positions at the time of your birth, we glimpse not just personality, but potential. Nothing in your chart dooms you. Nor does anything guarantee you greatness. The stars are not tyrants; they are teachers. They reveal tendencies, gifts, pitfalls... and then they hand you the choice.

"The chart is a map. The planets are players in a grand story—your story. Their relationships to each other tell of your talents, your burdens, your instincts, your fears. It is my belief," Cosimo said gently, "that before birth, our souls choose their moment of arrival to offer themselves the precise conditions needed for growth."

A few students exchanged skeptical glances, but Cosimo merely smiled. "You need not share this belief to benefit from astrology. All that is required is a willingness to learn, and a commitment to becoming more self-aware. The chart is a tool, and what you build with it is yours alone."

Remo's heart thudded as he listened. A portrait of potential, not fate. A path of self-awareness, not predestination. For the first time since his arrival, he felt a flicker of belonging.

Cosimo pointed again to the chart. "Let's begin with the glyphs for the planets. Copy them as I explain their natures."

Remo bent over his parchment, eager to begin.

"How was your first class?" Andrea asked as they made their way through Mavortis' streets.

They crossed over the bridge that spanned the Veil River, heading toward the Briar District, a cleaner, brighter part of the kingdom than the Iron District they'd left behind.

"It was interesting," Remo said carefully. "I see what you mean about Cosimo. He's very..."

"Say no more. You'll get used to the way he teaches. He likes riddles. And questions. And more riddles. Are you nervous about your hospital interview tomorrow?" Andrea asked.

It had almost slipped Remo's mind. "I am, a little. The head physician is a bit of a prick."

Andrea tossed a copper coin to a beggar seated along the bridge. "That's unfortunate. All pricks have heads, but not all heads have to be pricks."

Remo barked out a surprised laugh. "You're not wrong." He hesitated, emboldened by Andrea's easygoing mood. "Speaking of work, will you finally tell me what kind of business you had back in Lunaria?"

"Sly attempt," Andrea noted, amused but no more forthcoming.

"Well?" Remo prompted. "Seems only fair, seeing as you now know the truth of my intentions in coming to Mavortis."

Andrea considered him for a moment. "I'll tell you later," he promised. "Tonight."

Remo opened his mouth in surprise, and then froze. Across the street, sunlight caught a familiar figure in a royal blue dress with crimson bows. Long, dark hair glinted in the light. For a breathless moment, he thought he was imagining it.

But it truly was her—Sabelle.

Remo didn't even think. He broke into a jog, weaving through the crowd toward her.

Sabelle turned, her face lighting up in genuine shock and delight as she caught sight of him. Without hesitation, she grabbed both his hands in hers.

"Remo?" Sabelle laughed, looking as astonished to see him as he felt to see her. "What are you doing here? I thought you were on your way to Lunaria!"

"I was on my way to Lunaria to reach Mavortis," Remo said, beaming. "It's so good to see you again."

Andrea caught up, his expression one of pure mischief. Remo, remembering his manners, turned and gestured.

"Sabelle, this is my friend Andrea. Andrea, this is—this is Sabelle."

Andrea gave an elegant bow. "Pleased to meet you, Sabelle. Remo's told me absolutely nothing about you, which I must say seems a grievous oversight on his part."

Sabelle laughed again, the sound like bells. "Well, we'll have to rectify that."

Andrea winked at Remo. "Alas, my company pales in comparison. I'll leave you two to your reunion."

He gave them a short bow and disappeared back into the crowd with an exaggerated saunter.

Sabelle turned back to Remo, her cheeks still flushed from surprise. "When did you arrive in Mavortis?"

"Just the other night," he said, grinning. "What about you?"

"This morning," she said, linking her arm with his easily. "Are you settled with work yet?"

Remo shook his head, still half in disbelief that she was standing before him. "I have an interview at a hospital tomorrow, a practical exam of sorts. It seems like a prestigious place, though. I'm not sure they'll want to hire someone with my age and background."

She shot him a look of fierce loyalty. "Well, I healed perfectly well after your careful tending," she said, her tone daring him to say one more word against himself.

He smiled, searching her face for any remnant of a scar and failing to find one. "I'm glad for it. Although no scar could ever hope to mar your beauty."

The words slipped out smoothly, without calculation. Sabelle's flirtatious smile widened, and together they began walking along the cobble-stone street, neither one exactly leading the way, both willing to be led.

As they strolled, Remo glanced around, noting the absence of a certain overbearing older brother. "Is Cecco here as well?"

"No, he's managing the family business back in Juno," she said breezily. "I should have a little more freedom here without him breathing down my neck, if I can manage to outrun my father's watchful eye too."

Remo smiled at her irreverence. "So you'll be running wild through Mavortis instead for a change?"

She tossed her hair over her shoulder. "Naturally."

"And why is your father in Mavortis? Isn't he a Senator in Saffiro?" he asked.

"Aren't you the nosy one?" she teased, side-stepping the question with a sparkle in her eye that dared him to keep digging.

Recognizing the warning and not wishing to annoy her, Remo relented. "Have you eaten yet? Would you like to join me for lunch?"

Despite all logic advising caution, his heart beat faster with hope. Fate, or something like it, had crossed their paths again. He wanted to court her properly, though he knew the odds were stacked against him.

Healing was a respectable profession, and he had clawed his way higher than the simple farm boy he had once been. But Sabelle was the daughter of a member of the royal court, her future no doubt mapped by grander ambitions than a village healer could offer. Still, of all the risks he had taken lately, what was one more?

Sabelle's expression blossomed into pure delight. "I thought you'd never ask. I was worried I'd have to resort to dropping hints soon."

Goosebumps prickled along Remo's skin where their arms touched. "I've been known to be oblivious to subtleties," he admitted with a bashful smile. "You'll have to use more direct methods with me."

"Not to worry," Sabelle said, smoothing an invisible wrinkle from the extravagant silk of her gown. "I've been called many things, but subtle has never been one."

Remo returned to Andrea's living quarters hours later, the afternoon slipping into twilight.

Andrea was bent over his desk, carefully pouring a scarlet liquid into a thin glass cylinder, a blue flame flickering beneath it. He glanced up with a wide, teasing grin. "Welcome back, lover boy. I'm almost disappointed to see you home so soon. The moon isn't even out yet."

Remo closed the door behind him and dropped his bag by the settee, bracing himself for whatever teasing lay ahead.
"I know, I know. I'm sorry to disappoint."

Andrea swirled the liquid thoughtfully. "So. How was your afternoon with Sabelle?"

Remo put his hand behind his head, absentmindedly mussing his hair. He opened his mouth, closed it, and finally said, "Expensive."

Andrea chortled. "Ah. That serious, is it?" He tossed Remo a look that was half sympathy, half amusement. "At least tell me the meal was worth it."

When their bowls of fragrant lamb stew, baskets of herb-crusted bread, and glasses of pale, sweet wine had arrived, Remo had barely noticed the extravagance. What was a few denarii compared to the memory of Sabelle's tinkling laughter at his jokes, or her own quick-witted quips?

For a little while, the rest of the world had dissolved. There were no looming hospital interviews, no empire tightening its grip across the kingdoms, no whispered warnings tucked inside glass bottles. There was only the table between them and the feeling, new and terrifying and precious, that he was exactly where he was meant to be.

He smiled despite himself. "It was worth every last coin."

Andrea snorted. "How do you two know one another?"

"I met her a few days ago in Juno. It was serendipitous that we ran into each other again. Although we kept bumping into one another on the island, seeing her here again so unexpectedly makes me feel like it's fate. And I'm not sure I even believe in fate."

Andrea shook his head. "You only met her a few days ago and you're already invoking fate? You're in deep shit, my friend. Where did you take her for lunch?"

"Some tavern called Pellegrino's."

Andrea let out a low whistle. "And here I am, hosting you freely. I would've charged you rent if I thought you had denarii enough for a place like that."

Remo chuckled. "You'll be martyred for your sacrifice."

"I suppose you had to take her somewhere fitting." Andrea lifted the vial, watching the red swirl within. "Based on her dress, I'd wager she's from a wealthy family."

All humor faded from Remo's face as reality slapped him back into place. "Her father is a Senator of the Saffiran Court."

Andrea stiffened. It occurred to Remo that if Andrea was indeed nobility from Saffiro, he might be familiar with the court's members. "Do you know her last name?" Andrea asked.

"Er—yes, it's Fattura."

Andrea nodded, though no recognition lit his face. "I wonder what her business is in Mavortis," he mused aloud, then turned his attention back to Remo.

"I wondered that myself. She kept sidestepping the question, but eventually muttered something about her father meeting with business contacts. The family made their fortune as merchants."

Andrea shrugged, still absentmindedly swishing the solution in his hands. "Well, regardless of the circumstances, I'm glad you have another familiar face in Mavortis. And hers is certainly a beautiful one."

"Indeed," Remo said with a twinge of regret. "I wonder how long I can continue meeting with her until her family finds out and puts an end to it."

Andrea gave him a sympathetic look. "I don't wish to give you false hope. Juno is a small island, and if she was vague with you about her presence here, it could be because her family is seeking a match for her. Senators are independently wealthy and pay for their power and influence. They're probably looking to match her with someone of greater rank. Royal courts are saturated with daughters of lesser nobles, all vying to be pawned off to the highest bidder."

Remo appreciated Andrea's honesty, even as it bit. He had assumed as much himself, but hearing it aloud from someone in the know solidified his fears, and deepened his curiosity about Andrea's noble background.

"I wonder what her family would make of us dining at The Crooked Cupola," Remo said. "Perhaps if Sevo wore a dress and played the harp... or cleaned up what looks suspiciously like a blood stain on the ceiling..."

Andrea roared with laughter, and Remo smiled, satisfied with the effect of his joke. When Andrea's laughter subsided, Remo sank into the vermillion settee, the memory of his earlier question resurfacing.

"Earlier you said you'd tell me what sort of business you had back in Lunaria."

Andrea hesitated, then sat beside him. "Do you recall what we discussed while we walked along the forest path?"

"You mean the rumors of the empire trying to expand?"

Andrea gave a solemn nod. "Yes. Emperor Varro has been escalating the authority of the Knights of Saffiro. He's been sending them into other kingdoms in greater numbers and granting them imperium, the power to act however they deem necessary in Saffiro's interest, without oversight and without consequences. There have even been reports of them in Anxur."

A chill ran down Remo's spine. "It's true," he said quietly. "I saw at least two before I left."

Andrea looked grim. "My business in Lunaria involved discussing the issue with influential individuals. Pushing back against Saffiro. Gathering any information I could. I report to people who wish to keep vigilant."

"I don't understand," Remo said, shaking his head. "Are you an emissary? A spy? Why is this yours to fix?"

Andrea's handsome face suddenly looked twenty years older. He stared into the fire. "Because if my father starts a war, the blood spilled will be on my hands too."

Remo's breath caught. "You—your father is Emperor Varro?"

Andrea met his eyes and dipped his chin in affirmation.

Remo froze, the implications crashing over him like a wave. Andrea wasn't just minor nobility. He was a prince—the disinherited son of the most powerful man in Terramundi.

The guards' deference at the gate at the sight of Andrea's signet ring and the way he carried himself, effortlessly regal, all corroborated his confession.

"The guards at the gate—they called you 'lord' when you showed them your ring," Remo said, struggling to catch up.

"They assumed I was a relative of the royal family," Andrea said with a wry smile. "Because no prince, even an exiled one, would travel alone, without a carriage or guards."

Andrea leaned back against the settee, looking lost in memory. "I grew up in the palace of Saffiro, the Kingdom of the Sun. I had every material comfort. Educated by the best tutors. Of course, I would learn much later that the history they told me was slanted. I was trained in battle from the time I could walk. The only times my father seemed to vaguely approve of me were when I was covered in someone else's blood, acting like the brute he wanted me to be. But no matter how many fights I won, or how my skills improved, the only true affection afforded to me as a child came from my mother. She died when I was still very young."

Remo's heart ached at the words. He knew what it was like to live under the shadow of a cruel father, but Andrea's suffering was etched even deeper.

Andrea's voice hardened. "Three years ago, my father sent me to Satria to train the Satrians to raise a legion of soldiers for Saffiro's protection. To monsters like my father, Satrians are nothing more than fodder—hasta-ti—to die in the front lines, sparing worthier Saffiran lives."

He grimaced, as if the memory physically pained him. "But when I got there, I saw the truth. I saw the poverty. The brutality. I was an angry, cocky bastard back then, but I wasn't without compassion."

His voice dropped lower, rougher. "One night, I caught a Knight assaulting a Satrian girl. He was pulling her towards an alley, pulling off her dress. I snapped. I broke his hand. Beat him bloody."

Remo shivered. He could believe it. Andrea's easygoing manner only made his capacity for violence, when roused to defend others, all the more striking.

"The other knights, my father's men, stood by and watched as she was being attacked. While I attacked one of their own. They viewed my actions as treasonous. In their eyes, I was no leader—only a weak, sentimental boy unfit to command. I lost their loyalty, my authority. I lost my mission."

Andrea shook his head. "When I returned to Saffiro and confessed what happened, my father made his displeasure known. Then he exiled me. Stripped me of my title and cast me out."

Andrea rubbed a hand absently along his forearm, as if feeling old bruises. "It was a mercy. Being torn from his shadow remains the only true blessing my father ever gave me. I have no siblings; in exiling me, he cast aside his only blood heir. Another mercy. I never wanted the throne, least of all a throne built on centuries of rot. Emperors were meant to be chosen by the Senate, not handed down like heirlooms. But law bends easily to greed, and ambition has long since hollowed out the empire's bones."

He sounded aloof, removed from the event as though he were telling another person's story, not his own.

"Andrea, I'm so sorry," Remo said.

Andrea shrugged as if to prove how little he was affected by the event. "But, to answer your question, that is why it's my responsibility to make sure the empire does not expand. Because it's built on fear and cruelty, and every time it grows, more innocent people pay the price. If I do nothing, then I'm no better than the ones who looked away. I couldn't stop being born into it, but I can damn well stop it from devouring what's still good in this world."

The air surrounding them was electrified with energy as a breeze from Andrea's opened balcony doors blew in, the night sky exposed as if the stars themselves awaited this moment where Remo felt his destiny and free will converge.

"You won't do it alone," he said, voice firm. "If the empire rises against Anxur, I'll fight with you."

Light returned to Andrea's eyes for the first time since he began his story. Gratitude softened the exiled prince's striking features as he offered Remo a small, sorrowful smile.

Without hesitation, Remo clapped a hand on his friend's shoulder. Andrea gave his shoulder a firm pat in return before retreating to his workstation, the silence between them rich with understanding. Neither was comfortable with outward displays of emotion, but the bond forged between them needed no words.

The rest of the night passed in an easy, reverent quiet.

# Chapter Nine

R EMO'S PRACTICAL EXAM AT the hospital ended in success, though he wouldn't have guessed it from Arlo Acerbi's relentless criticism. Despite Remo performing every task with skill and precision, the physician seized every opportunity to belittle him.

One look around the hospital told Remo that Acerbi was in no position to be so selective. Only five healers were tending to forty-five patients, and it was painfully obvious that even the most basic care was falling through the cracks.

His first assignment was straightforward; he was to clean and re-bandage an infected wound. When Remo finished, Acerbi sniffed and deemed him *"not a complete halfwit"*—a generous review, by Acerbi's standards.

Remo was then saddled with an even less glamorous challenge of performing an enema on a patient who hadn't moved their bowels in days, all while Acerbi hounded him with hypothetical questions and biting commentary. He anticipated he'd be given the tasks Acerbi considered beneath him, but he didn't complain. It was the nature of the work, and his nature to work hard.

Later, weary to the bone, Remo scrubbed the day off himself in a washing basin, his skin raw and his mind fogged with exhaustion. All he could think about was a hot meal and the familiar, golden glow of The Crooked Cupola. He dried off, dressed, and headed straight for the inn.

The tavern was alive with the easy noise of dinner chatter. Andrea sat near the hearth, talking to a fair-haired girl Remo didn't recognize. As soon as he caught sight of Remo, Andrea waved him over with an encouraging grin. Remo crossed the room, greeting Andrea before turning to acknowledge the girl, and faltered.

Everything about her appearance lived somewhere in shades of in-between: hair not quite gold, not quite brown, spilling over her shoulders in soft waves; skin kissed by sunlight; eyes the color of molten gold, shimmering between shades of tawny and light brown. Her nose lent a definitiveness to her otherwise changeable features, elegant and sharp.

She smiled shyly at Remo as he stared a second longer than appropriate by his standards, making a study of her. He felt guilty acknowledging her unique features and averted his eyes at last. Whatever existed, or didn't exist, between him and Sabelle, he owed her loyalty in thought as well as deed.

Still, there was something familiar about this girl. Something that stirred a memory just beyond his reach. Her scent, vanilla and amber, enveloped him like a long-forgotten memory.

"Remo, meet Lyra, my best friend and greatest critic," Andrea said with a grin. "Lyra, this is my new roommate."

"It's you," Remo blurted. "I mean, it's nice to meet you. Andrea's mentioned you many times."

She smiled widely, the act only multiplying her already immeasurable beauty. Her cheeks seemed to be recovering from a faint blush, likely a lingering consequence of his stare. "Likewise, Remo. Andrea was just telling me about you as well."

Her voice surprised him—low and velvety, with a lilting accent he couldn't place. Remo had heard the trade accents of half the continent, but Lyra's didn't match any of them.

He quirked a brow at Andrea in mock suspicion. "All good things, I hope?"

"Well, that depends on where you stand on the issue of obnoxious snoring," Andrea said matter-of-factly.

Lyra flashed a mischievous smile. "Don't worry, Remo. I know Andrea well enough to never take a word he says seriously."

Andrea placed a hand on his heart in a display of exaggerated hurt. "You wound me, woman."

Sevo appeared with three tankards of Satrian cider and a towering plate of fried rice balls. The scent of cheese and herbs made Remo's mouth water.

Andrea raised his tankard. "So? How'd the big day go?"

Remo shrugged, spearing a rice ball. "Well enough. I was hired and then immediately put to work."

Lyra's head cocked in polite curiosity. "What do you do?"

"I'm a healer."

"Oh, that's wonderful! I mean—" she stumbled. "It's probably grueling and heartbreaking, too—death and sickness and—"

"You're doing a great job selling it," Andrea said, his dry, sarcastic tone at odds with the playfulness in his eyes.

Lyra threw him a glare. "What I mean to say is that it takes a caring sort of person to do healing work."

Remo smiled kindly, understanding her intended meaning all along. "Thanks. And you spoke true, it's very unpleasant work most of the time. Honestly, if I start thinking about what I saw today, I might lose my appetite."

Lyra's amber eyes widened. "I can imagine. Though, I'd prefer not to."

Andrea, resting his chin on one hand, looked ever-so-slightly bored by the brief departure of attention away from himself. Remo wondered, not unkindly, whether Andrea's need for constant notice was a side effect of having grown up a prince.

Remo turned to him with mock seriousness. "Well, thanks to today's successful practical exam, I'll finally be able to afford lodgings of my own. Unless, of course, you'll secretly miss my alleged snoring."

Andrea's full lips curled into a grin. "Oh, I'm sure I'll weep bitterly for the first few nights. But with a maiden or two warming my bed again, I expect my tears will dry rather quickly."

Lyra tutted. "And to think Nella's been asking about you."

Andrea, suddenly sharper, straightened slightly. "What does she want to know?"

Lyra took a slow sip of her drink, luxuriating in her power to make him squirm.

Remo, amused, cut in. "Who's Nella?"

Lyra looked to Andrea, giving him a pointed invitation to answer.

Andrea huffed and gave in. "Nella is my past lover. And Lyra's roommate."

"Every couple of months, Andrea and Nella get back together... and then promptly end things again," Lyra explained, deadpan.

"Ah," Remo said, wisely deciding not to comment further.

Andrea took a long pull from his drink, then repeated his question, more urgent this time. "Well? What does she want to know?"

"Whether or not you're seeing anyone else. So—are you?"

"No," Andrea groaned stubbornly, as if admitting defeat.

Lyra look pleased.

Remo, sensing the chance to steer the conversation to safer waters, turned back to Lyra. "Do you work?"

"I'm a minstrel," she said with an almost apologetic smile. "I perform at different taverns."

"Really? What instrument?"

"The lyre," she admitted, sheepish again.

Remo was fascinated by the oxymoron of her: a shy performer. She had the gentle air of someone who had wandered into the wrong world by accident and decided to stay. "I should've guessed as much, given your name."

"She sings beautifully," Andrea chimed in sincerely. "I damn near cried the first time I heard her play."

Lyra beamed at him, the fondness between them obvious despite their teasing banter. Watching them stirred something bittersweet in Remo, a longing for that kind of easy familiarity.

"I'd love to hear you sometime," Remo said. "I'll make sure to bring a handkerchief."

Her honeyed eyes avoided his as she laughed and ducked her head in thanks.

"And I," Andrea said gravely, "shall boil myself alive in alchemical equipment if my workload grows any heavier."

"I feel the same way," Remo admitted. "I never imagined that there was so much math involved in my subject. We're learning calculations for tomorrow's lesson. What's your subject like?" he asked Lyra.

Andrea rolled his eyes. "Don't even bother asking, Remo. Her subject makes no sense to me."

"That's because you have all the concentration powers of an old sock. All it takes is a woman to be within twenty meters for your attention to wander," Lyra snapped.

Andrea looked torn between amusement and annoyance. "Is it my fault that ladies practically trip over themselves to try and catch my attention?"

Lyra scowled. "The only thing bigger than your heart, Andrea, is your ego."

Andrea grinned stupidly. "I can think of something of mine that's even bigger—"

"My subject!" Lyra interrupted loudly, her cheeks faintly pink again. She turned to Remo, leaving Andrea chuckling to himself. "It's about learning to discipline your mind, to focus your attention, and to explore different states of consciousness. We study ancient texts and practice moving between realms of existence."

*That explains her appearance,* Remo thought. Perhaps her physicality, in all its in-between colors, had borne changes from her spiritual travels in between worlds. He still didn't remotely understand her subject but nodded politely.

A part of him wondered if they became friends, he might someday tell her about his strange experience in Jupiter's temple, and what an Awareness student might make of it.

"You know, in Alchemy, we have five elements instead of four," Andrea cut in. "Astrology only deals with fire, air, water, and earth. We alchemists get one extra."

Remo blinked. "What's the fifth?"

"Quintessence," Andrea said dramatically, waggling his fingers like a magician.

Remo suppressed a smile. "What's that supposed to be?"

"The stuff of stars," Andrea said. "The material between all things. The divine breath of the universe."

Across the table, Lyra leaned toward Remo and whispered, "And he calls *my* subject silly."

Telescopes lined the circular dovecote's outer balcony, their brass bodies gleaming under the moonlight.

It was their first night class under the open sky, and Professor Cosimo had brought them here to practice star charting. The heavens were clear and glittering, the constellations stitched across velvet-black sky.

Cosimo strolled between students, his staff tapping gently against the stones. When he reached Remo's side, Remo ventured a question. "Professor—you specified *visible* planets. Do you think there are others out there, ones we can't see yet?"

Cosimo's smile deepened into something secret. "I suspect so, Mr. Renato. Just as I suspect the world is larger than Terramundi and that life exists beyond the Great Beyond. Perhaps, one day, we'll invent telescopes strong enough to prove it."

Remo frowned thoughtfully. "But what would that mean for astrology? Would unknown planets still affect us?"

Stroking his beard, Cosimo gazed upward. "If they exist, and if human consciousness ever comes to know them, astrologers of that era will have the task of interpreting their influence. Until then"—he patted Remo's shoulder lightly—"don't lose sleep over hidden dragons while today's fire still burns your back."

As Cosimo turned away toward other students, Remo considered his words as he stared at the stars.

They twinkled at him indifferently, not caring whether or not he believed they affected his life. He wondered if they were laughing at him from above; he envied their advantageous perspective.

For a moment, he stopped trying to understand the world and instead stared back at the stars, mirroring their indifference.

The heat of mid-July scorched Mavortis as the setting sun passed through the last stretch of Cancer season, waves of visible heat wafting off the clay roofs of the city.

Between long shifts at the hospital and nightly lessons at the Academy, Remo had little time for anything but work and exhaustion. His studies, both astrological and medical, piled up faster than he could clear them.

Still, moments of reprieve graced him amid the grind in the form of meals at The Crooked Cupola with Andrea and Lyra, and occasional, stolen afternoons with Sabelle.

It was one such rare evening now, the sky burnished gold, as Remo and Sabelle strolled through the public gardens. Fields of red poppies swayed around them, vibrant against the heat-hazed air.

"I'm half-tempted to fake an illness just to admit myself to your hospital," Sabelle said dramatically. "At least then I'd see more of you."

Remo laughed, offering his hand. "If you were my patient, I'd tend to you so carefully you'd be discharged by morning. We'll need a better plan."

Sabelle pouted, and her hand brushed his. Even the smallest of physical contact with her made every nerve ending within his body attentive.

"Don't you dare sway me from my righteous anger!" she scolded. "I've been forced to suffer the dullest company imaginable."

Remo gave her a quizzical look. "Who would that be?"

"My father's friends," she sighed, disgusted. "The local nobility. My family has money but no title, and that alone makes us beneath them."

Remo solemnly tapped his chin. "Sounds serious. You should bring them to my hospital immediately."

She blinked. "For what?"

"To have the sticks surgically removed from up their asses," he said gravely.

She gasped at the shock value of what he'd said, then threw back her head while laughing. He liked saying ridiculous things just to make her laugh. There was no sight more intoxicating to him than her smile, and no better feeling than to be the cause behind it, using whatever cheap means necessary.

"I shouldn't make such jokes in front of a lady," Remo teased, making a small apologetic bow.

Sabelle's bow-shaped lips curled upwards. "I'll have to think of some way to punish you for your language."

"Not being with you every day is punishment enough," he said.

It came out more honestly than he intended; he'd meant for it to be a mawkish joke. Perhaps she felt the sincerity behind his words because she didn't roll her eyes as he expected. She instead softened, her green eyes glazed as though she were deep in unpleasant thoughts.

"What's wrong?" he asked.

"I think my father only allowed me to stay here to parade me in front of higher society," she admitted, staring at the path ahead. "To meet someone they'd approve of."

Remo's heart sank; her situation was as Andrea predicted. "Maybe we should rethink things, then."

She stopped walking and faced him, her green eyes flashing. "No. I won't be ordered about—not by them, and not by you." Her voice softened, almost breaking. "Unless you don't want my company."

The defiance in her voice only made his heart ache more. He lifted a hand and brushed a loose strand of hair from her face, his knuckles grazing her cheek.

"Anyone blind to your worth would be as unworthy of you as those who judge by titles." His voice dropped to a near whisper. "You're a fairy tale come to life."

Wistfulness replaced the uncertainty in her gaze. He willed himself to choose his next words carefully before he lost his resolve to ever mention them again. "But if ending our brief understanding now is what's best for you, then that's what I'll do," he said.

However rebellious Sabelle claimed to be, she was still dependent on her family's status and money. He didn't want her to risk either for his sake, not when they were still only getting to know one another.

"I will always do as I please," she said firmly. "My family knows that.

We can meet in secret, on your side of town if we must. And it's not a crime to be seen with you. We haven't done anything scandalous or indecent."

Remo stepped closer, the jasmine-sweet air swirling between them. "There's just one thing false about what you've said," he murmured.

She blinked, caught off guard. "What's that?"

"That we haven't done anything indecent."

He brushed her hair back again, exposing the delicate curve of her neck. His lips found hers already slightly parted for him. Their joining felt inevitable. Her arms slid around his neck as his hand tangled in her hair, the taste of pomegranate and summer heat flooding his senses.

He gathered enough strength of will to force his lips to part from hers at last, the both of them somewhat breathless in each other's embrace. And though he managed to break from their kiss, he knew it would take a strength he was glad he didn't possess to end their understanding.

If there was something he couldn't abide, it was abandoning a story halfway through. He needed to see everything he did through to some end because he couldn't stand questioning what might have been. And whether they had a future together or not, they couldn't seem to stay away from one another.

Remo lingered on the walk back to Andrea's home, savoring the heady afterglow. Was this how Milena and Devlan had felt in their stories—so full of hope, so brimming with wonder that it felt dangerous?

He stepped into the apartment and instantly sensed a different energy. Andrea wasn't alone. Fortunately, both occupants were fully clothed as Remo caught sight of a sharp-eyed girl perched on the settee.

Andrea rose and cleared his throat. "Remo, this is Nella." No other introduction followed. *Complicated, indeed.*

Nella had fierce hazel eyes framed by sharp brows and a tight bun that only emphasized the sternness of her features. A smattering of freckles softened her severity, but Remo doubted she'd appreciate anyone pointing that out.

She greeted Remo without so much as a smile, although the mood within the room did not indicate that he had interrupted a lovers' quarrel—quite the contrary.

Andrea, usually so self-assured, actually looked hesitant. That alone made Remo stand up a little straighter.

"So. You're the healer," Nella said, her tone as warm as a slap.

Remo, unsure how to meet such bluntness, scrambled for neutral ground. "Yes. And you study at university?"

She merely nodded, leaving Remo with the unenviable task of introducing the next conversation topic. "What do you study?"

"Medicine," she said. No elaboration. No softening. She could certainly give Arlo Acerbi a run for his money in the art of intimidation.

"That's impressive," Remo offered, and meant it. Becoming a healer was tough enough, but training to be a physician was practically a pact with hell.

"What's your subject at the Academy?" she pressed.

Remo felt all the blood drain from his face as he looked to Andrea for the correct answer.

"Relax," Andrea said lightly. "She's known about the Academy for a long time. Cosimo allowed it."

Remo still hesitated, but Nella's stare was merciless. "Astrology. We've only just gone over the foundational things. Now we're doing calculations; it's mostly been mathematical formulas and astronomy so far."

"Fascinating," she deadpanned, sounding anything but.

Something about her borderline rudeness made Remo want to laugh. Maybe it was her lack of pretense, clearly not caring whether or not she was likable. Part of him admired how little she appeared to care what he might have thought about her. Or maybe it was the contrast between her and Andrea; the good-natured, amiable prince and his fierce, abrupt lover—or whatever they were to one another.

"I'm off. See you tomorrow," she said, more command than farewell.

"You will," Andrea said, without missing a beat.

"Remo," she added with a curt nod.

"Goodnight," he answered, taking a cue from her curt farewell. Normally, he might have added "It was nice to meet you," but he decided that honesty and brevity were more valued by Nella than niceties.

As she left, Andrea looked as though he were bracing himself to answer the torrent of questions Remo would undoubtedly ask regarding her. Remo began with, "Aren't you going to walk her home?"

Andrea blinked, then gave a lazy wave toward the window. "No need. She lives just across the way."

To prove it, he swung open the balcony doors. Sure enough, they spotted Nella slipping into the opposite building without a backward glance.

Remo leaned against the doorframe with folded arms. "So. You two are back together, huh?"

Andrea sighed the sigh of a man both ashamed and delighted. "It would appear so." His smile gave him away.

Remo snorted. "Blink twice if she's holding you hostage."

Andrea looked as though he were suppressing a laugh. "Careful. I know she comes across as intense. Maybe even cold. And I suppose she is. But she thaws as you get to know her better."

Remo laughed at his friend's choice of words. "Well, that's a relief."

"I suppose some of that hardened edge comes from the way she was raised. Nella is a noblewoman, although, like me, she doesn't like people knowing so or treating her as such. She's the seventh child of the King of Vecontii. Therefore, she will never inherit the throne, nor is she the family's only chance of a powerful alliance through marriage, so, her family begrudgingly allowed her to study medicine at university as she wished."

"So you two met in Mavortis?" Remo asked.

"Well, no, but we didn't start courting until we ran into one another here. Our families have met several times during balls and events, and our fathers would meet occasionally to discuss political matters. Vecontii is the wealthiest kingdom besides Saffiro due to its dominance of trade routes at sea. So naturally, a marriage between the households of Saffiro and Vecontii would be encouraged. I think that's why we hated each other so much at first—because neither of us is very keen on doing anything our families would approve of.

"But part of what brought us together was our similar backgrounds. Although she's on far better terms with her family than I ever was with my father, she still holds some resentment towards them. We understand each other in that way. I know what it's like growing up in a powerful family, to be viewed as a weapon and not a child, not as a *human* with needs."

Andrea's smirk faded into something quieter. "Long story short, we met again here. Cosimo gave me express permission to tell her about the Academy, because... Well, there's something you should know. About him—and me."

A ripple of unease ran through Remo. He straightened, every instinct telling him that Andrea was about to lower a heavy secret onto his shoulders. Information was Remo's greatest weakness, but the deeper he sank into Andrea and Cosimo's world, the harder it became to pretend he could ever go back. His hands were already stained.

Andrea spoke low, as if the very walls could betray them. "Cosimo isn't just a headmaster. He's a member of the Order of Aquarius—a secret resistance against the empire."

Remo went still. "And he's fine with you telling me this?"

Andrea shot him a significant look. "I would never divulge anything about the Academy or the Order that I was not granted permission to reveal. Cosimo mastered Awareness in his day in addition to the other subjects, and while I don't pretend to know how Awareness works, I know he has some sort of ability. He can read people's energy and intentions, and he trusts you. I do as well."

Remo sensed it intuitively; the integrity of Andrea's word was as good as gold. Andrea's tone was defiant, and Remo had the feeling that the prince didn't take questions of his loyalty lightly. He suspected that to have earned the loyalty of one like Andrea meant that you could always depend upon it.

"I know," Remo said. "I just didn't want you risking yourself for my sake. I'm honored you trust me. I won't betray it."

Andrea's voice softened. "Like I said, Cosimo trusts you too. Maybe it's because of Trota. Maybe it's something more. He thinks you might play a bigger role than either of us can see yet."

Remo shook his head, half laughing. "Me? I'm no one. I'm not a knight, or a lord, or a trained fighter."

The former qualifications particularly weighed on him, the front of his mind not quite rid of Sabelle even with the critical discussion taking place.

"Take my word as proof that prestige of title and wealth have no bearing on one's value and on what that individual may contribute to the betterment of the world," Andrea said.

Remo, too preoccupied with digesting the information being disseminated, didn't fight Andrea on this point despite his doubts. He remained quiet as Andrea continued.

"The Order of Aquarius formed at the same time as the Academy, right after the Calamity of Emperor Septimus' making. It should go without saying that they both function in secret. It was Cosimo who gave me the order to gather information about the Knights of Saffiro, on their numbers and moves. All of the other professors of the Academy are involved in the Order, as well as some alumni."

Remo recalled how easily Andrea had been looped into his first conversation with Cosimo. Now it all made sense. Andrea wasn't just a favorite student. He was part of something much deeper.

"Saffiro's been courting Vecontii's favor for years," Andrea went on. "Nella's family, the Valentias, are rich from trade—too powerful to strong-arm, but too useful to ignore. What my father really wants is their fleet. He's used light taxes as bait, hoping to get a naval alliance in return," Andrea scoffed. "But my father doesn't make friends. He makes assets. Bardi's been playing nice, but he won't be able to stall much longer.

"Anyway, with more and more concerns about Saffiro expanding again, Cosimo knew we needed more powerful allies in place. And it just so happened that my girlfriend is a princess from Vecontii. I asked Cosimo whether or not he thought it was a good idea to reveal the Order to her, and he, who had been looking for a closer in with the Valentia family, encouraged me to. It's likely why he allowed me to tell her about the Academy in the first place. Her information has been indispensable."

"You said you hated each other at first. How did you end up courting?" Remo asked.

Andrea grinned wolfishly. "That's a story for another time. One I'll enjoy telling more."

"How'd she react when you told her about the Order?"

"Badly," Andrea sighed. "She thought I was using her. Can't blame her, it looked that way. But we were together before the Order needed her. My feelings were always real; the rest was a useful coincidence. I think part of her was relieved to finally have an explanation, though. She knew I was keeping something from her. She knew I made salves and elixirs for apothecaries and sold my metalwork, but that didn't explain the absences. Why would an alchemist need to travel across kingdoms?"

"Well, at least she came around and trusted you in the end," Remo replied. "I suppose we'll be seeing much more of her now since your, ah,"—he gave a pointed glance at the bed's rumpled sheets—"reunion?"

"You're awfully invested in my romantic life tonight. Should I assume this has something to do with your afternoon with Sabelle?"

Remo made a gesture as if to suggest that Andrea's statement was correct as he strolled back towards the balcony. "In fact, it does. I'm trying to learn exactly what to *avoid* in romantic relationships."

The cushion Andrea hurled at Remo's head was well-earned, but the action didn't quite cover the sound of Andrea's laugh.

# Chapter Ten

ANOTHER ROOM OPENED IN Andrea's boarding house, much to Remo's relief, and likely Andrea's, given Nella's now-frequent visits. The new room was smaller, the furniture shabbier, but Remo didn't mind. It was his own space and affordable enough with tuition and Sabelle to budget for.

Workdays blurred into each other. Acerbi clearly enjoyed handing him the most difficult patients and dirtiest tasks, but Remo endured it all with steady resolve. He wasn't squeamish—not at blood, bile, or pressure. He pushed through each challenge for the patients' sake, and to deny Acerbi the satisfaction of seeing him fail. His patients noticed. They welcomed him as one of the few healers who truly cared.

"Healer Remo. Thank goodness you're here," one such patient sighed with relief as Remo approached.

"Hello, Ludovico," Remo said, pulling on gloves. The man had gout. He'd been treated with an autumn crocus elixir. "How are you feeling?"

"Dismal," Ludovico groaned.

Remo checked the swelling. It was less red now, and Ludovico didn't flinch as much. The elixir had helped.

"Bless you, boy," Ludovico said. "That odious man left me to rot again. Same as always."

Remo didn't need to ask whom he referred to. Acerbi's detachment went beyond professionalism; his disdain for anything "beneath" him bordered on cruelty. He wasn't in medicine to help people; he was in it to wield power.

Remo offered reassurance and quickly returned with the medicine.

Ludovico wouldn't be neglected, not while he was on duty.

Acerbi intercepted Remo in the hallway, snapping his fingers like one might summon a dog. "You. The woman in the long-term ward. Prostitute. Incurable case. Undoubtedly deserved," he sneered.

Remo's jaw tensed at Acerbi's words. If Acerbi's contempt could reduce even he to a worm, how must he have treated her during the exam? Remo could only imagine her shame. Sure enough, the patient was weeping when he arrived.

Remo softened his voice in an attempt to make himself smaller, gentler. "I'm here to help," he said. She didn't answer, just hid behind her hands. Her arms showed a telltale rash. "Can you tell me what you're feeling?" he asked.

She gave no sign she'd heard him. He didn't push. "I'll be back in an hour," he promised, and gently withdrew.

When he returned an hour later, the tears had stopped, though her face was still pale. The worst hadn't set in yet. There'd be no cure, only comfort, pain relief, and the dignity she'd been denied.

"Are you up for talking now?" he asked, voice just as gentle.

She didn't meet his eye, but she nodded.

"What's your name?" he asked.

No answer. He didn't press. "Can you tell me how you're feeling?" he offered instead.

Silence stretched between them. He waited. At last, in a raspy voice, she said, "My whole body aches."

Venus pox. The aches were only the beginning; it would get worse.

"I'll bring something for the pain," he said. "Any other symptoms?"

She shivered before she could reply.

"May I check your temperature?" he asked, and waited until she nodded before approaching.

Her skin burned under his hand. "I'll bring water, a blanket, and something for the pain," he said.

The nameless patient didn't respond, and he left quietly, heart heavy.

"Here," Cosimo began, "is where the paths of astronomer and astrologer diverge. We've charted the heavens. Now, we seek their meaning."

Remo sat up straighter, eager.

"The zodiac," Cosimo explained, pacing the room, "is seasonal, not stellar. Aries begins at the vernal equinox, signaling spring. Cancer follows at the summer solstice, marking the longest day of the year, Libra at the autumnal equinox, bringing forth balance and a gradual shortening of days, and Capricorn at the winter solstice, ushering in winter's stillness on the longest night.

"These four—Aries, Cancer, Libra, and Capricorn—are the cardinal signs. They open each season and herald change. After them come the fixed signs, which sustain the essence of each season, and finally, the mutable signs, which signal an approaching transition."

Remo quickly scribbled notes, sensing the importance of every word. He felt suddenly aware of astrology as a profound, living rhythm, a dance of light, seasons, and human experience far richer than he'd ever imagined.

"First, you will learn the classifications of the zodiac signs, meaning their elements and modes. Each is equally important in understanding the quality of the sign. We will start with Aries, as it is at the head of the zodiac calendar," Cosimo said, pausing expectantly. He huffed at the silence. "I suppose you'll learn to laugh at that later, once you learn the signs' anatomical rulerships.

"Now, to understand fire signs, you need only study nature itself. Everyone, look at one of the lanterns around you. Imagine yourself seated by a roaring hearth. What do you feel? Consider what fire truly does."

Remo gazed thoughtfully into the candle flame nearest him, hypnotized by its restless flicker. He had always found fire mesmerizing.

Cosimo continued, his voice warm and compelling, "Fire begins with an initiatory spark, much like Aries, the sign that sparks the zodiac's cycle in spring. Notice how flames leap into existence, boldly, impatiently—this is Aries energy, eager to act and assert itself."

He took a slow step forward, letting the class absorb his words. "Fire provides heat, vitality, consciousness itself—qualities embodied in our next fire sign, Leo. Leo sustains the warmth of summer, passionate and generous, like the steady glow of a flame illuminating the darkest spaces. See how fire dances confidently, captivating the eye? That's Leo's charisma, its natural urge to entertain and inspire."

Cosimo's eyes brightened with enthusiasm as he gestured toward a flickering candle by the window. "Finally, consider Sagittarius, the mutable fire sign. Its energy is adventurous and restless, just like the flame that bends and shifts with every breeze. Sagittarius seeks wisdom through exploration, always drawn outward into the unknown. Like candlelight guiding us through darkness, Sagittarius' optimism lights our path, ever-curious and adaptable."

Remo stared deeper into the flame, feeling something inside him resonate powerfully with Cosimo's words. It wasn't scientific or quantifiable, yet a profound truth stirred within him. It was an intuitive knowing, as if Cosimo's lesson had reawakened ancient wisdom long hidden in his unconscious. The realization felt less like learning something new and more like rediscovering something vital he'd once forgotten.

As Remo made to dismiss himself through the common room exit into The Crooked Cupola, he saw Lyra. She wore a floaty lilac dress with a lace-trimmed bodice, reminding him, fleetingly, of a sugared violet. She noticed him and gave a shy wave as he approached.

"Has your class just ended?" Lyra asked.

"Yes, I'm heading back now. What about you?"

"Oh, I'm not here for class today. I just came to use the library. We can't bring any books on arcane studies home. If caught, we'd face arrest and questioning." She paused, clearly uneasy at even mentioning such a risk.

Encouraged by her vulnerability, Remo confessed, "Does the fear ever fade?"

Lyra met his eyes, sympathy flickering across her gentle features. "Somewhat. But never completely. At least for me." She gave a small, self-conscious smile, clearly grateful someone else shared her apprehension.

Remo's eyes flickered above Lyra's head, at the archway for Awareness, noting the engraved sun glyph above it. "Why a sun for Awareness?"

Lyra spun, thoughtful. "It symbolizes our conscious mind—the awareness we have when awake."

Curiosity piqued, he motioned toward the other arches. "Then why does Astrology have a moon, and Alchemy a star?"

Lyra's gaze drifted to follow his. "The moon symbolizes our unconscious. Astrological forces influence us without our conscious realization.

"Do you know much astrology?" he asked.

"Only a bit," she replied. "I'm Satrian, and the people there still hold fast to the Old Religion of which astrological knowledge is deeply intertwined."

Remo recognized her accent now. It was rarely heard in Anxur, given Satria's impoverishment and isolation after the Calamity and Saffiran domination.

"As for why the star represents Alchemy," Lyra tapped a finger to her lip in a contemplative gesture. "I think Andrea would probably tell you it's because he's in the class."

A surprised laugh burst from Remo. "I don't doubt it. How long have you known each other?"

Her expression briefly shifted, unreadable. "A few years," she said simply, offering no further explanation.

Remo wasn't sure if he had imagined the change, but he decided not to pursue the topic further. "How many years does it take students to master each subject?"

Lyra's smile returned, clearly pleased by the safer topic. "Technically, mastery is lifelong. There's always more to uncover. These are spiritual pursuits, so no official titles exist. Alumni frequently return to consult teachers or access the library.

"Astrology, being the most structured of the three subjects, typically takes a year of formal lessons. But most students stick around longer than that to continue their research.

"Alchemy is more variable, typically taking anywhere from three to five years. Much depends on the specialty each student pursues and their spiritual development. Andrea would tell you it's equally scientific and spiritual, so that adds complexity.

"Awareness is different. It usually takes about three years. The first year is primarily devoted to reading ancient texts and introductory mental discipline exercises to focus and steady our minds. The second year involves deeper mental training, exploring different states of consciousness. By the third year, these practices intensify significantly.

"Ultimately, true mastery of any of these disciplines is demonstrated through some profound personal work or experience. Professor Cosimo mastered all three subjects, you know. That's almost unheard of."

As they neared the exit toward The Crooked Cupola, they saw the headmaster himself approaching, his eyes twinkling warmly as he greeted them. His gaze lingered curiously in the space between them, a thoughtful smile forming on his lips as if observing something fascinating yet invisible to their eyes. "Excuse my intrusion. May I speak with you privately, Mr. Renato?"

Startled by the unexpected request, Remo nodded politely, bidding Lyra farewell before following Cosimo through the Astrology classroom toward his private office.

The headmaster's office was comfortably furnished, centered around a broad, polished wooden desk. Behind it sat a burnt-orange leather wingback chair, its upholstery worn from frequent use. On the wall directly behind hung a large embroidered tapestry, boldly displaying the Academy's coat of arms: symbols representing Awareness, Astrology, and Alchemy intertwined in vivid hues of realgar, cobalt blue, and shimmering gold, reminiscent of the lapis lazuli tokens students carried.

A golden telescope stood proudly nearby, clearly a treasured keepsake from Cosimo's previous career as an astronomer, now serving merely as ornate decoration. Along the adjacent wall stretched an expansive bookshelf filled meticulously with leather-bound tomes. Cosimo gestured toward the chair opposite his desk, but Remo's attention caught on a padlocked wooden trunk just behind the headmaster's seat.

Cosimo noticed Remo's interest and smiled. "Few things ignite imagination like a locked box. Treasure, secrets, power—all possibilities dance in our minds until we see inside." He laughed softly. "To satisfy your curiosity, this box simply contains lapis lazuli stones awaiting new students.

"Yet," Cosimo continued, "sometimes the unknown holds greater joy than reality. Before we open the box, we dream freely. Once opened, we're left with what truly is, often disappointing compared to what we hoped."

The headmaster leaned forward, voice sincere. "Beliefs shape our world, Remo. Believe the box holds treasures, and your heart is rich, regardless of what's truly there. Mind your beliefs carefully. They create your reality."

Remo mused over what he would wish to see within a locked box, questioning what his soul would dare to imagine lying behind the padlocked trunk. The freedom to imagine such a thing made him feel overwhelmed and miserable. Whatever he wanted out of life couldn't fit inside a small, wooden chest.

The familiar sensation of his heart's lonely descent to his stomach filled him as he remembered that this world would never match up to his fantasy books. What he truly desired was not only immaterial; it did not exist. He wondered if he could ever feel satisfied with his reality when none of it contained the magic of the stories he clung to.

Cosimo's voice gently drew him back. "How are you finding your Astrology lessons?"

Remo took a second to consider his reply, deciding on honesty. "They aren't quite what I expected. I'm not sure what my expectations were to begin with, but I very much enjoyed today's lesson."

Cosimo's knowing smile warmed his features. "Indeed. Today's lesson introduced the more philosophical components, based on millennia of astrologers' observations of the signs and planets. I'm pleased you enjoyed it, as more such lessons await." His expression suddenly grew serious. "However, I didn't call you here just to discuss your studies."

Remo tensed. "Yes, Professor?"

Cosimo stood, leaning on his ornamented walking stick, his presence suddenly profound. "Beyond my astronomy career, I am an alumnus of this Academy. My lifetime of study in these arcane arts gives weight to my intuition, and if you'll forgive my immodesty, I must tell you this intuition rarely misleads me. I sense we stand on the brink of profound change."

Remo was mystified as to why Cosimo should be attempting to prove his credentials, feeling as though he were dancing around some fact that perhaps Remo couldn't yet handle the full truth of.

"Andrea has told you of recent developments with the Order and Saffiro?" Cosimo asked.

"He has," responded Remo, more uncertain than ever where Cosimo would lead this discussion.

Cosimo's eyes were steady. "Remo, your arrival here, sent by Trota and bearing that poem, was no mere coincidence. I sensed immediately it was guided by fate."

Remo shifted anxiously, unsure of Cosimo's meaning.

Cosimo leaned closer, voice low and compelling. "Let me speak plainly. I'm inviting you to join the Order of Aquarius. Trota is a member of the Order as well."

Remo's mouth went dry as he rapidly revisited every casual conversation he'd ever shared with Trota, searching desperately for any hint that she was involved with the Order. "Oh," he murmured weakly, Cosimo politely silent as Remo processed this revelation.

He inhaled sharply, recalling suddenly her curiosity about the Knights of Saffiro in their village. Discovering Trota was an astrologer had been shocking enough, but to realize she secretly supported a rebellion against the empire was almost unimaginable.

Remo's pulse quickened, surprise mingling with a burgeoning sense of excitement and trepidation. "Professor, I—I'm not sure what I could possibly contribute. Andrea explained some of what the Order does, and frankly, I'm hardly equipped to fight or strategize against an empire."

Cosimo didn't appear to expect that reply. Remo suspected more concealed knowledge rested behind the headmaster's onyx eyes as he gave his student a meaningful look. "Do you think Trota is stabbing knights with her scalpels? Not all strength is brute, Remo. Battles are not always won by violence. Ultimate victory is obtained without any physical fighting. Intelligence, cunning, information, planning—these are just as important to know how to wield as one might a sword, and our goal is to *prevent* war. To prevent Saffiro from conquering Anxur."

"Even so, what is it that you want me to do? Become a spy, like Andrea?"

It had come out more direct, more accusatory than Remo had meant it. Cosimo didn't seem to notice. He looked to be engaged in an internal debate, perhaps deciding how much to reveal. Remo wondered which side of Cosimo's silent argument emerged victorious as he opened his mouth to speak.

"No, Remo. I seek nothing you aren't ready to give willingly. Joining the Order must be your own choice. Yet everything about your arrival—Andrea, Trota, that poem—suggests fate has brought you here."

Cosimo approached a bookshelf, retrieving a weathered leather volume and returning to place it before Remo. He opened it carefully, revealing a detailed image. "What do you see?"

Remo leaned forward to look at it, studying the ancient, detailed drawing. "A dragon eating its tail."

Cosimo stared at his student expectantly, waiting for Remo to come to the realization on his own. He saw the moment the recognition reached Remo's eyes as the poem from the message in the bottle replayed in his head:

> *The dragon's head*
> *The dragon's tail*

"Is this related to the poem?"

"Precisely." Cosimo tapped the page. "This picture represents one of the most important astrological concepts there is to learn. It's an astrological allegory representing the lunar nodes: the North Node—the dragon's head—and the South Node, its tail. Your South Node signifies past lives, talents, and comfort zones, skills you've long perfected. But lingering too long there limits your growth." He recited softly:

> *You have done this many times*
> *You've mastered these lessons*

*You've served for your crimes*
*But at the opposite, you'll always fail*
*If you chase the dragon's tail.*

"The North Node," Cosimo continued, "is your greatest challenge. It's unfamiliar territory that promises profound growth. We must actively seek out our North Node, which I daresay you have started the task of doing by journeying to Mavortis."

*The opposite does not come easily to you*
*You may even fear it*
*It is completely new*
*Now you're where you've never tread*
*If you chase the dragon's head*

Remo listened intently. "What are my placements?"

"Your North Node in Sagittarius is conjunct your moon and Saturn," Cosimo said. "This indicates that your basic instincts are entwined with your soul's mission. Not all of us meet the challenge of our North Nodes in one lifetime. You are intuitively drawn to it, yet afraid of it. You must overcome this fear, and you'll be tested again and again through events and external circumstances. You cannot fight your karmic mission in this life, Remo. Saturn's influence will not let you escape it.

"You must let go of the past, be it the residual karma of past lives or old patterns of thinking. It's an attraction and a repulsion, a karmic pull that lives in your seventh house of other people. Relationships, particularly abroad, will be the arena of your greatest growth. You must allow others to challenge and change you. That vulnerability," he said, "is your key to fulfillment."

He paused, observing Remo carefully. "Your South Node in Gemini shows a past life spent cultivating knowledge and communication. This remains your natural comfort zone; your Gemini ascendant reinforces this. Yet, you must venture beyond familiarity, exploring new environments and deepening relationships. Your instincts led you here for a reason. You've made significant leaps already, but there's more to come, especially emotionally.

"Your greatest rewards lie within your relationships if you can only be brave enough to remain open to them. The right people will come to you who are meant to help you do so. It was all arranged and agreed upon before you incarnated, though you have forgotten that now. Not to mention that Saturn conjunct the North Node means that when a wise old person gives you advice, you will be sure to benefit from heeding them."

Remo almost smiled, then realized that Cosimo most likely wasn't joking: He learned in class that Saturn ruled older people, as well as things like time, limitations, responsibility, and discipline. It was a lot to absorb and accept, though Remo felt that he'd chosen his fate the moment he decided to move to Mavortis.

Cosimo's interpretation of his North and South Node made him feel assured, in a way, that he was correct to feel confident in taking those life-changing leaps because his gut instincts had led him to choose the path of his soul's highest growth. He felt that somehow, even if he made his way back to Anxur, something or someone would sweep him back towards change, towards what was meant for him.

Cosimo continued, "Eclipses bring dramatic change and fated events into our lives, and the North Node transiting the first house tends to change *us* as we align with who we are truly meant to be. A recent astrological transit, the eclipse and North Node in your first house, confirms that dramatic, fated change brought you here. Meeting Andrea, Trota's involvement, and the poem itself—none of these events are mere coincidence.

"When I drew your natal chart after our first meeting, the North Node transit seemed to confirm signs of what I already suspected regarding your arrival here. I'd be remiss not to admit that your being sent by Trota, a member of the Order and my favorite student, also made an impression. And as if I needed further convincing that you are on a far greater journey than the one you've traveled physically, you arrive with the poem."

"What special significance is the poem, beyond its message of the moon's nodes?" Remo asked.

Cosimo stood once more, making his way slowly towards the door. Recognizing his dismissal, Remo stood and walked towards him.

"That, I'm afraid, you'll have to wait to learn. Will you agree to come to an Order meeting before you decide whether you'd like to join? I think you'll find that more of your questions will be answered there," Cosimo said.

Surely, Remo thought, this counted as weaponizing information, because Cosimo knew that withholding information from him would drive him crazy enough to agree to anything. Cosimo needn't have resorted to that sort of trickery to make Remo agree to come to an Order meeting, though.

In his mind, he had agreed to join the Order the moment he promised Andrea his aid in protecting peace throughout Terramundi. Nonetheless, he was grateful for all the information he gained from Cosimo in his efforts to convince him to join.

"I don't need time to decide that. I'd like to join the Order. Just tell me the place and time of the meeting."

Cosimo cast a wide smile as he opened the door for Remo. "On the second Jupiter's day of August, after sunset. Andrea will guide you. It will be here, at the Academy."

Remo nodded, stepping outside, the poem's final stanza echoing ominously:

*The dragon's head*
*The dragon's tail*
*Chase the former in this life*
*And lest you fail*
*You must not in the next*
*May you prevail on the eternal quest*

# Chapter Eleven

"VESTA'S ALMIGHTY HEARTH, WOMAN. You had a rough day, I gather?"

Nella made a sound akin to a growl at Andrea's greeting, slamming books onto their table at The Crooked Cupola. Remo tried not to wince at her rough handling of them; he couldn't accept folded pages nor book vandalism of any kind. Nella's menacing look challenged him to comment, which he wisely refrained from doing.

Her usually sleek hair was ruffled as if she'd been pulling it, her eyes rimmed with red. She aimed for a chair, but Andrea smoothly intercepted her movement and pulled her into his lap. If any man was brave enough to weather the storm that was Nella, it was Andrea. She didn't resist and instead collapsed into his muscled shoulders.

"Exams," she muttered.

Andrea rubbed her back soothingly. Lyra smiled at the scene, and Remo, seeing her approval, found himself silently rooting for the couple.

"So," Lyra said, picking up their earlier conversation. "What did Cosimo want from you?"

Andrea met Remo's questioning eyes, then answered low, "She's in the Order too."

Remo sputtered into his wine. "Are we sure this organization operates in *secret?* Seems everyone knows of it."

"You exaggerate," Andrea said. "It's only us here. Oh, and Sevo."

Lyra looked at Remo curiously. "So you've joined, then?"

He nodded, and her answering warm smile made him feel instantly at ease. He studied her for a moment, remembering how she'd admitted that the risk of attending the Academy still unnerved her. And yet, she was part of the Order. Either she was braver than she let on, or her sense of justice ran deeper than her fear.

Nella still hadn't emerged from Andrea's shoulder, though there seemed to be some movement of her head. Remo realized that she was kissing his neck. A moment later, Andrea stood while still holding her. "Would you two mind carrying her books home?"

"Of course," Lyra said, amused.

Andrea carried Nella out in his arms, the image of a gallant knight in shining armor. Remo suspected Nella's current distress was of a sort far too inappropriate for the damsels of children's tales.

Remo quipped, "How come he never carries *me* home?"

Lyra laughed, and he wasn't sure if it was his wine or the sound that warmed him. "Perhaps he doesn't want to make Nella jealous."

"That must be it."

She smiled and shook her head. "I'm glad you joined the Order. You're part of our little family now."

Remo's chest tightened at the word *family*. He was surprised by how much he wanted to be around his new friends, considering his typical habit of keeping the world at arm's length.

Cosimo's earlier words echoed in his head as he searched for a response that accurately conveyed his feelings: *Your greatest rewards lie within your relationships if you can only be brave enough to remain open to them.*

"Thank you," he said, feeling out of his element. "Moving here would've been lonely without you both. I'm grateful to you and Andrea for including me as you both have."

Not that he was a stranger to loneliness. Ironically, loneliness was his greatest companion; he found himself frequently in its company.

Lyra's ochre eyes glimmered. "Of course. You fit right in with us. It already feels like we've all known one another for a long time. And I know Andrea loves having another man around when Nella and I discuss things he doesn't care about. Although, keep making jokes about wanting him to carry you home in his arms, and he may have some regrets."

Another laugh spilled from Remo's lips as he found conversation with her as effortless as breathing. "How is it that you came to be in the Order?"

Lyra's open expression immediately hardened; not in response to him, he realized, but to some memory that the question had triggered. Cheering in the room echoed from a raucous group at a nearby table, the noise so incongruent with the heavy look she now wore.

"Did Andrea ever tell you the story of how we met?" she asked, a lilt of her accent revealing itself.

"No, he hasn't."

She made a small smile. "Of course not. I tease him about being vain, but his kindest deeds always go unmentioned." She looked far away, lost in thoughts he felt he sorry to have spurred.

Remo stepped in gently. "You don't have to tell me. Saffiro's cruelty is reason enough."

She gave a grateful nod, slowly returning to the present.

He frowned, wondering why she would ever have felt she had to reveal anything she didn't want to for his sake. He would have respected any boundaries she erected. It was another reason for him to feel justified in his decision to join the Order. He would fight any threat that would cause injury to Lyra. His friend.

Remo reached for his coin pouch, but the glint of denarii on the table stopped him; Andrea had already paid. With a playful raise of his brow, he turned to Lyra. "Think it's safe to head back, or do you suppose Nella and Andrea still need, ah... privacy?"

Lyra smirked, though the expression didn't fully reach her eyes. "Knowing them? We'll need to give it another half hour. I'm sure they went to my place so Nella won't have to drag herself back."

Remo wondered if he imagined the note of bitterness he detected in Lyra's words. She seemed happy for Andrea and Nella, but even the happiest third wheel could grow weary of balancing. Then again, perhaps he was projecting. Lyra was stunning; surely she had admirers, perhaps even a partner he didn't know about. Or maybe she simply valued her space and was understandably tired of making room for her friends' romantic escapades.

"Another round it is," he said, signaling to Sevo. The innkeeper returned with two glasses of wine and a slice of iced almond cake—also pre-paid by Andrea.

"I suppose the cake is recompense for temporarily kicking me out of my room," Lyra said.

A smirk played at the corner of Remo's lips. "And does it indeed compensate?"

She moaned as she bit into the spongey cake. "Yes. Damn them both. My fatal flaw is my sweet tooth."

He chuckled, mentally filing that detail away as she slid the plate toward him in invitation. "Typical royals. Always buying everyone off to suit their whims," he teased.

Lyra sighed with exaggerated weariness. "Mock all you want now, but the moment you bring your girlfriend around, I'm sure you'll be just as nauseatingly affectionate. Thank the seven gods you at least have your own lodgings."

Remo feigned innocence, turning away. "I don't know what you mean."

Lyra dropped her voice into a deadpan. "Forgive me. I forgot your heart belongs to Andrea."

He grinned, nodding as if to graciously pardon the accusation. "I'm not sure it'd be wise to bring Sabelle around here. It's already difficult enough to keep quiet about the Order and the Academy. And her father is a Senator of Saffiro. I'm worried our time together is running out."

Saying it aloud stung. He took a long sip of wine to hide the look he was certain had reached his face.

Lyra's voice softened. "You have my word that neither Andrea, Nella, nor I would be careless enough to say something in front of her. Too much is at stake. As for her family being a bunch of snobs..." She bit her lip, searching for a solution she knew wasn't there. "Well, this isn't the worst part of town. Where's she staying?"

"The Briar District."

Lyra exhaled. "I know the proprietor of a tavern called Scappi's—only nobles and merchants dine there. I can secure you a table. If you're seen there, no one will question your standing. They'll assume you belong."

Remo smiled. "That would be great. Thank you."

"No trouble." She leaned her head into her hand as she sipped. "Though perhaps I'd be wiser to stay out of it, lest I must endure more lovers kissing at the table, leaving me to carry their things home for them."

"You're doing the work of Venus herself," he said solemnly.

She rolled her eyes, a cheerful sparkle in them once more as he carried the books.

Light flowed onto the street from tavern windows and shone on them as they walked, swaying into and away from each other as if they were both moth and flame, their pace unhurried not for their friends' sake, but for their own.

By August, Remo had found his footing in his work at the hospital. On good days, he didn't see Acerbi at all. The cases were often beyond anything he'd encountered, so he buried himself in research to give his patients the care they deserved.

The patient Acerbi had assigned to him in the long-term ward grew progressively worse, as was inevitable with her condition. Painful abscesses and pocks covered her body. Some nights she writhed in agony, and all Remo could do was offer stronger doses of willow bark elixir and cooling herbal salves for her skin. Emotionally, he tried to be a steady presence. Because of her past and appearance, even the hospital staff kept their distance. The injustice made Remo work twice as hard to ensure she would, at the very least, receive quality care under his watch.

After weeks of consistent dedication to her needs, he had finally earned a semblance of the patient's trust. She began acknowledging him, sometimes answering his questions, though ventured nothing in the way of real conversation, and still never offered her name.

The hospital had a hothouse and garden where healers gathered herbs. Remo spent hours there. For one stubborn patient, he prepared a soothing throat elixir using saffron, cloves, frankincense, sugar candy, and honey. He ground and strained it all carefully before bottling it.

On the way back, he admired a rose blooming with vivid orange and shocking-pink petals. On a whim, he clipped it.

Although Remo often preferred solitude, he didn't always want to be alone. Had it not been for Andrea's warmth and easy charm, he doubted he would've made a single friend in Mavortis. Andrea had a way of drawing people in, making them feel like they belonged, even when Remo himself wasn't sure he ever truly did.

He noticed his patient never received visitors. That sort of ache was familiar. So he decided he would be *her* Andrea—the one to offer kindness freely, without expectation.

Back in Anxur, Remo had often sought refuge in nature when the sting of solitude became too much. There was healing, somehow, in the hush between trees, in the warm breath of sunlight, in the way the world opened up beneath a wide sky. It silenced the thoughts that curled in on themselves.

He imagined how it must feel to be shut away in a narrow room, pain your only companion, the hours stretching long and empty. So on the milder days, he would ask if she might like to visit the gardens with him. A simple question, never pressed. She always declined, but still, he asked.

"It's beautiful outside," he said on his return from the hothouse. "But if you're not up for a walk, then the garden can come to you."

He placed the rose gently on the table beside her bed. She stared at it, expression unreadable. He cleaned her wounds, applied fresh salve, and spoke softly as he worked, narrating small things to fill the silence.

As he left, halfway through the door, he heard her speak. Her voice was gravelly, barely above a whisper. "Thank you."

He smiled faintly, nodded once, and quietly shut the door behind him. The next time he entered her room, the rose was in her water cup.

# Chapter Twelve

"I N OUR CLASSES, WE have learned how to calculate natal charts and foundational astronomy," Cosimo began. "We have covered topics such as the motions and significations of planets, the twelve zodiac signs and their rulerships, astrological houses, aspects, and the nodes of the moon. Today, we will learn how to combine all this information to create a clear and accurate portrait of a person."

Remo was looking forward to this particular lesson. Ever since Cosimo had described his North and South Node, the dragon's head and dragon's tail, Remo had become more convinced of astrology's validity, accepting it as a discipline that worked. He'd watched its patterns play out in his studies and his own life.

Cosimo raised a hand, his burgundy robes flowing at the sleeves. "As astrologers, I must impress upon you the importance of guarding your natal chart. I realize I've collected each of your birth times, and I ask you to trust that the Academy keeps this information protected. We require it for a few reasons.

"First, so I can understand you as a teacher must. Second, so you can compare your own rendering with the chart I prepared. If there's a discrepancy, it will be easily spotted."

He walked the aisles between their desks. "We never share this information with outsiders. Not all astrologers use birth charts for good. History has shown us that astrology can be twisted toward darker ends."

Emperor Septimus and his astrologer Serafina swam to the forefront of Remo's mind. It felt like a lifetime ago that Trota had told him the true version of that legend.

"If your chart falls into the wrong hands, it can be used against you. I won't detail the methods, but know that it's possible. Your chart is a map of your soul. Guard it. Keep it from those who would use it to uncover your weaknesses or cast the Evil Eye upon you."

*So*, Remo thought bemusedly, *they believe in the Evil Eye here, too*. He'd come to trust astrology, but remained skeptical of other occult claims. A snort from a classmate echoed his doubt.

"Is something amusing, Xavier?" Cosimo's voice was cold.

Xavier flinched. "No, sir. My mom used to warn me about it. I just thought the Evil Eye was an old wives' tale."

Remo heard a soft smack. His classmate Rinta had slapped her forehead, while Estelle's eyes grew comically more round at Xavier's folly. Remo was relieved he didn't air his own doubts.

"I see today's astrology lesson must wait," Cosimo said gravely. "It seems we need an essential lesson in Awareness."

Xavier's face turned red. Remo leaned forward slightly, curious. Awareness was the most mysterious of the Academy's three disciplines.

"Malocchio, or the Evil Eye," Cosimo began, "is the belief that someone can harm you physically, emotionally, or spiritually by looking at you with malice. It can be intentional or unconscious. The symptoms vary: headaches, anxiety, fatigue, confusion... If strong enough, it can inflict extended periods of misfortune. If this can be done with a glance, imagine what can be done with access to your birth chart. Your natal chart in the hands of your enemies is a set of instructions on how to destroy you."

Remo shivered. He remembered what Trota had said about Septimus collecting the charts of potential rivals and having them executed.

Cosimo continued, "Intention is the most powerful force in the universe. When someone feels a strong emotion, whether it's hatred, gratitude, or anything in between, and combines it with clear intent, the universe organizes around them. It listens.

"We are all magicians, and intention is our magic. Your energy is the wand; your attention, the spell. You energize whatever you focus on. Every emotion you experience emits a frequency—a signal cast into your environment. And when you truly understand the power of what I've just told you, when you see it work for yourself, nothing in this universe will be impossible for you."

Remo felt as though Cosimo used the analogy of magic for his sole benefit. Remo, who dreamed of the magical universes in his fantasy books, longed to believe that what Cosimo had said held truth. Maybe he could try to see things in that light, too.

Perhaps he could accept that the universe contained an understated magic system. He felt as though a door had opened in a hidden place in the universe just for him to explore and that lying beyond it were truths that made him a little more content to belong to this world.

When class ended, Remo made his way toward the Academy's library, still buzzing from Cosimo's unexpected lesson in Awareness. He entered the common area, where he spotted Lyra seated on a bench near the Awareness archway, utterly absorbed in a book. She only looked up when he sat beside her, startled, snapping the book shut as pink bloomed across her cheeks.

"I've just gotten out of class," Remo said, feigning oblivion. "Cosimo talked about Awareness today."

"Did he?" Lyra asked quickly, tucking her book into her bag before he could catch the title. "What did he say?"

Remo tried to recall the words before they slipped from memory. He had scrambled to write down the professor's words during class; he had a compulsive need to capture anything that inspired him onto paper. "That intention is powerful. Like magic."

Lyra nodded. "That's one of the first Awareness lessons. Learning how to direct your energy with focus."

"I'd like to read more about it. Would you show me where the library is?"

Her honeyed eyes brightened. "You haven't been yet?"

She stood, leading him a few paces along the wall. Her fingers skimmed the smooth stone, searching with purpose. Before he could ask what she was doing, she pressed against an invisible seam and the wall gave way, revealing a narrow entrance.

She smiled, clearly satisfied by his awe. "You'll learn to spot it with time. But until then, best not to lean against this wall without warning.

A few first-years got squished by accident."

Remo burst into laughter, unable to help himself. She eyed his reaction with a mixture of disapproval and amusement.

"They were okay though, right?" he asked, belatedly trying to sound like a concerned healer.

"Obviously. Still awful of you to laugh."

The corridor led to an expansive underground library with shelf after towering shelf, each one fitted with rolling ladders and tiny reading nooks. Though underground, the space was bathed in candlelight and gentle lamplight, making it feel both vast and intimate.

"Vesta's hearth," Remo whispered. "This is dangerous. I may never leave."

"I didn't know you liked to read!" she exclaimed, delighted. "Now I won't have to drag Andrea along every time I want company."

"If anything, you'll have to drag me out."

She grinned, then led him to the Awareness section. "If you'd like my recommendation on a basic introductory book,"—she grabbed a lantern and walked along the shelves with purpose—"Here. *On Intention* by Alma Amalle."

"Thanks," he said. "Is it all just Academy books here?"

"Seven gods, no. Something in my soul would die if I had only educational books to read."

Remo thought he had never felt more understood. "What do you like to read?"

Her face lit up. "I'll show you."

She led him to a tucked-away fiction section. "This one's my favorite," she said, handing him a volume entitled *Fates of the Fae.*

"I haven't read that one yet. I'll give it a try," he said.

She looked sheepish as she released the book. "I don't know if you'll like it. It's got fantasy elements, but it's kind of, um... romantic."

Remo glanced at the cover, then flipped it open. Of course—it was a love story. That explained her hesitance. But he wouldn't tease her, not when he secretly cherished the love stories hidden in all his favorite books.

"I'm sure I will," he said with sincerity. "I like these kinds of novels too. One of my favorites is *Milena and Devlan*."

The change in her was immediate. Her wariness melted into surprise, her eyes lighting like candles suddenly caught by flame. "Really? I didn't expect that from you."

"I love fantasy," he said, smiling faintly. "I never grew out of it."

Lyra toyed with a loose strand of hair, nodding. "Me neither. I'd never want to. Growing too old for fantasy... it's like growing too old to dream."

Remo sighed as if he could breathe easier knowing he'd met a kindred spirit. "Thank you for that. It's nice to know someone else feels the same way."

She gave him a thoughtful look and smiled, perhaps experiencing the same phenomenon. She tucked her hair behind her as she turned to face the books once again. "*Milena and Devlan*, you said? I've been meaning to read it."

"I can lend you my copy," he offered. "So you can read it outside the library."

Lyra turned back to the shelves, scanning the spines with practiced ease. "Thanks, but we're allowed to take the fiction books home. I don't see that one here, though... ah—never mind! Found it." She plucked the book from the shelf, and they carried their selections to a nearby table.

They read together in easy silence, occasionally pausing to share a line, a laugh, or a thought sparked by their respective stories. When their eyes began to blur and their stomachs reminded them of time's passing, they checked out their novels and headed up toward The Crooked Cupola, the warmth of the afternoon lingering between them.

Sevo jumped as Remo and Lyra emerged from the trap door in the back room, sloshing the jug of ale he'd been carrying. "Fantastic," he muttered, "more students traipsing mud through my inn."

He turned sharply to fetch a mop, grumbling under his breath. Remo and Lyra exchanged blank looks. "You'd think he'd be used to this by now," Lyra murmured.

Remo felt a twinge of guilt and scanned the room for a rag or broom. Before he could find anything, Sevo came back, still muttering, and snapped, "I've got it. Just go."

They stammered apologies and slipped into the main room.

"He seemed a bit high-strung, don't you think?" Remo asked.

"That's just Sevo. Though yes, he's especially twitchy today."

They left Sevo in peace and decided to check if Andrea was free for dinner. He was holed up in his room, elbows-deep in an Alchemy project and looking very much like he'd rather be anywhere else.

"If alchemy's supposed goal is eternal life," Andrea groaned from his settee, "then death sounds preferable to doing this forever."

Lyra tutted. "Drama prince."

He stuck his tongue out in reply.

"So you're not trying to live forever, then?" Remo teased.

"Please don't insult me in my own home," Andrea said flatly.

Remo turned to Lyra, who gave a helpless shrug.

"No, alchemists aren't searching for eternal life," Andrea explained with a grunt. "That was always metaphor. Same with the philosopher's stone. Spiritually speaking, we're already immortal. Consciousness just moves between forms." He sighed. "But please, can we stop talking about it now? I need a break."

"We haven't eaten yet," Remo offered. "Came to see if you'd join us."

Andrea was already pulling on his boots. "Crooked Cupola?"

"No. Sevo's in rare form tonight," Lyra said.

Andrea paused, mid-lace. "Makes sense. Two Knights of Saffiro came by earlier. Didn't cause trouble, but it shook him. They usually don't come near the inn."

"Did they seem suspicious?" Remo asked. "Did Sevo hear anything useful?"

Andrea shook his head. "No. Probably just passing through from the gate. He said they mostly gossiped about other knights."

"Typical," Lyra's tawny eyes narrowed. "And yet women get the gossiping reputation."

Andrea raised a hand to his chest in mock offense. "I take that personally. Anyways, Remo, did you hear about Mateo and Elena from Astrology?"

Remo spent his next free afternoon visiting Sabelle's boarding house to see if she was in. The man at the counter, eyeing him with marked distaste, said she wasn't.

The clerk's expression made Remo instantly self-conscious about his appearance. He wore a plain white shirt with rolled-up sleeves, a dark leather jerkin, and cotton breeches: simple, clean, and woefully common.

He wondered if Sabelle ever felt embarrassed by the humble few garments he rotated between, so stark beside her lavish, ever-changing wardrobe. He didn't want to dress like the puffed-up lordlings parading through the Briar district, with their over-tailored coats and smug expressions, but something about today made him linger on the difference.

He walked aimlessly through the polished streets, window-shopping without intent. On impulse, he stepped into the first tailor's shop he saw.

A stout, kindly man in his middle years looked up. "What can I get for you, lad?"

Remo glanced down at his clothes, then up at the tailor, floundering. "Uh... A doublet and shirt, maybe new breeches, too. Nothing too ornate. Something I could wear during the day but still..."

The tailor offered a knowing smile. "Something fit to accompany a fine young lady around these parts of town?"

Remo flushed. "Yes, that's about the measure of it."

The tailor hummed cheerfully as he took Remo's measurements, flitting around his shop. Remo chose a silk brocade in a soft silver-blue for the doublet and a cream-colored fabric for the shirt. They spent nearly an hour deciding, the whole time Remo's thoughts circling the divide between Sabelle's class and his.

A familiar worry tugged at him: What if she had been at the boarding house and simply told them to lie, avoiding him entirely? What if she'd seen sense and ended things before it grew more complicated?

He left the shop with a lighter coin purse and heavier thoughts, too uncertain to stop by Sabelle's boarding house again. He'd wanted to take her to the theater and their favorite wine window. But now, all plans drifted into dusk as he walked home. He ran into Andrea, Nella, and Lyra on their way to The Crooked Cupola. They didn't notice him approach; all three were listening intently as Lyra animatedly told a story.

"...And the owner of the Sleepy Steed Inn threw him out. He was back inside ten minutes later, though how he got past the guard at the door is a mystery. He..."

Lyra broke into a tinkling laugh, unable to finish the sentence as her giggles crescendoed into a full-blown cackle.

Andrea rolled his eyes with fondness while Nella raised her brows in mild amusement. Remo chuckled too; her joy was infectious.

"She always does this," Andrea said to Remo once he spotted him. "She never gets through a good story without laughing herself silly."

Lyra attempted a breath to calm herself. "He pulled—" she tried again, but the memory overtook her, and she collapsed into laughter once more. This time, they all joined her.

Nella half-guided her into The Crooked Cupola, where Sevo, thankfully in a better mood, served them drinks and warm blackberry custard.

They were all in need of blowing off steam and thus drank more than normal. Even Nella, who usually nursed her wine with the posture of a wary cat, had let her shoulders drop and her judgmental stare relax into a small, contented smile.

Remo had only been properly drunk a handful of times back in Anxur, and all of them had taken place during Saturnalia, the old feast day once dedicated to Saturn, now a celebration of the winter solstice. As a healer, he generally disapproved of overindulgence. But as the insecure, lovesick fool he currently felt like, he allowed himself to indulge more than usual.

They stumbled together through the lamplit streets toward Andrea's lodgings, not ready to part just yet. Lyra and Andrea were midway through a raucous duet of a tavern song called "The Nasty Knave." The lyrics that made it through Remo's alcohol-soaked brain were absurd and riddled with innuendo.

Nella and Remo exchanged a long-suffering look, an unspoken pact between the last two adults in the room. If anyone was going to haul the others out of trouble tonight, it would be them.

"Is *this* the singing of Lyra's that first brought tears to your eyes, Andrea?" Remo called over the singing. "Because now I understand. That screeching could make a grown man weep in a plea to make it stop."

Lyra gasped theatrically and placed a hand to her chest. "Shame on you! People pay good coin to hear me sing, you know. Well... not that voice. But still."

"I'll consider it a rare honor to be subjected to this version, then," Remo replied, deadpan.

Lyra gave a mocking bow in reply as they reached Andrea's front door. He lit the lanterns while Nella claimed her usual spot on the velvet settee. "Home at last," Andrea sighed, draping an arm over her shoulder with exaggerated relief.

Remo seated himself in the armchair next to the fireplace. Lyra and Nella were soon engaged in a side conversation. The flickering lamplight caught on the glint of Andrea's small gold earring. It was the only piece of ornament Andrea wore daily, the merest hint that he may have come from a wealthy background.

"I want one," Remo blurted.

Andrea raised a brow. "One what?"

"Your ear."

There was a beat of silence. Andrea blinked. "Mate, you already have two."

Remo let out a frustrated noise. "No, I mean the sparkly bit. The earring. It looks... fashionable. Interesting."

"Brand new clothes, now an earring... Is this all an effort to impress Sabelle?"

"Yes. Exactly."

Andrea sighed. "I suppose we all do stupid things for love. And I'm not one to discourage stupid things. Hold on, I'll get my needle."

At that, the girls turned to look. Andrea passed the needle through the flame, sterilizing it. Lyra gave Remo a pitying look. Nella looked bored, as if the whole thing were a predictable comedy.

"If this ends badly, you lucky bastards have a medical student at your service," Nella said.

Remo smirked as he swabbed his ear with alcohol. "It's the healers who would tend to such minor things. You physicians are too high and mighty for such menial tasks as badly pierced ears."

Nella looked as if she might retort, but simply inclined her head in agreement. "You're right. I *am* too important."

The needle pricked his right earlobe with no warning. "Any last words, soldier?" Andrea asked in an impersonation of a warrior at battle, his needle a sword lodged in an enemy's chest.

Remo squared his shoulders. "Only that I wish I'd asked someone sober."

Andrea snorted. "Too late. It's off-center."

He pulled the needle free and rummaged in a box until he found a small silver hoop. "Here. Lunarian silver. I bought it on my last trip through the kingdom, but gold suits me better anyway. Keep it in."

Andrea tossed him a clean cloth and washed his hands in a nearby basin. Remo dabbed at the blood trailing down his jawline.

"So when will we meet this Sabelle you're bloodying yourself for?" Nella asked coolly.

Remo shrugged. "Soon, maybe. We can plan something."

"What's she like?" she pressed.

Remo turned toward the fire, watching the flames flicker and dance. He thought of Cosimo's lesson about staring into fire to understand its nature—how flames reflected one's essence, one's chart. Sabelle felt like fire to him: unpredictable, magnetic, dangerous.

"She's clever," he said at last. "Exciting to be around."

Nella narrowed her eyes, unconvinced. She glanced toward Andrea, who had met Sabelle briefly.

Andrea chuckled. "He's leaving out a few minor details. Like the fact she's beautiful. And a Senator's daughter."

Nella turned back to Remo, giving him an accusatory stare for intentionally withholding those details from her. He wasn't sure why he didn't want to talk about Sabelle with them. Maybe because he didn't want them to misunderstand what she meant to him. Or maybe because he didn't understand it himself.

Andrea seemed to pick up on the fact that Remo didn't want to remain on the subject for too long and quelled any would-be comments or questions from Nella with a stern look.

Eventually, their gathering drew to a close. Nella stayed over. From Andrea's balcony, they watched Lyra cross the street to her lodgings, waving from her own balcony.

"You can stop playing nursemaid to me now!" she called before ducking inside.

Remo took that as his cue. He returned to his quarters, peeled off his clothes, and lay in bed with his thoughts. Sabelle was there in the dark with him—her green eyes, her bronze skin... her soft curves. He blamed his Gemini rising on his insatiable curiosity to learn every inch of her body, to know how she felt, how she tasted.

He had always longed for the impossible. And Sabelle Fattura was quickly becoming his favorite new fantasy. One he knew he could never fully belong to.

# Chapter Thirteen

F LOWERING BUSHES AND TREES lined the garden path, illuminated by the last remnants of dusk's fading light. Remo and Sabelle strolled side by side, their arms occasionally brushing as they passed the maze-like pockets that diverged from the walkway. The air was thick with a heady floral scent.

"So, where did you step out to yesterday afternoon?" Remo asked, affecting a light tone. "I tried to visit, but the man at the boarding house said you weren't in." He bent slightly to inspect a nearby bleeding heart, feigning interest in the drooping blossoms.

There was a pause, too long to be casual. "My father commissioned a portrait," she said, her voice lined with a trace of regret.

Crestfallen, Remo realized why. A portrait meant to advertise her beauty and pedigree to noble suitors. But he spent enough time worrying about that. He wouldn't allow himself to mope about it and ruin his time with her. He forced a smile. "A face as stunning as yours ought to be immortalized in paint."

Her lips curved into a smile that stole his breath. He couldn't understand why her beauty hurt to behold.

Quiet fell between them as they reached a small enclosure surrounded by tall hedges. A carved stone bench stood by the far wall, framed by fig trees and flowering bushes. Remo set down a basket and pulled out two glasses and a bottle of honeyed wine, despite his recent recovery from the night before.

"To be safe, perhaps you shouldn't attempt to visit me at the boarding house again unless we've already agreed on a time and place," Sabelle said, plucking ripe figs from a nearby tree without looking at him. "You know, in case the man at the desk reports to my father."

Though Remo understood their circumstances all too well, her words still hit like a blow. He wished, just once, he could stop seeing things from both sides: either remain logical and unaffected by the reminder that he was her secret, or feel the full sting of it, untempered by understanding. At least then, walking away might be easier.

Aware he'd gone silent, he looked at her, which was always a reliable way to stop spiraling. "You're right. That was stupid of me. I'm sorry. No more surprise visits."

She must've sensed the hurt behind his words, because she rose on tiptoe and kissed his cheek then did it again and again like a pecking bird until he laughed. Just like that, they were alright again.

"Trust me, avoiding my father is more for your sake than mine," Sabelle said.

"You don't have to spare this humble peasant's feelings," he teased.

"Honestly, I think it's more about you being Anxurian than, well, titleless," she admitted, looking apologetic. "Of course, neither is his ideal..."

"Thanks, darling. That makes me feel much better," he said flatly, though the curve of his lips revealed his good humor. "But why should he dislike Anxurians when his children are from Juno?"

She sighed and bit into a fig. "I'm not sure he doesn't hate his children, too. He's hardly around. My brother's more of a father to me than he ever was."

He couldn't gauge her feelings, though she appeared unaffected. His brow pinched as he listened, but she shook her head dismissively as if to say she wasn't bothered.

"Anyway, his prejudice probably comes from spending too much time in Saffiro. Some in the empire still resent Anxur for resisting their conquest centuries ago. He calls Anxurians 'feeble-minded fishmongers,'" she added with embarrassment. "It would serve him right if I proudly announced I was courting one."

Remo let out a long breath. "At this point, I honestly can't tell if you're keeping me a secret or using me to horrify your family," he said, dryly. The quip was doing its best to mask a ripple of real insecurity.

She shot him a flat look which made him feel oddly comforted. "The only thing I'm using you for is your height," she replied, stretching theatrically for a fig just beyond her reach.

As she reached for another fig, Remo found her honesty startlingly refreshing, like a bite of cold wind. It should have reminded him their future was impossible, but instead, it made him feel closer to her, lulled by the illusion that there were no secrets between them. And yet, a sharper truth twisted in his gut: his own secrets were piling up fast.

With either admirable tenacity or brazenness, Sabelle jumped on him without warning to use his body as leverage, climbing him to reach the branches. He caught her instinctively, laughing in spite of himself as she retrieved her prize, grinning with pride.

"You know," he said, valiantly keeping his eyes anywhere but the breasts inches from his face, "your impeccable manners are definitely the most distracting thing about you."

She chortled as he let her down and poured the wine. He hoped the stifling nobility she kept company with wouldn't snuff out her person-ality like wildfire in all its improper manifestations.

"Here's to...," he started, wishing he'd thought of something clever earlier.

"Us continuing to meet again," she finished.

Remo's eyes twinkled with remembrance at the phrase they had now repeated twice, each time followed by a reunion. As he clinked his glass to hers, he wondered whether he could learn to be content with these continued chance encounters or with chasing scraps of her company.

"I wish I had my tarocchi cards," Sabelle said, reclining on the linen blanket.

"What would you ask?"

"About us."

"And what do you want them to say?"

A flicker of emotion, unspoken but unmistakable, passed across her features. She reached toward his ear, her fingers brushing the silver ear-ring gently, as if checking whether it was real. "When did you get this? Or have I just never noticed?"

He was confident he would have immediately noticed such an addition on her, but he never seemed able to tear his eyes from her. Not wanting to retell the slightly pathetic, wine-sodden story, he kept his expression impassive. "Answering my question with two of your own... hmm," he said, sipping his wine in deflection.

He hoped she would assume he had always worn the earring, rather than learn the sad truth that he had pierced it to emulate the swaggering nobility he saw around the wealthy quarter, where the fashion was popular. In hindsight, hoping he could somehow trick his way into being seen as Sabelle's class equal was a lot of pressure to place on one little piece of Lunarian silver.

Sabelle smirked and bit into another fig, clearly enjoying the fruit—and just as clearly savoring his gaze on her lips and tongue.

He cleared his throat. "Well, since you seem to be at a loss for words, I guess I'll have to play fortune-teller for us both. Fortunately, I know a thing or two about the stars."

He laid back on the blanket and looked up at the night sky, now deep blue and clear, the stars winking as if in on the joke. "Do you see that reddish one there?" he asked, pointing to the planet he now recognized as Mars.

Sabelle nodded as she lay beside him, equal parts amused and cautious, likely suspecting she was about to endure one of his unfortunate jokes.

"Good. That star means..." He made a show of measuring angles with his fingers. "Oh, this is uncanny. It says you're about to go on a date with a devastatingly handsome young man."

She played along with mock seriousness. "And how does this date end?"

"Let's see. The devilishly attractive gentleman is reaching for the lady's hand... Oh dear, what an embarrassing coincidence." He intertwined his fingers with hers.

She shook her head, lips curling into a small, sad smile. "And what happens next? How many more dates will they have?" she asked, her voice barely above a whisper.

Her concern for their relationship both warmed and pained him. It meant she recognized that something external could tear them apart.

It seemed some outside force had cooled the passion behind her earlier insinuation that any consequences of their relationship could be damned to hell.

He wasn't upset by the shift; in truth, he thought she should be more afraid of what their forbidden romance might cost them. Remo sat up slightly, voice soft. "As many as you want. But if you don't... he'll vanish faster than those figs you picked. He's completely yours."

Her returning serene smile told him he'd chosen the right words. Whatever she saw in his eyes stirred desire in her own. "I think I saw something else in the stars about how this date will end."

She leaned in, her fingers trailing from his neck to his chest. He leaned into her, drawn to the warmth of her body, the hunger in her gaze. He brushed his lips against hers in a gentle tease but she had no patience for restraint. With a low, urgent sound, she crashed her mouth to his, devouring the kiss. His hand slid to her waist, gripping tight as she clawed at his chest, dragging him closer. There was no space between them, no room to think, and no desire to stop.

Their mouths met in hurried, heated strokes. The feel of her hips under his hands banished every rational thought. She was the one temptation he had no strength to resist. His whole body surged with need, and she felt every bit of it. Her hand slid down, deliberate now, past his chest and stomach until she found the hard line of him beneath his breeches.

She gasped into his mouth, the sound soft and utterly thrilled. Her fingers curled, exploring, and he groaned low in his throat, hips twitching against her palm. The fabric between them barely dulled the sensation. Her hand moved, slow and curious, and it took every ounce of restraint he had not to let it go further. It was only a taste, dangerous and forbidden, and gods, he wanted more, but not like this.

With aching reluctance, he caught her hand and brought it to his lips, pressing a kiss into her knuckles like a promise. His eyes met hers, still burning, with a silent plea for mercy. He was still drowning in her touch, her mouth, the pounding rhythm of his own pulse, when a voice cut through the garden like a blade.

"Any luck finding them?"

Another voice, rougher, answered, "No."

"Let's keep looking."

Sabelle held a finger to his lips, eyes suddenly sharp. Then, without a word, she seized his hand and tugged him toward the thick hedge behind them. He followed, dazed, every nerve still on fire from the way she'd touched him just moments ago. Through a gap in the leaves, he spotted a Knight of Saffiro sweeping his gaze across the enclosure. Remo's heart pounded so loudly he was sure it would give them away. He didn't dare move, didn't breathe, just stared as the knight paused, then turned away.

He opened his mouth to ask why, but Sabelle was already creeping along the hedge line like a thief. She peeked both ways down the path, grabbed his hand, and broke into a run. Her laugh came out like a thrill-drunk giggle. They sprinted through the garden, her skirts whipping behind her, the wine still buzzing through his veins. He barely had time to think before—

"Over here! They're running!"

Remo yanked her down the right path, breath ragged as steps thundered behind them. They ducked into the nearest hedge enclosure, hiding behind a wide-boughed tree. She was laughing again, wild and breathless. He clamped a hand over her mouth, but not before she licked his palm with slow, deliberate mischief.

She arched her body against his, pressing into him with maddening precision. *Vesta's hearth, this girl is trouble,* Remo thought as her hips moved, grinding into his with devastating effect. He silently cursed her, cursed himself, cursed the timing. He heard a guard entering the enclosure and whispered a prayer to Jupiter, because only luck would help them escape now.

From somewhere in the maze, a voice barked, "Wyll! Where are you?"

The guard closing in on them sighed in response, the sound coming from just a few feet away. Remo held his breath as he could have sworn lightning flashed overhead.

"Fuck's sake," the guard muttered, leaving the enclosure. "I'm over here! Follow my voice."

They broke into a run the moment the guard's voice disappeared into the distance, tearing through the garden path like fugitives. Sabelle was still laughing as if they hadn't just been nearly caught by royal guards.

"Are you going to tell me what that was about?!" Remo demanded as they reached the edge of the garden, breathless.

With an infuriatingly mocking grin, Sabelle teased, "You mean you didn't see that coming in your interpretation of the stars?"

He didn't return her smile. He reminded himself that she didn't know about his involvement with the Academy of the Arcane Arts, and therefore couldn't understand how dangerous it was for him to be noticed by Knights of Saffiro.

"Poor baby," she cooed mockingly, giving him a once-over like he was a nervous colt. "I had no idea you were such an anxious person." She brushed imaginary dust from her skirts. "Don't worry about them. They were probably just keeping watch for my father. I lose his watchmen all the time."

He stared at her, disbelieving. "You do forgive me, don't you?" she asked sweetly, eyes wide with feigned innocence. "Wasn't that exciting?"

It was hard to look at her, wild and radiant and utterly unapologetic, and stay angry. His breath still hadn't fully returned, and neither had his common sense.

"I suppose I can't deny that a... part of me was excited during that," he said, his voice low, his gaze suggestive.

She giggled, impulsive and unrepentant, and kissed him again.

He shook his head, exasperated and aching for her. "Promise me you won't do that again. I mean it, Sabelle. I don't like games like that."

Something shifted in her expression—not guilt, exactly, but something close. She studied him as if seeing him differently for the first time. Her voice softened.

"Okay," she said quietly. "I promise. I'm sorry."

Remo nodded, and she gave him a shy grin he almost found believable. A laugh escaped him despite the dread still lingering in his body. "You know, I'm starting to see why Cecco kept you on so tight a leash. You're unhinged."

Her grin was immediate and wicked. "No one leashes me. And if you ever try, I'll run away laughing. But I know you secretly love my wild side, so don't pretend to be a choirboy with me, Remo. Besides..." Her gaze drifted downward. "I'm now quite certain you're no eunuch. Thank

Venus for that," she winked.

Holding hands, they reached the street outside Sabelle's boarding house, the night alive with voices and tavern light. A finely dressed gentleman exited a nearby establishment called The Silver Spoon, catching Remo's attention.

They had just neared the front steps when a male voice called out, smooth and smug— "Sabelle!"

She dropped Remo's hand instantly, the ghost of her warmth still lingering in his palm.

A tall man with aristocratic polish and sharp blue eyes strode toward them, smiling at her with the smug assurance of someone confident she'd been reserved for him. The smile vanished the moment he saw Remo, replaced by one more polished, and far more venomous.

"Oh—Good evening, Your Highness," Sabelle said with strained civility, offering a quick curtsy.

"Your Highness?" Remo repeated, stunned.

"Well," the man drawled, "if it isn't my most mediocre healer. I didn't expect to find you this far from your side of town outside of work hours."

Sabelle blinked between them, clearly as thrown as Remo felt. The insult was blatant, the possessiveness undeniable. Arlo wanted to embarrass him and stake a claim.

Remo forced himself to remain calm. "A pleasant surprise to run into you as well, Physician Acerbi."

Sabelle snapped out of it, her smile quick and polished. "I suppose introductions are redundant, but just to be proper: Remo, this is Prince Arlo, a family friend. He's been kind enough to show me around and help me settle into polite society. I feel silly now; I never thought to ask which hospital you worked at, Your Highness."

Remo should have realized that Acerbi's arrogance came from a royal title. Only someone with wealth or a powerful patron could afford university and physician training. It made sense now—he must be a spare royal. Remo vaguely recalled Andrea mentioning a Crown Prince Marcellus. That would explain Acerbi's hunger for status; he had no throne, so he reached for power in other ways.

Sabelle hesitated. "Prince Arlo, this is Remo. He's my—"

"Friend," Remo cut in, sparing her the danger of honesty.

Arlo Acerbi was no fool. He'd likely seen them holding hands. Remo knew he would assume the relationship was romantic, but he didn't want to put Sabelle in the position of having to explain it, especially if her family found out. Acerbi would make sure they forbade her from seeing him. A small part of Remo wondered if she might have admitted to it, had he stayed silent.

Sabelle blinked once, revealing neither hurt nor relief at his interjection. Remo continued for her. "Sabelle and I met on Juno, while I was traveling to find work in Mavortis. By chance, we ran into each other here and were catching up."

Acerbi's expression twisted into a caricature of surprise. "How delightful for you, Remo. Sabelle is generous with her time, isn't she?" He turned to her. "With your grace, etiquette, and beauty, you could do very well in the right company."

The dig landed with surgical precision. Remo felt the heat of humiliation rise, his self-worth clashing with bitter awareness. He tried to collect himself.

"I'll escort Sabelle from here," Acerbi said smoothly. "I'll see you at work tomorrow."

The veiled threat in Acerbi's parting words made Remo dread seeing him more than usual. Sabelle looked guilty, as if she wanted nothing more than to be rid of the prince's company and speak to Remo, perhaps to explain why she had dropped his hand the moment Acerbi appeared, though she didn't need to.

Remo understood it had been instinct, a reaction to the looming threat of her family finding out. He didn't blame her. In his eyes, she had done the right thing. It only confirmed what he already suspected, that on some level, she did care what her family and others thought about their relationship. And though the hurt of that realization settled heavily in his chest, he couldn't fault her for it. It was just more proof that she saw the complications, too, no matter what she'd said before.

"Goodnight, Physician Acerbi. Sabelle." Remo bowed his head toward her and gave her the faintest smile he could manage, hoping it conveyed that he understood, that it was alright. Then he walked away before she could finish a reply. He wouldn't have left her alone with Acerbi if they hadn't already been standing at her boarding house doorstep.

He had a sinking feeling in his gut that this night marked the beginning of something worse. Still, he didn't grasp the full extent until he stepped into the hospital the next morning and was summoned to Acerbi's office. He expected a threat, that he'd be told to stay away from Sabelle or risk everything. He knew Arlo wanted her; that was obvious. The thought of someone like him courting her made Remo's stomach churn. He'd hoped to keep his head down, but Acerbi had no intention of letting him.

Remo closed the door and braced himself.

"Don't bother to sit," Acerbi said coldly. "I'll make this quick and very clear. If you ever steal from the hospital again, I'll fire you and ensure no one hires you anywhere in Mavortis."

Remo stared at him. "What?"

Acerbi stood, voice sharp. "I won't tolerate that impertinent tone from a subordinate. You stole a rose from the hospital's hothouse to give to that whore in the hospice ward. Who knows what else you've helped yourself to? If we weren't short on healers, I'd dismiss you outright. I wonder, does Sabelle know that the man she's been entertaining is a petty thief courting a dying prostitute?"

A triumphant smirk twisted Arlo's mouth as Remo's scowl deepened. It wasn't just a threat to his job. Acerbi was trying to destroy him in Sabelle's eyes, which somehow felt worse. And Remo didn't doubt for a moment that, as a prince, Acerbi could ensure no hospital in Mavortis would ever hire him again.

"You're ambitious, trying to court a senator's daughter," Acerbi continued. "But Sabelle is far too good for you, and I'll make sure she knows it. I haven't told her father of your... friendship, only to spare her the humiliation. But consider this your final warning: stay away from her, if you value your place here. As for the rose, if you want to waste money buying one for the whore next time, be my guest. At least she's your equal."

Remo nearly stepped forward, not out of pride, but rage. Not for himself, but for the woman Arlo had degraded without flinching. It was clear now that Acerbi was the kind of man who only saw value in women with beauty, titles, or wealth.

"Leave," Acerbi hissed.

Remo walked out of his office as calmly as he could. His head was clouded with anger, and he wasn't sure how he'd make it through the rest of the day feeling the way he did. He did his best not to let it affect the care he gave his patients, although he was certain they noticed he wasn't in his usual spirits. But when he entered the hospice ward, everything shifted. There, in a chipped cup of water, sat the rose, wilting but still alive.

"Good morning," he said softly.

The woman looked up. And for the first time, she smiled.

That tiny gesture undid him. The cost of that single rose might have been high, had Acerbi chosen to twist its perfectly reasonable use into an excuse to fire him out of petty jealousy. But as Remo returned his name-less patient's trusting smile with equal gentleness, he knew he would never regret that small gesture, that little reminder to her that she was a human being worthy of respect and dignity.

Remo ate alone that night, stopping at a modest inn he'd never been to before. He didn't want to burden Andrea or Lyra with his mood; he needed time to think. The soup was thick, warm, and tasteless. Afterward, he walked a longer route home than necessary, letting the night air cool the rage still simmering beneath his skin.

He concluded there was nothing else for it. He'd have to stay away from Sabelle. Were it not for the Academy and the Order of Aquarius, he might have thrown caution to the wind and pursued their relationship anyway. But he felt certain his time in Mavortis wasn't over. To stay, he needed his job at the hospital. It paid for the Academy, for his room, for his life here. And though he hated enduring Acerbi's vile treatment and bowing to his threats, something deeper told him he had to stay the course.

Whatever forces had drawn him to Mavortis hadn't finished with him yet. He felt it in his bones that his purpose here wasn't fulfilled. And beyond that, he *liked* it here. He had Lyra and Andrea. He had meaning.

Even his cramped little room had started to feel like home. He wouldn't risk that, no matter how much it hurt to admit he could no longer fight for what he had with Sabelle. It wasn't a battle he could fight alone, and he wasn't convinced she thought it was worth fighting at all.

When he finally reached his lodgings, he had no energy left for anything but opening the window and collapsing into the chair by it. The night wind slipped through the room, brushing over him like a balm. He glanced toward his small desk and spotted the fantasy book Lyra had recommended. The promise of getting lost in a world that wasn't his own held a particular appeal at the moment.

*Well,* Remo thought with a mirthless laugh, *at least I can read about love that works out.*

Fortunately, Acerbi wasn't working the next day, and for once, Remo moved through the hospital without dread trailing his steps. He was mid-round when his quietest patient surprised him.

In response to his usual soft-spoken question— *Would you like a turn around the garden today?*—she whispered a single word.

"Yes."

He masked his surprise, shifting instantly into action as he helped her rise. Her body was stiff, the strain of her illness weighing on her bones. She leaned heavily into him, and he bore it without hesitation, offering his arm as they walked toward the small garden reserved for long-term patients, a space few healers bothered to visit.

But Remo believed the spirit needed healing as much as the body, maybe more. And if a few minutes of sun and silence could ease someone's suffering, even for a breath, then it was worth everything.

He didn't like thinking about death. He never had a patient die under his care. And now, as he supported her toward the sunlight, he tried to suppress the shape that thought was already taking.

She blinked as they stepped into the sun, the first time its warmth had touched her face in weeks. They made a slow, careful loop past the flowerbeds. Remo said nothing, letting her set the pace, her breath shallow but steady.

He inclined his head toward a cluster of butterfly bushes swaying in the breeze. "What's your favorite flower?"

She took so long to answer that he assumed she'd ignored him, as she often did when the weight of her silence grew too heavy to break. "Roses," she rasped after a long pause, her voice hoarse from the effort. She met his eyes—hesitant, steady, present—for the first time.

Remo's smile was gentle. "Then it seems I made a lucky guess."

She turned away, but not before he saw it: the faint curve of a smile, lingering on her lips as she watched the butterflies flit.

# Chapter Fourteen

REMO SAT IN THE Academy's library, immersed in the Awareness book Lyra had recommended. It laid out three core principles:

1. You are not your thoughts; you are the observer of your thoughts.

2. Your power lies within your focus.

3. To direct your focus with intention, you must discipline mind, body, and spirit.

The book included breathing techniques meant to clear the mind and soothe emotional turbulence. Remo resolved to try them later when alone. A scraping chair broke his concentration, and he looked up to see Lyra settling into the seat across from him.

She nodded toward his book. "Are you enjoying it?"

"I am," he said. "I've never read anything like it, but it makes sense. Awareness class must be fascinating if it's anything like this."

Lyra rested her arms on the table, gazing at him with a dreamy smile. "Will you say that in front of Andrea for me?"

Remo chuckled. Their banter about their chosen disciplines was a familiar routine. "Gladly."

Her starry-eyed expression faded into concern as her gaze dropped to the redness beneath his eyes. "Are you alright? Andrea and I didn't see you yesterday."

He hadn't slept, too preoccupied with Sabelle and Acerbi's warning. Her worry surprised him, stirring something tender. He offered a crooked smile. "Bad day at work. I'm okay."

She didn't press further. She opened her book, and they read in companionable silence for half an hour before heading to The Crooked Cupola.

Andrea and Nella were already seated, and Remo felt relieved that, for once, the lovers weren't pawing at each other. He wasn't sure he could endure that tonight.

Andrea gave him a once-over. "Look who decided to grace us with his presence—and looking worse for wear."

Remo welcomed the teasing. Sweet as Lyra's concern was, he didn't want attention drawn to him. "Clearly, a day without your company destroys me."

Andrea snorted but didn't probe. He likely understood Remo didn't want to explain anything in mixed company.

Remo glanced at the hefty tome Nella was buried in. "Anatomy?"

Without looking up, she nodded. "Galenus. I might offer myself up for dissection next class just to escape all this studying."

Remo laughed softly. He understood the exhaustion well.

Andrea looked between them in amazement. "Why do you do this to yourselves? I glanced at that book once and broke into a cold sweat. It was in the common tongue, and I still didn't understand a word."

Nella shut the book with a sigh, then kissed Andrea's forehead. "Don't trouble that pretty head of yours. It's my curse to carry."

Andrea narrowed his eyes, but his smirk gave him away. "Are you saying my *ruggedly handsome* head is all bone and no brain?"

Nella's grin turned wicked, a retort already dancing in her hazel eyes. "No. Galenus assures me we all have brains. I'm just saying yours is best used between my—"

"Ahem," Lyra coughed loudly.

Nella shrugged and stood. "Impossible to study in such conditions." She departed without ceremony, a classic Nella goodbye.

The others turned their attention to the upcoming Order of Aquarius meeting, discussing it in hushed tones. Remo leaned in, listening closely.

"There are never more than thirty or so people at these meetings, though the Order has far more members," Lyra explained. "They happen about twice a year. Cosimo leads them and gives a briefing on recent developments and goals. After that, the floor opens to anyone who wants to contribute."

Remo bounced his leg, frenetic energy buzzing through him as they waited for the meeting to begin. Andrea looked out the window as the sky shifted from burning orange to deep fuchsia. "It's time," he said.

They made their way down to the Academy, walking the torch-lit stone corridor. Instead of turning through any of the usual arches, Andrea pressed against a section of wall opposite the library. A hidden door swung open, smacking Remo in the arm.

"How many of these damned doors are there?" Remo muttered, rubbing his arm.

Lyra gave him a sympathetic look, fighting a smile. "Just the two, as far as I know."

They stepped into a wide, circular chamber built of stone. It resembled an ancient amphitheater. At the center, a zodiac wheel was mosaiced into the floor, surrounded by white pillars holding planet-like crystal orbs. Remo realized the orbs mirrored the planets' current positions in the sky.

They settled on a middle bench, eyes scanning the gathering crowd. Remo counted thirty-two others present. He noted they were the youngest among them. Most chatted like old friends. Sevo arrived soon after, having closed the inn for the evening. Cosimo stood at the center, and when he spotted them, inclined his head in greeting.

Minutes later, Cosimo cleared his throat and raised a hand for silence. The simple gesture was enough for every conversation to still, all attention turning toward him. He dipped his chin again in thanks before speaking.

"I would like to begin by thanking all of you for being here. In these uncertain times, seeing the familiar faces of our veteran members reminds me of the unwavering loyalty behind our cause. The newer faces give me hope for the future we are striving to create.

"Our first order of business is to address the rumors circulating about

Emperor Varro's mission to expand the empire."

A ripple of whispers stirred across the room.

Cosimo nodded. "Yes, the rumors are true. Several Order members have confirmed them. Knights of Saffiro have been seen in Anxur, the last free kingdom in Terramundi.

"You may recall Prince Andrea's report from three years ago that his father attempted to build a legion of Satrian men. It appears that effort continued under a new commander. We now have reports of 10,000 trained Satrian soldiers, skilled in combat and primed to take a kingdom. Though that's a smaller force than past battalions, it's not one we can afford to dismiss.

"The exact number of Knights of Saffiro working alongside them remains unknown, but estimates suggest a formidable force. We must also consider that the King of Mavortis is a strong ally of Emperor Varro. The Salii soldiers under his command are likely to join the cause. Together, the combined forces of Knights of Saffiro, Salii, and Satrian hastati number at least 30,000.

"You may ask, if this is true, and they hold the upper hand, what can we do? A fair question, with a layered answer.

"Firstly, we have the potential to renew relationships with our powerful allies of old. When the Order was founded 227 years ago, the rulers of Merucia, Lunaria, and Vecontii joined us in protest of Saffiran conquest. They passed their knowledge and allegiance to their descendants, vowing that the devastation wrought on Satria would never be repeated. We've already begun efforts to secure their support once more. Prince Andrea, would you care to elaborate?"

Andrea stood, jaw tight. "Queen Silvia of Lunaria granted me an audience on the Order's behalf, but she's hesitant to oppose Saffiro directly. She fears what it could cost her kingdom. Lunaria is a small kingdom with no standing army. We'd have to raise a covert campaign. The queen would rather avoid interfering in the affairs of other nations than risk depleting her kingdom's resources—or the lives of her people."

As Remo listened, he processed that just before their fateful meeting in the forest, Andrea had returned from visiting Lunaria's queen.

Cosimo nodded in thanks as Andrea sat. "The leaders of Merucia, however, remain steadfast in their support. They're prepared to weather any storm for the cause. They know this goes beyond Anxur. It's about resisting Varro and his tyranny.

"But like Lunaria, Merucia has no standing army. We're dependent on their militia and mercenaries—and Merucian mercenaries are markedly mercurial."

"Try saying that five times fast," Remo muttered to Lyra.

They both tried, and failed, earning a few muffled laughs before Andrea silenced them with a glare.

"Therefore," Cosimo resumed, "the number of Merucian mercenaries willing to fight beside Anxur is insufficient to challenge Saffiro, even when combined with Anxur's own legion. Our numbers sit around 10,000—a third of what Saffiro commands. We need a third ally. One powerful enough to make Saffiro think twice. We need Vecontii.

"Vecontii is the wealthiest kingdom outside of Saffiro, and we believe they have enough reason to oppose Emperor Varro. We will send Prince Andrea as our envoy on a diplomatic visit to King Bardi. If all goes well, he will call upon his navy to join Merucia in Anxur's defense."

Andrea stared at the floor, his jaw still clenched. From the corner of his eye, Remo studied him. He suspected Cosimo had already informed Andrea of the mission, and that it complicated things with Nella. Despite the couple's sometimes unbearable public affection, Remo genuinely enjoyed seeing his friend happy. He silently hoped, for Andrea's sake, and for the sake of all the kingdoms, that Nella would understand the need for him to leverage his connection to Vecontii through her.

"If Vecontii, Merucia, and Anxur stand united against Mavortis, Saffiro, and their Satrian legions, we have a fighting chance of holding Anxur. But let me be clear: preserving one free kingdom won't weaken the empire. It only prevents it from gaining more power.

"All nations have suffered under Saffiro's rule. The forced conditions of Satrians, the crushing taxes that starve the poor and feed the Saffiran elite, the cruelty of the Knights—these are signs of a broken world.

"Balance must be restored. For the people of Terramundi to truly flourish, they must do so under a new ruler. Not a tyrant, but someone who wields power to serve, not rule. Someone who values humanity over conquest. A ruler who governs with compassion, justice, and a steady hand." Cosimo looked at Andrea, bowing his head in respect.

Despite Andrea's effortless grace, Remo often forgot he was a prince, an exiled one who always seemed slightly affronted by gestures like Cosimo's, as if the idea of inheriting the throne sickened him.

Cosimo paused his monologue, pacing the breadth of the amphitheater. He lifted his gaze to the rows above before speaking again. "Those of you who've studied Astrology here at the Academy know that Aquarius, the sign our Order is named for, is ruled by the malefic planet Saturn.

"Saturn, guardian deity of Satria, has long been feared for its difficult influence. It may be the least understood of all the planets. It's true that Saturn's influence can leave us feeling lonely, cynical, even depressed, but only if we fail to rise to its challenges. If we don't cultivate discipline in the part of life Saturn touches in our charts, we suffer its harshest traits.

"But Saturn also rules Capricorn, the sea goat who climbs difficult terrain, slow but sure. Each of us has a mountain to climb in this life, a trial only we can face. Saturn is both the obstacle and the reward for overcoming it. Without trials, we'd never know the pride of resilience. Without climbing the mountain, we'd never appreciate the view from the top, or the mastery it took to get there.

"Together, Capricorn and Aquarius paint the full portrait of Saturn. Aquarius sees a future worth climbing for. It holds the vision that fuels our ascent. It asks, 'What is your dream? What do you wish upon the stars for?' Capricorn replies, 'Then earn it.'"

Cosimo slowed his steps, pausing at the edge of the mosaic circle. His hand drifted lightly over the pillar holding the crystal orb resembling Saturn, as if in silent reverence. "Well, my friends, here is our mountain. To ascend it, we must first remember our Aquarian wish: freedom. Freedom is Aquarius' greatest ideal, and the ultimate mission of our Order. The histories of the Order and the Academy are intertwined. They were born of the same tragedy. It's only right they stand together now, against a tyrant once more."

A buzz spread through the room. Cosimo raised a withered hand, and the sound dissolved into silence. "Even with Merucia, Anxur, and possibly Vecontii standing against Saffiro," he said, "it still may not be enough. We must use every advantage to ensure Anxur doesn't fall, both for its sake, and for every kingdom in Terramundi. Nothing will change as long as we live beneath Saffiro's chokehold, letting them drain us of our resources and our freedoms.

"Our advantages may seem few, but that is not the truth. We have ancient knowledge at our fingertips. The Academy has preserved the tradition of astrology and remembers its influence throughout history. It is a living art, unfolding through millennia. There was once an attempt to use astrology as a weapon before Satria's fall. And now, we will use it again, but this time to restore balance."

Cosimo turned toward Remo, his gaze intent. "Recently, I was shown a treasure I thought lost to time. Toward the end of her life, the astrologer Serafina was said to have become manic, driven by a fear that her life's work would be erased. A master of Astrology and Awareness, she re-portedly received prophetic visions, though no one knows if any came to pass.

"After founding the Academy and the Order, she spent her final days fleeing Saffiran soldiers at sea. One survivor of the shipwreck that claimed her life said she would write obsessively in her last days. She feared her knowledge, and perhaps her story, would vanish, so she sealed her prophecies and allegories in bottles and cast them into the sea.

"One such bottle has been found. Inside it was an engraved precious stone. I believe this stone is a fragment of a talisman she and her teacher once began, intended to stop Emperor Septimus' designs, but never completed."

Remo's eyes widened as Cosimo looked at him. He had unwittingly stumbled upon one of the last remnants of the woman who had founded the very Academy in which he now sat. After 227 years, he had found it—or perhaps, it had found him, leading him to lands he never dreamed he'd see, and a journey that only continued to widen in scope.

"Her teacher, Zeno—the Academy's first headmaster—kept the in-complete talisman here," Cosimo continued. "It has remained safe for two centuries. The time for its use has come. I believe the bottle's reap-pearance is no coincidence. It is a sign from Serafina herself that the mo-ment has arrived, and astrology must rise again as part of this revolution.

Astrology is our gift. It is our weapon. And we will use it to win.

"In times of old when people still believed in magic, talismans were crafted to harness planetary power toward a specific aim. Timing was everything. The maker chose a goal, then the planet best suited to empower it. I believe that by crafting a single talisman imbued with all planetary forces, each drawn from its temple in its respective kingdom, we can forge a powerful weapon against Saffiro.

"Such a talisman might stop war and unite all seven kingdoms through their planetary ties. It will require planning, astrology, and above all, intention. Stealth will be vital to move through the kingdoms unnoticed. Make no mistake; this is no simple task. But it may mean the difference between life and death. Between freedom and subjugation."

Cosimo fell silent again, but this time the pause stretched. He stopped pacing, folding his hands as if waiting.

Remo knew what he was waiting for. Blood roaring in his ears, he stood. "I'll do it."

# Chapter Fifteen

R EMO COULDN'T RECALL THE final thirty minutes of the meeting after volunteering for the harrowing mission.

Cosimo had looked at him with reverence, offered a compliment he hadn't absorbed, and instructed him and his two friends to meet in his office after the gathering to discuss the mission's details. The remainder of the session passed in a blur, with Order members posing questions and sharing information. Andrea appeared undaunted, as if ready to lead troops into battle at any moment.

Lyra, on the other hand, looked as though she were grieving the loss of something precious. Her expression shifted when her eyes found Remo, filling with curiosity. "Why did Cosimo look at you when he spoke about Serafina's bottle?" she asked, her voice laced with urgency.

Remo, feigning interest in the golden telescope near Cosimo's desk, replied, "Because I was the one who found it."

"You... you just found it?" Lyra repeated, her mouth falling open.

Remo wondered at her disbelief. "Yes. In a cave in Anxur. My brother and I used to look for things that floated in from the sea. That's mostly why I came to Mavortis—my mentor Trota told me to ask Cosimo what it might mean. But I never imagined—"

He didn't finish the sentence. Andrea and Lyra exchanged a glance so loaded with meaning it stopped him cold.

"What?" Remo blurted, confused by their sudden clarity.

Lyra looked away from Andrea slowly, as if weighing her next words.

"Didn't it occur to you that—Trota, right?—might have known exactly what that bottle meant? Who wrote it? And that she sent you to

Cosimo instead of going herself?"

Remo had never thought of that. He'd assumed that since he found it, he ought to be the one to bring it forward. If he had known the message's importance, he likely wouldn't have trusted himself with it. But Trota, as an alumna of the Academy, might have understood its history and trusted him anyway. Cosimo had returned the artifact to him, too, which still felt impossible. Yet that didn't fully explain the awe in Lyra's voice. There was something deeper in it, something he hadn't yet understood.

Lyra shook her head. "Remo, if Trota knew what that bottle was and sent you here, then she must've believed you had a part in this. So does Cosimo."

Remo ran a hand along his jaw, her words settling uneasily in his chest. "Maybe. But it could just as easily mean she didn't know what it was, or only suspected it was important and wanted Cosimo to confirm. Either way, does it change anything? Even if she trusted me with it, that alone wouldn't have made me take up the mantle. That choice had to be mine."

Lyra tilted her head, considering. "I suppose that's true. But who's to say how much control we really have? Maybe it's both fate and free will that brought you here."

Andrea spoke for the first time in a while, his gaze fixed on something distant. "Maybe we choose our fate with our free will."

Lyra's eyes widened. "Wait—is it true? There was a gemstone in the bottle?"

Remo blinked. "Yes, I have it. It's an amethyst."

Before either could reply, Cosimo entered briskly. "Ah, good! You're all here." He turned to Remo. "Now, then. You've volunteered to create the talisman that may be our greatest weapon against Saffiro. Are you certain you wish to undertake this mission?"

Andrea and Lyra did their best not to look at Remo, as though worried their attention might pressure him, but Remo didn't hesitate. He gave a single, resolute nod. "I want to do this. I feel like it's meant to be me. Everything that's happened since I found the bottle... Maybe it's all part of something larger." He looked at Andrea. "Besides," he said, "I promised I'd help however I could. This is that promise kept."

Andrea gave Remo a meaningful look. Cosimo's dark eyes held a softness as they danced between the men.

Then he turned to Lyra. "And you, Ms. Calandre? Professor Cimbri tells me you are well on your way to mastering Awareness. However, you are under no obligation to take part if you do not wish to. Like Mr. Renato, you have a choice. No one will think less of you if you decide not to take the risk. We can send other Order members."

Lyra's amber eyes blazed. "It would be an honor to help my friends." She looked to Andrea. "I once also made a promise, though unspoken. I swore to myself I'd repay the kindness you once showed me."

Andrea's expression was strained, as though recalling a painful memory. "You don't owe me anything, Lyra. You never have. This quest might be dangerous—"

"I knew the risks when I joined the Order. And besides, I won't be alone. I'll be with both of you." She lifted her chin, defiant, daring Andrea to argue.

Andrea exhaled, a sound between a sigh and a laugh, as he conceded. But the breath of resignation didn't reach his eyes. They shimmered with something deeper, a mix of resolve, gratitude, and the weight of knowing his friends had chosen to stand beside him in the fight that mattered most.

"Of course, I would ask you as well, Andrea," Cosimo said, turning back to him, "whether you're prepared to take on the talisman quest alongside your diplomatic mission. But that would be a waste of my breath and your time."

Andrea smiled grimly. "Your instincts serve you well. I accept both. I wouldn't let these two try it alone."

"I'm relieved the three of you are embarking together," Cosimo said. "All your talents will be vital to the talisman's creation." He turned to Remo. "The first step is identifying the ideal astrological configurations. I'll help with that. Do you recall from class the exalted placements of each planet?"

Remo rolled up his sleeves and recited, "The Sun is exalted at 19 degrees Aries, the Moon at 3 degrees Taurus, Mercury at 15 degrees Virgo, Venus at 27 degrees Pisces, Mars at 28 degrees Capricorn, Jupiter at 15 degrees Cancer, and Saturn at 21 degrees Libra."

"Correct," Cosimo said with a pleased nod.

Andrea frowned. "What does all that mean?"

Cosimo gestured to Remo.

"A planet's exalted position is its most powerful and comfortable placement. Its energy flows easily and expresses itself at its highest potential," Remo explained.

"Correct again," Cosimo beamed. "And since you found the amethyst linked to Jupiter, that means three stones are already accounted for. I have the incomplete talisman that Headmaster Zeno safeguarded over two centuries ago. It contains a ruby engraved with Mars' symbol, and a sapphire engraved with Saturn's. This means you don't need to harness Jupiter, Mars, or Saturn, as they've already been prepared."

"But Professor," Lyra asked, "how do you know Serafina finished the ritual for the amethyst?"

Cosimo smiled. "A good question, Ms. Calandre. I'm confident because the amethyst bears Jupiter's engraved symbol, and that step comes at the crafting stage, indicating a successful invocation. More importantly, there is an overwhelming presence of Jupiter's energy within the stone, which tells me unmistakably that the intention was set successfully.

"Now," Cosimo continued, "once Remo and I chart the dates of upcoming exaltations, the three of you must journey to each kingdom ruled by the respective planetary deity. These deities are the tutelary, or guardian, spirits of their lands. For instance, Mercury will reach 15 degrees Virgo in two weeks. That means you must be in Merucia when the time comes. The ritual should take place in Mercury's temple; it amplifies the power of the talisman.

"Continuing with this example, since it will be the first you face," Cosimo said, "once you're within the temple of the planet whose energy you're harnessing, you'll begin with a plant offering. For Mercury, appropriate herbs include horehound or licorice. Burning the plant creates suffumigation smoke, which strengthens the connection between the heavens and earth. The rising smoke is more than symbolism; it's the medium through which intention and atmosphere meet.

"The presence of sunthematic objects, items associated with the planet, will make the talisman even stronger. Next comes the invocation. The ancient texts don't give specific wording, but you must say the planet's name and call upon it for help. I leave the creative details to you, Remo. You know from class the qualities of each planet and the realms they govern.

"After the invocation, the talisman must be constructed. Andrea, your alchemical expertise will be crucial for this step. Since you're experienced with metals and gemstones, your task is to engrave the stones with their planetary symbols and set them into the golden plate. You're familiar with intagli from Alchemy, yes?"

Andrea nodded. "An intaglio is an engraved stone with magical properties."

"Exactly. That's what these stones become after the ritual. Once the invocation is complete, engrave and set the stones into the plate. You can prepare the bevels in advance using the Alchemy lab's equipment."

Andrea nodded again, and Cosimo continued.

"When that's done, pass the suffumigation smoke over the talisman while setting your intention. Speak to it. Be precise. Give it specific instructions. The talisman's ultimate purpose is to protect Anxur and all kingdoms from Saffiro's imperial reach. But when invoking Mercury's influence, tailor your intention to Mercury's domain. Ask Mercury to grant the wearer persuasive eloquence to sway the King of Vecontii. Ask for the power to broker peace among divided kingdoms. Ask for intellect, clarity, and sharpness in every moment of difficulty.

"Remo, this part will be strongest if you perform it with Lyra. Lyra, I suggest you give Remo some foundational lessons in Awareness to help strengthen his abilities."

Lyra nodded, the fire in her amber eyes undimmed.

"The final part of the ritual," Cosimo continued, "is where Lyra's skill in Awareness becomes essential. Lyra, you must meditate on the planet and the talisman, attuning yourself to it spiritually to ensure its presence is sealed. As the suffumigation smoke fades, show gratitude to the planet for honoring your request. Once the smoke has fully burned out, the ritual is complete. Now, we'll go over this again at a later time," Cosimo said, with a gentler tone. "I imagine this is quite enough information for one night.

"Remo, stay after Astrology on the Moon's day so we can look ahead at the planetary exaltations. I'd like to begin offering you private instruction as well, to ensure you're fully prepared."

"Yes, sir."

Cosimo's black eyes twinkled with amusement. "Go on, ask the question I see still burning behind your eyes."

Remo held his gaze, hoping his sincerity would soften the ignorance in his question. "I understand the ritual, but... logically, I don't understand how a talisman works. How the planets' powers could be captured inside an object."

Apparently, Remo's doubt was no great hindrance to their quest as Cosimo chuckled and stood to see them out. "My boy," he said warmly, "if you understood it logically, it wouldn't be magic, now would it? Magic is, by its nature, that which resists the bounds of ordinary awareness. Stop trying to dissect it. The harder you try to trap magic under a microscope, the faster it slips away. The mundane and the arcane exist in the same world. You must let them coexist inside you, too."

Something clicked into place for Remo. For the first time, he felt permitted to believe in something beyond his understanding. Releasing his need to understand everything gave him peace he hadn't expected. He was beginning to realize that belief itself was its own kind of magic.

"What happens after the talisman is complete?" Andrea asked. "Say it works and we stop this war. What's to stop our enemies from stealing it?"

Cosimo shook his head. "A talisman is not an everlasting charm. It burns with purpose, and when that purpose is fulfilled, the flame dies. What remains is only a relic—beautiful, perhaps, but powerless."

Cosimo held the door open as he looked over them with fondness. "As a wise man once said, 'Saturn loves no halfwits, nor Mars weaklings—nor I, either.' And I take great comfort knowing this mission rests with those the gods themselves would not refuse."

None of them felt ready to part ways just yet, so they returned to Andrea's chambers. He sank into the chair by the fire, rubbing his temples.

"Well, I'm glad that was just a quick check-in and nothing important is expected of us," Remo said.

Lyra caught his eye, and his wry smile made her shake her head. She tried to suppress her laughter, but it broke loose, slightly hysterical. Andrea and Remo joined in, their shared laughter bringing the first lightness they'd felt in hours.

Wiping tears from her cheeks, Lyra exhaled and drifted into a pensive silence. Remo recalled her earlier words: *I swore to myself I'd repay the kindness you once showed me.* He turned the phrase over in his mind, his brow furrowing.

She offered them both a sad smile. "So, I suppose we'll plan our trip to Vecontii around an auspicious Venus alignment?"

Remo tapped the arm of the settee. "Seems like it. If Venus exalts at 27 degrees Pisces, that's our best bet for both the talisman and to sway King Bardi. We'll already be there; no point planning two trips."

Andrea looked between them, disbelief flickering across his face. "You mean you'd both come with me?"

Lyra arched a brow. "Naturally. Don't you think I'm curious about the people who raised the lovely monster we know as Nella?"

Remo tried to smother his laughter, noting the mix of amusement and dread on Andrea's face—the face of a former legion commander.

"She's going to be furious with me," Andrea muttered. "I haven't told her yet that Cosimo asked me to meet with her father. She'll have to come with me to smooth things over. And besides, my dear father banned other royal courts from hosting me long ago, fearing I might rally support and challenge him. Since I joined the Order, some allied rulers have been more willing to receive me, though cautiously.

"Vecontii sympathizes with the Order, but King Bardi still fears Saffiro. War is coming, and sides must be chosen. And if Bardi believes I might have a legitimate claim to the throne after whatever chaos unfolds in Anxur... he might be more inclined to support me. Especially if his daughter has a chance to become Queen of Saffiro," Andrea added bitterly.

"Wouldn't she become empress?" Remo asked.

Andrea shook his head. "My father holds the titles of Emperor of Terramundi and King of Saffiro. My mother was called queen but held no real power. The wife of the emperor does not become empress."

A charged silence settled between them. The weight of responsibility seemed to land on all three at once.

"Why would Nella be upset about the mission?" Remo asked.

Andrea looked weary. "She's felt used by me before because of my work with the Order. I'm afraid she'll think our getting back together was just a way to gain her father's trust."

"Oh, Andrea... that's not true, is it?" Lyra asked hesitantly.

Andrea stiffened. "Do you doubt my feelings for her now, too? After everything? You, of all people, should know how little I want this. The title. The burden. Any of it. But if I'm the only one with any amount of power who gives a damn, and I don't do anything to help others and to change their situations, then I'm as much of a selfish piece of shit as my father."

"Oh, Andrea," she breathed. "I didn't mean it like that. I'm sorry. I know you don't. I really am sorry."

Andrea's frustration dissolved. The smallness of her voice broke through his anger. He rose from his chair and sat beside her, offering his hands gently, as though expecting her to reject them. She rested her hands in his, and he brought one to his cheek, gentler than Remo had ever seen him.

"No. I'm sorry," Andrea said. "You were just thinking of Nella." He kissed the back of her hand.

The gesture left Remo feeling strangely hollow. He realized then that there was a part of their bond he'd never touch. They would likely always be closer to each other than he would be to either of them, and the thought made Remo want to leave before they left him behind. Remo longed for that kind of intimate friendship and feared, more than anything, that he might never attain the kind he'd only read about in books and now witnessed between Andrea and Lyra.

He had felt lonely for most of his life, and while he often enjoyed solitude, he suspected he'd learned to enjoy it out of necessity, because it might be all he would ever have. He thought of his beloved fictional companions, Milena and Devlan, and the close-knit circle of friends they shared. The idea of a chosen family, woven together by loyalty and love, moved him more deeply than any romantic ideal ever had.

Lyra and Andrea released each other's hands, and Remo suddenly felt he no longer belonged in the room. He stared at his own hands, reminding himself that his current feelings didn't matter in the grand scheme of things. He had a mission to complete, one far greater than his own self-pity.

Lyra's voice was calm now. "Whatever Nella feels, she'll understand this matters more than all of us. If needed, I'll help her see that. I know she'll be invaluable to us in Vecontii. Her presence will smooth our entry into the kingdom, at the very least. But that's a problem for another day. First, we go to Merucia."

Silence settled again as each of them retreated into their thoughts. Remo stood, aching to be alone. "Goodnight," he said.

But before he could leave, Andrea reached out, placing a hand on his shoulder. "Thank you for choosing to go through this with me—with us," Andrea said. "You owe me nothing, but your choice brings me comfort. That we met at all is proof enough for me that the stars do, in fact, watch over us."

Remo grasped Andrea's shoulder in return and felt a knot in his chest begin to untangle—a thread he hoped might, in time, weave a storied friendship with Andrea and Lyra, one he wouldn't find a way to exclude himself from.

# Chapter Sixteen

T HE AMIABLE TAILOR BOUNCED on his heels as Remo stepped out wearing the silken brocade doublet. The pale blue fabric brought out the grey in his eyes. It fit perfectly, though a knot lingered in his stomach. He wouldn't need it to impress Sabelle anymore.

"You cut quite the figure in that doublet," Andrea said, joining him for an afternoon stroll through the Briar District. "It'll be perfect for Vecontii."

Remo felt marginally better about the investment. "Thank you. I'll keep telling myself that was the only reason I bought it."

"Am I to finally hear what happened with Sabelle?" Andrea asked.

"How did you know something happened?"

Andrea gave him a flat look. "You've been walking around like your spirit left your body. Work stress can be shrugged off, but matters of the heart? Not so much."

Remo mimed tipping an invisible hat. "I suppose I'm less mysterious than I thought."

"So out with it. What happened?"

Remo recounted everything, including Acerbi's threats.

"That bastard," Andrea growled.

"You know Acerbi?"

"Not well," Andrea said. "His father, King Ultor, is close to mine. I had the misfortune of being around him a few times back in Saffiro, but I haven't crossed paths with him in Mavortis. He has twin siblings, Marcellus and Marzia, so he'll likely never inherit the throne."

Remo mentally congratulated himself for having guessed as much.

They stopped at a tavern for a typical Mavortian meal of spiced meat, hot peppers, and a bottle of chilled mead to chase the heat.

"You're right not to risk seeing Sabelle," Andrea said. "I still can't believe that prick is your supervising physician. I wish I could say I had enough influence here to counter his, but I don't. Hardly anyone in Mavortis knows who I am, and those who might recognize me don't realize I live here. Honestly, I prefer it that way.

"My father may have banned the royal courts from showing me favor, but he didn't need to. Nobody cares about an exiled prince who has nothing to offer. So I kept my identity to myself. Nothing disgusts me more than people who kiss ass to gain status."

"Then I'm not sure politics would've suited you," Remo said with a smirk.

Andrea raised his glass in salute and took a long drink. "No, I don't suppose it would. But that means I've got no sway if Acerbi ever decides to make good on his threats. I wouldn't be able to help you keep your job."

"I'd never expect you to," Remo said. "Not being able to talk to Sabelle about any of this hurts. But maybe it's for the best. I don't see a way forward for us. I suppose that's a mercy for her. She should be with some lordling."

Andrea leaned in, lowering his voice. "When the mission's complete—if all goes well, and I'm in a position to follow through on it—I could give you a title. A lord, a duke... a Sir-my-tights-are-indecently-cupping-my-balls—"

Remo guffawed, mead spilling out of his nose.

Andrea didn't flinch. "I'm serious, Remo. Terramundi will owe you for your service. And if Cosimo's vision comes to pass, I'd be honored to grant you a title. Then, if Sabelle's still worth it, her family won't have a leg to stand on. No more secrets, and no more sneaking around."

Remo wiped his face with a cloth napkin, then hesitated, unsure whether a future lord would leave it crumpled on the table. "That's too generous. I don't know if I could accept something like that. I'm not exactly lordly."

Andrea raised an eyebrow. "And Acerbi is? You think he's princely?

Titles are just names. You don't have to act a part. You're more of a gentleman than half the nobles I've met. Titles don't change people, only how the world treats them."

Remo couldn't think of a reason to refuse and didn't want to. The offer was too tempting. "Well then, if things play out in our favor, I'd accept and owe you yet another unpayable debt. Thank you."

Andrea waved a hand dismissively, as if he'd offered no more than to pay for lunch. "Then consider it a certainty. Something to look forward to once our goal is achieved."

Remo thanked him again. But before his thoughts could spiral into the implications of Andrea's offer, he shifted the topic. "Enough about my troubles. What about you and Nella? Have you told her about our trip to Vecontii yet?"

Andrea frowned into his mead. "No. She's been overwhelmed with schoolwork. I didn't want to add to her stress."

Remo held his gaze, unconvinced. Under the weight of that stare, Andrea exhaled. "Fine. I've also avoided telling her because I'm afraid of how she'll react. Things have been good between us—peaceful, for once. I don't want another fight. Not in that part of my life. Not on a battlefield, either. I want peace."

Remo's expression softened. "You deserve peace. I won't pretend to be an expert on relationships, but it doesn't seem right to feel like you're always walking on eggshells around someone you love. A partner worthy of you would understand." He hesitated, then added gently, "Maybe she *will* understand this time. But you won't know unless you give her the chance. You have to tell her."

Andrea slumped in his chair with a sigh. "You speak wisely. I'll tell her tonight. At least then, the dreading will be over."

Remo hesitated, then asked, "You implied King Bardi would support your marriage to Nella if he believed you had a real shot at the Saffiran throne. So... would you marry her?"

Andrea's whole body seemed to recoil from the question, as though he'd done his best not to consider it himself. "She's already my queen, though I have no throne," he said. "But I'm certain she wouldn't want the title. I wouldn't ask her to give up her studies, or take on a role she didn't want. As queen, she'd have the freedom to do whatever she pleased... but I know her. The title itself would feel like a cage, no matter how free she truly was."

He ran a hand through his hair. "We both grew up in the system. And returning to it isn't something she wants. It's not something I want either, but I've accepted it as necessary, if only to help build a better world. I'd use her father's hope of seeing her crowned to further our cause, but it would serve him right if that hope never came to pass."

Andrea's voice hardened. "Even if he's a decent man, there's no excuse for using your daughter as a pawn and ignoring what *she* wants for her life. I know they miss her. I know they hope she'll give up medicine and marry well. And yes, we're going to exploit that hope."

Remo noticed how Andrea had completely sidestepped the question of his own feelings. His answer revealed only his worries about Nella and the strategy ahead. They finished their drinks in silence, then rose and made their way back toward their quarter of Mavortis.

As they neared the fountain at the edge of the square near the Veil River bridge, Andrea broke the quiet. "What would you say to Sabelle," he asked, "if you had the chance to talk to her about what happened?"

Remo tilted his head, caught off guard by the question and uncertain where he'd even begin.

Andrea suddenly raised a hand, halting him mid-step. He looked Remo straight in the eye. "Think fast. Because Sabelle is standing right there."

Remo's heart lurched. He followed Andrea's gaze and spotted Sabelle pacing along the fountain's edge in a long, dark pink dress. She looked anxious, scanning the faces of strangers as if searching for someone she hadn't yet found.

He tore his eyes away from her to glance at Andrea, who clapped a hand on his shoulder before turning to leave. "Be careful," Andrea murmured.

Remo gave a small nod, watching his friend disappear into the streets behind him, then turned back toward the fountain. It was the same fountain where he had first seen her in Mavortis.

Sabelle glanced his way, started to look away, then did a double take.

In an instant, her expression shifted from anxious to overjoyed as she ran toward him, her dress swaying around her legs.

"What are you doing here?" Remo asked. He already suspected the reason, but he needed to hear it from her lips.

"Remo," she breathed, gazing up at him like she couldn't believe he was real. She took his hands in hers. "I've seen you in every stranger's face since we last parted. I knew something was off between you and Prince Arlo, and I figured you probably wouldn't seek me out again. So I came to the one place I thought I might find you. We have to talk."

He stiffened. Just the thought of the moment Acerbi belittled him in front of her still burned. She hadn't defended him. He hadn't expected her to, but the childish ache of disappointment lingered. He scanned the square, Acerbi's threat echoing in his mind.

"We can't be seen together," he said. "Where can we go that's safe? Somewhere Acerbi or his people won't find us. Are you being followed again?"

Sabelle shook her head. "No. I made sure of it. Where do you usually go? Could we go somewhere near where you live?"

Remo couldn't think of a better alternative and needed to get out of the open. He led her toward The Crooked Cupola. Once they were seated in a quiet corner, Sabelle's expression turned remorseful.

"I wanted to apologize for pulling my hand away," she said. "It was a gut reaction to seeing someone who knows my family. If I could go back, I wouldn't have done it."

Whatever bitterness he'd held toward her softened as he saw the sorrow in her face.

She continued, "And I'm sorry I let Arlo speak to you that way. I was shocked. I thought he was teasing, because it was so out of character. I'd always believed he was... kinder than that." Her voice faltered, her excuse flimsy.

Remo held back a bitter laugh. Acerbi, he thought, would make a better actor than a physician, if he'd managed to conceal his venom from her for so long. Her jade-green eyes met his, pleading silently for forgiveness.

"You don't have to apologize," he said. "I understood. You did the right thing by pulling away." Each word hurt, but it was true.

She looked stricken. "No. I didn't act the way I should have. And you deserve an apology for that."

Truthfully, Remo didn't feel he deserved her apology. Acerbi's words echoed in his mind: *Sabelle is far too good for you.* He believed them. The phrase repeated like a mantra, unwavering in its affirmation.

"If you want forgiveness, then it's yours," he said. "But we can't be together, Sabelle. I'm sorry."

Her face fell, devastation distorting her features. His stomach turned; he had caused that pain. He had reached for something he never should have touched. Maybe he'd been fooling himself, mistaking proximity to Andrea for worth. But Remo wasn't a prince.

"Why?" Sabelle demanded, her voice taut with anger and grief.

He said nothing. Better, he thought, to let her believe this was his choice, not something forced upon him.

She wiped a tear from her cheek, her voice suddenly sharp. "Did Arlo threaten you?"

Remo flinched. He turned toward her too quickly.

Her scorn vanished the moment she saw his face. "He *actually* threatened you?" she gasped, her eyes wide in disbelief.

He hesitated. The truth hovered, heavy on his tongue. He hated seeing her upset almost as much as he hated the idea of her thinking he wanted this separation. At last, he spoke, recounting the threat Acerbi had made in his office that morning. By the time he finished, Sabelle's expression had hardened. Her eyes could have pierced armor.

"We'll find a way around it," she said fiercely. "We can't let him win. We won't let him separate us, not if we still want to be together. We'll just have to be even more discreet."

Only hours ago, Remo would've accepted that keeping his distance was the wisest course. He had too much to lose. But Andrea's offer had changed everything. A future that once seemed impossible was now within reach. If they succeeded in their mission and Andrea reclaimed his title, Remo could be granted a title of his own. A title that would make him Sabelle's equal.

He was ready to earn it. If they could navigate these next steps carefully, maybe there was hope for them.

"Are you sure this is what you want?" he asked quietly, his heart still brittle. "To sneak around, constantly afraid of being seen? Feeling like we're criminals instead of lovers?"

Sabelle leaned in, her lips brushing his ear as she whispered, "If you're trying to talk me out of this, you'll have to make it sound far less thrilling. Honestly, you're only enticing me more."

A grin broke across Remo's face, sudden and irrepressible, like sunlight cracking through storm clouds.

She smiled back, pleased by the effect her words had on him. Then, more softly, more vulnerably: "I want to be with you, Remo."

He reached across the table and took her hand, meeting her gaze with steady warmth. "Then we'll find a way."

"Promise me we'll keep meeting?"

"It seems to be our fate to keep crossing paths like this," he said. "And I'm happy to be fate's fool for you."

# Chapter Seventeen

O N THE MOON'S DAY after their private lesson, Remo and Cosimo mapped the planets' exaltation dates.

"Mercury will be moving into 15 degrees Virgo on August 26th. From here, it's about two days' travel to the temple," Cosimo said.

Remo hesitated, voicing the question he had avoided. "Professor, what should I tell my employer about being away?"

Cosimo looked at him in mild surprise. "Ah, yes. The dates are spaced apart enough that your absences won't raise suspicion. Invent any reason you must; the Order can provide forged documentation if needed. And of course, your work here will be compensated."

Remo nodded, his mind racing for a plausible excuse to offer Acerbi. He would have willingly sought employment elsewhere if not for the patients under his care; he couldn't bear leaving them vulnerable to Acerbi's negligence.

Cosimo moved slowly toward his desk, unlocking a drawer and retrieving something carefully. "You'll need to familiarize yourself with this."

He revealed a circular pendant of gold, about the size of Remo's palm. Engraved around its edge were the twelve zodiac signs, encircling seven distinct rings. Each ring had raised gold settings, clearly meant for stones prepared by Andrea. Already set into two rings were a sapphire for Saturn and a ruby for Mars. The pendant was beautiful, an artifact radiating ancient craftsmanship. Yet its weight felt greater than mere gold would suggest, a heaviness Remo attributed to the potent energies of Saturn and Mars emanating from within.

Cosimo regarded him closely, evidently sensing Remo's reaction. "Do not fear it. While the energies of Mars and Saturn are indeed powerful, this talisman channels only their highest virtues. Each stone is specifically charged to harness the planets' most benevolent influences. Did you bring Jupiter's amethyst, as I requested?"

Remo fished the precious stone from his pocket as Cosimo explained, "Jupiter's benefic energy will lend the pendant a lighter yet equally powerful presence. Andrea will set this stone into place before the three of you depart for Merucia. I'll provide each gemstone as needed; they will remain safely guarded here in the meantime."

Remo felt relief wash over him at not yet having responsibility for the talisman, easing the heaviness that had settled in his chest. As was their habit, he met Lyra and Andrea for dinner at The Crooked Cupola. Lyra excused herself early, scheduled to sing at a tavern in the Briar district within the hour, leaving Remo alone with Andrea.

Suddenly, a loud commotion erupted outside. Sevo went out to investigate and returned quickly, reporting it was just a scuffle between two drunken patrons. Remo, sipping his ale thoughtfully, found himself pondering something he had never considered before. "Does Lyra walk home alone from the Briar district?"

Something indefinable passed through Andrea's eyes as he observed Remo closely. "No," he answered carefully. "They arrange a covered wagon for her whenever she performs at certain establishments."

Impressed, Remo nodded appreciatively. "She must be quite talented for that arrangement."

Andrea merely nodded, looking distant and rubbing his temples. Remo took the chance to ask how Andrea's talk with Nella had gone.

"Not as badly as I feared," Andrea admitted. "She hates going back to Vecontii, and was furious about using our potential marriage as leverage, but she saw the sense in it. Bardi loves to keep his options open. We agreed following through with the marriage would remain our decision afterward. Then she kicked me out for the night."

"Better reaction than I anticipated," Remo joked lightly. "For a moment, I thought you'd stop at 'then she kicked me.'"

Andrea laughed darkly, a touch of bitterness in his voice. "She sees the necessity and is putting aside personal grievances for the greater good. Thankfully, she didn't suspect our reunion was mere convenience, because it truly wasn't. I'm relieved she trusts me."

Despite Andrea's apparent exhaustion, a faint smile played across his face, hinting at a private detail of their conversation he'd tactfully omitted. Remo felt a genuine happiness for his friend, hopeful that Andrea found real contentment in his complicated relationship.

Remo raised his ale in a toast. "Then here's to partnership. May yours be as persistent and enduring as the stubborn acne on Acerbi's left cheek."

Andrea nearly spat out his drink, coughing. "Promise me you'll improve your romantic sentiments before we reach Venus' temple."

The next week focused entirely on preparations for Merucia. Cosimo taught Remo to use an astrolabe to accurately track celestial movements.

Remo spent extensive hours in the library, studying astrology books. He noted materials considered sunthemata, or sympathetic, to Mercury, suitable as offerings and for suffumigation. He carefully crafted the invocation to Mercury for the ritual, finding it came naturally to him. His Gemini rising and South Node, he learned, indicated Mercury's influence: a sharp wit, intellectual agility, boundless curiosity, and adeptness with language—qualities he'd possessed even in a past life.

Each evening, he diligently tracked star movements from his window, carefully noting their shifts. Lyra continued guiding him in Awareness, frequently joining him in the library to reinforce the key concepts from the Awareness text he had recently completed.

"It's wonderful you're studying the theory," she advised gently, "but remember, theory alone is meaningless without practice. Spiritual learning requires firsthand experience. It must be felt, not just intellectually grasped."

Remo nodded. "You're right. I understand the basics well enough, but applying them feels far more challenging."

She smiled sympathetically. "Exactly. Awareness books quickly grow repetitive. Principles remain consistent despite different wording. Without active practice, theory is useless."

Lyra introduced practical exercises like mentally retracing daily events backward each night. Remo practiced maintaining awareness during sleep, briefly achieving lucidity within a dream before losing focus.

His hospital duties remained intense. Encouraged by his nameless patient's slow but steady trust in him, Remo enjoyed brief garden walks with her when possible. Their conversations gradually grew deeper and more detailed, a sign of her emotional improvement since physical recovery wasn't possible for her.

Remo told Acerbi he'd miss two workdays visiting an elderly, ill relative in Merucia, conveniently overlapping his days off. Acerbi gave no response, deliberately ignoring him—a silence Remo welcomed, relieved to avoid the physician's snide remarks.

The day before departing, Remo visited the local apothecary, acquiring horehound, licorice, and valerian, all herbs associated with Mercury's domain, essential for the ritual. He then retrieved the talisman from Cosimo along with Mercury's designated gem, an aquamarine stone.

"Guard these diligently," Cosimo advised him gravely. "Rotate watch duties and never leave them unprotected. Andrea and Lyra understand their roles. Trust Andrea's instincts and heed his advice. Lyra will assist with intention-setting and lend her considerable focus to empowering the talisman. And Remo, your astrological skills are crucial. Begin the ritual exactly when planned. May Mercury's swift influence be with you."

Remo thanked Cosimo and then met Andrea and Lyra at Andrea's residence. When he presented the talisman and aquamarine gemstone, Lyra's eyes widened, mouth forming a perfect 'o' as the gem shimmered in the candlelight.

"What do you think are aquamarine's properties?" Lyra asked.

Before Andrea could reply seriously, Remo assumed a mock-mystical voice that sounded uncannily like Cosimo's, teasing, "Legend says if you wear an aquamarine necklace and leap from a high tower, the stone will remain unharmed."

Andrea laughed, gripping his stomach, while Lyra pretended to disapprove but couldn't hide her smile. Remo tucked the items safely into his bag, then they revisited their plans carefully.

Andrea was well-traveled, having journeyed many times for the Order, and was therefore familiar with the territory they would cover. He studied a map of Merucia, plotting the quickest route to the temple located near the kingdom's border, as some believed the gods protected these borders from invaders and citizens attempting to leave.

"Although Merucia is allied closely with the Order," Andrea explained, "Cosimo wants to keep the talisman hidden from even our closest royal allies. A talisman of this magnitude carries immense power. If someone with corrupt motives gains possession, the consequences would be catastrophic. Even honorable individuals may succumb to the lure of such strength, so secrecy is paramount."

He continued, "Cosimo also insists we avoid using my royal signet to ease our passage through borders. Any spies observing our movements could raise alarms about a Saffiran royal traveling covertly. Thus, we can expect no assistance from friendly kingdoms in navigating their lands or crossing their frontiers. We must evade inspections at all costs to keep the talisman undiscovered.

"We'll review escape strategies if necessary. Fortunately, Merucia's border guards are generally lenient toward travelers, posing minimal threat. Vecontii will similarly pose less risk since we'll be accompanied by Nella, but that journey remains months ahead."

Remo and Cosimo's astrological calculations indicated Venus would reach its exaltation at 27 degrees Pisces in January, so their diplomatic visit with King Bardi was set for then.

They strategized ways to evade or outwit the Knights of Saffiro should they encounter them during their travels and meticulously reviewed the ritual steps until fatigue overtook them. Agreeing to meet outside their quarters before dawn, they planned to head to The Crooked Cupola, where Cosimo had arranged horses ready in the stable.

A dim glow inside the inn signaled Sevo's early rise and Cosimo's readiness. Entering, they were welcomed by the inviting scent of hot tea with frothy milk and sweet, warm porridge. Cosimo, seated with Sevo, motioned them to eat while he spoke.

"Sevo packed provisions for your journey. Remo, track the stars closely. Andrea, stick firmly to the route. Lyra, maintain the Awareness state we practiced. I have complete confidence in you all. Upon return, meet me in my office. Any questions?"

They shook their heads silently.

"Then good luck. I'll see you in four days." With that, Cosimo stood and disappeared into the back room.

After finishing breakfast, they thanked Sevo and proceeded to the stables. Lyra beamed, gently stroking her horse's shiny grey coat in the predawn light. They secured their belongings to the saddles and set off toward the northern border of Mavortis.

Gradually, the city gave way to sparser woodlands, less dense than the forest where Remo first encountered Andrea.

By the time the sun fully emerged, they had traveled approximately three miles. A berry-pink dawn filtered through the leaves above, and a fresh, earth-scented breeze swept through, lifting Lyra's dark blonde hair. They intentionally strayed from main paths to avoid travelers or potential encounters with the Knights of Saffiro.

For hours, the only sounds were birdsong and the rhythmic clopping of their horses' hooves against the dirt. Conversation was minimal during their brief lunch of bread and hard cheese. Fatigue and underlying nerves subdued them until evening approached, and they reached the edge of the forest. Deciding to camp under cover before continuing over the green hills beyond, they dismounted and began unpacking their gear.

Lyra fed the horses carrots, speaking to them gently with affection and gratitude. Remo watched the scene with a mix of amusement and respect, believing anyone who treated animals so tenderly must be honorable.

Andrea sighed dramatically, shaking his head. "Look at the fuss she makes over animals. She laughed at me last year when I nearly broke my neck falling down the stairs to my lodgings. No 'Oh, Andrea, are you okay?' But if a horse looks even slightly tired from carrying me around, she's ready to empty our entire food supply for it."

Lyra shot Andrea a teasing look. "You stumbled drunkenly down a few stairs; that's hardly near death. If you wanted sympathy, you should've brought Nella."

Andrea snorted. "Sympathy from Nella? I'm half-convinced she pushed me."

Remo laughed, gathering twigs for the fire. Lyra finally stepped away from the horses, her expression caught between pity and amusement at Andrea's comment. She affectionately tugged at the hood of Andrea's cloak as he secured the horses to nearby trees for the night. Andrea responded with a deadpan look, which made her giggle. A reluctant smile spread across his face, and he winked at her. Satisfied, Lyra triumphantly joined Remo in collecting firewood.

He watched her, noticing how she seemed to delight disproportionately in these small interactions with Andrea.

Soon, they sat huddled around a small, crackling fire as the night grew cool, enveloped by the smoky scent of burning wood. Lyra's eyes twinkled in anticipation. "Time for stories," she announced, looking pointedly at Remo.

"Yes, Remo," Andrea drawled, amused. "Please entertain us before Lyra starts a story she can't finish because she dissolves into giggles halfway through."

Lyra tossed her hair back and rounded on Andrea. "That's because my stories are hilarious. *Yours* always revolve around lovemaking."

Andrea reclined, flashing a teasing grin. "Guilty as charged. I enjoy happy endings."

Lyra blushed fiercely, giving Remo a pleading look, clearly wanting to avoid one of Andrea's provocative tales. Remo considered his limited options. "Happy, sad, amusing? Real or fairy tale?"

Andrea replied promptly, "Real life."

Remo immediately regretted offering that option, doubting he had anything sufficiently intriguing for his worldly friends. Lyra seemed briefly distant, then refocused, meeting Remo's eyes intently. "I read enough fairy tales. A true story would be good," she said decisively.

Remo hesitated, then recalled the single compelling experience from his life in Anxur: the mystical encounter at Jupiter's temple, where he'd possibly hallucinated or entered an altered state, connecting with Jupiter's spirit.

When he finished recounting the tale, Lyra straightened up, her eyes wide but composed. Andrea, typically blasé, looked visibly astonished.

"That night, I decided I had to leave Anxur," Remo concluded softly. "It didn't matter if it was just a dream or an effect of the tea. I knew Mavortis was the next step for me."

Lyra opened her mouth to speak but hesitated, instead studying Remo closely as if seeking more hidden details. Feeling vulnerable under her scrutiny, Remo asked hesitantly, "Do you think I'm... crazy?"

"Heavens, no," she said, scooting closer to him reassuringly. "If you're crazy, there's no hope for me or anyone else in Awareness class. You mentioned drinking purple lotus tea, correct? It sounds like you experienced an altered state of consciousness. That flower is known to heighten receptivity to other planes, though it's remarkable you had such a powerful experience unintentionally."

Remo looked into her amber eyes, comforted by her words. "So you don't think it was merely a dream?" he asked.

Lyra hesitated. "It could have been, I suppose, but given the circumstances—that you held Serafina's amethyst imbued with Jupiter's essence, within Jupiter's own temple in Anxur, the kingdom dedicated specifically to Jupiter—it feels too coincidental. I truly believe you connected deeply with Jupiter, perhaps even more intensely than Cosimo expects of us in creating the talisman."

"Have you—" Andrea started, breaking his long silence, and they both turned toward him. "Have you told Cosimo about this?"

"No," Remo admitted. "I wasn't sure what had happened. I was afraid I was just..."

"Crazy," finished Lyra with another sympathetic smile.

Remo nodded gratefully.

Andrea shook his head. "But isn't it a bit... *strange* how everything unfolded afterward? That you ended up being one of three chosen to connect with the planets in crafting this talisman? I mean, this happened before you even knew about the Order. It's almost as if it worked out perfectly. How could Cosimo have known?"

"Know what?" Remo asked.

Andrea looked at him, his shock still apparent. "I told you that Cosimo had his private reasons for believing that you would be an important addition to the Order. But it's like he knew you could intuitively connect with the planets. He talked to me like he knew you had some special quality that made you necessary to the Order."

Despite the warmth of the nearby fire, Remo felt a sudden chill. "But maybe I don't," he said cautiously, worried they'd begun to expect too much from him. "Maybe it was just an isolated incident, or perhaps the tea affected me."

"Even if the tea influenced you, it doesn't make your experience less real," Lyra responded gently. "We sleep every night, our perceived reality dissolving into dreams we fully believe. Who's to say dreams aren't genuine experiences in another realm?"

Remo sat quietly, absorbing Lyra's words. Andrea's revelation unsettled him deeply. What exactly had Cosimo said to Andrea that implied Remo had a special purpose? The irony wasn't lost on him: the Jupiter experience had steered him down an unexpected path that mirrored the way his journey had begun—connecting with planets within their temples, each time holding a precious stone associated with them.

"I'll take first watch," Remo finally offered, knowing sleep would be impossible for now as he pondered his situation.

Andrea and Lyra thanked him, settling onto the moss-covered ground. Remo placed the pack containing the talisman securely beside him, carefully observing the stars and tracking their movements as he'd promised Cosimo. After several hours, he woke Andrea to take over the watch.

At dawn, they rose to continue their journey, riding for hours over gently rolling hills cloaked in lush, emerald green. Andrea frequently checked his map to ensure they stayed on course. They skipped lunch, pressing on determinedly to reach Mercury's temple before the following sunrise. By late afternoon, they ascended the final hill separating them from Merucia, passing without issue from the kingdom's border guards.

If Mavortis glowed reddish from its buildings, Merucia was blanketed in silvery-blue. From their hilltop vantage point, they saw the kingdom's nearest city spread below, filled with tall, grey stone structures and slender towers of varying heights, some serving as lookouts, others as dovecotes for Merucia's famed messenger pigeons.

"We've arrived," Andrea announced as they descended into the bustling city.

As they traversed the lively cobblestone streets, Remo immediately felt fond of Merucia, finding it warm and inviting. Children laughed and played in open squares while their mothers bartered and shopped at market stalls. They rode past orderly rows of quaint shops with pale blue shutters, the streets filled with friendly chatter as locals went about their daily routines. Despite the city's charm, Remo felt a pang of disappointment knowing their schedule allowed no time for leisurely exploration.

"I've heard there's an incredible library here," Lyra said wistfully. "Supposedly, it holds some of Terramundi's oldest books."

"Perhaps someday we can return and spend as much time as we'd like exploring it," Remo suggested, pleased by how she beamed at the idea. He sincerely hoped they'd have that opportunity.

An unnatural silence settled over the town square. Before the friends could exchange questioning glances, the cause became clear. Four Knights of Saffiro stalked through, prompting mothers to urgently grasp their children's hands and steer them away.

A mix of relief and dread surged through Remo when the knights turned sharply toward one of the shops, loudly pounding on a board-ed-up door. A man screamed as he was forcibly dragged outside and surrounded by the knights. Within moments, the bustling village square was deserted.

Remo felt guilt tighten his chest, aware they couldn't intervene. They couldn't risk exposing the talisman, and even if they wanted to help, their weapons were inadequate, carrying only discreet daggers, as swords would have drawn unwanted attention.

Andrea appeared to battle internally, his protective instincts urging him to help the elderly shopkeeper. Remo, recalling Andrea's similar act of bravery toward himself, spoke up regretfully, "We can't, Andrea. We can't risk being searched, and we're not adequately armed."

Andrea reluctantly tore his gaze from the troubling scene, prepared to argue until his eyes landed on Lyra standing behind Remo. Understanding dawned, and he nodded grimly, urging them onward. By evening, they had ridden completely through the city, arriving at another hill topped with a stone tower and an old mill. Andrea checked the map, confirming it was Mercury's temple.

Before making camp, they stopped by a freshwater spring to let the horses drink, splashing cool water over their faces and hands. Under a clear, starlit sky, they made camp in the grassy expanse near the temple, relieved they'd reached their destination in time.

Remo carefully checked his bag, reassuring himself that the talisman, aquamarine stone, plants, and suffumigation materials were all securely in place. Finding everything intact, he exhaled deeply. Famished from skipping lunch, the three friends hungrily consumed more bread, cheese, and fruit than planned, knowing their rations would be sparse the following day.

"It's my turn for first watch tonight," Lyra said firmly, pulling the bag containing the talisman close, eyeing it as though it might escape on its own. She glanced at the two men. "You both get some rest."

Groaning their weary thanks, Remo and Andrea swiftly fell asleep. Lyra woke Remo as requested, letting him track the stars and prepare ritual materials. Remo woke the others fifteen minutes before sunrise, ensuring they were ready in the temple at dawn. They entered the ruined tower, lanterns lighting the dim predawn gloom. Grass carpeted the circular floor, and twin staircases rose like wings toward an unseen upper level, Mercury shining overhead. Andrea climbed upward to investigate.

"Be careful," Lyra called, helping Remo unpack their supplies.

Remo handed her a scribe's robe matching his own. "Scribes are Mercury's servants, translating and writing, so I, uh... thought we should dress accordingly," he explained, feeling slightly embarrassed despite

Cosimo's encouragement.

Lyra giggled, and Remo's face flushed as he wondered if Cosimo was playing a trick, now laughing at his expense with Sevo. Lyra pulled the robes over her dress, glancing first at herself and then at Remo before bursting into louder laughter. "We lead ridiculous lives, don't we?"

"We truly do," he replied, finding himself laughing despite his embarrassment.

Andrea returned shortly after, confirming that the upper level opened onto an exterior platform.

"We should perform the ritual down here," Remo decided. "If we're connecting heaven and Earth with suffumigation, it makes sense to remain on the ground."

Lyra settled near the tower's center. "I think you're right."

Remo nodded decisively. "Then let's begin."

Lyra lit the horehound, placing it gently in a small bowl as its smoke curled skyward. Andrea prepared his engraving tools and burnisher, readying the precious gemstone to be set into the raised bezels of the golden pendant. Remo carefully arranged offerings of licorice and valerian plants, quills and ink, an ancient book, and a copy of a beloved poem.

Lyra closed her eyes, attuning herself to Mercury's energy. Remo held the aquamarine, reciting his invocation and offering—a poem honoring Mercury, planet of poets:

*"We humbly begin our invocation,*
*calling upon you, Mercury, planet of Communication,*
*Master of Poetry and Deliberation,*
*as you reside in your most powerful station.*

*We seek your intelligence, quickness of wit,*
*your boundless knowledge of all that's writ.*
*Mercury, Articulate and Cunning of Mind,*
*Master of Skills of every kind,*

*Imbue this stone with your essence,*
*knowledge of all seen and unseen.*

*Infuse your eloquent, quicksilver presence*
*into this aquamarine."*

He bowed his head, feeling the gem tingle softly in his palm. Andrea approached, engraving and burnishing the aquamarine into the talisman with precise tools. Remo recognized only abrasive powder and a small drill. As Andrea worked to set the aquamarine firmly into the golden pendant, sunlight began to pour through the tower's open windows, heralding the arrival of dawn.

Remo joined Lyra in attuning to Mercury's energy: words, thoughts, and ideas, the essence of the planet and of his own soul. He tapped into the influence of his Gemini rising and South Node, the astrological roots of his lifelong love of books and reading.

He felt the immense power Mercury had held over his life. Through books, he had lived a thousand lives, traveled to extraordinary realms, and fallen in love with countless characters. His heart was filled with people and places born from fiction, a private sanctuary he could enter at will. He let the emotion swell inside him, his energy rising with the intensity of his memories and longing. These emotions gave strength and clarity to his intention.

Andrea handed him the completed talisman, the aquamarine now set into its golden bezel, for the final stage of the ritual, intention-setting. Remo waved the suffumigation smoke over the pendant and spoke aloud.

"Mercury, please imbibe this aquamarine stone and talisman with your powers of communication and clarity of mind, for the purpose of enabling the wearer to establish peace in Terramundi. Grant the bearer effective skills of persuasion, diplomacy, and intelligence. We thank you for granting our request."

He lowered the suffumigation bowl and held the talisman between himself and Lyra. They concentrated their shared intention for what felt like half an hour, feeling energy pulse around them, a wordless knowing that their ritual had worked.

"The smoke has burned out," Andrea murmured.

Lyra and Remo opened their eyes simultaneously. Lyra's serene smile mirrored his own certainty. She let go of the talisman, allowing it to settle into Remo's palm. It was still warm from her touch.

"We did it," he whispered, stowing the pendant safely in his bag while leaving the sunthemata as an offering to Mercury.

They climbed to the tower's peak and drank in the view of Merucia. A flock of messenger pigeons soared past, hundreds strong, their feathers in soft greys, blues, and whites, some shimmering with green, violet, and black iridescence in the morning sun. The friends stood silently, letting the morning wind kiss their skin.

"Now, we return home," Lyra said.

Andrea gave her a serious look. "No. First, we get something to eat."

# Chapter Eighteen

THE JOURNEY HOME PROVED far more pleasant now that the anxiety surrounding the ritual had passed. Though weary from long days of riding and restless nights on the forest floor, the friends joked more easily with one another. On the second evening, they gathered once again around a small fire in the woods, grateful for its warmth.

"So," Andrea asked, "did you connect with Mercury the way you did with Jupiter?"

A flicker of uncertainty passed through Remo. He shook his head. "No, it wasn't the same. I'm not sure what I was supposed to feel, but I did sense Mercury's vibration inside me." He glanced at Lyra, unconsciously seeking reassurance.

She nodded. "It was the same for me," she said. "I focused on Mercury's energy, and it sort of permeated me. I imagined a blue light flowing from above, through me, and into the talisman. I just knew it was working. I felt it just as much as you did."

Andrea looked thoughtful. "Maybe you're just more connected to Jupiter, being born in Anxur and all."

Remo tilted his head. "Maybe. Jupiter does feature heavily in my natal chart. But so does the sign of Gemini, which is ruled by Mercury."

Andrea scratched his beard. "You should dig into it more when we're back. Maybe the library's Awareness or Astrology sections have something that'll help you make sense of it."

Lyra warmed her hands by the fire, the flames dancing in her eyes as she looked at Remo. He thought, absently, that she looked like a fire priestess. The image stirred something inside him, a memory buried deep, like a door locked tight in the recesses of his mind. The sensation flickered and vanished.

"I'll help you research," she offered. "I think I know a few books where we can start."

A yawn escaped Andrea's lips, which he tried and failed to stifle. Unfooled, Lyra looked at him, her expression firm as she commanded, "Sleep."

"No, I think it's my turn to keep watch," he protested, sitting up straighter and crossing his arms with stubborn resolve.

"I'm not tired," Lyra said. "I'll take the first shift and wake you for the second."

Andrea attempted a look of protest, but his heavy-lidded eyes betrayed him, only making him appear more exhausted.

"Sleep," Lyra said again, more gently this time.

He sighed and murmured a thank-you before lying down. Within minutes, his slow, even breathing signaled he'd slipped into sleep.

Remo remained awake, leaning against the same tree as Lyra, the talisman bag resting between them. "I don't think I can sleep just yet. If you're tired, I could—"

"I'm not," Lyra cut in. She glanced sideways at him. "But thank you. I'm glad for the company."

Nearby, Andrea let out an exaggerated snore and shifted positions. Lyra smiled, then looked at Remo. They both laughed quietly.

"And to think he accused *me* of snoring on his settee," Remo said.

Lyra shook her head in amused disbelief. "Nella used to leave his lodgings to return to ours in the middle of the night just to escape his snoring."

Remo's smile tugged at one corner of his mouth, but it faded as thoughts of Andrea's relationship weighed on him.

He glanced at Andrea to make sure he was still asleep, then looked to Lyra, who met his eyes. "Do you think he and Nella are good for each other?" he asked.

Lyra bit her lip in thought. "In truth, I'm not sure. When things are good between them, they both seem so happy. And when they're together, I get to enjoy their company at the same time. But when things are bad... I've never felt like I could say anything. It's not really ours to interfere with."

She glanced at him again, something fragile sparkling in her eyes. "It's more complicated than it looks, for a few reasons. One of them is... they're soulmates."

Remo searched her citrine gaze, stunned. "Soulmates?"

He'd heard the term before; it was an idea rooted in the Ancient Religion. The belief that certain people were destined to find and connect with each other, usually in a romantic sense.

It sounded about as fanciful as the fated lovers in his favorite fantasy novels. But instead of wonder, the notion filled him with sadness.

He couldn't imagine anyone being destined to love him the way heroes in stories were loved. Soulmates felt like just another beautiful fantasy not meant for him, another idealistic wish destined to go unfulfilled.

"Yes. Cosimo told Andrea they were, though he's not really supposed to. It can disrupt the natural order of things." She tucked her hair behind her ear. "Masters of Awareness can see soul threads—connections between people. Not all soulmates are meant to be lovers, and not all are meant to last. Some meet to teach a lesson and then part."

She hesitated, then continued. "Cosimo said we all have multiple soulmates. The threads come in colors. Red means unfinished business, temporary connections not meant to last. He wouldn't tell Andrea the color of the thread between him and Nella." Her voice softened. "But when souls choose each other, again and again in every lifetime, the thread is purple. That's the rarest kind."

Remo chewed on his lip. "Like the fae in your favorite stories?"

"Exactly like them," Lyra said.

"Do you think you'll be able to see soulmate bonds someday?"

"Maybe," Lyra breathed, the weight of it visible in her expression. "But when it comes to Andrea and Nella, we just have to let them figure it out and be there when they need us."

Remo stared into the fire, entranced by the shifting light. "You're right. It's their path to walk. Still, I think his tiredness runs deeper than the journey. I just want what's best for him."

"As do I," Lyra whispered. "He's been so good to me. Since the night we met."

The night deepened around them, firewood crackling, owls calling from the trees, Andrea's soft breaths nearby. A heaviness settled over Remo, as if he already knew what Lyra was about to share.

"We met in Satria," Lyra said softly. "That's where I was born. My mother died giving birth to my little sister. I was only three. My grandmother and father raised me. He's a kind man. Loving. He did his best for us. But we were poor, like most in Satria. I started working in a tavern when I was still young to ease his burden."

Remo listened closely, the warmth in his gaze inviting her to go on.

"The tavern was popular with the Knights of Saffiro stationed nearby. They drank heavily, got loud, sometimes violent with each other. My father didn't want me working there, but we had no choice. We needed the money, and it was reliable work."

She inhaled, her breath shuddering as she did so. Through the brief pause, Remo did not waver in his attention to her, though dread sluiced through him as he thought he knew how this story ended.

"Like I said, the Knights of Saffiro would get drunk and act like beasts. There was one guard who..." She paused, struggling for the words. "He was always very attentive. He'd touch me as I passed by, just trying to work. Little things at first. Unwelcome, but small. Then he started grabbing me, and..."

Her chest rose with the effort of steadying her breath. "There was an alley next to the tavern," she said quietly. "He violated me there one night."

Remo's fists curled so tightly his nails bit into his palms, but he didn't move, didn't speak. He would have gladly broken his healer's vow if the man who hurt Lyra stood before him. The fury surging through him warred with the urge to comfort her, yet he knew this moment wasn't his to fix, only to bear witness.

The anger drained from him the instant he saw a tear slip down her cheek, replaced by a heartbreak deeper than anything he'd ever known. Her voice cracked as she added, "I was only sixteen then."

Her pain flooded into him as if it were his own. Then it struck him; she always used the entrance through The Crooked Cupola, deliberately avoiding the alleys.

"I told my father, and he tried to take justice into his own hands. But striking a royal guard comes at a price. He was imprisoned without trial. After that, I became the sole provider for my sister and grandmother. I stayed at the tavern; I had no other options. The guard was sent away for a while, and I managed to avoid him. But he came back. And he hadn't forgotten my father's retaliation.

"One night, the same knight dragged me from my work, and no one stopped him. Not the other soldiers. Not the innkeepers. They just watched as he shoved me outside, back into the alley. I screamed. I fought. But he was stronger. I felt completely powerless. But that was the night I met Andrea."

The memory came to Remo all at once, Andrea's story about Satria. About the girl. The knight. The moment he intervened.

"Andrea pulled the guard off me. Beat him bloody," she whispered, her eyes far away. "He saved me from living that nightmare twice. Then he walked me home. Asked about my family. Gave my grandmother money. He arranged for us to move to a camp for widows and children, far from that place. My grandmother cried. She'd never known such kindness. She begged him to take me with him.

"I used to sing around the house," Lyra said. "She believed I could do well outside Satria. She wanted a better life for me. Said the camp would care for her and my sister. They wouldn't need me anymore.

"Andrea agreed. He didn't yet realize what his kindness would cost him—his father's exile, his men's respect. But he knew I couldn't go to Saffiro. So he paid for a wagon, helped see me settled in Mavortis. All for a stranger.

"And he's looked out for me ever since. He still sends a wagon to take me home safely after I sing at taverns across town. I don't deserve his friendship. I could never repay what he's done, what he keeps doing."

Remo recalled how Andrea once told him that the taverns arranged Lyra's rides home. Of course, Andrea had downplayed his role. In true Andrea fashion, he never took credit for his quiet kindness. They teased him for his ego, but in truth, his most noble acts were always the most humble.

Looking at Lyra, her face still streaked with tears, Remo didn't fight the ones that welled in his own eyes. Mercury's essence still lingered in him, giving voice to the words that came.

"I'm so sorry that happened to you, Lyra. I'm sorry about your father and for everything you've had to endure. Thank you for trusting me with your story."

Sensing her retreat, he spoke quickly. "You're the bravest person I know. You deserve everything Andrea's done, and more. I'm glad we met. Count me among the friends who'd move heaven for you."

Tears welled again as Lyra met his grey eyes. She didn't speak but reached out, offering her hand. He took it, and she squeezed it, crying softly.

When the tears stopped, he whispered, "Rest now."

She didn't resist him, likely to avoid speaking at all. She let go of his hand as she lay down, turning her back to him.

He didn't want her staying awake to keep watch, not with those memories replaying in her mind. The thought of all Lyra had endured made Remo feel like he'd been punched in the gut. He felt sick with the weight of it.

In the still woods, Remo sat with his thoughts, thinking of the trauma both his friends carried. Lyra's breathing deepened. Her dark gold hair caught the moonlight.

Just as he had once promised Andrea his support, he now made a silent vow to Lyra too, there in the silence beneath the stars.

The three resumed their journey after sunrise. Andrea was in good spirits on the ride back to Mavortis. If he noticed anything off about Lyra, he didn't mention it.

Remo glanced at her shyly. She didn't look at him. He understood. Secrets were easier spoken in night's hush than in daylight's glare.

The dark cloaked confessions, the moon and stars silent witnesses to every nightmare. But the sun made everything visible, harsh, and impossible to hide.

He wished he could give her a signal that she had nothing to regret, that she was safe with him. But he didn't know how to say it without reopening the wound. And he wouldn't do that unless she chose to.

By dusk, they reached Mavortis and slipped through The Crooked Cupola into the Academy. Andrea knocked on Cosimo's office door. An ancient voice beckoned them to enter.

Cosimo stood behind his desk, bracing himself on the back of his chair. His gaze swept over the three of them, seeming satisfied to find no visible injuries.

He took up his walking stick and rounded the desk to study them more closely. "Was your trip successful?" he asked.

Andrea looked to Remo, who handed over the talisman. "We believe so."

Cosimo examined the aquamarine, a wide smile spreading across his lined face. "Oh yes," he murmured, closing his eyes. "Mercury's presence is strong. Well done, all of you." His eyes opened sharply. "Any trouble on the road? Any encounters with Knights of Saffiro?"

Andrea shook his head. "None." He sank into the chair before Cosimo's desk, reclining slightly. "Out of morbid curiosity," he said, "what would've happened if we hadn't succeeded? What if we hadn't reached the temple in time, for example?"

Cosimo returned to his desk, tucking the talisman into a velvet-lined box and snapping it shut. He locked the container, then secured it in a drawer, which he also locked. "Well, intention is more important than the geographical location, but I'd prefer not to take any risks. We'd have had to try again when Mercury was next well-positioned, at time's mercy. And time, just now, is rather in short supply. So let us simply be grateful that you did succeed."

He opened another drawer and retrieved three small pouches, each clinking with the sound of denarii. "Your payment," he said, gesturing for them to take their earnings.

They thanked him, but as they turned to go, Cosimo added, "Ah—one last thing. If you plan to celebrate tonight, kindly take it elsewhere. Sevo's in one of his moods. Someone accidentally lit another tapestry on fire."

With heavier pockets, the three decided to treat themselves to one of the nicer taverns nearby. After freshening up, Nella joined them. Andrea quietly updated her as they strolled hand in hand. Lyra and Remo trailed behind, giving the couple some space. Remo kept stealing glances at Lyra, hoping she'd meet his gaze just long enough for him to offer a smile, anything to make her feel at ease again.

At the tavern, they dined on pepper steaks and meat pies, except Lyra, who, never eating animals, chose a fragrant pumpkin stew instead. They washed it all down with pear ciders. The meal passed comfortably, the warmth between friends easing any tension lingering between Lyra and Remo. Nella and Andrea, true to form, eventually started kissing at the table. Not long after, they left, leaving Lyra and Remo to take a slow walk home together.

"Lyra," he said. At last, she met his eyes, the first time all day.

Though he'd longed for this moment, he realized he had no idea what to say. He wished for the talisman, for Mercury's influence. But his eyes said more than he could, and whatever they said, it softened her expression.

"I know you shared something vulnerable with me yesterday," he began. "I just want you to know it was safe to do that. You're safe with me. Nothing changed between us, except now I get to care about you even more. I know how you're feeling. I know how terrifying it is to let someone see that part of you, how easy it is to want to disappear. But you don't have to hide from me. Please don't."

She drew a breath, her eyes glistening. His words seemed to lift something from her chest. "Thank you, Remo. I know I'm safe with you," she said, her soft smile reassuring him. "No hiding," she added, her words a sacred agreement between them.

"By the way," she said, a sly smile forming, "where did you get those scribes' robes for the ritual?"

"Let's just say," he grinned, "somewhere in the Briar District's bathhouse, there are two very confused and very naked monks."

Lyra threw back her head in laughter. The sound untethered a burden in Remo's heart, leaving him light enough to float.

# Chapter Nineteen

Acerbi didn't ask any questions about the condition of Remo's supposedly ill relative in Merucia. Remo considered himself fortunate; any interaction with Acerbi was one too many. Still, he paid for his absence.

He found nothing amusing about the volume of the four humors he had to deal with that week. He was once again saddled with the least desirable tasks, a silent punishment for his time off.

His nameless patient also regressed. Though he'd warned her he'd be gone, she withdrew when he returned, as if the absence had undone their fragile progress. Guilt gnawed at him. He tried to reconnect by suggesting a walk through the gardens for some fresh air, but she declined, citing muscle aches.

"Here, this will help *salve* that issue," Remo joked, waggling the jar. It was the sort of terrible pun Lyra might've made to get him to laugh, and he cringed inwardly while waiting for her reaction.

She blinked, staring at the jar, then at him. A reluctant grin tugged at the corners of her mouth. "Please go away for another few days to atone for that awful joke."

Before leaving for Merucia, Remo had asked Sabelle to meet him at the fountain on Venus' day. He was running out of new places to take her.

"How about your room?" Sabelle had suggested, maddeningly playful.

He fought to stay composed, though the idea made his pulse spike. "I'm serious. What do you want to do tonight?"

Sabelle raised a brow. "I've already told you where I'd like to go."

Remo fumbled. "Are you sure that's what you'd—"

"Yes," she said firmly. "And before you come up with another objection, I don't know anyone on this side of town. No one will recognize me."

Still stunned, he nodded and led them to his building. At his small room, a flush of self-consciousness crept in.

Sabelle smiled, taking in the room as if it were charming. She sat on the edge of his bed, eyes drifting to the window.

Remo sat in his desk chair, rubbing the back of his neck, caught between dread and desire. How many times had he imagined this moment?

Her turquoise dress spilled across his bed. Before his mind could wander too far, he said, "I have something for you."

Her eyes lit with curiosity as he reached into his pocket and pulled out a small, rectangular parcel wrapped in brown paper and string.

"You darling!" she cried, delicately unwrapping it, eyes ablaze. She squealed with delight.

"A new set of tarocchi cards," he said. "You mentioned missing yours, so I got you a set for here. They're the Mavortian version..."

She looked briefly puzzled, though pleased. He wondered if he'd misread her earlier comment, but her response eased his concern.

"They're perfect. The artwork is beautiful," she said, fingers brushing the jewel-colored designs. "Where'd you find them?"

He smiled, aiming for mystery, pleased by her delight. He'd asked Cosimo where to find a deck. The headmaster gave him a look, but no questions. Remo recalled the conversation:

*"You can't buy them. They're not made or sold in shops for obvious reasons; they're illegal. I'll give you a spare—our Awareness students use them to develop intuition."*

The look in Cosimo's eyes lingered in Remo's mind, and the warning that followed stuck with him more. *"Remember, Remo, more is at stake than your livelihood. The Academy's survival, and the Order's, depend on your discretion. Stay vigilant."*

The warning had thrown Remo, though he'd promised Cosimo his discretion. Back in the present, he saw Sabelle's expression shift from contentment to concern.

"I have to tell you something, Remo."

His eyes locked onto hers, dread stirring in his chest.

She exhaled. "I'm going to be leaving Mavortis for a little while. I'm returning to Juno for a month, but my father's agreed to let me come back afterward."

His heart slowed. A month wasn't so bad. He could manage that. Still, he gave her the dramatic reaction she was expecting.

"A whole month?" he feigned outrage. He *would* miss her. But between the Order, his healing duties, and the Academy, his days were full. Though he'd much rather have his hands full of Sabelle than any of his other obligations, they were obligations he didn't take lightly.

Her smile returned at his theatrics. She gave an exaggerated pout and nodded. "Will you miss me?"

"Like crazy. I'm half tempted to lock my door right now and keep you here as my prisoner."

Sabelle leaned back on his bed. "I don't think that's how the fairy tale goes," she mused. "The beast locks up the princess, and the prince comes to rescue her. How can you be both my beast and my prince?"

She was playing directly to his love of fantasy. His eyes dropped, briefly tracing the curve of her body.

"In some tales, the beast is the prince," he murmured. "Maybe you haven't met that side of me yet."

She stood and sauntered toward him, slow and deliberate. "I think we've met briefly," she cooed, bending to slide a hand up his thigh. "Though I'd like to get better acquainted..."

As he rose, she straightened too, their bodies brushing as they moved in tandem. He kissed her, slow and tender, lips pulling on hers with an intimacy that contrasted the heat building elsewhere in his body. He pulled on her lips with his own, a slow, tender kiss at odds with the passion mounting inside him. He ached for her, his body straining for more. She kissed him harder, tugging him close, both hungry for friction.

They moved together, backing up until the edge of the bed pressed against the backs of her knees. She sat and drew him down with her, fingers deftly unfastening his pants. He didn't break their connection, his mouth sliding to her neck, then lower, exploring skin he had only imagined.

As his hands roamed her soft hips and thighs, his mouth continued its slow descent, plotting a use for his tongue far more gratifying than anything Mercury's favor had ever required.

"Hello? Remo." Andrea waved a hand in front of his face. Remo blinked, finally registering him.

"Where in Vesta's blazing hearth is your mind?" Andrea asked, incredulous. "I've been calling your name for a full minute, and you haven't even looked up."

Remo cleared his throat, silently relieved Lyra was still in Awareness class. He took a slow sip of his drink, dodging the question.

Disbelief gave way to amusement on Andrea's face. He folded his arms, watching Remo with obvious delight.

"Ah," Andrea said with a wicked grin. "Your mind must be wherever your body was when I heard all those... *enthusiastic* noises coming from your room yesterday."

Mortified, Remo propped an elbow on the table and half-covered his face.

Andrea laughed at his reaction. "I was coming to see if you wanted to grab a drink. But before I could knock, it sounded like you already had company. Did you two—"

"No," Remo cut in, his tone gruff. They had pleasured each other, mouths, hands, lips, and stopped there.

Andrea raised his hands in mock surrender, his voice gentler now. "I don't mean to be crude, or offend you. I only want to remind you to be careful. Nella and I are different. She's removed herself from all society ties here. But Sabelle? There could be eyes and ears anywhere. Just... don't get careless."

Remo bristled at the warning, even though he knew it came from concern. With a sigh, he said, "I know. We won't do that again. It was a mistake. I didn't want to risk it, but she seemed so confident we'd be safe. And we were, but it was a risk. I just can't stop thinking about her."

Maddeningly smug, Andrea watched Remo with the air of an older, wiser brother. "You know," he said, "there are other physical outlets for all that energy. As an alchemist, I know a thing or two about transmutation. Why not train with me? I could teach you some of the fighting techniques I learned during my time in Saffiro. Besides, it might come in handy if we run into trouble on the road during our mission."

Remo eyed the prince's solid frame. Andrea had a warrior's build, broad and brawny. Remo wasn't weak by any means, but his own frame was leaner. Still, the idea of bulking up and distracting himself from thoughts of Sabelle sounded appealing.

"When do we start?" Remo asked.

"How about Mars' day next week?"

"Aptly timed, astrologically. To do an activity of Mars—fighting—on Mars' day. In Mavortis nonetheless, where Mars is the tutelary deity," Remo pointed out. "Ironically, Mars also rules, er, *other* physical outlets."

Andrea snorted. "Naturally. Makes perfect sense that I was drawn to the kingdom ruled by the planet of fighting and fucking."

Over the next few afternoons, Lyra and Remo spent hours tucked away in the Academy's library, searching for anything that could explain the mystical experience he'd described to her and Andrea. They scoured Awareness texts, hoping to find something relevant. When their efforts in that section came up short, Lyra branched into Astrology for a wider net.

Tilting her head as a thought struck her, Lyra looked up. "Do you still have the tea you drank that night?"

Remo shut the book in front of him; it was useless anyway. "I do. I haven't had it since."

"Why not?"

"I sort of forgot about it," he admitted. "Do you think the same thing would happen if I drank it again?"

Lyra shrugged, closing another book and adding it to their ever-growing pile of rejects. "Only one way to find out. It's worth a try. I'll keep reading in the meantime. Maybe something will match what you experienced."

Remo gathered the books they'd finished and stood to return them to their shelves. "Thanks for all your help, Lyra."

"Don't mention it," she said, already absorbed in another volume.

At five in the morning on Jupiter's day, Remo brewed another cup of the purple lotus tea. He practiced the breathing exercises Lyra had taught him, working to slip into a relaxed, open state. He drank slowly, hoping the tea's effects would reveal themselves soon. He tried to release all expectations, knowing that anticipation might block the state of openness required for the experience.

He let go of his thoughts, his body, his sense of self. He became nothing, pure awareness. Peace flooded him, lifting him to a place beyond time, where forms began to swirl. From the void, something emerged. Standing before him was Jupiter just as he had appeared months ago, though now garbed in monk's robes.

The being gave a jovial smile. "I didn't expect to be summoned, but this is a pleasant surprise."

Remo kept his awe in check, fearing the vision might vanish. "I summoned you? Where is *here?*"

Jupiter stroked his beard. "You entered a state of receptivity, mind and body aligned, while intending to see me again, on the day sacred to me. And yet, you're surprised I appeared?"

Remo glanced around. He had expected to see Jupiter's temple in Anxur, where he'd met the god before—and so, that was exactly what surrounded him now.

"This is all happening in my head, isn't it?" he asked, staring at his hands. "It feels so real."

Jupiter clasped his hands behind his back, his gaze piercing. "All that manifests in the physical world begins in the mental realm. Your reality is shaped by belief. If you believe I'm real, then I am. If you think I'm a figment of your imagination, then I am that, too. Reality is entirely subjective."

The words stirred something in Remo. He tried to mentally bookmark Jupiter's words; there were more pressing questions.

"Then why did you come to me?" he asked.

Jupiter's eyes narrowed slightly, his chin lifting. "Because you called for me."

"Thank you for coming," Remo said quickly, not wanting to offend a god. "I meant the first time. Why did you come to me back then?"

"We had an appointment. You held my stone within my temple and induced the same receptive state that allowed you to call upon me now. You summoned me there, but believe it or not, we agreed to meet there long ago."

If Remo had still been grounded in his body, he was certain his pulse would've quickened and a chill would've swept down his spine. "You mean... before I incarnated?"

"Precisely," Jupiter nodded. "We arranged the push you'd need to leave Anxur. But I can't say more. Ask no further."

The command in Jupiter's voice stopped Remo from pressing the subject, though curiosity still burned in him. "Can you tell me why I can speak with you like this, but not with Mercury? I held their stone too, at their temple, but nothing happened."

Jupiter stepped closer, his piercing gaze igniting something in Remo, a spark of understanding so clear, words felt unnecessary. Still, Jupiter spoke. "Because I am your daemon."

And Remo understood. Jupiter had been assigned to him at birth—a guardian, a guide.

Nodding, as if affirming Remo's realization, Jupiter added, "I am here to ensure you fulfill your purpose."

Remo swallowed. "So... am I some kind of chosen one?"

Jupiter's laughter boomed, echoing like thunder. "You're not particularly special, no. But no one is. Because *everyone* is.

"Each of us has a unique purpose, vital to our own growth and to the greater whole. Yes, if you fulfill yours, great good could come from it. But if you refuse it, the world won't stop turning. The universe won't crumble. You matter. And yet, you don't. That's the paradox. You are a microcosm of the macrocosm. A story within a greater story."

Somehow, being told he wasn't particularly special by a divine being left Remo feeling strangely free.

"Then what is my purpose?" he asked.

Jupiter's gaze sharpened. "You know. It brought you here. It shaped everything you've done. You must finish the talisman. The day of reckoning approaches. Balance must be restored before the future can unfold."

Understanding rushed in. Clear, whole. He only wished he could hold onto it always. In silence, he asked if he'd made the right choices for his soul's growth.

"Yes," Jupiter replied, reading his thoughts. "You've made great progress, Remo. But don't become complacent. Many outcomes remain possible, depending on the choices still ahead. Just remember, you control what you experience. And if you ever dislike the path you're on, you can always choose another."

Above them, the night sky shimmered deep violet, stars blazing brighter than Remo had ever seen. "Where are we?"

Jupiter glanced around them. "The in-between, I suppose you could call it."

The stars pulsed with an impossible energy. The more Remo looked, the more vivid the details around him became. Shooting stars shimmered across the horizon, and he felt certain his imagination had conjured them.

He turned to Jupiter to make sure he hadn't disappeared. "Will you come again, if I need you?"

Jupiter nodded. "You know how to find me."

The reassurance lifted a weight Remo hadn't realized he'd been carrying. But he sensed the moment was ending. He couldn't stay in this liminal space much longer. "Is there anything I should know about what lies ahead?"

Jupiter chuckled. "Remo, after all this time, you still don't listen. I told you, your future changes with the choices you make. There are many possible futures, but I can't reveal any of them. It's against the rules. If we knew our futures, we'd be paralyzed by fear. And that fear would keep us from ever truly living."

He paused, then added gently, "The best advice I can give is to carry on as you are. Keep your faith, whether in yourself, in the universe, or in something greater. It doesn't matter what you call it. But nurture it. Without it, we're all lost."

Remo felt his awareness begin to shift. Tingling spread through his arms as he was drawn back into his body. The image of Jupiter faded as effortlessly as it had come.

He sat still in his room, fully returned, trying to commit every detail of the conversation to memory.

Remo saw Lyra first that morning and told her everything.

"Jupiter is your *daemon?*" she repeated, astonished.

"You know what a daemon is, then?"

Lyra shook her head. "No, but it sounds like a spiritual guardian. I'm going to research it—see you!"

She dashed toward the Academy's library, leaving Remo to make his way to Astrology class, where Cosimo was teaching about house systems.

"There are many different methods for calculating and interpreting the astrological houses," Cosimo explained. "Each astrologer has their preferred system, one they believe yields the most truth. It's a matter of experimentation and preference."

Remo raised his hand, unsettled. "But, sir, how can there be multiple ways to interpret the houses? How can two systems be true at once? Isn't that illogical?"

Cosimo's knowing smile suggested he had expected that question. "Let me ask you something," he said. "Your life experiences have shaped how you see the world, yes?"

Remo nodded, and Cosimo gestured to another student. "And Xavier here has his own worldview, shaped by *his* experiences."

Xavier looked startled to be mentioned.

"So," Cosimo continued, "neither of your perspectives is wrong. You each interpret reality based on your lived experience. So how could I say Xavier's view is right, and Remo's is wrong?

"Reality is subjective," Cosimo said, his voice calm. "It's shaped by how each person sees the world and processes what happens to them. Astrology is no different. The house system, or lens through which you interpret a chart, is also subjective."

His gaze settled on Remo. "You must let go of the need to fit everything into tidy black-and-white boxes. Let your grey eyes see the grey that exists in others, and in yourself."

Still unsatisfied, Remo said nothing. Jupiter had told him the same thing just hours earlier, that reality was subjective. And still, despite all the magic and mystery he'd encountered, he struggled to let go of his need to separate reason from faith. Over dinner at The Crooked Cupola, Remo told Andrea all about his second meeting with Jupiter.

"A daemon?" Andrea repeated. "That sounds familiar... but—seven gods! Jupiter is on your side? How can we possibly fail with the planet of luck rooting for us? This is fantastic news!"

Not wanting Andrea to get the wrong idea, Remo repeated Jupiter's warning that events would still unfold as they must, and overconfidence could be dangerous.

"But surely we can use your daemon to our advantage?" Andrea pressed.

"Let's hope so. I'm still not entirely convinced it wasn't just the tea making me hallucinate."

Andrea scowled. "You're awfully cerebral for someone enrolled in a school for arcane arts."

Remo sighed, taking a swig. "I *am*, aren't I? Damn Geminis," he said, chuckling, remembering Trota saying the same.

# Chapter Twenty

THE FOLLOWING MARS' DAY found Remo and Andrea on the outskirts of the Iron District, near the Academy's hidden dovecote entrance.

"Good. Lower your elbow slightly," Andrea instructed.

Remo adjusted his stance and glanced at Andrea, who nodded in approval. Andrea had been guiding him through basic stances and exercises, building the foundation of a warrior's balance before advancing to more complex techniques.

"That's good enough for today," Andrea said, clapping him on the back. "You did well."

Remo dropped into the grass, sipping from his waterskin. "How old were you when you started learning this stuff?" he asked, already feeling the soreness creep in.

"I was young, about eleven," Andrea replied, his tone flat. "Saffirans are known for their battle prowess. And naturally, a prince of Saffiro has to be a fierce warrior to be seen as a competent leader."

Remo glanced up. During training, he'd noticed several scars on Andrea's body—marks he hadn't seen before. He silently wondered about their origins, and the invisible wounds they might have left behind. The memory of the night Andrea had opened up to him resurfaced. Remo had never shared his own painful memories in return; they had seemed trivial beside what Andrea and Lyra had survived.

But then he recalled how left out he'd felt at times witnessing the bond between Andrea and Lyra, forged in shared pain. He was beginning to understand that vulnerability had to go both ways. To grow closer, you had to be willing to be seen. Cosimo's words echoed in his mind.

Before he could overthink it, Remo spoke. "At eleven, I was still playing with sticks, pretending they were swords. My father would've sent me to Saffiro to train if he could've. One time, I forgot a chore. I thought I was done for the day, just reading in my room. My father stormed in, ripped the book from my hands, and beat me with it until I bled."

Remo let out a hollow laugh. "I never felt so ashamed. I was a disappointment to him; I was always more interested in books than anything else. Another time, I came home bloodied after a fight with this older kid who used to torment me. I'd tried to fight back, but he was huge, and he beat me. I came home sniffling, nursing my wounds. My father heard me and beat me further. Told me to take it like a man. Said I was an embarrassment."

The memory made Remo feel small again. "I know it's nothing compared to what your father did to you. It probably sounds laughable. And I know mine just wanted me to be tough, to turn into a man who could handle anything. Maybe he was right. My childhood ended early anyway. He died when I was nine."

A patient silence stretched between them. Andrea, it seemed, knew the story wasn't over.

"I had to help my mother by taking on his responsibilities. Later, Aemilian helped too. That's when I could finally start my training as a healer. My mother never stopped grieving. A part of her died with him. I don't blame her; they did the best they knew how. I just tried to be the kind of brother I wish I'd had. Sorry, I don't know why I'm saying all this."

Remo stared ahead, aware of Andrea's eyes on him. He was beginning to feel foolish for opening up, uncomfortable showing the parts of himself he usually avoided.

"I'm glad you did," Andrea said. "And what you went through isn't laughable. It's very similar to what I experienced with my father. I could never impress him, no matter how hard I trained, how well I performed, or how much blood I spilled."

"Same," Remo said quietly. "I never earned his approval either."

A breeze swept past, cooling Remo's sweat. He closed his eyes and let it pass over him, wishing it would take the sad memories with it.

"My father hates me. And I hate him," Andrea said.

"As do I. For everything he's done to you."

Andrea glanced at Remo, a trace of gratitude in his expression. He looked like he wanted to smile but couldn't quite manage it. Remo kept going until he did.

"I've seen his face on the new denarii," Remo said. "Ugly as sin. You had to get your good looks from your mother."

Andrea gave him an exasperated look that said he saw right through the effort, but he didn't stop it.

"Honestly, I think he exiled you out of jealousy. No ruler wants a son better looking than him."

Andrea finally smiled and playfully shoved him. "I hate your father too. Damn him to hell," he said with mock bravado.

Remo laughed at the darkness of the sentiment. "Is it considered treason if I say the same?"

"As if everything we do isn't already treason?"

"Fair point."

Andrea let out a long sigh. "Sometimes, it all feels so heavy. Other times, like it's just a game."

"Whoever designed the game must be a sadist," Remo muttered.

"Maybe we design it ourselves with our karma," Andrea replied. "In that case, we're all masochists."

Remo rolled his eyes. "You're starting to sound like Cosimo."

Andrea chuckled, but his gaze darkened as he looked past the horizon, beyond the boundaries of Mavortis.

"At the Order meeting, it sounded like Cosimo thinks you'd make a strong candidate to replace your father on the throne," Remo said cautiously, eyeing his friend, careful not to tread too hard on what he knew was sensitive ground. "Did you ever want to become emperor?"

Andrea looked older than his years as he met Remo's gaze. "Never. And it never mattered what I wanted. Only what was best for Terramundi. The Senate is supposed to elect a new emperor when one dies," he continued. "But ever since the first emperor, the Senate has been easily manipulated. Intimidated. They've allowed the sons of emperors to inherit the throne instead of choosing the person best suited to rule.

"If my father died today," Andrea said bitterly, "you can bet the snakes would slither out from their courts to stake a claim to the throne. And despite everything he's said about me, about how lacking I am, I think, deep down, he saw me as a threat. Why else would he exile and humiliate me so thoroughly?"

Remo could see it clearly, the leader Andrea could be. Competent, principled, and brave enough to undo the cruel laws his father had put in place to serve his own greed. Andrea would give up his happiness if it meant Terramundi's people could live safer, fairer lives. And though Remo had never been fond of kings or crowns, he knew no one was more worthy of the emperor's seat than his fierce friend who lived and breathed kindness.

After supper, Remo curled up with *Fates of the Fae,* Lyra's favorite fantasy novel. He liked it more than he wanted to admit for something so clearly aimed at a feminine audience. A new character had just appeared, and Remo had a feeling they would become important.

Curious, Remo leaned out his window to see if Nella and Lyra's window was open. He called Lyra's name. She appeared moments later, puzzled, searching for the voice. "Up here!"

She spotted him and grinned. "Everything okay?"

"I'm not sure," he said with mock seriousness. "This new character Fiora meets—is that who she ends up with? What about Tomand?"

Lyra lit up. "You'll have to finish and then read the next one."

"How many books are in this series?"

"Six."

"Oh, is that all?" Remo deadpanned.

"You'll be begging for a seventh when you're done. Trust me."

"And have you finished *Milena and Devlan?*" Remo asked.

"Not yet. I'm halfway through, but I really love it so far."

Remo sighed. "I wish I could read it again for the first time. You never get that same feeling twice."

Lyra groaned in agreement, settling on her wide windowsill. "Although, rereading a book feels like coming home. It's a comfort you don't get the first time, because then you don't yet know how much you'll come to love it. Sometimes, you find things you missed on the first read. It's a bit like falling in love, I suppose. The initial flutters wear off after the newness fades, but then you're hopefully left with a more enduring appreciation that time can't threaten."

Remo watched her with quiet admiration. Every so often, Lyra would say something that offered him a glimpse into her inner world, a vignette framed in rose-colored glass. He longed to press his eyes against that glass and take in all the wonders he was certain he'd find there.

A bird fluttered from Lyra's room to her shoulder with blue-grey wings and a snowy white body.

"Oh, I didn't realize you had company," Remo teased, a smile tugging at his lips.

Lyra blinked, then laughed. "This is Turi. He was a gift to Nella from Merucian royalty, but she gave him to me. He's the smartest messenger pigeon in all of Terramundi, aren't you, sweetheart?" she cooed, stroking his feathers.

Remo chuckled. Under Lyra's care, that pigeon was probably the most pampered bird in the realm.

"Nice to meet you, Turi. Well, I've got five more books to get through, so I should get back to it."

"Get a move on, then," Lyra said with a grin before disappearing into her room.

Remo lingered at his window, gazing toward hers a moment longer, then returned to the book in his hands.

At the hospital, Remo's nameless patient had taken a turn for the worse. She was no longer well enough to leave her bed for their daily stroll through the garden.

Instead, he sat at her bedside and told her stories, trying to distract her from her pain. There wasn't much else he could offer her. Seeing her suffer hurt him deeply, but she bore it with strength. After tending to some of the more severe blisters on her skin, he gave her willow bark for the muscle aches. As he worked, he recounted a story he'd read long ago called *Master of the Air.*

He'd asked what kind of story she wanted. She said "tragic," so he obliged.

"Clovis falls in love with Dalia, though nothing ever becomes of it. It's never clear whether or not Dalia loves Clovis in turn because she's flighty and can't have any commitments tie her down. While Clovis is learning magic, he is also trying to avenge his parents' murder. What Clovis doesn't know is that Dalia is working for the people who killed his family, and those people are technically working towards an honorable aim. So the two were never quite lovers before they were forced to become enemies."

Her throaty voice broke the following silence. "I can tell you a story more tragic than that."

Remo schooled his features, careful not to show his surprise. He responded in a low, gentle tone. "I'm here to listen should you ever want to tell it."

With a wary look, she began. "My parents weren't murdered, but they might as well have been. I was born here in Mavortis—eight of us, and my mother couldn't care for us all. She didn't even know who my father was. So when I was old enough, she sent me to work in her brothel. I never learned to read or write. Had no trades, no options. It was one of the better brothels. More... refined clients. The kind like that awful man," she added, shuddering.

Remo didn't need to ask. She meant Acerbi.

"There was one man who used to come in often. He was gentler than most and always paid me well. He'd tell me about his life, his world. It was so different from mine. He was about my age. He gave me attention, made me feel... human. I loved him. And I thought he loved me. He promised to take me away, to marry me. I should have known it was a fantasy. But I held onto the hope anyway.

"He made me promise to stop seeing other men. Said if I wanted to marry him, I had to stop being a whore. Promised to pay me. So I quit. But my mother wouldn't let me come home. She was furious I couldn't give her money anymore. One day, I saw him on the street. I ran up to him, started talking. He looked horrified, and I didn't understand why until I saw the young woman behind him. His betrothed."

Her voice faded. "He slapped me. Said he didn't know me. Called me a presumptuous whore. Took her hand and walked away. I tried going back to the brothel. They wouldn't take me. I never saw him again."

Remo sat silently, horrified that her already tragic life had held so much more pain.

Tears ran down her scarred face. Remo handed her a clean handkerchief, aching with the knowledge that he had no true remedy, only hollow words. "I'm so sorry. You didn't deserve that."

Her mind had drifted far from the present, lost in memories. Remo wished he had something, anything, that could heal her unseen wounds. It was the worst kind of helplessness, knowing he could do nothing. He sat with her in silence, offering the only thing he had left: his presence. And he stayed that way until duty called him back to his other patients. He carried her sorrow with him the rest of the day, heavy and quiet like a shadow.

That evening after Astrology class, Cosimo pulled him aside to discuss the next part of their mission, a journey to Lunaria in October, when the moon would be exalted at 3 degrees Taurus at sunset. Remo sat in his usual spot before Cosimo's desk, heart still heavy.

Cosimo watched him closely. "May I ask what burdens your thoughts, Mr. Renato?"

Shifting in his chair, Remo met his gaze. "How do you know something's bothering me?"

A ghost of amusement flickered on Cosimo's face. "Let's just say your Gemini rising doesn't do much to hide your emotions. You wear them plainly. And I happen to be quite sensitive to the energy others emit. All emotions carry a vibration. They're electrical signals cast into the environment, and for someone as attuned to subtlety as I am, reading them comes naturally." He leaned forward slightly. "So tell me, what weighs on you? Is it about your mission?"

"No," Remo said quickly. He knew Cosimo wouldn't let him hide behind deflection. Worse, he sensed Cosimo wanted him to confront his discomfort with vulnerability and would know if he lied, so he told the truth.

"It's just... you say we have free will. That our fate is a product of our choices and past actions. But if that's true, how can some people live such miserable lives? Why would anyone choose that? Is that really the price of spiritual growth? I can't understand it. I don't think I can believe it. No one would choose to suffer."

The words came fast and defiant. Cosimo's calm only made Remo angrier. He wanted a fight. He wanted hypocrisy, to uncover a crack in the saintly mask. But Cosimo just sat there, infuriatingly composed. Remo read his calm as sanctimonious. Cosimo waited in silence. Remo held his tongue. He knew anything more would be said in anger.

Finally, Cosimo folded his hands and spoke. "You have an empathetic heart, Remo. You feel others' pain deeply. That is a gift. This world is cruel, and it needs more hearts like yours."

The words caught Remo off guard. He stiffened. He wanted to be met with his own anger, not disarmed by understanding.

"You are not required to accept my beliefs as your own, Remo," Cosimo said gently. "As I mentioned once before, astrology functions just fine outside any spiritual framework. What I offer now is merely one lens through which to understand the world. It is not a prescription, nor a certain truth. Only the foolish are certain of anything."

Cosimo studied him. "You asked about suffering, why some endure so much. I won't claim to have a complete answer. Only theories, shaped by experience and study. Personally, I believe fate is not something imposed upon us by a god, but something that unfolds from the hidden patterns within us. Some ancient impulse, perhaps, echoing across lifetimes.

"I don't believe anyone chooses suffering, not consciously, and certainly not with perfect understanding. But I do believe that in the mystery of our existence, across lives, maybe even planes, we encounter opportunities for growth that can only come through certain challenges. Why one soul experiences more than another? I don't know. I suspect it's less about earning pain and more about how much one can illuminate within it. But I would never tell someone in pain that they chose it. That would be cruel. It's not about deserving, it's about becoming."

Cosimo's voice softened. "We incarnate to feel. To experience the full spectrum of life; not to be punished, but to awaken. And some awaken through joy, others through loss, some through moments no one else would ever recognize as sacred. Pain is not a virtue. But what we *do* with pain—how we hold it, how we witness others through it—that might be where meaning lives. And that is always a choice."

He looked Remo in the eye. "It may take time to reconcile your intellect with your spirit, and that's alright. The only belief worth holding is the one that brings you closer to compassion. Toward yourself, and toward others."

By the time Cosimo finished speaking, Remo's frustration had faded. He thought again of his nameless patient, how her suffering had raised all these questions. For now, it was enough to hope that maybe her pain meant something. That maybe there was a bigger picture, just out of sight.

Remo gave a small nod, signaling his acceptance and his desire to move on. Cosimo took the cue and shifted into instructions for the next stage of their talisman construction.

After their meeting, Remo made his way to the Academy's library to research lunar-aligned plants. He spent hours poring over *The Astrology of Plants and Herbs* by Niccolo Culpepper, compiling lists for the final three phases of the mission.

But when it came to the invocation, inspiration failed him. He spent hours flipping through books, thumbing pages without purpose. Eventually, he gave up and left through one of the Academy's alley exits.

Outside, on his way back to his quarters, he spotted two Salii soldiers deep in conversation. One of them, he thought, glanced at him a little too closely. He rarely used that alleyway, so he convinced himself he was being paranoid. They didn't follow him when he turned the corner onto his street.

# Chapter Twenty-one

THE NIGHT BEFORE THEIR journey to Lunaria, the three friends gathered in the private room of The Crooked Cupola, eating warm baked apples drizzled with cream and dusted with cinnamon and cloves.

Remo found it far more difficult to compose an invocation for the moon's ritual than he had for Mercury's poem. He suspected it had something to do with his natal chart; his moon conjunct Saturn made emotional expression feel awkward and constricted. At least, that's the excuse he gave himself for the delay.

If all went according to plan, they would arrive in Lunaria just in time to perform the ritual on the second night of their trip. Cosimo had arranged for a messenger to inform the hospital that Remo had fallen too ill to work. He assured Remo the messenger was trustworthy and would carry out the cover story convincingly. The details would be passed along when Remo returned.

Lunar transits moved much faster than planetary ones, so the trio felt less pressure than during Mercury's alignment. Worst case, they'd only have to wait a month for the next moon in Taurus, its sign of exaltation.

Still, they hoped to complete the task now. Five other planets were currently in feminine signs, earth and water, making the moon's divine feminine energy more accessible. Cosimo had handed Remo the talisman and a small iridescent pearl, the moon's sacred stone, harvested from an oyster off the coast of Lunaria.

On the morning of their departure, the dark sky threatened rain. They took the familiar path through the Forest of Numa, the same route where

Remo and Andrea had first met. As the sun slipped behind the thick clouds after midday, rain began to fall, gentle and steady. Their horses splashed through mossy ground as autumn leaves in warm reds, oranges, and golds clung stubbornly to the branches above.

They paused for a quick lunch, more for the horses' sake than their own. The trees were too damp to offer much comfort. Remo threw his cloak over his pack to shield the sunthemata. Wet hair clung to his face as he bit into a soggy piece of bread. It was a miserable lunch. No one seemed inclined to speak beyond what was necessary.

The dreary weather did little to ease Remo's fatigue. With the moon in Taurus transiting his twelfth house of sleep and set to reach fullness in two days, he longed for nothing more than a warm, dry bed. But that luxury would have to wait.

Andrea's attempt at building a fire had failed; the steel and flint sparked, but the damp twigs and leaves refused to catch. The group huddled beneath a dense cluster of trees, which offered some relief from the rain. The only warmth to be had came from their shared body heat. Lyra volunteered to take the first watch, insisting she could never sleep well in the cold, and put a little distance between herself and the men.

Andrea gave her a dubious look, a mix of concern and pity, that seemed to suspect some underlying motive, though he didn't comment, only asking her to wake him for the second watch. By dawn, no one had slept well. No waking was required.

The night before, struck by sudden inspiration, Remo had taken a glass vial and let the rain fill it. By morning, the vial overflowed. He corked it carefully; it would serve as a sympathetic offering to the moon, ruler of water.

Wet and weary, they pressed on horseback down the forest path, grateful at least that the rain had stopped. They arrived in Lunaria before midday, riding past the small, bustling city Remo had briefly passed on his way to Mavortis.

The countryside, dressed in rich autumn hues, glowed in the sunlight. They passed an orchard of apple trees beneath a pale blue sky, stars already beginning to shimmer. Remo watched the sky anxiously. According to his calculations, they had just one hour left until the moon reached exaltation in Taurus.

"We're nearly there," Andrea assured him.

Half an hour later, they arrived. The temple stood at the heart of a clear spring, backed by a waterfall. White wildflowers dotted the surrounding grass. The temple resembled a roofless stone tower from a distance. Arched stained-glass windows encircled it, each one portraying a phase of the moon in golden yellow and red against a deep royal blue.

They dismounted and tied their horses to a nearby tree. The three friends exchanged a look—there was no path forward but through the spring. Andrea stepped in first, leading the way. Lyra followed, her hair trailing in the water, its usual in-between hue darkened in wetness. Remo brought up the rear, holding his bag above his head to keep the contents dry.

Together, they climbed onto the raised platform and stepped into the temple. They lit candles to amplify the lantern's glow. Light spilled through the stained glass, casting colors across the walls. It felt like standing inside a jewel box.

Remo retrieved the still-dry offering materials from his bag, which included a vial of rainwater, honeydew melon, white poppies, adder's tongue, almonds, and moonwort for the suffumigation.

Andrea narrowed his eyes at the melon. "You've been carrying a *melon,* and we've been eating soggy bread?"

"It's an offering," Lyra said, her tone strict.

Andrea's stomach growled in protest. He moped as he prepared his own materials. Lyra settled cross-legged and began steadying her breath. Remo, more nervous than he'd been for Mercury's ritual, lit the moonwort. As the smoke curled upward, it symbolized the link between earth and sky. He watched the tendrils reach for the moon overhead, shining clearly now.

He couldn't help but worry: would the Moon be less receptive to someone like him? His natal moon conjunct Saturn—what kind of mother, divine or not, would respond to that? If he'd felt emotionally starved by his own mother, how could a celestial one be any different?

Lyra had already begun, eyes closed, features serene as she held the talisman. Remo took a calming breath and grasped the talisman, the pearl in his other hand, and began.

"We call upon you, the Moon—our Divine Mother, Womb of All Creation. You are the divine feminine, the essence of life itself. You enable us to feel. You are our soul, our imagination. You rule the depths of the sea, the rivers, and all life-giving water within and without.

"Moon, symbol of women, of sensitivity and emotion. We call upon you to bless this talisman with your essence. These objects are offered to you, along with a gift of my own energy."

Remo closed his eyes and took a deep breath. After weeks of struggling with the moon's invocation, he realized he'd been approaching it all wrong. He'd been thinking, when he should have been feeling. That, after all, was the moon's way. He gave her what she asked for: emotion, raw and powerful. Something that radiated from him like heat, like light. A force as real as anything else in that sacred place.

He thought of his mother, how he had longed for her approval and never quite received it. At times, he felt more like her parent than her child. He'd had to learn how to care for himself. He ached for affection, for her validation. He'd needed to hear that he was loved, but the words had never come. That need hadn't faded; he'd only grown better at hiding it.

Deep down, he feared there was something inherently unlovable about him. That he didn't deserve love. That no one ever truly could. Remo offered these thoughts to the moon—his fears, his silent grief. A hot tear traced his cheek and fell to the cold temple floor.

And the moon answered. He felt it, a wholeness settling in his chest, a motherly tenderness that filled in every crack. She had heard him. She accepted his offering. And somehow, he felt... enough.

Andrea approached and began engraving the pearl into the talisman. The suffumigation still burned strong. Remo steadied his focus, directing it toward the moon and the talisman. For the first time that day, he felt whole. For the first time in his life, he knew he was loved. A breeze brushed his hair back, soft as a mother's hand. He thanked the moon silently, then opened his eyes as Andrea returned the talisman.

Lyra smiled at him, serene. They held the talisman between them as Remo waved the suffumigation smoke over it.

"Moon, we ask you to imbue this talisman and pearl with your essence," he said. "Protect its wearer, as a mother would her child. Grant emotional strength, resilience, sensitivity, and deep empathy. May its wearer know peace—an ocean of calm. We thank you, Divine Mother, the Moon."

Lyra and Remo held the talisman a moment longer, focusing on their shared intention. When the smoke faded, they left their offerings behind. Lyra looked reluctant to leave. Remo noticed how the moonlight seemed to illuminate her, as if the moon itself had lent her its glow.

A whim to tell her so stirred in him just before Andrea said, "Let's go."

They waded back through the spring and mounted their horses once more, riding toward the edge of the woods, the lot of them cold, tired, and quiet. They reached the woods before long and made camp along its border.

Remo volunteered to take first watch. Though the ground was damp and the night bitter, he noticed Lyra curling up alone, several feet away from them. He knew why, and it made his heart ache.

He looked up at the moon, feeling a warmth he'd never associated with it before. He never imagined it had been watching him all these years while he read by its light, dreaming of distant adventures. Then he looked at his sleeping friends. He had found two real companions in this strange new world. He smiled at them, silently wishing them sweet dreams as he imagined the moon smiling down on him, too.

The next morning brought fair weather, making the journey back far more bearable. They chatted eagerly about what they would eat and drink upon their return to Mavortis. They allowed themselves a longer break than usual, basking in the satisfaction of completing their second mission for the Order.

When night fell again, Andrea took first watch. But just as Remo was about to fall asleep, he thought he heard the sharp crack of twigs nearby. His eyes darted to Andrea's. In the soft lamplight, he saw Andrea raise a finger to his lips; he'd heard it too. No further sounds followed, and eventually Remo fell asleep.

A jolt woke him, rough hands shaking his shoulders. Lyra sat up nearby, wide-eyed and alarmed. Andrea's lamp had gone out. In a whisper barely louder than breath, Andrea said, "I think we're being watched. I saw a figure ahead. Stay alert. Be ready."

Andrea reached for the knife at his side. His calm expression carried the composure of a seasoned commander. Remo drew strength from it and turned to whisper instructions to Lyra in case things escalated. She nodded, clutching the bag as he moved to shield her.

Footsteps grew louder. Two figures appeared through the trees. By their outlines and the clink of armor, Remo knew they were Knights of Saffiro. One carried a lamp, revealing a strong nose beneath his helm and a scar running across his brow. The travelers remained seated as the knights approached. They had rehearsed this moment before; they were to stay calm and act like they had nothing to hide.

"Hello, sirs," Andrea greeted with a slight nod. "Can we help you?"

"You can, as a matter of fact," replied the man with the strong nose. "You can tell us what brings you to these woods at this hour, looking so rough." Their clothes were still wrinkled and grimy from sleeping on the ground and traveling through yesterday's downpour.

"We're a band of traveling musicians," Andrea said. "We were on our way to Mavortis when we were robbed in Lunaria. Our instruments are gone. Probably sold to a pawnbroker in another kingdom by now."

"I see," the knight said flatly. "But your generous thief left you a bag." He gestured toward the pack beside Lyra, the one with a few rations and the talisman tucked in a hidden pocket.

"Yes, well, I suppose moldy bread didn't seem worth stealing," Andrea replied, bitterness laced just enough to feel real.

The knight turned his gaze on Lyra. His companion's eyes remained locked on Remo. "And what do you play, pretty?"

Lyra's fear was palpable. She couldn't look at him, just lifted her chin and stared past him. Her chest rose and fell too quickly, breath trying to keep pace with her pulse. She was shaking.

"She sings," Remo said evenly, a note of warning beneath the calm.

The knight grinned like a predator. "Does she? Let's hear it, then, sweetheart."

"She does. But not for you." Remo's voice was ice. He kept his eyes on the knight, Lyra's shaking figure in his periphery. He'd risk everything before letting this man touch her fear.

Stepping in to preserve their cover, Andrea said smoothly, "Forgive his tone, sir. We're tired and miserable. It's been a long day. We're just three minstrels hoping to get some sleep before we move on. Was there something else you needed?"

The knight turned from Remo to glare at Andrea. "Actually, yes. I want the truth. What are you doing in these woods?"

Tension thickened the air. A long pause followed before Andrea, composed as ever, replied, "We're on our way to Mavortis to ask a patron to fund new instruments."

"Liar. Seize him," the knight said, eyes full of scorn. His companion stepped forward.

Andrea rose and unsheathed his knife in one motion, daring the knight to come closer.

"Insolent bastard," the guard growled, drawing his sword.

Remo grabbed his own knife, significantly smaller than the swords now pointed at them. Knives were the only weapons the three of them could carry without drawing suspicion, though he now regretted that reasoning.

No one moved. Two swords pointed at them; two daggers pointed back. Lyra stood between and just behind Andrea and Remo, like the fifth point in a deadly star.

"You won't get out of this alive with those pitiful excuses for steel," the knight sneered. "So I'll ask again: Why did you leave Mavortis, *Remo?*"

Remo's pulse thundered. This was worse than he'd imagined. How long had they been followed? Did they know about the talisman? His mind raced, but no words came.

"Perhaps this will loosen your tongue," the knight sneered, reaching for Lyra.

He didn't make it a step before Andrea lunged. Remo barely dodged the other guard's blade, hearing it strike a tree where his chest had been.

"Idiot! We need him alive!" the first knight yelled, locked in combat with Andrea. Despite the smaller weapon, Andrea held his ground.

Remo wasn't so fortunate. His knife was knocked from his grip, and the guard seized him in a crushing hold. He struggled, watching helplessly.

Andrea moved with the fluidity of a trained warrior, angling his body to deflect the blows. He struck fast and hard, aiming for the gaps in the knight's armor with quick, targeted jabs.

Remo knew brute strength alone wouldn't free him; the knight restraining him was too large. So he drove his foot backward with all his might, striking the guard in the groin. The man cried out and doubled over. Seizing the moment, Remo snatched the knight's sword and shouted for Andrea. He threw the weapon to him.

The other knight had just disarmed Andrea, who now lay vulnerable on the ground, until the sword landed near him. Andrea seized it, raising it just in time to block the incoming strike. Focused on helping Andrea, Remo didn't see the punch coming. The second knight's fist slammed into his face, the taste of blood blooming in his mouth.

Remo reacted fast, turning to what he knew best—anatomy. He jabbed the knight's neck, aiming for the vagus nerve. The result was immediate; the man collapsed. The remaining knight turned in shock just in time for Andrea to recover. But the fight was already over.

A heavy branch cracked against the knight's skull, sending him crumpling to the ground, unconscious. Standing over him, the talisman glinting at her throat, was Lyra.

The three grabbed their horses and didn't stop riding until they reached The Crooked Cupola. By the time they arrived, the sun had already risen, and they looked spectacularly bedraggled. Hoods pulled low over their faces to avoid drawing attention, they made straight for Cosimo's study.

The headmaster stood as they entered, his posture sharp with alarm. Bruises and scratches marred their weary faces. They weren't expected back until later in the day, and certainly not in their condition. "What happened?" Cosimo asked, voice taut with urgency.

"Two Knights of Saffiro harassed us last night," Andrea said. He hesitated, seeming reluctant to say more, as if worried Remo might get into trouble.

Remo spared him the burden. "One of them knew my name. He looked familiar. I think I've seen him in Mavortis before, possibly in Salii armor. Could've been the same man. A few days ago, I exited one of the alleyway entrances to the Academy and thought one of the guards was watching me."

Cosimo's face remained unreadable. "Do you believe they suspected anything about the talisman or the Academy?"

"No," Remo replied truthfully.

"Very well. Report any further incidents to me immediately. Going forward, avoid your usual haunts, especially The Crooked Cupola, and begin using alternative entrances to the Academy. Stay alert for any Saffiran or Salii knights following you. Fortunately, you'll travel with Nella to Vecontii by carriage. It's safer than sailing, and easier to escape trouble on the road than at sea. I'll have Sevo prepare food and hot water for you here. Rest in the vacant rooms until then."

The three bathed in separate rooms, soothed and refreshed by the hot water. Sevo served them roasted orange squash with salted butter, along with creamy risotto. Bellies full, they returned to their rooms for a long-overdue nap. Remo woke at dusk, the first of the three to rise.

He thanked Sevo and tried to pay for the meal and lodging, but the innkeeper waved him off. "Consider it a perk of being in the Order," he said dryly.

Remo considered his bruised face and the heavy weight of coins in his pocket, payment from the Order. He had thought it would feel better than it did. But money couldn't buy any of the things he truly longed for. He'd always known that, but now he *felt* it.

The next morning, Remo walked into the hospital with a flicker of optimism. Acerbi had been called away on urgent personal business, meaning he wouldn't have to see him.

The relief was short-lived. His patient, his nameless companion, was worse than ever. Her pale face and body were mottled with sores and angry pustules. Her forehead burned with fever, and her breaths were shallow and thin. She noticed his black eye, worry flashing in her gaze, but he didn't register it. His focus was on her condition, which was quickly becoming terminal.

"I'm glad to see you one last time," she rasped, her voice raw, as though each word took the last of her strength.

He'd never witnessed death, but he knew what it looked like. And now, all he could do was hold her hand and stay. She squeezed his hand with more strength than he expected, as if he were her last tether.

"I told myself I wouldn't die until I saw you again," she said. "And here you are."

A hot tear slid down Remo's cheek. *"Please,"* he said, but the rest of the sentence never came. *Please don't say that. Please don't die.*

"Thank you," she said, voice cracked. "For trying. For listening."

"You don't need to thank me," he whispered hoarsely. "I was happy to be there with you."

She shivered despite her fever. Tears filled her eyes. "Rose."

Remo leaned in, confused until she added, "My real name. The only part of me they couldn't take. Someone should know it. My name was Rose."

And then, with one final breath, the spark in her eyes faded. Rose looked peaceful in death.

# Chapter Twenty-two

"THERE'S THE INVALID. How generous of you to show up," Acerbi sneered as Remo passed. "Feeling better from your fake illness? Or shall I fetch some leeches?"

"I'm well now, thank you," Remo said calmly, pretending he hadn't heard the accusation. He found Acerbi's taunts harder to endure now. He hadn't realized just how much abuse he'd swallowed to stay by Rose's side and provide the care she deserved.

"Tell me, how *did* you get that black eye while convalescing? Did that strange little man who brought your message give it to you? If so, I should like to invite him for a drink."

Remo wouldn't give Acerbi the satisfaction of a reply or a reaction. What struck him as odd was that Acerbi hadn't, as usual, threatened to sack him over his absence. The hospital's desperation for healers had eased recently, and there was now enough coverage that firing him wouldn't cause a crisis. Remo could only assume that Acerbi simply enjoyed tormenting him, perhaps curious to see how much abuse he could endure before finally breaking.

"I'll be sure to raise a glass in honor of that prostitute you were so fond of. Sorry for your loss, Remo. But don't worry. There are plenty of other whores in this city."

Remo stared at him, rage simmering just beneath control. He thought of Sabelle, of the dinner they would share when she returned from Juno. That was his revenge, an evening she'd spend with him, not Acerbi—because Sabelle liked *Remo*. He walked away, clinging to that thought like armor.

A pensive mood had haunted Remo since Rose's passing. He withdrew into himself, avoiding his friends. Dusk was falling as he lay on the grass outside the dovecote exit on the outskirts of the Iron District, Cosimo's recommended route to avoid detection by the Knights of Saffiro, in case they were still watching him. When the tall grasses nearby rustled, Remo sat up, instantly alert.

"Remo?" a gentle voice called. His pulse eased; it was Lyra.

"I thought I might find you here," she said, concern etched across her face. "Are you alright? Andrea and I are worried. We haven't seen much of you these last few days."

Remo stared ahead. "I'm sorry. I didn't mean to worry you. I just needed some time alone."

"Please don't hide from us. No hiding, remember?" Lyra said softly, her tawny eyes wide and pleading.

He wasn't sure why he didn't just tell her, why the words caught in his throat when his thoughts were so full. She had cared enough to come find him, to ask what was wrong. She had opened up to him, and with her, he knew he could be vulnerable. With Lyra, he found that he wanted to be. Her words, once his own, unlocked something, and he found the courage to speak.

"A patient of mine died a few days ago," he said. "She had a miserable life, and I couldn't save her. While we were in Lunaria, she got worse. And the day I came back to the hospital, I watched her die."

Understanding spanned across Lyra's face as Remo looked away. He said nothing more. The grief in his throat was too much.

"I'm so sorry, Remo," Lyra whispered.

He nodded in thanks, still unable to speak.

"I know you did everything you could to make her last moments comfortable," she added.

As if sensing what weighed heaviest on him, she continued, her gaze now turned to the sky. "Life can be painful. Terrible things happen. We don't always understand why or if there's any meaning in it. But I believe there is, even when we can't see it from here." She turned to him. "Death isn't the end, Remo. Don't fear for her. We're more than these bodies. Our consciousness moves on until we're ready to return."

Remo looked at her, serious. "I don't know if I want to do this shit again."

Lyra gave a small, sad smile. "There must be a reason we keep coming back. Maybe," Lyra mused, "if we knew why we came back, we'd finally know what makes life worthwhile."

The image of the dragon eating its own tail from Cosimo's book rose in Remo's mind, the symbol of an eternal cycle. He wondered what it would take for that dragon to shed its skin for good.

They sat in silence as the stars emerged. Even without speaking, Lyra's presence made him feel less alone. If he had given Rose even a fraction of the ease he felt now, perhaps she hadn't been afraid when death came for her.

As they walked home, the conversation brightened. Lyra had gotten him and Sabelle a reservation at Scappi's, one of the Briar District's most exclusive taverns.

"Will you be singing there tomorrow?" Remo asked, still eager to hear her voice.

Lyra shook her head. "No, I'll be singing elsewhere. But I hope you two have a lovely time."

"I'm sure we will. Thanks again for the reservation." He knew he wouldn't have gotten it without her.

It was risky for him to be seen in that part of town, but Sabelle had promised her father's men wouldn't be looking for them.

Lyra grinned. "Don't mention it. But are you sure it's worth the risk of Acerbi finding you?"

"I'm sure. Honestly, I almost hope I run into him just to see him fume."

Lyra chewed her lip. "I hope she's worth risking your job. It seems like an awful amount of effort just to impress someone."

He knew she was right, but his pride kept him from admitting it. "It's not about impressing her. It's about quietly punishing Acerbi for being such a prick."

Lyra blinked. "Is that supposed to be a more acceptable reason?"

Remo gave the question a half-second of serious thought. "Absolutely."

She shrugged, clearly unconvinced.

Scappi's was every bit as pretentious as Remo imagined. White linen cloths draped candlelit tables, silverware and trays gleamed under the soft lighting, and a man played a lute on a raised platform. They dined on lamb with herb dumplings and stuffed mushrooms, though Remo's real hunger was for Sabelle. She dazzled in an emerald green gown, drawing the attention of every diner in the room.

"So, what did you get up to in Juno?" Remo asked, shifting in his chair.

Sabelle sipped from her glass, her eyes fixed on him over the rim. "Mostly I wished I were back in Mavortis with you. I had a few more dresses made. Spent as much time in the caves as I could. What about you? Will you finally tell me how you got that black eye?"

The bruise had faded to a yellow shadow beneath his eye.

"I've been sparring with my friend Andrea. He's teaching me self-defense. One punch landed harder than planned," Remo said. It wasn't wholly a lie, just not the correct truth.

Sabelle gave him a skeptical look but didn't push. "Is that the friend who helped get us into this place?"

Remo shook his head. "No, that was Lyra. She's a singer here."

"Ah," was all Sabelle said. "And how did you two meet?"

Remo tilted his head, surprised by her sudden interest in his friends. "Through Andrea. They've both been very kind to me."

She nodded in understanding, though her expression was far from pleased.

"Would you like to meet them?" he asked, a little unsure.

Her eyes lit up. "Oh yes, I'd love that."

"Maybe we could all have dinner. Andrea could bring his girlfriend, Nella. You met him that day we bumped into each other."

Sabelle's eyes flickered in recognition. "I remember. He's quite good-looking."

A flash of jealousy sparked in Remo's chest. "Yes. He is," he said tightly.

As he glanced around the tavern, self-consciousness crept in. Everyone was dressed in fine clothes that probably cost more than he made in a month. He wore his best, but it still felt like everyone could tell he didn't belong.

Remo felt Sabelle should be with someone like Andrea, a handsome prince, the protagonist in a fairy tale. He began to feel foolish, like an imposter. This wasn't his world. He didn't deserve her company. He wondered if she regretted their connection, if she questioned being with him at all.

He wished he were back in his room, reading about love from a safe distance. He wanted Sabelle to be his Milena, but he didn't feel like her equal. No matter how much she insisted she wanted to be with him, he couldn't shake the memory of how quickly she'd thrown his hand aside at the sight of Acerbi.

Remo spiraled deeper into the thread of dark thoughts until he remembered his one glimmer of hope—the title Andrea had promised him. If the Order mission succeeded, if he earned that title, maybe he could earn Sabelle's hand. Perhaps there was still hope for a happily ever after.

A darker thought crept in: what if he made a love talisman in Vecontii? Maybe Venus could help him win her heart. He didn't linger on the idea; the Order's talisman needed his full focus, and splitting his energy could ruin both. Truthfully, he hated the idea of begging the gods for help with love. If it was real, it should be theirs to earn, not the gods' to grant.

The evening of the group dinner arrived, and Remo found himself unexpectedly anxious, unsure whether he feared Sabelle wouldn't like his friends, or that she'd like them more than she liked him.

The tavern filled with evening noise as they gathered. Sabelle, poised and glowing, turned to Andrea. "How did you and Remo meet?"

Without hesitation, Andrea lied. "I work at the apothecary. He pretends we're friends for the discounts and to exploit my unmatched skills."

Remo's mouth twitched with amusement. "He's also incredibly humble." He hadn't asked Andrea to lie, but was grateful. If Sabelle already liked Andrea, as Remo suspected she did, a tale of heroism would only worsen things. He shot Andrea a grateful look. Andrea winked.

Lyra shifted in her seat, catching Remo's eye. She forced a smile he could see straight through. He was glad Sabelle met his friends, but Lyra looked like a fifth wheel, and knowing her Libra sun craved partnership made his guilt worse. Worse, he sensed a subtle shift in Sabelle's energy when Lyra spoke.

"Well, I have to run," Lyra said brightly. "I'm performing elsewhere tonight. It was lovely meeting you, Sabelle."

"Likewise," Sabelle replied, her tone clipped.

Remo frowned as he said goodbye, hoping Lyra wasn't hurt. She smiled at him, soft and knowing, before slipping away.

The night ended better than expected. Conversation flowed, and everyone seemed to get along. Later, at Andrea's lodgings, the two men reflected on the evening.

"She's certainly charming," Andrea said of Sabelle. "And of course, beautiful. Nella thought so too," he added with an unreadable tone.

Remo arched a brow. Andrea gazed at the fire. "Nella's attracted to both men and women."

Andrea seemed lost in thought. Remo gave him space, not pressing.

"Well, Sabelle has made it worryingly clear that she finds you handsome. Thank you, by the way, for lying about saving my life in the forest. I fear she'd be quite in love with you otherwise," Remo said in an effort to lift Andrea's spirits.

Andrea gave him a soft, bittersweet smile. "No danger of that, brother. I just hope she appreciates what you're risking to be with her."

Remo mirrored the smile, thin and forced just like Lyra's had been, and made for the door.

Cosimo gathered Remo, Andrea, and Lyra to share a troubling development concerning Saffiro.

"An Order member has reported that dozens of Knights of Saffiro are now stationed in Anxur," Cosimo said. "King Lars has ordered his legion to cooperate with the royal guards—for now. They know Saffiro has the numbers to decimate them. There haven't been outright attacks yet. So far, the knights are extorting Anxurians for money, supplies, and shelter."

Remo's thoughts immediately flew to his mother and brother. Panic rose in his chest as he considered whether he should be there now, but he remembered that Cosimo had told him the knights were monitoring all travel in and out of the kingdom.

He couldn't return, not without putting himself, and possibly all of them, in danger. All he could do was hope they were safe, and take small comfort in the fact that no violence had yet erupted.

"The people are too afraid to fight back," Cosimo went on. "They remember what happened in Satria. And the last time Anxur stood against Saffiro, it nearly cost them everything. King Lars needs his soldiers ready for the larger war ahead. A fight now would only drain our defenses when we'll need them most.

"We need a plan," Cosimo said. "One that gets the three of you into Saffiro undetected. More importantly, we'll need time inside the Sun's temple to complete the final talismanic ritual. Andrea, are there any secret routes leading directly to the temple?"

Andrea frowned, thinking. "Not that I know of. We'll need a major distraction to get past the temple guards."

Cosimo tapped a finger to his lips. "We'll work on a strategy to pull their focus long enough to complete the ritual. Someone will have to stand watch outside. Perhaps King Bardi will agree to send men to accompany you without knowing exactly what you're doing. Ask him, if he seems receptive, once you arrive in Vecontii."

Andrea nodded. "We'll need the Vecontiians. Let's hope they fight as well as they're rumored to love."

# Chapter Twenty-three

D ECEMBER BROUGHT A CHILL that swept through Remo's window. The overcast sky threatened more snow. Though snowfall
was rare in Mavortis, a thin layer now blanketed the rooftops and cobbled streets, frosting the red buildings like icing on gingerbread.

Remo sat reading another volume of *Fates of the Fae*. The series was
as addictive as Lyra had warned.

Saturnalia was fast approaching. The festival, which honored Saturn
during the first days of Capricorn season, was masked as a celebration of
agriculture in kingdoms outside Satria, where the Ancient Gods were no
longer openly worshipped. Lyra had described what Saturnalia was like
in Satria, where Saturn remained the tutelary deity.

*"Of course, being poor, Satria never has the abundance of gifts and
excess you see in other kingdoms,"* she had said. *"But it's the one time of
year when Satrians feel united. As children, we were told stories about the
Saturnalias before the Calamity, when servants became masters, masters
became servants, and food and wine flowed like water. Green and gold
decorations were everywhere.*

*"I might not have known seven-course feasts, but there was still a certain
magic,"* Lyra had said, eyes shining at the memory. *"My father would
dance with me and my sister, and my grandmother always made me sing
the old songs to Saturn."*

Remo smiled, grateful for the glimpse into her life. He found himself
wondering what to give her, Sabelle, and Andrea for Saturnalia, since
gift-giving was customary.

Sabelle was spending the holiday with her family, who were visiting

Mavortis, so she and Remo had exchanged gifts a day early. She adored the necklace he had chosen for her—an emerald piece that matched her eyes. In return, she gave him a poesy ring carved from what looked suspiciously like bone, inscribed with their shared phrase: *May We Meet Again.*

For Lyra, he wanted something inspired by *Fates of the Fae*, her favorite series. Suddenly inspired, he ran to Andrea's room and knocked.

"Come in," Andrea called. Remo entered and found him hunched over a half-finished experiment.

"How would you like a special commission, alchemist?" Remo asked.

"What do you need me to make?"

Remo sketched his idea for Lyra's gift. A wide grin spread across Andrea's face as he studied the drawing.

The three friends celebrated Saturnalia together at The Crooked Cupola on the festival's first night. Cosimo had deemed it safe enough for Remo to return without fear of being watched.

Golden candles glowed in every corner, greenery and sugared berries hung from the beams, and suits of armor wore jester hats. The whole inn brimmed with merriment. In true Saturnalia fashion, they switched roles with Sevo, serving guests while Sevo lounged, feet up, singing rowdy tavern songs.

They drank honeyed mead and feasted on spiced meat and roasted vegetables, the flavors rich and warming. Remo handed Lyra her gift. He had never been so excited to give one. She gingerly untied the green cloth wrapping, and her eyes widened as she lifted the delicate, pointed bronze accessories.

"They go on your ears," Remo explained, watching realization dawn on her face. "Andrea made them for you. Now you can look like the fae from your favorite books."

Lyra squealed, bouncing with joy, and hurried off to find a mirror. She returned beaming, eyes glossy, and squeezed his hands tight.

"This is... the most thoughtful present I've ever received. I love them. I can't believe you thought of this for me!" she said, shaking her head with a disbelieving smile. She turned and thanked Andrea for his craftsmanship.

Andrea beamed at her, then turned to Remo with gratitude. "Thank you," he said softly.

They watched Lyra flit between Academy friends across the inn, proudly showing off her new gift.

Remo gave Andrea a questioning look. Andrea added, "Thank you for treating her the way you do. The way she deserves."

Lyra didn't take off her elven ears for the rest of the night.

The unseasonable chill of midwinter lingered into January, and all traces of Saturnalia's festive décor had vanished from The Crooked Cupola. Remo drank deeply, savoring the way the spiced wine warmed him like a fire in his belly.

Nella sat poring over her textbooks, as diligent as ever in her physician training. Remo nodded toward her open pages. "How many years of university do you have left?"

"One," Nella replied. "Before you can become a physician, you have to study the seven liberal arts. Each used to have a planetary association: Arithmetic for the Sun, Grammar for the Moon, Logic for Mercury, Rhetoric for Venus, Music for Mars, Geometry for Jupiter, and Astronomy for Saturn. Then, four years of medicine and six months of experience."

"Interesting," Remo said, taking another sip.

Lyra grinned. "That's why it's called a universe-ity."

Groans followed from Nella, Andrea, and Remo. Lyra giggled.

Maintaining a deadpan expression, Remo set his drink down and pointed toward the exit. "That's enough. Into the Veil River."

Lyra laughed impishly, delighted by her bad pun and Remo's dry reaction. He fought a grin; he liked how her personality, like personified sunshine, played off his introverted, often dry nature.

Nella rolled her eyes, then closed her book with a sigh. "Let's go home," she said to Andrea.

Andrea stood and drained his drink. "As you wish."

The four of them walked toward home, Lyra and Remo trailing behind Andrea and Nella, as usual. Remo noticed Lyra clutching her cloak tightly. It was too thin for the cold. Without a word, he took off his own cloak and offered it to her.

Lyra's eyes widened. "Oh, no—I'm fine. Put it back on, you'll freeze!"

But Remo didn't mind the cold. He'd always tolerated it well; he found the bite of it bracing, almost energizing. He draped the cloak around her shoulders. Her protests faded into visible relief as the warmth settled in.

As they approached his building, Remo froze; Sabelle was waiting outside. "Sabelle? What are you doing here? Is everything okay?"

It was too late for her to be out alone. But her anxious expression turned cold the moment she saw Lyra wearing his cloak.

Lyra quickly removed it, returning it without a word. "Goodnight," she said, her voice tight. Sabelle didn't bother hiding her displeasure.

Andrea and Nella followed Lyra's lead, leaving Remo alone with Sabelle.

"Sabelle, why are you here so late? You shouldn't have traveled alone. It's not safe," Remo said.

"If I'd known you were out, I wouldn't have come," she said curtly. "Clearly, you had other company."

Remo frowned. "Are you upset?"

Sabelle turned on him, her voice tight. "Your cloak was around *her.*"

Remo blinked. "Lyra? She was cold. She's my friend."

"You treat your friends an awful lot like lovers," Sabelle replied, her voice tight.

Understanding hit him, and he felt foolish for not seeing it sooner. "You're jealous?"

The question struck her like a slap. Her face hardened with indignation, but before she could deny it, Remo stepped toward her. *"You're* my girlfriend, Sabelle. And I like you very much."

But she still looked wounded, turning to leave. "Where are you going?" Remo asked quickly.

She turned, eyes burning. "I came because I wanted you. But I'm not sure you feel the same."

Remo's head spun. He wished she spoke with that much certainty whenever they talked about what stood between them. He didn't know what more he could do. He had already risked his job, his reputation—maybe even his freedom—just to be with her.

"I want you too, Sabelle," was all he could manage, though his fears still lurked in the corners of his mind.

She didn't move. "Do you want me the way I want you?"

He hesitated. "And how is it that you want me?"

They stood too close, her body brushing against his. She said nothing. Instead, she beckoned him inside, and gave him her answer without a single word.

They lay in Remo's bed for some time afterward. Sabelle was unusually quiet, idly winding her fingers through his. At last, long after he'd forgotten the question, she whispered her first words since. "I want you like this. I want you at my side."

He nudged her chin up, coaxing her to meet his eyes, eyes that blazed with a fire he longed to burn in forever. "Then I shall stay at your side for as long as you want me."

His words seemed to ease her. She nodded faintly. He stroked her cheek, sensing something heavy pressing on her spirit, though he didn't ask. He didn't want to know. He only wanted to hold onto the feeling of being hers and pretend, for a little longer, that she was his. He chose the illusion over the looming truth, because even if their love wasn't perfect, it was real, unlike the fantasies he used to crave in novels.

When it came time to part, he walked her to the Briar District, where he arranged a carriage to take her the rest of the way, both to avoid being seen and to shield her from the rain that threatened to fall from the cloudy sky. As he made his way home, his mind spun with the memory of what they'd just shared. He was so distracted he didn't notice the two Salii, soldiers of Mavortis, tailing him in the dark.

They closed in as he turned a corner just streets from his home. The moment he heard their steps, cold dread surged through him. He spun around to see them lurking, and his blood ran cold. His heart slammed in his chest as he bolted into a run. But he wasn't fast enough. They chased him like hunters, driving him into a cul-de-sac and closing in.

"Thought you'd have a quick little roll in the hay with someone else's betrothed, did you?" one sneered.

"What?" Remo blurted, the implication of the man's words eclipsing the concern he felt for his own life.

They grabbed him, slammed him to the cobbled ground, and began pounding him with fists. He tried to fight back, scrambling under their weight and reaching for one of their blades, desperate to use the skills Andrea had taught him. But it was no use. They were stronger.

He couldn't see their faces beneath the reddish-bronze armor, but he imagined the voice belonged to the same knight he'd encountered in the Forest of Numa, though that man had worn Saffiro's armor then. If Remo's hunch was right, it was the same soldier he'd seen watching him leave the Academy, now dressed again in the uniform of the Salii.

Before Remo could further question it, another of the guard's fists crashed into his face. Blood filled his mouth with a sharp, metallic tang. His head slammed into the stone, vision flickering with dark spots just before another punch struck his eye. One of the Salii kicked him squarely, and his ribs gave a brutal crack that sounded as painful as it felt. Agony overtook him, and he struggled to remain conscious.

The last thing he heard was thunder crashing overhead, and one soldier snarling, "Compliments of Arlo Acerbi. He wishes to tell you that you're dismissed from the hospital."

They left him there, bleeding on the street, rain mixing with his blood. His eyes fluttered as the pain and night swallowed him whole. Lightning flashed. He wondered, bitterly, where his guardian daemon was now.

A moment—or was it hours?—later, he felt himself being lifted. For a second, he wondered if he was floating; if he'd died, just as he'd feared he might when this mad journey began. But death couldn't hurt this much. Pain pulsed through every nerve.

He slipped in and out of consciousness, unable to resist the wave of exhaustion. A fever set in, dragging with it strange dreams of fire, a ship, and a crown of sapphires. He thought he saw an angel once, but dismissed it as fevered hallucination.

He preferred the oblivion of sleep over wakefulness, as pain rippled through his every limb. He groaned, barely able to open his swollen eyes or move his inflamed face. At least, he noted distantly, he was in dry clothes.

"Remo?" came a familiar, friendly voice.

Remo couldn't lift his head, but he knew the voice. Andrea. He groaned in acknowledgment, relieved to be alive and in bed.

"How are you feeling? And what in Vesta's blazing hearth happened to you last night?"

Remo forced one eye open, wincing as he tried to sit up straighter. "Is this the part where I bestow true love's kiss upon my knight in shining armor?"

A relieved sigh escaped Andrea's lips before they twitched with amusement. "As long as Nella doesn't find out afterward, my sweet."

Remo blew out a breath, the closest thing to a laugh he could manage, then cringed as pain flared in his ribs.

"I found you nearly bleeding to death after Lyra came knocking on my door," Andrea said. "She said she had a 'feeling' and came to check on you. When you weren't in your room, she got worried. Thank the stars for whatever Awareness she has; you might've died if she hadn't come asking. She stayed with you all night and just left to get ready for class. Nella will be back soon, too. She patched you up after I brought you home."

Remo squinted at his body, noticing the bandages for the first time. "Did I ever tell you what a gem I think Nella is?" he muttered dryly.

Andrea laughed with relief to find his friend's sense of humor intact, even if his body was in tatters. "Since you're awake enough to play jester, you can tell me who did this to you and why."

Remo told him everything. The words of the Salii soldier stung as much as the bruises.

"You think those Salii were the same ones who attacked us in Lunaria? But why would they wear Saffiran armor?" Andrea asked.

"The Salii had to have been hired by Acerbi," Remo said, his voice strained. "They basically said as much. And you once told me his brother, Marcellus, is their leader. I'm not positive they're the same royal guards from the woods—it's just a guess. The question is, how long has the Salian Order been following me? If they knew about the Order or the Academy, I'd already be in prison... or worse."

Andrea nodded thoughtfully. "I think we're safe on that front. This felt more like personal vengeance. Do you really think Sabelle is Arlo's betrothed?"

At those words, Remo's heart twisted like it was trying to strangle itself. "She did seem upset yesterday when I first saw her. Maybe she was going to tell me, but got distracted. She was worked up about seeing my cloak on Lyra's shoulders."

Andrea snorted without humor. "Typical." His tone turned serious. "Aren't you bothered she didn't tell you?"

"Of course it concerns me," Remo said, broken inside. "And if she's betrothed to Acerbi, of all people..." He trailed off, unable to accept the idea of her marrying such a monster.

Andrea's face twisted with a mix of pity and fury. Remo could tell he was holding something back, maybe because he didn't want to sound like a hypocrite, given the chaos of his own relationship. Remo now found himself without a job, without a future in Mavortis, and, presumably, without Sabelle.

And yet, he wasn't sure he'd trade this aching low for the numbness he'd felt in Anxur. Pain meant he was alive. And while truly living had brought heartbreak, it had also brought friends who would search for him in the dead of night and carry him home.

"Shit," Remo muttered as a memory crashed down on him. Andrea cocked his head, waiting.

"Sabelle and I were chased by two Knights of Saffiro once in the public gardens of the Briar District. She said they were probably sent by her father to keep an eye on her, but... what if they were sent by Acerbi? He must've wanted her even back then."

Andrea's restraint snapped. "You've lost everything for this girl, brother—nearly even your life. She's not good for you. I don't care if she comes crawling back, which frankly, I doubt she will. You shouldn't let her in again. She's not worth it. She could endanger us all."

Remo didn't reply. He couldn't contradict anything Andrea had said. If Sabelle truly was betrothed and hadn't told him, it was easier to let anger take root.

Andrea left soon after for Alchemy class, and Lyra arrived to take a turn watching over Remo, though he insisted it wasn't necessary. He'd never been fussed over so much in his life, and though he wouldn't admit it, he didn't entirely mind.

She entered with a tankard and covered plate from The Crooked Cupola. She winced at the sight of him and set the food beside his bed. "I brought you some food," she said, unnecessarily.

"Thanks, Lyra," he murmured, groggy from Nella's pain medication.

She pulled his desk chair up to the bed, her brow pinched as she examined his bruised frame. "Andrea told Cosimo what happened. Cosimo said not to worry about paying for your room; the Order will cover everything. He also said you'll be well paid for our quest in Vecontii in a few weeks. His orders are to take care of yourself. You'll need to be healthy by then."

*But what of Sabelle?* he thought hopelessly, despair creeping in. He wouldn't have peace until he heard the truth from her lips, but he wasn't in any shape to seek her out again.

Maybe she'd think the worst of him. That after everything, he had no intention of seeing her again. That he only wanted her body. The thought made him sick. He didn't know how, but he had to find a way to get a message to her.

He looked at Lyra, her eyes mirroring his pain, though something uncertain lingered there.

"Andrea told me you were the one who checked on me last night, and that I'd probably be dead without you. I... Thank you, Lyra," he said, unsure how to begin repaying such a debt.

She shook her head, refusing the praise. "It was Nella who stitched you up and tended your wounds."

"But you were the one who came looking."

She shook her head again, as if rejecting even that small role. "Remo, I'm... I'm sorry," she whispered, fear flashing in her eyes.

"What in the world could you be apologizing for? I owe you my life, Lyra."

"But your cloak... did it cause a fight between you two?"

Remo couldn't believe she was blaming herself over something as small as a cloak. "Of course not," he lied. He didn't want her to feel guilty over something that never should have mattered to Sabelle in the first place. *I gave it to you; there's no blame on you. I lent you my cloak, not my hand in marriage."

She laughed shakily and nodded, looking relieved. His own joke burned, but he pushed his thoughts of Sabelle and Acerbi aside.

Lyra leaned over and picked up a book from his nightstand, one he hadn't put there. She must have brought it at some point during the night.

"Since you've got... spare time," she said softly, "I brought you something new to read."

Amusement danced in his swollen eyes as he replied, "That's kind of you. What book is this?"

She tucked a strand of hair behind her ear and shifted in her seat. "It's called *The Tale of Skyloft*. It's about a wizard who meddles in shadows that unleash darkness into the world, which he then tries to quell." Her gaze drifted to his swollen eye. "I can read it to you, if you'd like. But I won't bother you if you want to be alone." A faint blush spread across her high cheekbones, as if she assumed her presence would be more a nuisance than a comfort.

"I would like that very much," he said quietly.

Her answering smile was full of relief as she began. The story was interesting, and Remo found comfort in hearing it from her lips, her lilting Satrian accent wrapping around the words in a way he liked. It struck him, mid-chapter, that no one had ever read to him before, not even in childhood.

In the days that followed, Remo made a point to walk around his room as per Nella's strict orders. He never went to the Academy alone; Andrea always escorted him, eyes sharp for Knights of Saffiro or Salii. Remo threw himself twice as hard into his astrological studies and began helping plan their mission to Vecontii and the eventual journey to

Saffiro.

With his romantic life in ruins, Remo found it difficult to plan the ritual offering to Venus, planet of love. Lyra, thrilled by the idea, offered to take over the offering portion of the ritual. Remo was happy to let her.

Two weeks had passed since the attack. Although Remo's body was healing, his heart was not. He hadn't seen or heard from Sabelle.

Andrea entered his room, a grim look etched into his handsome features. His voice held unmistakable distaste as he said, "You have a visitor."

When he stepped aside, Sabelle appeared. She looked angry at first, but the moment she saw the bruising on Remo's face, her expression softened.

Andrea looked as though he already regretted letting her in, as if it went against his better judgment. Though hesitant to leave, he finally stepped out. "I'll leave you two."

As the door clicked shut, Sabelle stepped closer. "What—what happened?" she asked, breathless.

Remo stood. "I've wanted to come see you. But on my way home that night, I was attacked by two Salii, sent by Acerbi. I've been dismissed from the hospital and barred from working anywhere in Mavortis. They said... Is it true you're betrothed?"

The question tumbled out. He needed to hear it from her, though the truth was already in her eyes.

"I'm not betrothed yet," she said. "I came to tell you that night that he proposed, but I haven't answered. And I wanted to tell you then, but when I saw your cloak around that girl"—her face twisted—"I realized I wasn't ready to lose you. That moment made me realize how much I want to be with you."

Remo sank back down. It was all too much, all too complicated. "So—you're not betrothed to Acerbi?"

"No," she repeated. "But my family's pressuring me. I'm running out of time. I needed to know why you never came to visit."

Nausea twisted through him. His heart and mind split in two. "Did you and Acerbi have an understanding like I thought we did?"

She shook her head. "No. I knew he liked me, but there's nothing between us. He offered a marriage of convenience, that's all."

Remo absorbed her words. He didn't see how a Mavortian prince would benefit politically from marrying a Saffiran senator's daughter, but that was the least of his concerns. He figured Sabelle's beauty made up for what Acerbi might otherwise deem an inferior match.

"I haven't come to see you because Acerbi would kill me. I've already lost my livelihood. My life is the last thing I have to lose for you, Sabelle, and yet you speak as if you're still considering marrying him after what he did to me. After what he's taken from me. After what he'd do if I gave him another chance." His voice cracked with disbelief and desperation.

Sabelle bristled. "And what was I supposed to think? You vanished."

Remo's gaze pleaded. "I'm sorry. It tore me up thinking you'd believe I just walked away. But I couldn't risk it; I could barely move."

Her posture stiffened, but some of the coldness in her expression melted. He pressed on.

"I understand now," she said at last. Her eyes brimmed. "And I'm so sorry he did this to you."

"Did he hurt you?"

"What? No. Why would he?"

"Because his soldiers knew we'd been... together," Remo said. He was relieved she hadn't been harmed, but baffled Acerbi would still want to marry her, knowing what had passed between them. Nobler women had suffered for far less, and Acerbi didn't seem the forgiving type.

"My affairs are my own. At least until I'm married," Sabelle said.

Remo couldn't fathom how a monster like Acerbi could be unbothered by Sabelle sleeping with another man outside of marriage. The idea of her being bound to someone so cruel made him sick. He would fear for her every moment.

Their connection had already cost him so much, but Remo saw it as the price of love and being worthy of Sabelle. He would give every ounce of blood and pain to earn it. And maybe if he just tried a little harder, if he pushed a little further...

"Sabelle, I'm leaving for a few weeks. I can't say why, but I'm doing it for us. If things go well, I might be given a title someday."

Her eyes widened in shock. Something about the glimmer in her gaze unsettled him, but he pushed it aside.

"But how—"

"Please don't ask," he interrupted. "I'm not punishing you. I just can't say."

She only nodded, gaze sharp. "Then I'll decline Acerbi's proposal."

Something felt off; doubt sank into his gut. It was as if his body knew something he didn't, like a message clawing to be seen, but his conscious mind locked it away.

"When do you leave? Can I come say goodbye?" Sabelle asked.

"We should say our goodbyes now. I leave in two days, at first light," he said.

"May I at least know where you're going?"

He hesitated, then said, "Vecontii."

Excitement lit her face, turning her beauty sharp, almost dangerous. She stepped closer, lowered her lashes, and took his face in her hands. Her kiss was slow, coaxing, her tongue promising things he wasn't sure her heart truly meant.

"Safe travels, my love. I'll wait for you. May we meet again," she whispered before slipping from the room.

Remo sat staring at the door long after she'd gone. Deep inside, the message clawed at its locked box, slamming against its cage.

He ignored it again.

# Chapter Twenty-four

A SKY-BLUE CARRIAGE WAITED outside, its cream-colored horses pawing the ground impatiently.

Andrea, Lyra, Remo, and Nella would ride together for over a week to reach Vecontii before the ritual. With Nella's princess status, they could travel in comfort without fear of the Knights of Saffiro or other threats.

Remo tucked the talisman into his bag and loaded it into the carriage. He was about to climb in when he heard her voice. He whirled around to see Sabelle, stunning in a dramatic red, high-necked cloak with black beading.

Her eyes swept over the carriage. "I came to say one last goodbye," she said, still absorbing the sight of his grand entourage. "Whose wagon is this?"

"It's Nella's. I'm traveling to Vecontii with her, Andrea, and Lyra."

All excitement drained from her expression at the last name. "Lyra?" she repeated.

"Yes," he said, heart racing. He hated how she always made him feel like he'd done something wrong.

"So you're traveling with *her*, and yet you won't tell me why or share any details about the journey?"

Panic rose in him, threatening to shatter everything. He felt like his world was breaking apart, and if he couldn't gather the pieces, he'd be nothing—especially without her approval. "Sabelle, it isn't like that. I told you—"

She glanced inside the carriage and fixed her gaze on Lyra. The others were far enough away not to hear their conversation.

"I no longer believe anything you told me," she said. "You're clearly keeping secrets. So go. I don't care anymore. The cards were right all those months ago. They warned me of betrayal. I should have known it would come from you."

Remo's mind worked furiously to make sense of what she meant. At last, he realized she must be referring to the tarocchi reading she'd given him back on Juno. "You can't seriously believe I would betray you based on the possible meaning of a card you pulled?" he said, stung by the accusation.

"The cards never lie," she said. "I tried to ignore them. But they were right. I can't trust you. Don't come looking for me." Tears slid down her furious face.

"Are you really jealous, Sabelle? Lyra is my *friend*. You seemed to understand the concept of friendship when you pretended to be mine after you pulled your hand away from me in front of Acerbi." He delivered the words with all the anguish the memory still carried.

Sabelle's mouth fell open. "I didn't ask you to say we were friends. I told you, it was an instinct. I didn't mean anything by it."

Remo ignored her excuse; the dam of his pent-up resentment had broken. *"You're* the one practically betrothed to the man who tried to have me killed. I've done nothing to betray you. Meanwhile, you've barely reassured me you won't marry the man who's made my life hell for loving you. Don't talk to me about secrets—you've kept plenty."

He'd spoken the words that had festered like a wound inside him for months. He regretted it immediately, even though they were his truth. It was clear that sharing his feelings only enraged Sabelle further. He cursed himself, thinking he should have learned by now that his feelings didn't matter, that nothing ever came from expressing them except more pain.

"I have nothing else to say to you. Goodbye, Remo." She said it with such finality that his eyes widened as if desperate to catch one last glimpse of her.

"Sabelle," he called after her, pleading for her to believe him. She didn't look back. The horses pawed the ground behind him. He climbed into the carriage.

"Is everything alright?" Andrea asked cautiously.

Remo was determined not to betray his emotions to his friends. He wouldn't burden them anymore. He kept a stiff upper lip, refusing to let himself appear weak. His father's voice echoed in his mind, tempering the storm inside him. The ghost of the man was disgusted with him for feeling so deeply.

It felt like an old wound had been torn open, bleeding fresh. He blamed himself. He should have told Sabelle earlier that Lyra would be joining them, but he suspected it wouldn't have changed anything. She had chosen to believe what she thought the cards foretold.

His friends clearly noticed the fight but respected his silence. The carriage rode on in silence for several minutes before Lyra let out a soft groan. Remo looked over. Her face had gone pale, a sheen of sweat across her brow. She looked faint, pressing her fingers to her forehead as if battling sudden pain.

"What's wrong?" Nella snapped, instantly alert.

"My head... I feel... awful," Lyra muttered, rubbing her temples.

Remo shifted into healer mode, scanning her for signs. Nella placed a hand on Lyra's forehead but said nothing. Lyra swayed in her seat, as if on the verge of collapse. Panic surged through Remo. Normally calm in a crisis, he felt something primal twist inside him.

His mind jumped to what Cosimo had once explained in Astrology class: the Evil Eye. The image of Sabelle staring daggers at Lyra came roaring back. Wittingly or not, she must have passed it on. Afterward, he had read about it in Awareness texts, wanting to protect himself and know what to do if anyone ever had cause to envy him—though why anyone would was beyond him.

"It's the Evil Eye. Sabelle cast it on her," Remo blurted.

Andrea looked helpless as Lyra's eyes fluttered closed, heavy with fatigue. Nella's eyes widened at the diagnosis, but she quickly composed herself and unclasped her necklace, fastening it around Lyra's neck.

"Lyra," Remo called, trying to keep her awake. She opened her eyes slowly, straining to meet his gaze.

"I need you to spit, three times," he told her, pulling back the blue curtain from the carriage window. She leaned out and spat onto the road three times as the wagon rumbled forward.

Nella held Lyra's hand and gripped the charm, reciting:

*"Mother, Father, Moon and Sun,*
*Drive away what has been done.*
*Through the Night and through the Day*
*Destroy our enemies, make them pay.*
*Cast away the eye that harms,*
*And place protection in this charm."*

Lyra inhaled sharply, her gaze suddenly clear. Relief passed between Andrea and Nella as normalcy returned. Remo, too, felt relief. He wanted to join in their calm, but instead he felt worse. Sabelle had wished harm on Lyra and he'd failed to stop it. Despite their fight, he couldn't bring himself to believe she had done it intentionally. He'd never understood her coldness toward Lyra, but now he could finally name its source: her belief in those cursed cards.

As she returned to herself, Lyra insisted she was fine. "Of all days to forget my lunula amulet," she sighed.

Remo learned that lunula amulets were crescent-shaped charms given to girls at birth. They were believed to act as talismans, protecting against the Evil Eye and dark forces. Boys received similar charms called bullae, which were removed before they reached manhood. The tradition wasn't practiced on Anxur, though Remo imagined that if it had been, his father would never have considered him manly enough to remove his bulla.

"But, Nella... where did you learn that *carmen malum?*" Lyra asked.

Nella hesitated. Lyra's eyes pleaded. Nella sighed, then gave a rare look of guilt. "A servant in my family's house was Satrian. I was closer to her than to most relatives. She taught it to me and said I should only use it to protect someone who truly deserves it."

Remo thought he understood Nella's hesitation. Satrians, especially Satrian women, were often treated as lesser citizens, relegated to servant roles in noble households.

"Wait, what's a carmen malum?" Andrea asked.

"A carmen is a kind of chant or spell," Lyra explained warily. "A carmen malum is a potentially harmful or protective incantation. Satrians are deeply superstitious and wary of witchcraft—probably because, historically, women were once seen as powerful because of it."

Remo was surprised that Nella, a physician-in-training, had taken the Evil Eye seriously enough to learn protection against it. He told her as much and got a glare sharp enough to curse him on the spot.

"That bitch should pray I don't do worse to her for this," Nella growled.

"Nella," Andrea said sharply, his tone making it clear she should leave Remo alone.

Part of Remo agreed with Nella's fury over what the Evil Eye had done to Lyra. But another part of him still wanted to believe Sabelle hadn't meant it, despite everything she'd put him through. He reconciled those parts of himself by saying nothing, brooding in silence for the rest of the week-and-a-half-long journey to Vecontii.

Time dragged. Remo stayed quiet, lost in thoughts of Sabelle, only speaking when they discussed the talisman. Meadows, woods, and winding roads passed by the windows, all touched by winter's decay. Bare trees with gnarled limbs stretched toward the grey sky as they passed through the end of a thicket and approached a broad stone bridge spanning Lovers' Lagoon.

At the far end of the bridge, the copper gates of Vecontii gleamed in the distance. Beyond the gates stood what Remo thought might be the most beautiful place he had ever seen.

Vecontii looked like something out of every fairy tale he'd ever read, the kind where a prince and princess lived happily ever after, which felt fitting for the kingdom ruled by Venus. Part of the kingdom floated on a lagoon, its stone bridges lacing from one side to the other. In the distance, a grand white palace rose above the city, crowned with dozens of turrets and copper spires.

The innermost towers shimmered with a faint pastel-pink hue, like rose quartz. The setting sun painted the sky in soft gold and pink, fluffy clouds glowing behind the palace, their brightness mirrored in the metalwork.

He could only imagine how beautiful Vecontii must be in springtime, with pastel flowers climbing its gates and appearing around every corner. Even in winter, the kingdom was a dream in shades of pink, gold, and blue. It was so enchanting, he half expected a fairy or mythical creature to flit by; something magical would not have looked out of place in this romantic realm.

Although he knew the land was associated with Venus as its tutelary deity, Remo suspected that knowing Nella had skewed his expectations. Instead of the beauty before him, he'd imagined severed heads atop the spikes of a gothic castle.

The carriage approached the gate without issue. It had been sent by King Bardi himself for his daughter, who had arranged its arrival. The cream-colored horses clopped through the streets, drawing stares from passersby. They headed straight to the palace, Nella's family home.

Nella briefed Lyra and Remo on palace etiquette before their introduction to her father, King Bardi. They were to bow deeply and address him as *Your Majesty* when he first spoke to them. After that, he should be called *Your Highness* or *Your Grace.*

Lyra and Remo shared a nervous glance. As the only commoners among nobles, they were glad to face this together.

"It's clear I've been terribly rude to both Your Highnesses," Remo quipped, nodding dramatically to Nella and Andrea. "I repent and acknowledge you could have me hanged from the parapets."

Andrea shook his head, mildly annoyed but amused.

Nella simply lifted her chin in acknowledgment. "And you'd do well to remember that, boy."

The carriage stopped at the palace entrance. Attendants escorted them inside while servants hauled their belongings. The entry hall sparkled with dove-grey tiles and a blinding crystal chandelier. Gilded panels adorned the walls and ceiling, and white columns framed the space in regal symmetry.

An elegant olive-skinned woman in her fifties, clearly Nella's mother, entered with a radiant smile. They bowed as she nodded graciously in greeting. Nella greeted her mother with the same formality as the others. They looked alike, though her mother's features were softer, her hair a rich chestnut.

"Andrea, how lovely it is to see you again," said the Queen of Vecontii with a smile, notably omitting his title due to his exiled status. Her warm demeanor made it clear this wasn't a slight, but a subtle nod to heraldic rules.

"Thank you, Your Highness. You're most gracious to welcome us into your home," Andrea responded.

Queen Maddalena turned to Remo and Lyra as Nella introduced them. They bowed again and offered their thanks for her generosity.

"It's a pleasure to meet my daughter's friends at last," the Queen said, then motioned for a servant to guide them to their rooms before dinner.

They ascended a grand staircase toward the east wing, where the guest rooms were located.

Remo's suite was magnificent. A four-poster bed draped in forget-me-not blue silk curtains stood against a vanilla-paneled wall trimmed in gold. He thanked the servant, who promised to send someone to draw his bath.

In the adjoining bathing chamber, a polished clawfoot basin was already being filled with steaming water. Remo relished the chance to scrub the road dust from his skin. Crystal vials of perfumed oils sat on a side table, and he chose one scented with woodsy musk. He lathered up, breathing in the clean, rich aroma. He dressed in his best doublet for the feast and headed down just before eight.

Andrea was already there, speaking with a strapping man in his early thirties whom Remo assumed was one of Nella's older brothers. The planes of his aristocratic, tanned face were chiseled and framed by shoulder-length golden hair and hazel eyes. Standing beside them, Remo felt like an ugly duckling.

"Prince Amaury, this is my friend Remo," Andrea offered.

"A pleasure to meet you, Remo," Amaury said, the words an invitation for Remo to address him.

"Your Grace," Remo said with a respectful bow. "The honor is mine."

Prince Amaury responded with polite diplomacy, studying Remo as if trying to determine the purpose of his presence. A few minutes later, Nella, Lyra, and a pretty woman Remo assumed was Nella's sister descended the stairs.

Nella wore a pink dress, unlike anything he'd ever seen her wear in Mavortis. A defiant challenge flickered in her eyes, daring anyone to comment on the frilly gown. He guessed she wore it to please her parents.

Time seemed to slow as Lyra descended the staircase in a rust-colored velvet gown, looking ethereal. Her long, light bronze hair fell to her waist, while the upper half had been braided into a coronet. From beneath her carefully styled hair, Remo glimpsed the tips of the brass elven ear cuffs he had given her for Saturnalia.

It thrilled him to see she'd chosen to wear them for such an important occasion. She looked like a queen lifted straight from the pages of one of their beloved fantasy books. With the elven accessory, she appeared positively otherworldly.

Remo glanced toward Amaury, who seemed utterly entranced. He didn't even take his eyes off Lyra when he asked, "Is she with you?"

"No, Your Highness. We're not romantically involved," Remo replied. If only Sabelle believed that, he might actually look forward to the feast.

He frowned as Amaury continued to watch Lyra. A protective feeling rose in him, one he couldn't quite explain.

Lyra reached the last step and smiled, and the warmth of it felt like sunlight falling over all of them.

"Amaury," Nella said with a cursory nod.

"Hello, Nella," he replied, barely glancing her way. His eyes stayed on Lyra, who offered a shy curtsy as Nella introduced her.

Amaury gave a bow, his hazel eyes meeting Lyra's amber ones as he rose. "Had I known my sister was friends with Venus herself, I'd have thrown a ball in your honor instead of a mere dinner."

A soft flush painted Lyra's cheeks, but she held his gaze and smiled. "Your Grace is too generous with your compliments."

"Please, call me Amaury," he said, just beginning to offer his arm when Nella stepped in and took Lyra's instead.

"You've always been my favorite brother, Amaury. Don't make me reconsider by subjecting my friend to your... well, to you," Nella teased, leading Lyra toward the Great Hall.

Andrea cleared his throat, and Nella paused. "Oh, right. Remo, that's my sister, Amata. Amata, meet Remo."

She continued walking Lyra out of Amaury's sight, while Amata reddened at her sister's lack of manners. Like their mother, Amata bore a resemblance to Nella, though her light brown hair lacked her sister's fiery tinge.

"Please forgive my sister's rudeness. I fear her time away from court has left her a bit... unpolished," Amata said, her doleful eyes downcast.

Remo bowed. "There is nothing to forgive, Your Highness."

Amaury seemed unfazed by Nella's jab and moved to follow them, with Amata trailing behind.

"If that's how she talks to her favorite brother, I'd love to hear what she says to her least favorite," Remo muttered to Andrea as they followed.

Andrea chuckled. "You won't get the chance. They're probably hanging upside down in the dungeon or locked in stocks somewhere in town."

The Great Hall mirrored the palace's design: diamond-tiled floors, towering marble fireplace, and crystal chandeliers overhead. A long carved table ran down the center, leading to King Bardi, seated on a grand throne upholstered in aquamarine velvet.

A mural of pale florals, pinks, blues, and beryl green spread behind him. The entire room resembled a pastel-frosted cake. They crossed the length of the hall until they stood just a few feet from King Bardi, Queen Maddalena seated on a matching throne at his side.

Nella stepped forward and bowed again. "Father," she said, then gestured for her companions. "This is Lyra Calandre, my best friend and roommate in Mavortis."

Lyra dropped into a deep curtsy, the gesture graceful and precise.

King Bardi tilted his chin in approval. "Welcome to Vecontii, Lyra," he said. She thanked him softly.

King Bardi looked like a man who had aged rapidly in just a few months. The lines on his tanned face suggested long hours spent worrying over something of great importance. His features had a slightly sunken quality, as if he'd lost significant weight; Nella had once described him as rounder, thanks to his fondness for the kingdom's famously rich pastries.

His gaze shifted to Remo as Nella continued. "This is Andrea's friend, Remo. He's also a member of the Order of Aquarius."

Remo bowed deeply, silently praying to Vesta that he looked half as natural as Lyra had during her curtsey.

"I trust your journey was safe?" King Bardi asked.

"Yes, Your Majesty. Thank you for the accommodations."

The king gave a nod, then turned to Andrea. "Andrea. How delightful to see you again. I imagine we have much to discuss."

Andrea bowed with practiced grace. "Likewise, Your Grace. Thank you for hosting us."

King Bardi's words did not seem to match his true feelings. He appeared anxious to host the exiled prince and his companions, his ringed fingers tapping against the arm of his throne before he finally rose.

His wife stood beside him as he gestured toward the long table prepared for the feast. "Please, be seated."

White Vecontiian wine filled their cups as the feast unfolded. Cured meats, cheeses, and fruit came first, followed by exquisitely prepared seafood—lobster, crab, scallops, and oysters gleaming on copper trays. Remo quickly understood why Vecontii was famed for its seafood. It rivaled the best he'd ever eaten on Anxur.

Dessert included sugared fruits, honey cakes with nuts, and cream-filled pastries known as *Nipples of Venus,* named for their rounded form and suggestively peaked icing. Remo noticed Amaury carefully savoring one while casting glances at Lyra, who either didn't notice or artfully ignored him.

Conversation stayed formal. Andrea would likely speak about Order matters once the king summoned him privately. After dinner, they didn't linger; everyone returned to their rooms. Remo fell asleep the moment he hit the bed, blissfully free of the carriage's jolts.

Morning sunlight streamed through the silken curtains as Remo stretched across the wide bed, slowly recalling where he was. A flicker of nerves stirred. Tonight, they would perform the talismanic ritual for Venus. He dressed and headed downstairs for breakfast.

The Great Hall dazzled in the morning light; sunbeams bent through the chandelier's crystals, scattering rainbows across the room. King Bardi and Queen Maddalena were absent, likely taking their breakfast in bed, as was customary for high-ranking nobles.

Amaury sat alone at the long table, idly pushing his golden utensils across his plate. He looked up as Remo entered, his expression briefly hopeful, then visibly disappointed. He gave Remo a curt nod.

Remo returned Amaury's gesture with a respectful nod and sat beside Andrea. Nella entered with Lyra and Amata. The men stood. Amaury pulled out Lyra's chair and ignored Nella's eye-roll.

"I trust you slept well?" Amaury asked, his eyes on Lyra.

Andrea jumped in. "Like a babe, Your Grace."

Lyra gave him a small smile, and he winked back. Then, leaning toward Remo, Andrea whispered, "It's true. My bed was so soft, it was like sleeping on Venus' bosom."

Remo nearly spat out his tea, trying to cover it up with a cough. He was convinced Andrea said things like this in public just to see him struggle.

"Yes, Your Grace. Thank you," Lyra said smoothly, trying to redirect attention from Remo's outburst while Andrea slapped his back with mock concern.

With Amaury's gaze still fixed on Lyra, Remo leaned toward Andrea. "Are you meeting with King Bardi today?"

Andrea shook his head. "Not yet. He hasn't summoned me."

When breakfast ended, Amata offered to show them the palace and gardens, slipping naturally into the role of hostess, since Nella clearly had no interest in doing so.

"We'll start inside, if you please," Nella said, wrapping her arms tightly around herself in front of the large fire.

Amata turned to her brother. "Will you be joining us?"

"Sadly not. I have business with Father," he replied.

"Then you mustn't be tardy for King Bardi," Lyra said, barely suppressing a laugh at her rhyme. Nella, Remo, and Andrea all groaned.

Remo pointed at her. "Stocks!" he declared, which only made her laugh harder. Nella looked moments away from summoning them herself.

Amaury tilted his head, a vaguely amused smile on his lips. "I look forward to rejoining your... *party*."

"Oh, fucking hell, these two," Nella muttered, burying her face in Andrea's shoulder as he chuckled. Lyra gave a surprised smile as Amaury inclined his head and left the room.

Amata led the tour; Andrea and Remo drifted a few paces behind the women.

"Do we know what time dinner is? Venus enters 27 degrees Pisces just after sunset," Remo whispered to Andrea, apprehension tightening his chest.

Andrea's expression didn't ease his worry. "Dunno. I'll ask Nella when we're expected. If it conflicts with the ritual, maybe she can move it. We could make up an excuse."

They kept their voices low while Amata described the corridor's history ahead of them.

"I don't think we should call attention to our absence or try to change anything," Remo said. "It might raise suspicions and make it harder to slip away to the temple."

Andrea nodded. "You're probably right. Worst case, we'll make up a reason for being late."

At the end of the corridor, they reached the ballroom, a grand space with slate-grey and gilt paneling and doors that opened onto a balcony overlooking the gardens. An ivory harpsichord stood in one corner.

"I hope you'll be able to attend a ball here one day," Amata said to Lyra, who lit up at the thought.

"If you do, I hope it's in summer," Nella grumbled, wrapping a scarf tighter around her head. "It never feels this cold in Mavortis."

Amata smirked. "I suppose winters down south are milder. And here I thought it was just Andrea tempting you to stay in Mavortis."

Nella shivered. "And, you know, my education," she snapped. "Perhaps you should visit. The warmer climate might feel nice on your old bones."

Amata looked momentarily wounded but quickly composed herself, continuing to describe the history of the ballroom to Lyra. The exchange hinted at sensitive history between the sisters, which Lyra and Remo dutifully ignored.

They moved on. Remo and Lyra entered the library—three times the size of the Academy's—and exchanged a look of silent awe. Shelves were packed with hundreds upon hundreds of books, both ancient and new. Remo turned to Amata, asking if he was allowed to touch one.

Amata giggled, apparently charmed by his enthusiasm. "Be my guest."

He gently opened a beautifully illuminated manuscript, breathing in the scent of its pages. Lyra hovered beside him, inhaling the scent too. She sighed dreamily.

Nella watched with thinly veiled judgment, her head leaning on Andrea's shoulder.

"Our best friends are freaks," Andrea muttered, while Amata covered her mouth to hide a laugh.

"Do you want to smell the book, too?" Remo asked, waving it under Andrea's nose.

"I'll pass," Andrea said, lips twitching.

They practically had to drag Remo and Lyra away. The two looked ready to spend the entire visit in the library.

The tour continued through the palace, each room more beautiful than the last. Aside from the library, Remo's favorite was a small tower room painted sky blue, its circular walls adorned with a woodland mural and a golden bed that nearly filled the space.

By the time they reached the gardens, it was noon. The grounds were bare in the dead of winter, but it wasn't hard to imagine how beautiful they'd be in springtime, full of blooming flowers and trees. Winged statues and fountains lined the manicured gardens. From the path, they glimpsed the Temple of Venus, the site of that night's ritual.

Its rose-stone façade appeared better preserved than any other temple they'd seen, likely due to its proximity to the Valentia family's ancestral home. It had clearly been maintained with care. Remo spotted two guards within the grounds, obstacles they'd have to distract before performing the talismanic ceremony.

Fortunately, dinner had been scheduled for eight, leaving enough time after nightfall to complete the ceremony unnoticed. It was a relief not to have to explain their absence. Still, the matter of the guards remained.

"Would they even suspect anything if we were in there?" Remo asked as they sat together in Andrea's room.

"If you're in there too long, they might. It's odd; guards on the grounds are normal, but they've never been stationed near the temple. I wonder whose orders that came from," Nella replied, frowning. "If they catch you mid-ritual, they'd throw you in prison. And my father wouldn't intervene—he can't. If he did, people might accuse him of harboring witches or practicing himself. And with Emperor Varro watching, he can't afford that."

"So what do we do?" Andrea asked quietly.

"I'll distract them so you can get in," Nella said. "I can't send them away, only my father has that authority. But I can buy you enough time to slip in unseen and begin the ritual. If they see you leave, that's fine. They won't know how long you were there, or what you did."

"Can't we just tell your father it's Order business and have him remove the guards?" Remo asked.

Andrea shook his head immediately. "No. Cosimo doesn't want the royals to know about the talisman. We can't risk telling King Bardi. He might grow even more wary of us and refuse to support Anxur's cause."

Remo gathered the ritual supplies of dried vervain, pennyroyal, damask roses, and a vial of rosewater. He would also offer Venus a decorative glass bottle of musk oil, a small box of cosmetic powder from an apothecary, and a ring shaped like a jeweled golden crown donated by Nella, who had declared it "too gaudy" for her taste.

Nella led them to a vantage point where they could observe the temple from a distance. They didn't ask what her distraction would be, but it seemed effective; moments later, the guards ran off in pursuit of a shadowy figure. With the path clear, the trio darted toward the temple, their tools tucked safely into their bags. Once inside, they lit several candles to illuminate the space.

The temple was breathtaking. Its vaulted ceiling depicted angels soaring through a sky of fluffy clouds. Though the fresco bore signs of age, it remained largely intact, its weathering adding character rather than detracting from its grandeur.

At the front stood an altar to Venus, bearing a pair of brass scales and faint traces of rose perfume. Behind it, a sea-green mural shimmered with a giant pink clamshell painted in the center. At its heart glowed the sigil of Venus, luminous under flickering candlelight.

They were already dressed in fine clothing, befitting their status as guests of King Bardi. These garments, rich and elegant, served as sunthemata, symbols of Venus' domain. As the sun dipped below the horizon, Remo lit the suffumigation smoke with the pennyroyal and placed Venus' offerings reverently upon the altar. He drew out the diamond to serve as her talismanic gem.

"We call upon you, Venus, the Fairest and Most Generous, Ruler of beauty, dancing, music, and all that is aesthetically pleasing. Peacemaker and seeker of justice. All that humans long for lies within your domain: love, relationships, marriage, pleasure, leisure, affection, wealth, beauty, and passion. We call upon you now to infuse this talisman with your divine essence. These objects are offered in your honor along with a gift of song."

Lyra, who had volunteered to lead the offering to Venus, had told them earlier she planned to sing a love song.

Andrea had teased, *"What if we all just kissed? Surely lusty old Venus would approve."*

Lyra had looked faint at the suggestion.

Now, she drew out her lyre, a delicate hand harp, and sat with poise as Remo waited for the first note. Around them, the silence felt charged, expectant.

Lyra began to pluck the first notes. Remo felt the resonance vibrate in his chest. She played with haunting grace, her posture as mesmerizing as the sound itself. He felt transported, part of something ancient, sacred. The whole of him hummed in tune with her song.

Then she sang. Her voice was honey and heartbreak—soft, aching, full of longing. Though the song was a love ballad, her voice held a wistful ache, rendered even more poignant in her native Satrian tongue. The melody rose and fell, reminiscent of the ebb and flow of the sea.

He wanted to bottle the feeling her voice summoned and keep it forever, afraid it would vanish and leave him hollow. It felt eternal and elusive, primordial and fleeting, of this world and yet beyond it. She plucked the final string of her song, and the universe itself seemed to mourn its ending.

As Andrea engraved and burnished the diamond into the talisman, Remo simply looked at her, still entranced, still searching for the song's remnants in her eyes. Even in the dim temple light, he could see a faint rosy hue rise on her cheekbones. It made him realize he had been staring. He quickly turned his focus back to the talisman, waving suffumigation smoke over it.

He didn't think of Sabelle, only Venus. Sabelle's memory brought pain. He pushed it down. This moment belonged to love, not loss.

Instead, Remo centered himself on the feeling Lyra's song had stirred within him, recognizing it as the essence of Venus. He thought of *Milena and Devlan,* the most romantic love story he'd ever read, and how it had left a lasting imprint on his heart and soul.

"Venus, we ask you to imbue this talisman and diamond with your energy. Grant its wearer the power of diplomacy. May they always have enough to live. Grant them a sense of justice, that they may rule with peace. Give them sound judgment, and help them love the people of Terramundi, and be loved in return. We thank you, ever-loving Venus."

They continued to set their intentions in reverent silence as the suffumigation smoke burned low. Minutes later, it faded. Remo quickly tucked the talisman into its protective case. Before they could even peek outside to check for guards, a cold voice echoed from the doorway.

"Explain yourselves," Amaury said, his tone sharp and threatening as he looked between Andrea and Remo.

# Chapter Twenty-five

T HE SCENT OF SMOKE still hung in the temple, and the offerings lay openly on Venus' altar—there was no denying they'd been up to something. Remo stood quickly, scrambling for a lie that would shift blame onto himself.

Any suspicions against Andrea would be devastating, as he still needed to ask King Bardi for men to stand as numbers against Saffiro. As for Lyra, Remo thought she had seen enough sorrow for one lifetime, and he wouldn't allow her to suffer the same fate as her father in prison. It might have been incriminating enough for all three of them to be caught in the temple, but he'd try to spare his friends.

"I can explain, Your Highness," Remo said. "This was my doing. I asked my friends to come because I—well, I needed Venus' help with a personal matter. A relationship, actually. I was desperate, and I didn't want to come alone. Please don't blame them for my foolishness."

Lyra shook her head, looking at Amaury pleadingly. "Your Grace, I wanted to see the temple myself. It's so beautiful, and I gave into the temptation. I'm Satrian, you see, and we still hold fast to the Old Religion."

The effect of her words was immediate. Amaury's expression lost its former hardness. "You hide your accent well, though I admit I detected it earlier."

Lyra stared at her feet. Remo was annoyed by Amaury's backhanded compliment. It seemed to suggest that being Satrian was something to be ashamed of. But Remo held his tongue; he was in no position to pick a fight with the Crown Prince of Vecontii.

Amaury turned, his face twisting into a mask of fury as he remembered Remo and Andrea's presence. "Do you comprehend the gravity of your actions? If anyone else had witnessed you three in here with offerings, you would be incarcerated on charges of witchcraft! And to compromise a lady by bringing her in the company of two men without an escort!"

It was obvious Amaury's fury stemmed from more than etiquette; he didn't like Lyra's closeness to Remo and Andrea.

"Yes, Your Grace," Remo said. "It was foolish. I'm in love with someone named Sabelle and things ended badly. I didn't know where else to turn, so I came here. The blame is mine. Please, forgive them."

Remo thought he had rendered himself just pathetic enough to get away with his lie. Indeed, Amaury looked reassured at Remo's profession of love for a woman other than the one standing next to him.

Though his tone had softened, Amaury's posture still bristled with authority. "I'll overlook this once. Do not let it happen again."

"Yes, Your Highness," the three answered in unison.

"May I ask what brought you here tonight, Amaury?" Andrea asked. Although Andrea was disgraced as an exile, he had been born Amaury's superior in rank as Emperor Varro's son, so it was less offensive coming from him.

Remo noticed Amaury's hand twitch toward a coat pocket. He was carrying something.

"Looking for you three," Amaury replied defensively. It seemed he had business of his own within Venus' temple and, in his shock at finding the three of them there, forgot how suspicious it would look for *him* to be there.

The question was a gentle reminder that Amaury's presence within the temple marked him as not a wholly innocent party either. Remo's gut told him that the Vecontiian prince was there for a personal reason. Maybe Amaury wanted Venus' help winning over a certain Satrian songstress.

Lyra, ever the peacemaker, turned to Amaury. Her eyes shimmered with remorse. "Will you forgive us, Your Highness?" she asked gently.

Amaury looked at her as if he had already forgotten their crime. "I suppose your intentions were innocent enough. I won't make mention of this to my father. But you three had better come with me; we'll all be late for dinner as it is."

They stalked out of the temple, unquestioned by the two guards nearby patrolling the gardens.

"Where is Nella?" Andrea anxiously asked Amaury.

"I'm afraid she had a fainting spell while walking through the gardens. Fortunately, the guards were there to see, and they helped her into the palace."

If Amaury had connected the two events in his mind, he didn't reveal it, perhaps because he had also taken the opportunity to enter the temple without prying eyes.

"I want to see her," Andrea said immediately.

"I'll send a servant," Amaury replied stiffly, still stewing over Lyra's unescorted visit.

Remo doubted that Amaury truly adhered to such rules of propriety. Nella had told scandalous stories of the affairs and raucous parties that took place within the Vecontiian court. Under Venus' tutelage, love, flirtation, and scandal thrived within the court of romance and poetry. Nella would undoubtedly dismiss any servant who came along with Andrea to allow them to talk in privacy.

Andrea discreetly took Lyra and Remo's things before leaving to see Nella and fill her in on the night's events. They entered the Great Hall for dinner seconds before the King and Queen's arrival. Nobody appeared to notice their absence, nor did they question their whereabouts during Nella's fainting spell.

Andrea apologized for his lateness after appearing during dinner, citing his desire to check on Nella after learning of her condition. That evening, Remo snuck into Andrea's room after struggling to find it with only a candlestick as his light through the expansive corridors. He knocked on the door once before Andrea swung it open.

"I told Nella the story. She doesn't seem to think there's any danger in Amaury finding us," Andrea explained, pacing the room as he filled Remo in on his conversation.

"That's a relief, although I can't say I was too concerned. He seemed to believe our story."

"Maybe. Or maybe he's waiting for the right moment to use it as leverage. He's not stupid."

Remo sighed, rubbing his eyes. "I'd prefer to believe he's just a handsome idiot."

"You'd do well to remember that he's Nella's brother and shares her acumen."

The comment reminded Remo of the tension between Amata and Nella earlier during their castle tour. He asked Andrea whether or not he had imagined the perceived strain between them.

"No, I'm afraid they do share some mutual hostility. You see, Nella resents her sister for being, well, more traditional and, therefore, receiving more approval from her parents despite her controversial past. And I think Amata resents Nella's independence on some level. Amata is two years older than Nella, making them the youngest siblings. The rest of Nella's siblings, aside from Amaury and Amata, are all off and married in other courts.

"Amaury stays here as heir, except when he's off sailing. Amata's scandal made her unmarriageable to other nobles. I think that's why Amaury got so tense about Lyra being alone with us—his sister's past left a mark."

Remo leaned forward, head in his hand, wordlessly urging Andrea on.

Andrea sighed. "We're becoming like two old gossiping hens."

Remo gasped in mock offense and countered, "I beg your pardon, sir. We are not gossiping. We're sharing information."

Andrea smirked and went on. "Amata fell for one of the palace guards. They carried on a secret affair for nearly a year before King Bardi found out. Out of mercy, the guard wasn't charged, but he accepted a bribe and vanished to another kingdom without a backward glance. To salvage her reputation, her parents hurried to marry her off to the suitor they'd arranged for her when she was twelve."

With an apologetic look, Andrea continued, "She was betrothed to Arlo Acerbi."

Blood swam through Remo's body, tensing for a fight at the mere mention of Acerbi's name. Remo steadied himself, trying to return his heart rate to a resting rhythm. "And naturally, she refused to marry his sorry ass?"

"She certainly had no love for him. She still mourned her relationship with the knight and didn't want Acerbi to marry her without knowing her past transgressions, feeling that a lie was a terrible way to start a marriage. She told Acerbi of her affair with the guard in the hopes that he would either extend the betrothal for a longer period, allowing her sufficient time to reconcile with the situation, or that he would break the arrangement entirely since she knew she could never love him.

"Arlo was furious that King Bardi tried to pass his 'ruined' daughter off on him. So he retaliated by spreading the scandal across the courts, destroying Amata's prospects. He called it justice, claiming the king humiliated him by hiding her past.

"Relations between Vecontii and Mavortis haven't been the same since, partly because of that and partly because of Mavortis's alignment with Saffiro. So now Amata's stuck here, unlikely to ever marry. Hence my wicked girlfriend's jab about her sister being an old maid."

Remo finally saw a piece of Acerbi's twisted logic. He'd been jilted by Amata for a man of lower station. Perhaps that explained why he'd been so eager to crush Remo and Sabelle's bond. But insight was not forgiveness. Acerbi's cruelty toward Rose, his threats, his manipulation—none of it could be excused.

The idea of Sabelle and Acerbi together sickened him more than ever. If Amata's scandal was too much for Acerbi, how hadn't he dropped Sabelle after learning of their relationship? Sabelle wasn't even nobility. It didn't make sense.

"Why didn't you tell me any of this before?" Remo demanded, uncertain why it would have mattered to him.

"Would it have changed anything, learning a story about a woman you didn't even know and her history with Acerbi? Would it have meant anything to you?" Andrea asked.

The answer was no to both questions. Remo supposed that the knowledge did nothing for him now, yet information about Acerbi's past felt like a safeguard against him.

Andrea clapped his hand on Remo's shoulder before a second knock was heard at the door. Nella let herself in, followed by Lyra. Now that they had accomplished the talismanic task, the four of them discussed the day's events and planned for the rest of their stay.

"I'm due to speak with King Bardi tomorrow afternoon. I doubt convincing him to lend roughly 20,000 soldiers to an exiled prince will be the work of one afternoon, but it will help me lay the groundwork for the Order's cause."

Remo noticed how tense Nella looked, perhaps resenting her relationship with Andrea being used as bait to lure her father into supporting the cause. But she seemed to be holding it together for the moment, dutifully playing her part for the Order.

"I suppose you two could use the rest of our time here enjoying the palace, smelling as many books as your strange little hearts desire," Nella said to Lyra and Remo, who looked enthralled by the prospect.

The next day, Remo took a quiet, contemplative walk through the winter woods beyond the palace. He wished to take advantage of his time in Vecontii by embracing the idyllic countryside around the palace. Mavortis didn't afford much in the way of nature, save for the outskirts of land around the dovecote entrance to the Academy and the public gardens in the Briar District.

The cold, clear winter air invigorated Remo as he ruminated over his present circumstance. He looked behind him at the white and light pink castle in the distance. The skinny, silver birch trees stood bare against the grey winter sky, threatening fresh snowfall. Remo spotted a doe in the distance, the scene bucolic.

Remo had acknowledged how far he'd come. He knew kings now, stayed in their palaces, and had come to expand his worldview and accept that there is a certain magic within the subtle energies of this world. More than that, his adventures with Andrea and Lyra had made him feel purposeful and alive. He mused that his waking life had become at least half as interesting as his beloved fantasy worlds.

But behind all the excitement lingered a faint discontent, a desire he didn't know how to sate. He feared it would follow him around for the rest of his life. Remo continued to ruminate over this unidentifiable feeling as he met Lyra and Amata in the library.

They planned to spend as much time as possible in the grand room before their time in Vecontii was over. They ate wild cherries preserved in syrup atop fresh snow as they browsed through books. A small smile gave way around Remo's lips as he witnessed Lyra's tangible pleasure at being surrounded by books and treats. He admired the contentment she took from both the smallest and greatest pleasures and remembered her humble upbringing.

He doubted she'd ever imagined anything so wonderful for herself while growing up in Satria and was certain she never took a moment of it for granted. Her head cocked at his faraway expression, and she asked him what was on his mind when Amata ventured to the other side of the library.

Of all the people he'd ever known, Remo thought Lyra might understand his obsession with fantasy and dissatisfaction with ordinary life. He expressed this to her, emphasizing that despite how much better he liked his life now, he sometimes still wished he could live within his fantasy worlds. With every nod of her head, Remo felt encouraged to continue, though self-conscious whenever he revealed a hidden part of himself.

"I understand how you feel," Lyra said. "I've wished the same. But the truth is, you carry yourself with you wherever you roam. You'd still be Remo with all of your problems, even in the backdrop of a fantasy world. You can't outrun your shadow. I love your idealism, but you mustn't let it trick you into believing satisfaction can be derived from our outside environment. I've learned from Awareness class that true contentment can only ever be found within. Nothing outside of yourself can fulfill you.

"I know this, and yet it's still so easy to get distracted by our longing for... well, whatever we want at the moment. Imagine achieving your wildest dreams—everything you've ever wanted is yours.

"And then what? You find something else to want. Its absence creates dissatisfaction, and the cycle begins again. Spend your life searching for fulfillment, and you'll miss what's already yours. Satisfaction begins with what you choose to see."

Lyra's words lifted something heavy from him. He couldn't explain why, but it felt more like the relief of being understood, and of understanding her, than the meaning of her words themselves.

"What are the odds that two minds so prone to escaping to other worlds could share so lovely a meeting in this strange place?" Remo mused.

Her mouth hooked up at the corner. "I don't know, but let's leave the numbers to others. I very much prefer words."

A servant arrived with marzipan cakes and tea, a sweet distraction from the anxious silence around Andrea's meeting with King Bardi. He wore the talisman under his clothes, and they could only hope Venus had heard their plea for diplomacy.

An hour before dinner, Remo and Lyra slipped into Andrea's room. Remo shot him a nervous look. "How'd it go?"

Andrea sighed, a weariness lining his face that set Remo on edge. "I'm not quite sure. He didn't flat-out refuse to lend support, for which I suppose we have the talisman to thank. I felt that the talisman helped me explain the situation to the best of my ability and that I made a great case for him.

"I mentioned how taking a firm stand against Saffiro would ensure that Vecontii could remain a strong force on the sea and a wealthy nation by preventing Saffiro from gaining any further power over them. I explained how we have the support of other nations and baited him with Nella potentially becoming Queen of Saffiro should I become emperor in the aftermath of a potential war.

"But Bardi is hesitant to lend his armada for the cause, let alone the numbers we'd need to equal Saffiro's. It's understandable. Saffiro is a close neighbor to Vecontii, and should Saffiro overpower our combined forces, it would mark Vecontii as an enemy and endanger them in future attacks. He said that we would discuss it more soon and that he'll give me a definitive answer before we leave."

Lyra fidgeted. "At least we'll know soon. But if he says no?"

With his hands behind his head, Andrea said, "Then Saffiro has the numbers to make any efforts the Order has prepared futile. Merucia and Anxur's numbers are insufficient against the estimated number of Knights of Saffiro in a potential battle. If Saffiro tries to up their presence in Anxur and invade sometime soon, I'm not sure there'd be enough numbers to stop them. Right now, the talisman is a hidden advantage. But should Vecontii refuse us men, the talisman would become our only hope of preventing another Calamity."

Lyra frowned, meeting Remo's concerned gaze. Andrea looked at his two friends guiltily before his expression hardened into self-loathing. He stood and walked to the window on the opposite side of the room, putting as much physical distance between himself and his friends as possible.

"Both of you would have been better off never meeting me. I'm sorry for entangling you in all of this. I won't blame either of you for walking away before it's too late."

In a cold, flat voice incongruent with the wounded look on Lyra's face, she commented, "Is that truly what you believe, even based on the circumstance of our meeting? I'd have been better off that night had I never met you?"

Andrea turned, the memory clearly haunting him. His eyes flicked to Remo, uncertain if he knew. He didn't realize Lyra had already shared that night with Remo, deep in the Forest of Numa.

"You act as though you forced us to join the Order. We volunteered, Andrea. With the agency I was given thanks to you, I chose to join the Order of Aquarius," Lyra said.

"As did I," Remo said. "Had I never met you, I probably would have died in those woods. I wouldn't exactly call that being 'better off.' We're standing beside you of our own free will. Or maybe it's our fate to do so. Either way, we're in this with you. Stop acting like we're your subjects forced to do your will; we're your friends. We're not involved in this just because of you. You're great, and we'd do anything for you, but this potential war will not be fought for your sake."

Andrea looked startled. For a heartbeat, the old royal glitter returned, sharp and defensive, as if Remo had overstepped. But then it dimmed, crumbled, and gave way to understanding. Remo recognized the tactic well. Andrea was looking for a way to blame and isolate himself.

Perhaps he grew afraid, though he'd never show it, that Lyra and Remo would decide that they resented him for dragging them into this political mess. So he'd try to reject them first, to suggest that they leave him so that when they inevitably did, they would take none of his power away from him. It would be a self-inflicted wound.

But Andrea appeared to accept that he didn't need to protect himself from his friends as they looked at him with as fierce a resolve as they did that evening in Cosimo's study when they decided to undertake this quest together. And despite his attempt to push them away, they stood alongside him.

Andrea's eyes watered with emotion, and Remo knew that the part of Andrea that was still whole, the part of him that his father had not yet managed to break, was shining through. Andrea wasn't quite crying, but it was a rare display of vulnerability. He nodded his head, seemingly unable to form words.

Lyra's brow furrowed as Remo crossed the room, tension carved into every step. His eyes burned, not with anger, but with the frustration of being shut out. Andrea braced, expecting a reprimand. Instead, Remo reached for him and pulled him into a solid, unyielding hug.

Andrea froze, as if uncertain how to receive the gesture. But Remo didn't let go. And slowly, Andrea's walls dropped. His hands came up in return, hesitant at first, then certain. He clung to Remo like someone who had forgotten what it meant to be held.

Across the room, Lyra watched them, her eyes soft. No words passed between them. None were needed.

Their week in Vecontii passed too quickly. Lyra and Remo read through three books each, spending long afternoons in the palace library. Andrea met often with Amaury to discuss political matters, while Nella drifted between groups, skillfully dodging her parents.

On their final Moon's Day, Amaury invited them to play a courtly game Remo barely understood involving glossy circle-shaped tiles in hues of pearl pink, turquoise, and mauve. Members of the Vecontii court lounged nearby, watching with detached amusement. A lovely young woman smiled coquettishly at Remo, but it only churned his stomach, his thoughts consisting only of Sabelle.

Offended by his disinterest, she redirected her attention toward Andrea, joining a growing number of women who had begun admiring the exiled prince from afar. Andrea's identity remained a closely guarded secret; word of his visit reaching Emperor Varro would be disastrous.

Nella hissed at one brazen courtier who stared a bit too long and intently for her liking. Remo thought that Lyra looked rather put out as well. Andrea, however, didn't appear to notice anyone outside of Nella and his circle of friends.

Upon the ending of one round, Remo sat out the next and warmed himself by the fire. He watched his friends from a distance, taking note of Amaury in particular. Remo felt he didn't have a good measure of the man yet and vowed to observe him closer during their last few days in Vecontii.

Nearby, he heard two courtiers whispering as they observed the game. "The prince appears attentive to her, but she's only a Satrian with no royal blood. They could never be matched; you would think his sister's scandal would have taught him that."

Remo's blood went cold. He kept his expression neutral, eyes fixed on the fire.

"The king is insistent that he finds a wife soon. If the rumors are true and war is near, Vecontii needs stronger ties to other kingdoms. The king must choose whose side he's on."

Another voice chimed in; he recognized it as the second woman who had tried to catch his eye earlier. "But I heard Prince Amaury refuses to marry. Evangeline said a servant overheard him and the king arguing again—probably about forcing him into an arranged match."

The memory of Amaury within Venus' temple flashed within Remo's mind. Perhaps Amaury's motivation for going to the temple was not to ask for Venus' help in courting Lyra, as Remo assumed, but to ask Venus for the freedom to choose whom he might marry.

That evening, as had become their routine, Remo slipped into Andrea's room to relay what he'd heard. Andrea listened, thoughtful.

"You might be onto something. I noticed his attention towards Lyra, but it was nothing more than his usual flirtation. He's always been a bit of a lover boy. He hasn't mentioned anything about his father wanting him to marry to secure Vecontii's ties with another kingdom. Perhaps I can broach the subject and learn something to our benefit," Andrea said.

"Like what?" Remo asked.

Andrea scratched his jaw. "I don't know. But if King Bardi is tempted by the thought of Nella potentially becoming the Queen of Saffiro, then perhaps Amaury would support that cause as well if he felt it would get his father off his own back when it comes to marrying for advantage."

"You think Amaury could help us sway the king?"

"Perhaps. But it wouldn't just be for selfish reasons. He's quite progressive, you know. He'd make a great ally; I enjoy our conversations. He asks thoughtful questions about the Academy and seems to desire changes in the world that his father resists. He's a bit older than me, and honestly, I learn from him. He's truly decent for a spoiled princeling."

"I knew that one day you'd replace me with someone richer and better-looking," Remo deadpanned.

Andrea smirked. "Replace you? Never. I need your earthy wisdom. It keeps me grounded in the world of the common folk," he said, a playful jab after enduring a week of Remo and Lyra's teasing about his royal upbringing.

"How gracious, Your Highness," Remo said with a theatrical bow. "Shall I wipe your ass before I go?"

With a shout that didn't cover his laughter, Andrea yelled an ungentlemanly suggestion of how Remo might occupy his time instead.

# Chapter Twenty-six

ON THEIR PENULTIMATE DAY in Vecontii, King Bardi told Andrea it was too dangerous to back the Order against Saffiro.

Andrea had done his best to push back, to make the king see that Vecontii's support could be the difference between victory and defeat. Nothing he said changed Bardi's mind, and now he sat in Remo's chamber, defeated, recounting the conversation.

"There was a skirmish," Andrea said. "Knights of Saffiro versus a rebel group in Anxur calling themselves the Light-Bringers."

Remo's heart twisted as he thought of his brother and mother, fearing for their safety. "Were there any deaths?"

"Twelve Anxurians. One Saffiran."

Remo's blood ran cold at the image of his little brother's body among the dead. He could almost hear his father's voice, sharp with judgment: *A real man wouldn't abandon his family to chase fantasies.* The sound faded only when a hand closed around his wrist—Andrea, grounding him.

"I'm sure your family is safe," Andrea said gently. "Write to them. Send a letter on one of the ships heading back; I'll cover the cost. And we'll go to Anxur when this is over. But the best way you can protect them now is by seeing the Order's mission through."

Remo exhaled, steadied. "Even without Bardi's support, it wasn't a wasted trip. The talisman carries Venus' blessing. That has to count for something."

Andrea groaned. "How do we know it even works? It didn't exactly charm Bardi."

Remo shared the worry. "Wear it today and tomorrow, just in case. A lot can change in a day."

Andrea followed his advice. After breakfast, Prince Amaury summoned them to his private office.

Remo admired the framed maps of Terramundi along the walls as Andrea sat opposite the Vecontiian prince's desk.

"What sort of business do you conduct within here, and how in Vesta's name do you get it done in such comfortable chairs?" Andrea asked, stretching out luxuriously.

Amaury leaned against his desk. "My father has me oversee much of the shipbuilding and communications with our merchants, on top of my duties within the armada. He might be the official commander of our fleets, but I'm the one who leads them. That said, I called you here for something else."

Remo's head snapped up; Andrea straightened. Amaury gestured for Remo to sit and circled behind his desk.

Sunlight poured through the window, casting a golden halo around Amaury as his tone turned severe. "What were you really doing in Venus' temple?"

They froze. Amaury stared them down. Remo didn't wait for Andrea's lead. "I told you—relationship trouble, I needed Venus' help—"

"Cut the bullshit," Amaury snapped.

Andrea raised an eyebrow. "Your time with the men of the armada has colored your tongue, Your Highness."

Amaury's gaze sharpened. "And Mavortis has made you forget your place. You may act the outcast, but you're still the emperor's son whether you like it or not."

Andrea cringed as Amaury addressed him, which the Vecontiian prince noticed.

"You say you want to be restored in Saffiro, yet bristle when addressed as royalty. You claim to oppose your father, but you hate the idea of being emperor. Still, you ask my father for support and tempt him with the prospect of my sister as your queen. So tell me: what is it you really want, Andrea? And why do you need a magician to get it?"

Remo's heart hammered with the weight of the accusations against him and Andrea. Despite this, Remo might've laughed at being referred to as a magician if the stakes hadn't felt so high.

Andrea responded through gritted teeth, "I won't deny that I hate the idea of being emperor. That I hate my father, and I want nothing to do with him. But do you know what I hate more? I hate the violence and abuse the rest of Terramundi suffers under my father's rule. I hate the people who stand by and watch it happen because it doesn't affect them. And I would count myself as one of them if I hid away in Mavortis for the rest of my life, doing nothing with my hatred but letting it fester within me instead of letting it push me to change something about this fucked up world."

All defensiveness fell from Amaury's expression as he regarded Andrea. "I admire that," Amaury said. "You'd sacrifice your will for peace. I won't even marry for my kingdom's sake. That's why I went to the temple. I asked Venus for a future where I could marry for love, if at all. But you'd give your life for Terramundi, even against the empire that cast you out."

"My father exiled me. Not Saffiro," Andrea corrected, the distinction seeming important to him.

Amaury ran a hand through his wavy blonde hair. "You're a good man, Andrea. And you'd make a just leader. I sympathize with your vision for a new Terramundi—a more tolerant world. I know my father denied your request for help should war reach Anxur, but I've been arguing with him about it.

"Our kingdom is divided. Some believe we should side with Saffiro, whether we like it or not, and trade away part of our resources for the security they offer. It would be the safer choice, though it would cost us our pride and possibly our economy. The alternative is to risk standing with the other kingdoms against Emperor Varro. If the collective defense fails, we'll be marked as enemies of Saffiro and face retaliation. But if it succeeds, we'll emerge as an independent power, without sacrificing any of our resources.

"As you know, I trained with our armada and have friends who could aid you, should you require greater numbers. It would be a gamble. I couldn't provide as many men as my father commands. But there are some loyal to me who would support your cause on my word alone.

"My father is a decent man with a mild temperament, concerned only with the safety of his kingdom. But some say he's too mild, too hesitant to stand up to Varro. He never served with the fleets as I have; he never spent time among the men, earning their respect. I'm confident I could rally at least 5,000 who would fight for the cause, even if it meant defying my father's will."

Remo and Andrea exchanged a significant look. Andrea turned to Amaury, stunned. "You'd go behind your father's back to protect Anxur?"

Amaury nodded, his mouth set in a grim line. "I'll keep trying to sway him. But if he won't act, I will. Consequences be damned. It will be us, and the generations after us, who have to live in this world when our fathers are dead. Therefore, I think the people who can do something to improve it should."

Andrea voiced his agreement, eyes full of admiration for the Vecontiian prince. He extended his hand to shake on their agreement, but Amaury stared at it, something weighing on his mind.

"Before I commit, I need to hear the truth," Amaury said. "I told you why I went into Venus' temple. Now I want your reason if I'm to trust you."

Andrea leaned back, met Remo's eye, and gave a small nod. If Amaury was going to be their ally, he deserved the truth of the Order's talisman quest—especially since they still had no plan for getting inside the Sun's temple. When Remo finished, Prince Amaury looked like he needed a large goblet of Vecontii's strongest wine.

"How, in the name of Venus' tits, do you plan on getting into the Sun's temple without notice?" Amaury asked, incredulous.

"You know, if I were Venus, I'd think twice before helping someone who profaned my divine décolletage," Andrea chided in a holier-than-thou tone.

Prince Amaury rolled his eyes. "In the name of Mars' ballsack, then. Do *either* of you have a plan?"

Remo and Andrea looked at one another helplessly. "We were sort of waiting for one to come to us," Remo admitted. "The sun goes into its degree of exaltation—19 degrees Aries—on March 31st. We have little over a month to figure out a plan before we have to begin traveling to Saffiro."

"Your father wouldn't even spare a handful of men," Andrea added. "Not that I blame him. I gave him no details; he looked suspicious enough already."

"Who wouldn't be? You're lucky he didn't arrest you for asking. You'll be in chains before you set foot in Saffiro," Amaury said.

"We're asking for help," Andrea muttered. "Not confirmation that we're doomed."

Amaury rolled up his sleeves, looking like he had already regretted involving himself. "Then we had better start planning."

Before they left Vecontii, Remo wrote a letter to his family, as Andrea suggested. Since he wouldn't have time to do so himself, Remo entrusted the letter and denarii to a servant who would take them to a ship headed to Anxur.

Nella's enthusiasm to leave her family behind was equal to Lyra's regret that they couldn't stay longer. Lyra and Amata became fast friends, and the latter promised to host a ball the next time Lyra should visit.

Amaury bowed to Lyra, who returned the gesture. "Whenever such a ball occurs, I hope you'll save a dance for me."

Lyra's answering smile did not match the hesitation in her eyes. "It would be my honor, Your Highness.

Remo realized something then. Lyra was never hesitant about touch around Nella. But with him and Andrea, even a fleeting brush seemed to pass through a moment of thought first, as though she were deciding whether it was safe.

King Bardi and Queen Maddalena, who came into the entrance hall to bid their guests farewell, distracted Remo from his thoughts. They thanked the king and queen for their hospitality and generosity. Amaury and Andrea shook hands, the unspoken understanding between the men's eyes that they would be in contact again soon.

They were silent in the carriage, each lost in their thoughts. Without Order business or books to distract him, Remo's mind once again drifted to Sabelle, wondering what would be left of their courtship upon his return. He would prefer to linger in the uncertainty, far removed from the situation, than be confronted with its reality. He felt powerless, as though he were headed towards his sentencing, as though Sabelle held all the power of his happiness within her hands.

After ten quiet days, they finally reached Mavortis and immediately visited The Crooked Cupola. Sevo greeted them and directed them below to Cosimo, Remo safeguarding the talisman. When Remo entered the Academy for the first time in weeks, he felt as if he had returned home.

Cosimo looked up from his desk, smiling warmly. "Good to see you all again—and always a pleasure, Miss Valentia." He bowed slightly.

Nella returned the gesture. "Likewise."

Remo handed the talisman to Cosimo, who closed his eyes, appearing to heighten his senses as he grasped the magical object. "Tell me—was Venus' temple as beautiful as described in old texts?"

"It was," Lyra admitted. "Nella's family has taken good care of it."

Nella nodded. "The Valentias have looked after the temple throughout the ages, even after the Old Religion died away. I was surprised by the presence of guards, however. I've been away from Vecontii for years, but I can't say I ever remember the temple being guarded."

"Strange indeed," Cosimo said, a shadow of worry crossing his usually unreadable eyes. "Did you learn whether that is a relatively new practice or if it started in recent years?"

Nella said she wasn't certain, and Andrea echoed her reply.

"We didn't think it wise to ask," Andrea said apologetically. "I feared I would draw attention to my curiosity surrounding it."

"Well-reasoned. I'm sure it's nothing to worry about, likely just a preservation effort," Cosimo reassured. "And as far as the talisman is concerned, the ritual went well?"

"Yes," Remo answered this time, unable to keep from glancing at Lyra, the memory of her singing during the ritual vivid in his mind.

Lyra caught his gaze and offered a shy smile before quickly looking away, possibly recalling the intensity of his stare.

Cosimo nodded, his expression brightening noticeably before returning the talisman to Remo, who regarded him with confusion. "I want you to hold onto the talisman for now. Keep it safe within your bag, along with this." He extended a sunstone toward Remo—the final precious gem needed for the talisman.

Perplexed, Remo accepted both items and carefully stored them away. Cosimo then turned his attention to Andrea. "And how did your conversations go with King Bardi?"

Andrea looked as curious as Remo felt but did not comment on the unusual exchange, shifting his focus back to Cosimo. "Not well. He declined to assist Anxur and the Order should war erupt. I assume news of the skirmish reached you?"

Cosimo inclined his head solemnly, prompting Andrea to continue. "King Bardi was unsettled by it, wary of what it signifies regarding Saffiro's power. Fortunately, Prince Amaury seems sympathetic to our cause. He pledged to aid us in reaching Saffiro's temple and promised to commit 5,000 soldiers if war breaks out."

Cosimo's eyes glittered with intrigue as he shifted his gaze to Nella. "Your brother has the authority to promise troops without your father's approval?"

Nella laughed bitterly. "The rules are different for men, it seems. My brother might openly defy my father and receive praise, yet I can't even pursue an education without becoming the family pariah. But yes—I trust my brother's word. He trained with Vecontii's fleets and holds influence there. They'd follow him before my father, who never served."

Cosimo's expression grew thoughtful, his mind visibly working to process this information. "Yes, yes, this is good," he murmured, seemingly to himself more than the others. "It just shows that we cannot dictate precisely how desired outcomes occur. We must remain open to the myriad ways our wishes might manifest. Once we define our desires, the universe arranges the rest."

Nella nearly rolled her eyes, while Lyra seemed inspired. Remo smiled slightly, familiar with his position somewhere between their reactions.

Their business concluded, they returned to their homes, the Order's payment more than compensating for missed work.

Entering his room, Remo's gaze locked onto an envelope by his door, yellowed parchment stark against the terracotta tiles. His heart raced, breath catching as the drifting dust mocked the turmoil inside him. After a long, frozen moment, he finally found the courage to bend and rip it open.

*Remo,*

*It took me forever to decide how to address you in this letter before settling on just your name. I can no longer call you "my," nor can I pretend you're "dear" to me anymore.*

*I don't know what to believe about your trip; your secrecy leaves me no choice but to make my own assumptions.*

*Your dishonesty about your actions suggests you've lied about Arlo as well. Clearly, you invented his threats to keep us apart. I've accepted his proposal—you've pushed me into his arms. I'm sure you'll find comfort crying on Lyra's shoulder.*

*Even if you return titled, Arlo would still outrank you in every manner. Leave me alone. I don't want to see you again.*

*No longer yours,*
*Sabelle*

Remo stared numbly at the letter, grief overwhelming him beyond the reach of tears. He felt lifeless inside as he clung to the last fragment of Sabelle he'd ever hold.

It was nearly noon, and Remo still hadn't left his room. He had an Astrology lesson later but couldn't summon the strength to face anyone before then. A loud knock startled him. Remo opened the door to

Andrea, whose eyes narrowed in immediate concern.

"Were you sleeping?" Andrea demanded, carefully analyzing his friend's sunken, exhausted eyes.

"No. Hardly slept at all." Remo handed him the letter. Andrea read it twice, anger evident on his face as he processed Sabelle's words.

"Remo, I'm sorry," Andrea said gently. "But consider this a mercy—she's gone. She's caused you nothing but grief, and the second things got difficult, she ran back to Acerbi."

Part of Remo wanted to, and indeed did, agree with Andrea, but he couldn't shake the feeling of responsibility. He blamed himself, echoing Sabelle's accusations internally. "If I had been honest with her about the Order, perhaps none of this would've happened."

Andrea now looked exasperated, frustrated with Remo rather than sympathetic. "You can't seriously believe her manipulative nonsense. She jumped to the worst conclusions about you, and you're convinced she deserves honesty after how she's treated you?"

"Your lies to Nella about the Order initially caused trouble between you," Remo pointed out. "Maybe honesty would help—"

"It's different between Nella and me," Andrea snapped defensively.

Remo's gaze hardened slightly. "How?"

"For one, Nella's father is already aware of the Order, and I knew I could trust Nella implicitly with the truth. But Sabelle—her feelings for you aren't even certain. Revealing our mission to her would put the entire Order at risk, jeopardizing everything we've worked for. I can't let you do it, Remo."

Remo felt as if he were being dragged out to sea in the midst of a relentless storm, utterly powerless to change his circumstances. He had lost any hope of convincing Sabelle of his true intentions; fighting against the inevitable was futile.

Glancing at the letter again, he slowly nodded. Andrea visibly relaxed at Remo's silent acknowledgment.

"I'm sorry," Andrea murmured softly, sincerity filling his voice.

Remo merely tilted his head again, unable to speak. He turned towards the window, away from Andrea.

Andrea hesitated briefly, as though wanting to say more, but eventually left, shutting the door softly. Remo wished he could similarly shut out the overwhelming grief that threatened to consume him.

A week after receiving Sabelle's letter, Remo remained withdrawn. Andrea and Lyra had respectfully kept their distance, understanding his need for solitude.

That morning, tapping at his window startled Remo awake. He rose groggily, threw on his shirt, and saw Turi, Lyra's messenger pigeon, outside. Opening the window, he allowed Turi in and removed the tiny note from his leg. It read simply: *Happy Birthday, Remo!*

He'd forgotten entirely. Glancing at Lyra's window, he saw her excitedly waving, her enthusiasm coaxing his first smile in days.

"Thank you, Lyra!"

"Meet Andrea and me at The Crooked Cupola for lunch later!" Lyra commanded cheerfully, leaving no opportunity for him to object.

Although Remo still felt the urge to wallow in self-pity, he couldn't deny how touched he was by his friends' persistence and care.

"I'll be there," he promised. Turi flew back to Lyra, who lovingly stroked him.

Later, at their usual table in The Crooked Cupola, Andrea handed Remo a small box, smiling tentatively. "Happy Birthday, Remo."

"Thanks, brother," Remo said, his answering grin sincere.

"This is from both of us. Lyra thought it up, and I helped make it."

Despite his recent gloom, Remo felt genuinely moved at receiving his first-ever birthday gift. Inside the box was an ornamentally carved wand made from pale, finely detailed wood set atop a silver handle, embedded with a luminous blue stone. It was unmistakably inspired by the wand wielded by the wizard in Remo's favorite book, *Milena and Devlan*.

Remo lifted his gaze to Lyra, aware that she must have drawn inspiration from the novel he had recommended to her. "I can't believe you thought of this," he said, laughing softly in disbelief as he admired the beautiful craftsmanship. "Thank you both—truly."

Lyra positively glowed at his reaction. "That's how your Saturnalia gift made me feel. We wanted you to experience that, too."

Still, Remo felt uneasy, guilty even, as if unworthy of their thoughtful effort.

"I already treasure it," Remo said, still examining its delicate features.

"It's also a practical gift," Andrea joked, snatching the wand and waving it dramatically toward the bar, mumbling nonsense words. Moments later, Sevo appeared with their lunch. Andrea looked theatrically astonished at the supposed results of his magical display.

Lyra laughed until tears formed in her eyes, and Remo joined her. Leaning toward Andrea, Remo teased softly, "Clearly, those Alchemy lessons are paying off. Who knew we had a real sorcerer among us?"

Throughout the day, Andrea kept up the playful act, each mock spell funnier than the last, bringing continuous laughter.

Remo placed the wand on his desk, appreciating it daily not just for its beauty or the story it represented, but for the reminder of the friends who had lovingly crafted it.

# Chapter Twenty-seven

E ACH MORNING BEGAN THE same for Remo. He would awaken far
too early, disturbed by a lingering sense of dread.

Inevitably, the source of this haunting would crystallize into the image
of Sabelle, beautiful and imperious. *Leave me alone. I don't want to see
you again.*

He took long, aimless walks around Mavortis to escape his tormenting
thoughts, though they always managed to keep pace. His only relief
came from intense physical training with Andrea several times weekly,
welcoming the distraction pain offered. If not for the Salii and Knights of
Saffiro who frequented Mavortis' infamous underground fighting pits,
he might have even considered joining.

Remo endlessly replayed every scenario with Sabelle, obsessively
questioning if he'd done enough. Her blame cut deeply, and her im-
pending marriage to Acerbi filled him with disgust and concern. He
wondered if knowing Acerbi's true cruelty, especially towards women,
would change her mind.

Yet Remo had warned her already, told her Acerbi had threatened
him, and it hadn't mattered. Revealing the full truth meant endangering
the Order, something he could never justify. Each day brought the same
painful realization. Nothing he revealed would ever make him enough
for her.

When not attending Astrology classes or studying in the Academy
library, Remo kept busy by finalizing plans for the talisman ritual in
Saffiro. On the first of March, after wandering Mavortis for hours, he
returned to the Academy through the eastern alleyway, determined to

spend another afternoon in the library, futilely trying to silence the anxious thoughts that never left him.

Perhaps it was the weather. Remo's already bleak mood deepened beneath the overcast sky. Determined to push past his discomfort, he pressed forward through the narrow street toward the Academy entrance, though his stomach twisted painfully with every step, urging him to turn back.

The Academy was unsettlingly silent, the usual murmur of students absent from the empty halls. Remo paused, straining to hear something, anything. His stomach tightened with instinctive fear. *Run,* it seemed to plead. *Turn around.* He brushed it off as paranoia; logic told him he had no reason to be afraid.

But at the hallway's end, Remo froze, a chill seizing him as Arlo Acerbi's voice sliced through the silence. "Tie him."

Two Salii soldiers seized Remo from behind. He fought back, striking one and nearly escaping before the other soldier slammed him to the stone floor, securing his wrists tightly behind him. With difficulty, they tied Remo firmly to a chair, trapping him helplessly. Acerbi stood by, smiling smugly, savoring Remo's futile struggle as he strained against his bindings.

Acerbi laughed mockingly, approaching with arrogant satisfaction. "Today's lesson won't be the one you planned."

He leaned closer, eyes gleaming with cruel delight. "I don't even have to invent your crime this time. Your occult studies already mark you guilty. You disgrace your profession as a healer."

Remo remained defiantly silent, seething with hatred, refusing to respond to Acerbi's taunting words.

"As a physician, my oath to do no harm prevents me from torturing you personally, so others will handle that after your imprisonment. Consider yourself lucky for now; you'll soon spend the rest of your life in darkness." Acerbi glanced at his two soldiers. "Though perhaps I should have had you properly killed last time."

Remo recognized one soldier immediately by his scar—the same man who'd attacked him, Lyra, and Andrea in the Forest of Numa. Acerbi's words confirmed his suspicion that these men had also been responsible for breaking his ribs.

Remo cursed himself silently. "How long have your men been following me?"

"Has your simple Anxurian mind finally caught up? I sent them to secretly follow Sabelle soon after she arrived—for her own protection, naturally. Since they were dressed as Saffiran guards, she assumed her father had sent them.

"When they reported she'd started meeting someone secretly, my curiosity was piqued. Imagine my disgust upon seeing you holding hands with her, until she pulled away in shame."

Acerbi openly relished the memory. "At least she had the decency to be embarrassed about being seen with you. I could hardly believe you were the one she'd stooped to meeting."

Acerbi's words stabbed Remo deeper than a physical blow. She had been ashamed of him. He masked his hurt, forcing neutrality onto his face.

"Once she confessed her misguided feelings for you, it was easy to encourage her doubts," Acerbi continued smugly. "I hinted you weren't loyal, perhaps seeing other women." His cruel smile widened.

Fury surged through Remo, realizing how Acerbi's lies had poisoned Sabelle's trust. At least this explained her mistrust better than a mere tarocchi card reading.

"It was almost too easy to turn Sabelle against you. All I had to do was suggest what she was already afraid to admit—that you seemed a little too taken with that Satrian girl always at your side. Pretty, I'll admit. Nearly on par with Sabelle in looks, though easily replaced. That kind always is. Sabelle may not have noble blood, but she carries herself like someone who matters. Not like the kind of women you gravitate toward at work. The broken ones. The used ones. Makes a man wonder if it's pity that draws you in... or preference."

Remo thrashed against his bonds, overtaken by a primal urge to tear out Acerbi's throat.

"Sabelle accepted the doubt I planted with remarkable ease," Acerbi said. "So much so, it was *her* idea to have you followed, before I even knew your name."

Remo's breath caught, his lungs seizing with disbelief. A sick part of him almost laughed at the irony. Sabelle had feared betrayal based on the warning of her tarocchi cards, yet in the end, she had betrayed *him*. She had put more trust in her divinations than in the person who loved her, and in doing so, she had fulfilled the very fate she feared. Acerbi might have been lying, but Sabelle's recent behavior made his account disturbingly believable.

"She didn't know you were doing more than breaking her heart; you were breaking the law. My men tracked your movements, noted your visits to that revolting little inn you and your friends adore."

Remo remembered Andrea's warning months ago—two Knights of Saffiro had visited The Crooked Cupola. It had been them. It had always been them.

"Then came your laughable excuse about visiting a 'sick relative' in Merucia. I nearly dismissed you for abandoning your duties, but curiosity won out. I never believed you. I kept Sabelle in the dark; she'd have warned you. I had my men pose as Knights of Saffiro to move freely beyond Mavortis, avoiding any ties to my family's command over the Salii.

"Of course, they were idiots and lost you more than once. Fortunately, they spotted you heading to Lunaria a month later. They watched you enter the Moon's temple—not illegal, not yet. But when they saw the offerings you left behind, even *they* realized something occult was happening. They tried to arrest you. Somehow, you got the better of them, likely thanks to Andrea."

Remo's head snapped toward Acerbi at the mention of Andrea's name.

"Oh yes, I know your friend is the exiled prince of Saffiro. He won't face consequences, of course. Not with Mavortis and Saffiro allied. Arresting the emperor's disgrace of a son would offend the wrong people. And my family values its place."

His grin widened. "I did inform my father, though. He's warned the other kingdoms to guard their temples. But here's the best part: had Sabelle known from the start that you practiced magic, she wouldn't have minded. Ever wonder why her father, a *Saffiran* Senator, was in

Mavortis for so long?"

Remo had. He'd asked her, and she'd brushed it off, pretending not to know. He kept his eyes away from Acerbi, who was clearly savoring the moment as he laughed.

"Seems you star-crossed lovers were both keeping secrets. She lied. Her father wasn't here. The business trip was a cover. *She's* the one here on business as Mavortis' Court Witch, my father's personal occultist. She's well-versed in all manner of arcane knowledge. I daresay you two may even share a few interests," Acerbi added, casting a knowing glance at the symbols above the archways.

"You'll rot for the same crimes she'll be praised for. That's what happens when commoners taste forbidden knowledge. You start thinking it means something. That *you* mean something. But you were born in the dirt, and you'll die in it. Sabelle will forget you soon enough."

Despite the rush of his heartbeat, time slowed for Remo. *Sabelle practiced witchcraft.*

His first instinct was denial. Acerbi must be lying. But then came the memories, the way she used her tarocchi, her strange reaction to the new deck. He'd misunderstood. She hadn't meant she lacked one, just that she didn't have it *with* her. She'd been practicing all along. And she'd kept it from him.

He couldn't forget the way Sabelle had looked at Lyra, or how Lyra had fallen sick moments later. If witchcraft meant bending reality to one's will, then yes, Remo could believe it. It was a darker shade of Awareness, really.

Other memories rushed in now, casting old conversations in a new light. Sabelle had once said her brother feared her. He now doubted she'd been joking. It even explained why Acerbi hadn't touched her after discovering their affair. He must fear her power. For him to propose beneath his station, she had to be formidable.

"Why would the King of Mavortis need a witch?" Remo asked, his voice rough. "And why would Varro approve?"

They were the only questions he could manage. He couldn't bear to ask another thing about Sabelle. But if the Acerbis had an interest in the arcane, the Order would want to know—if he ever got the chance to tell them.

Arlo froze mid-step, the flicker in his eyes betraying the crack in his composure. Remo's question had struck a nerve. In his eagerness to gloat about Sabelle, Acerbi had let something slip, and he knew it.

"You've no right to ask about your betters," Arlo snapped. "I should slit your throat just for that. But it's a harsher sentence to leave you rotting in prison, knowing I'm free... and bedding the woman you love."

Remo spat near his feet. "Fuck you."

Arlo's eyes flashed, but he recovered quickly, his sneer returning. "You'll die with the rest of the scum. Take him away."

The guards cut him loose and shoved him into the alley. He stumbled, hitting the stone and slicing his cheek as they dragged him from the Academy.

# Chapter Twenty-eight

I F TIME WAS WHAT separated one moment from the next, then Remo's cell seemed to exist outside of it, each moment unchanging, except for when the pain returned.

He didn't know how long it had been since they'd dragged him away from the Academy. There was no trial, only a sentence: guilty of practicing magic.

Even under torture by the Knights of Saffiro stationed in Mavortis, Remo said nothing. He refused to reveal which subject he had studied at the Academy, much less anything that could endanger the lives of his friends or the Order of Aquarius.

He'd known sorrow before, but the Mavortian prison taught him a new kind of torment. Whippings split open his back. They pulled out his nails. Through it all, he thought of Andrea. Of Lyra. He held onto their memory like lifelines.

His wounds were too deep to heal. As a healer, he knew infection would follow—and death, unless they found a crueler end for him first. He tried to use awareness techniques to block the pain, but they failed him. He thought of the path that led him here. He thought of Anxur, of the quiet life he used to lead, his only adventures once found in books.

And yet, even with death looming close, Remo didn't regret the choices that had led him to this cell. His life in Anxur wouldn't have lasted. The empire would've come for his homeland, one way or another. Danger was always coming. But more than that, he had met Andrea and Lyra. Friends he hadn't dared to dream of. People who made the pain worth it.

Before Andrea and Lyra, Remo had never known real friendship. It was the one thing in his life that surpassed even the stories in his beloved books. A bitter smile, closer to a grimace, tugged at his lips as he thought of them, the expression an act of defiance against the pain flooding his body. How poetic, he thought, to be willing to die for the very people who had finally made his life worth living.

No, Remo decided—he had no regrets. Not a single action leading to this moment would he take back. Even if the Knights of Saffiro never reached Anxur, he knew the dissatisfaction he'd felt gnawing at him last year would have devoured him eventually.

That unrest would have hollowed him out, stripped away the part of him that longed to shape the world, and left behind only a husk, a man who lived out a life of convention, doing what was expected, smothering his soul's craving for freedom. Better to die wounded and free than live as a polished lie. Remo felt he could die contentedly with the knowledge that he had, at least for a time, truly *lived*.

His battered body dulled his care for anything outside himself, silencing the questions stirring in the back of his mind. Something lingered—some forgotten thought, some dim knowing about Saffiro's deeper intentions—but he couldn't bring himself to care. Not while his back was torn open and blood seeped into the stone floor.

He thought of Jupiter, his daemon. Where was his guardian now? Maybe Jupiter had never been real, just a fever dream from the lotus tea. He tried to summon the daemon, but his pain drowned the effort.

He didn't know when sleep took him, only that it did, until the harsh clang of the cell door jolted him awake. Two Knights of Saffiro stood above him. For a moment, his heart plummeted in dread, unsure if he could survive more torture. Then one of them removed his helmet, and Andrea's face came into view. For a moment, Remo thought it was another hallucination.

"We're getting you out of here, Remo," Andrea said, firm and steady.

Remo nearly wept. The second knight, face still hidden behind his helmet, helped Remo into a third set of armor. The shirt beneath it clung to his shredded back, and the metal cut deeper with every move. Still, he forced himself upright.

"Hang in there, brother. We've got to move," Andrea whispered, supporting him.

The second knight led them forward while Andrea stayed close, supporting him. Remo clenched his jaw against the instinct to groan with every step, the movement slicing deeper into the welts across his back.

As they passed other guards patrolling the corridor, Remo prayed none would look too closely. The endless stretch of the damp prison finally gave way to a door. Two guards stood post.

One stepped forward. "Where do you think you're going? Shift just started. Who's on your post?"

Without hesitation, the second knight struck the questioning guard with the blunt end of his lance. Andrea felled the second with a swift punch. One scrambled up, shouting, "Imposters! Help!" as he drew his sword.

Remo's hand found a weapon at his belt. He drew it and fought, moving on instinct. Andrea intercepted the lunging blade of the lance-wielding guard, shielding their companion. Remo struck his opponent down again with all the desperation of a man who had nothing left to lose.

They didn't wait to see if more were coming. They ran, and they didn't look back. When they finally mounted horses and the chase fell behind them, Remo's pain surged, blinding and unbearable. The armor bit into his wounds with every gallop. He felt himself slipping, but Andrea's voice kept him tethered.

"Almost there, Remo. Just a little longer."

They reached a stretch of unfamiliar shoreline and dismounted their horses. Remo's eyes moved from the small rowboat waiting on the sand to the enormous ship anchored in the distance, its silhouette steady on the horizon. He turned just as the identity of his second rescuer was revealed; Amaury's blond hair tumbled free as he pulled off his helmet and tossed it into the boat.

Without speaking, he and Andrea pushed the vessel into the surf. Remo followed, dragging his aching body forward. They climbed in and began to row toward what was presumably Amaury's ship. Summoning the last of his strength, Remo hauled himself up the rope ladder and collapsed the moment he hit the deck. He didn't move. He didn't need to. He was safe now, and with that knowledge, he surrendered to unconsciousness. When he woke, the first thing he felt was the sharp sting of his wounds beneath fresh bandages.

"He's waking," said a soft, hopeful voice.

Remo forced his eyes open and found Andrea and Lyra at his side. For a moment, the image felt too peaceful to be real, like something his soul had conjured in death to ease the passage. But then Andrea smiled, and Lyra's tear-stained face came into focus. He blinked and smiled back. He was alive—and so were they.

Lyra eyes were swollen with tears. Andrea beamed, his winning smile as reassuring as the first time Remo saw it.

Remo groaned as he tried to sit up. Lyra rushed to help. "Thanks," he murmured, voice hoarse.

"Drink," Lyra whispered, offering water. He drank slowly, eyes closing as the cool liquid soothed his throat.

"How are you feeling?" Lyra asked, the question more comforting than any answer he could give.

"Like hell. But grateful." He paused, then added, "Who cleaned my wounds?"

"Nella. She's above deck with her brother. She said you'll heal just fine. By some miracle, you escaped infection. Your back will scar, but your fingernails will grow back. You'll mend."

Remo nodded, relieved to once again be in the care of Nella's capable hands, though he couldn't help but feel self-conscious about the weakened, scarred state of his body.

"How did you find me?"

Andrea looked to Lyra. She hesitated, then gave a small nod. Turning back to Remo, Andrea's tone was quiet, almost apologetic.

"For what it's worth... Sabelle came to our quarters to warn you. You were already gone. She found me instead. Said she thought you were in danger, and that it was her fault."

Remo's expression darkened. So she had felt guilty. "She wanted Acerbi to spy on me, even if he already was the moment he found out she was seeing someone. The two 'Knights of Saffiro' we ran into in the Forest of Numa? They were Salii soldiers Acerbi had on my trail. Same men Sevo saw at The Crooked Cupola. Same ones who attacked me. That's how they learned about the Academy."

His stomach dropped. "Shit. They *know* about the Academy. Were others arrested? Did they destroy it?"

Andrea's eyes were downcast. "They arrested Cosimo before you. No one dared return to the Academy after that; we figured it was crawling with Knights of Saffiro. But it looks like they didn't discover the Cupola entrance. I warned Sevo, and he sealed it off, spreading the word not to enter the school.

"We tried to rescue Cosimo too," Andrea added. "His cell was one floor above yours. But he wouldn't come. Said he'd slow us down, that more people escaping would raise suspicion. He told us to leave him behind. Didn't say what we were supposed to wait *for*. Just that he'd be in touch—something about prison being fitting due to some twelfth-house astrology thing. He said he'd communicate with Lyra if anything important came up. That's how we even knew he'd been arrested. That's how we warned the others. But we couldn't find *you* in time."

Remo explained his morning walk. He laughed grimly. "Twelfth house rules prison. The old codger was making astrology jokes while you were trying to rescue him." He turned to Lyra. "Has he actually communicated with you? How?"

"In the astral realm," Lyra said. "He showed me his memories—the prison's layout, your exact location. I don't know how he knew where you were. Maybe he overheard the guards talking, or maybe he left his body and explored the prison himself. He's a master of Awareness, after all. He can do things most of us can't begin to understand. When I came out of the trance, I drew the map he showed me and wrote down everything he told me. That's how Andrea and Amaury were able to find you."

"But how did Amaury get involved?"

"That was Lyra's quick thinking too," Andrea said. "I went to her after Sabelle showed up and warned me. I'd barely finished explaining when she grabbed a quill, scribbled a letter, and tied it to a bottle on Turi's back. Instead of waiting to meet us in Saffiro, Amaury left immediately with only a few trusted men."

Remo's heart dropped. "The talisman—do we still have it? What day is it?"

Lyra lifted a hand to calm him. "We have the talisman. And the sunstone. They're safe in your bag. We're headed for Saffiro now. We'll reach there in little over a week. We'll arrive a day or two before the ritual."

"I never collected the sunthemata. We'll need objects for the invocation," Remo said.

"We'll find them," Lyra assured him. "You don't need to worry about any of that right now. You've been through too much." Her golden eyes shone with gentle concern as she reached out and brushed a strand of hair from his face.

He closed his eyes at her touch. He couldn't remember being touched like that before—soothingly, without expectation. Part of him wanted to lean into her palm. As if she sensed it, her fingers drifted along the rough stubble on his jaw.

"A beard suits you," she murmured, her thumb drifting across his cheek with curiosity.

Andrea coughed lightly. Remo opened his eyes, but Lyra didn't look away. Andrea stood as though he were about to dismiss himself.

"Wait—don't go," Remo said. "I still have questions. I'm fine."

He groaned as he sat straighter, betraying the lie.

Andrea hesitated, and Lyra stood as if shaken from a trance. She brushed past him on her way to the door. "We'll be here when you wake. Rest now."

When Remo woke again, he felt more rested than he had in weeks.

A dull, persistent sensation pawed at the edge of his consciousness, like something important knocking from behind a wall in his mind. He sat up slowly, sorting through his earlier conversation with Andrea and Lyra—Cosimo, the Academy, the talisman, Sabelle...

Sabelle. She had betrayed him, deliberately or not, and then sealed it by accepting Acerbi's proposal. Whatever he was trying to recall, it had to do with her. Would he ever get to hear the truth from her lips?

Then it came to him. Remo shot upright, ignoring the jolt of pain. He fumbled his way through the dark, climbing toward the deck above. Each step burned, but urgency propelled him. When he reached the top, he spotted Lyra, Nella, Andrea, and Amaury mid-discussion.

Lyra saw him first. "What are you doing out of bed?"

"I remembered something. Acerbi said Sabelle was in Mavortis to perform witchcraft for King Ultor and to teach him arcane knowledge. He seemed to regret saying it."

Andrea and Amaury exchanged baffled glances. Lyra and Nella, however, shared something quieter.

It was Nella who broke the silence. "I suspected as much. Only a witch could cast the Evil Eye like that."

Amaury shifted, arms crossed over his chest. "Why would King Ultor be interested in occult knowledge?"

"I asked Acerbi that. He dodged the question. But I think it's the same reason we're making the talisman—to gain an advantage. As Varro's right hand, Ultor could be helping carry out whatever Sabelle's role as Court Witch entails."

Remo took a breath. "Which brings me to my next guess..."

They stared at Remo, waiting. He exhaled. It was only a hunch, but one he couldn't shake. "I think they're using astrology to time their attack on Anxur."

Acerbi hadn't said it outright, but Remo had seen the moment he slipped; Acerbi had no answer for why Varro would allow Mavortis to have a Court Witch when magic was banned everywhere else.

If Sabelle was guiding King Ultor, and Ultor was aligned with Varro, then Saffiro might be using astrology too. He couldn't prove it, not yet. But the thought chilled him.

No one argued. The logic was undeniable and deeply unsettling. They had thought the talisman gave them the upper hand, but if Saffiro had its own arcane resources and knew about the Academy, the Order's edge was gone.

"So what now, star boy?" Nella asked dryly. "What's their next move, if you're right?"

Remo clenched his jaw. "Saffiro is ruled by the Sun. And the Sun will be in exaltation on March 31st…"

Lyra's mouth fell open. Andrea bowed his head, bracing against the ship rail, the realization hitting both of them before Remo even finished the thought.

"I believe Saffiro will attack Anxur then," he said.

"That's far sooner than we expected," Amaury muttered, casting a doubtful glance at the small crew on his ship. "We'd need to send word to Vecontii now to rally reinforcements. Are you certain?"

Remo shook his head. "No. I have no proof—just instinct and astrology. But it would make sense. The Sun is their deity, their symbol. They'll want to strike while it's in its strongest position. Even with their superior numbers, they won't risk a stalemate like before. They'll use everything they have to make sure Anxur doesn't stand a chance.

"I would assume they plan to land in Anxur on that day," Remo said. "We should dock in Vecontii and send word to our Order contacts in Anxur, Merucia, and Lunaria—tell them to prepare their forces. Maybe Lunaria will reconsider if they know Vecontii is offering support. There's still time for them to reach Anxur. Better to prepare for a battle that doesn't come than be caught off guard by one that does."

Andrea cursed under his breath. "We're still over a week away from Saffiro. If you're right, by the time we complete the talisman, the Saffiran, Satrian, and Mavortian fleets will already be at Anxur's gates. A talisman is useless if its bearer isn't on the battlefield, and we can't be in two places at once."

Amaury stared out to sea. "No. But we can send Lyra's pigeon with a warning. If our allies act now, as Remo suggested, they might beat Saffiro to the strike. It would catch them off guard and force them onto the defensive."

Everyone turned to Amaury. "If Remo's guess is right, then we hold the advantage: we know the date. If we intercept them in the Anima Sea, they'll lose the element of surprise—and morale. They won't expect resistance at sea.

"Yes, we'd have to meet them closer to Anxur than we'd like and give up some distance. But the key is that they never reach the shore. Not one more Saffiran sets foot on Anxur's soil.

"And another thing—Satrian, Saffiran, and Mavortian soldiers may be formidable on land, but not at sea. Vecontii's navy gives us the upper hand. We'll have the 'high ground', in a manner of speaking. And we can learn a lesson in strategy from the sea itself; we have to adapt to circumstances, changing our shape accordingly. That's how we win."

Andrea rubbed a hand across his face, gaze sharp. "So you're saying we abandon the talisman quest entirely and meet them at sea instead? Even if your points hold, they'd still outnumber us. They might not be deterred, and without a completed talisman, we have no idea if it will work at all."

Amaury chewed on his lower lip, clearly weighing the risks. "You're right about their numbers. Even with Vecontii's naval advantage, we'd be outmanned, and the talisman wouldn't be at full power."

The wind brushed Remo's skin as he lifted his gaze skyward. There, Jupiter gleamed bright and still. A thought struck him, quick and electric.

"There might be another way," Remo said slowly. "A path to cut their numbers, complete the talisman, and avoid open conflict altogether."

Everyone turned to him, the air thick with anticipation.

Remo smiled faintly as he looked back up at the glowing planet. And for a heartbeat, he swore Jupiter wasn't twinkling, but winking.

That night, Amaury wrote a critical message to his trusted men in Vecontii, warning them of the suspected attack and urging them to prepare for battle.

Lyra carefully tied the message to the tiny bottle on Turi's back. The pigeon looked every bit as devoted to her as she was to him, nipping affectionately at her finger.

"I'll feed you berries and seeds when this is all over, my sweetling," she murmured, stroking his feathers and kissing his head. Amaury looked slightly jealous. Nella noticed and snorted with laughter.

Elsewhere on the ship, Andrea was deep in strategic conversation with Amaury's men, reviewing what he knew of Saffiro's tactics and sketching out possible scenarios and countermeasures.

Remo stood at the ship's edge, staring out at the open sea. A strange unease had settled over him like déjà vu, as though he'd lived this night once already in a dream. He watched Turi disappear into the dark, and soon Lyra came to stand beside him, her eyes gently searching his face.

"Are you okay?" she asked.

He met her eyes. He knew she assumed he was still haunted by what he'd endured, and she wasn't wrong.

As a healer, he knew well enough that the effects of the torture he had endured might linger not only physically in the form of scars, but mentally. And he would carry on through those nights, doing his best to keep himself whole.

But that wasn't what disturbed him now. It wasn't the past or even the looming future. It was something else. Something nameless and unsettled. Still, having Lyra beside him, and knowing Andrea was close, eased the weight of it for now.

Remo offered her a faint smile. "Right now, yes. I'm okay."

They reached the shores of Vecontii by late afternoon the next day, where they learned that Turi's message had been received. He now rested among a flurry of messenger pigeons tasked with carrying word to the Order's contacts in Anxur, Merucia, and Lunaria, warning them of the threat and urging them to prepare.

Tension ran high as they made preparations beneath King Bardi's nose. While docked, Lyra and Remo went to the apothecary to gather items for the sunthemata. Amaury, Andrea, and Nella oversaw the final arrangements for the rest of Amaury's men to join them at sea.

Remo and Lyra returned with saffron, citrus oil, dried St. John's Wort, rosemary, and a long list of strange ingredients Andrea had requested for some alchemical purpose he had yet to explain. He also gave them a Saffiran dagger, its golden hilt inlaid with a black stone veined in gold—to be used as a ritual offering. Remo, too, would wear the armor of a Knight of Saffiro, to serve as a sympathetic link to the sun in the upcoming ritual.

A day later, a pigeon from Merucia arrived. The Merucian militia and mercenaries would travel by night across kingdom lines to avoid detection. Even if Knights of Saffiro stationed throughout Merucia and Vecontii caught wind of the movement and tried to alert Saffiro, the fleets had likely already set sail toward Anxur. Any warning would arrive too late.

Five days later, the Merucians arrived. After boarding the Vecontiian ships, the armada set out for Anxur's shores. Cheers erupted from both Vecontiians and Merucians as they neared their destination and spotted an unexpected ally: a Lunarian fleet approaching from the east.

Queen Silvia of Lunaria stood proudly aboard one of the ships, her raven hair braided like a warrior's. She nodded once to Andrea, regal and restrained. Andrea, surprised but visibly moved, returned the gesture, silently conveying his gratitude.

Though smaller in number than the Vecontiians, Lunaria's presence offered a symbolic and emotional rallying point. Their support, coming at the eleventh hour, fortified the coalition's morale and bound them as citizens of Terramundi, united against Saffiro. Then the Anxurian fleet came into view, their flags billowing as they joined the coalition. They sailed in strong formation, proudly joining the allied fleet near the shores of their homeland.

The sight of Anxur's banner unfurling in the wind stirred something deep in Remo, an ancestral pride he hadn't expected. He remembered watching those ships as a boy, sitting on his family's garden wall. They felt like remnants of a life that no longer belonged to him. His heart clenched with worry. Was his younger brother aboard one of them, prepared to defend their homeland?

Days passed on the open sea. The final battle would come that afternoon—March 31st, the day of the Sun's exaltation. Remo stood alone at the stern, Nella's fresh bandages stinging against the breeze.

He had spent most of his life feeling alone, convinced that no one had ever truly understood or cared for him. The way he and Sabelle had parted—so cold and unresolved—weighed heavily on his heart, a burden he feared might linger long after the battle, if he survived it.

Before he could sink further into the ache of that ending, Andrea and Lyra flanked him. Andrea's calloused hand landed warmly on his shoulder, and Lyra's gaze met his with understanding. For the first time, Remo felt certain that he was not alone. If Andrea and Lyra kept showing up for him, there must be something within him worth loving, worth fighting for. Sabelle may not have seen it, but they did. And if he lived through this, he vowed to start believing in that worth himself.

Remo pushed past his doubts and looked forward. "This has been the greatest adventure of my life. And your friendships are the most important I've ever known. Thank you."

He couldn't bring himself to look at them. The emotion was too raw, and the intimacy of eye contact felt too exposing. He closed his eyes and said, "If this ends horribly, I'll find you both in the next life, and we'll share a new adventure."

Andrea's hand tightened on his shoulder. Lyra reached for his hand, curling her fingers gently around his. Remo opened his eyes. Lyra's gaze shimmered with unshed tears as she looked between him and Andrea.

The prince's brow furrowed, torn by some emotion he didn't voice, but he reached out and took Lyra's other hand.

Lyra spoke first, her voice soft but steady. "You will always have our friendship, Remo. Not even death can break that. It will guide us back to each other in every lifetime."

Andrea squeezed her hand. "You're both speaking like this is the end. It's not. We're going to survive. And when we do, we'll tempt fate and go on another adventure. But if we *are* planning for next lives, can we at least meet in Vecontii? I haven't stopped thinking about those pastries."

Lyra's laugh came out like a sob, and Remo threw his head back, allowing the laughter to lighten his heavy heart.

The three of them stood there, savoring one last perfect moment before the unknown arrived. As the sun climbed toward its zenith, the fated hour dawned, and Saffiro's legion crested the horizon.

# Chapter Twenty-nine

ONE OF AMAURY'S MEN called down from the crow's nest, telescope in hand. "Ahead! Our enemies approach!"

The wind seemed to whisper a warning. Faint shapes gathered on the horizon, inching closer. Remo tensed, giving Andrea and Lyra a final, silent look before they moved to the ship's bow.

Andrea and Amaury barked orders, making sure everyone was in position. Nella approached Lyra, who hesitated. Remo gave her a small nod, subtle but resolute. It was enough. Lyra's tawny eyes held his a moment longer before Nella led her away.

Remo sat and began his Awareness exercises. He focused on Jupiter, breathing deeply. There was no purple lotus tea this time. He would reach his daemon through will alone, because he chose to believe it was real.

Fifty enemy ships crept across the Anima Sea with deadly calm. As the danger outside became more real, Remo withdrew inward. His body dulled, his senses faded. And then he rose.

When he opened his inner eye, he found himself once again beneath the tree in Jupiter's temple. It was twilight here, as it always was in the liminal space between realms. Remo looked at his translucent hands. He was in his spirit form.

He turned. Jupiter was already there. The god smiled, serene and familiar. He looked younger now, dressed in white with a crown of laurel, the mark of a scholar.

In this realm, Remo felt safe, as though no danger could touch him, as though he had all the time in the world. The feeling emboldened him to tell Jupiter, "I liked your king's clothing better."

Jupiter chuckled, voice deep and amused. "You really do carry my influence, don't you? On the brink of battle, and instead of asking for help, you voice a blunt opinion I didn't request."

Remo grinned. "I was getting to that part. But why the simple clothes, if you can wear whatever you want?"

Jupiter arched a brow. "We see what we expect to see. Our perceptions reveal our values. Maybe it's not my wardrobe that's changed, but you. Perhaps you're no longer so impressed by appearances."

At Jupiter's words, a vague shape surfaced in his mind—a distant memory of someone he had once known. He knew it would hurt if he let the image sharpen, so he allowed it to drift away instead.

Jupiter inclined his head with kingly grace, as though he'd read Remo's thoughts and approved of his choice to let the memory go. "You've come far, Remo. I'm proud of you."

A warmth spread through him, unexpected and profound. He looked at his guide, his spiritual teacher, and heard the words he had never imagined a father figure would speak to him. For the first time since entering this space, Remo felt a flicker of doubt. Not about the vision or the journey, but about whether he was worthy of such pride. More unbelievable than any metaphysical experience was the idea that some-one might feel that way about *him*.

Jupiter seemed to sense this too. He stepped closer, voice gentle. "You wouldn't have been able to summon me this time without the aid of the purple lotus if not for your belief. Belief in me, yes—but more importantly, belief in your own ability to reach this state. In your trust that different layers of consciousness are real and attainable."

He paused, then added, "Your belief makes things real, Remo. Through that belief, anything becomes possible. This is the truth you've struggled with, and you've made progress. You've done well. But your path isn't finished. Keep seeking. Keep learning. This is the work you were meant to continue."

Remo absorbed Jupiter's words, though a question still tugged at him. "What's it all for? All this learning and seeking... What's the point?"

Jupiter laughed, exasperated but fond. "I'm not allowed to tell you that. But know this—it is the same goal all humans are moving toward. You don't need to know the ending to find purpose in the journey. Life isn't like the stories you read with neat beginnings and tidy morals. Each of us is the hero of our own tale, battling our dragons. Not the fire-breathers of myth, but fiercer ones: the shadows of our souls.

"Our individual stories may vanish with time, but the work endures. Your story is one among many, in a world that is one among many, in a universe that is ever expanding. And still, it matters.

"We must find and face our dragon, again and again. This is the work of many lifetimes. The dragon eating its tail symbolizes that endless cycle. The process will always outlast the momentary satisfaction of completing it, so learn to enjoy it. Our stories are never-ending. You must keep writing yours for the sake of writing and find fulfillment in the doing."

Pure magic thrummed within Remo's being as he resonated with Jupiter's words, recognizing a truth that touched the core of who he was. It was the same magic he felt when reading a line in a book that sparked something deep within him, connecting him to knowledge he had always known but never had the words to express.

The ever-present feeling that something was missing from his life vanished as he let the inspiration wash over him. The wisdom was like a glowing ember. He wanted nothing more than to keep that ember alive, feeding it with truth until his heart burned bright with a spiritual fire this harsh physical life could never extinguish.

"You must return now," Jupiter said. "And see this through."

The memory of what awaited him returned, and Remo nodded, accepting the challenge. He wished he could remain in this realm where nothing weighed on him, but his soul's work existed elsewhere. He wouldn't run from it. It would only pursue him, as surely as the dragon's head follows its tail.

"Will you still be with me?" he asked.

Jupiter's form radiated light, first amethyst, then periwinkle, brightening to an icy blue before turning white.

"The same light you see in me is in you," he said. "I'll always be with you. You'll always be able to find me."

The flash of white was the last thing Remo saw before darkness returned. Then came the chanting, cold and rhythmic. Phase one of the plan had begun.

The Saffiran, Mavortian, and Satrian ships were terrifyingly close now. As Amaury had predicted, the sight of Anxur, Merucia, Vecontii, and Lunaria united must have caught their opposition off guard.

They didn't attempt to grapple or board immediately. The sight of armed ballistae and crossbows bristling on the Vecontiian and Anxurian ships gave them momentary pause, even if the defending side was still outnumbered by at least ten thousand men.

But Saffirans were not known for diplomacy. Saffirans didn't negotiate, so the five friends launched their first wave of psychological warfare.

Lyra stood at the bow of the ship, visible to all. She began to chant, low, eerie, powerful, in the ancient language still spoken only in Satria. It was a carmen malum.

Remo nearly bowed at the sight of her, beautiful and terrifying as a goddess while she chanted. Her flaxen hair and skirts whipped behind her, as if she were summoning an ancient power that bent the world to her will. Her silken voice carried the repetitive chant, echoed by the allied soldiers in the strange, ominous tongue she had taught them.

Though it was difficult to tear his eyes from her, Remo shifted his gaze to assess the effect the chanting had on their enemies. The Saffiran and Mavortian forces looked confused, though not yet shaken. But the carmen malum wasn't meant for them. It was designed for the Satrians.

The sight of Lyra alone, powerful and unflinching, may have been enough to unnerve them. As the chant echoed across the sea, several Satrians spit to ward off its curse. Saffirans, proud and ignorant, hadn't cared to learn the depth of Satrian beliefs. It was the only thing, aside from Anxur, they'd never conquered. Now, the four-nation alliance held their attention.

Remo's gaze found Andrea, his expression calm but fierce, his eyes burning with purpose. He looked every bit the naval commander, undaunted and resolute. Beneath his armor, the talisman rested against his heart. Remo laid out the ritual offerings just as he had in every talismanic rite before.

With a strike of flint against steel, Andrea lit the rosemary in a half-sheltered brass bowl, summoning smoke for the suffumigation. Then, raising his arms to the sky, he began the second act of psychological warfare: the *evocatio,* a ritual calling forth Saffiro's tutelary deity as part of the talisman's completion.

"I invoke the Sun, Guardian of Saffiro," Andrea intoned, voice clear and strong. "I worship you, protector of this land and its people. You are the light of consciousness, the giver and sustainer of life. Please accept our offerings."

Andrea pulled the talisman from beneath his armor. Then he grasped the golden dagger, offered to the Sun, and slid it across a strip of exposed skin on his forearm.

Blood spilled, the ultimate offering of life-force, the sacred fuel of transformation. And coming from a Saffiran royal, it became a potent sympathetic gift to the Sun.

The black crucible now held white ash and vivid red blood, dripping steadily from the golden blade still clutched in the alchemist's hand, poised to complete his great work.

They hadn't reached the Sun's temple, which would have amplified their call, but with the sun overhead in exaltation, and the blood of a Saffiran prince offered in its name, Remo thought it might just be enough. Cosimo had once said the gods respond not to location, but to clarity of intent. Remo clung to that thought now.

Andrea affixed the sunstone to the nearly finished talisman, engraving it with care before passing the suffumigation smoke over the piece. His voice rang out, strong and sure. "Sun, I ask your favor. Abandon the Knights of Saffiro in their misguided cause. Let fear grip them. Bless the Anxurians, Vecontiians, Merucians, and Lunarians. Accept our devotion. Fill this talisman and this stone with your strength. Let its bearer be victorious."

Andrea had been a prince, then an exile, and now, a true alchemist. He united all three selves under the exalted Sun, the seat of ego, and transcended his own. Opposites merged, unconscious and conscious, fate and free will. As within, so without. His inner transformation rippled outward, ready to change the world.

Remo felt it in his bones. It was true. He watched with awe as several

Satrian ships turned back just as he had predicted. Their plan was working.

He glanced at Lyra, standing beside Andrea. Her eyes were closed, her expression serene, as she set silent intentions for the talisman's activation. The memory of their plan, carefully laid and now unfolding perfectly, flickered in his mind like a living flame.

*Remo lowered his gaze from Jupiter and turned to his friends. He addressed Lyra first. "Satrians are superstitious, right? And they're a third of the enemy's army."*

*Lyra nodded. "Yes. We are. We still follow the old ways."*

*Remo looked to Andrea. "You've said Saffiro and Mavortis treat the Satrians like cannon fodder—hastati. Poor, disposable, not human. They don't fight out of loyalty, but fear. And the gods are more fearsome than men."*

*He drew a steady breath. "We use that. We exploit their superstition, and Saffiro's arrogance."*

And Remo had been right. The carmen malum had unsettled the Satrians, but the evocatio and blood sacrifice unnerved them deeply. Now, they believed the Sun itself stood against them.

Recognizing the danger, many Satrians initiated a bloody retreat as mutinies broke out. Generals shouted orders while soldiers fought for control of the helm.

Some Satrians were heard frantically trying to explain why they needed to raise white flags immediately, but Saffiro and Mavortis refused to surrender. Those Satrians who seized control of their ships fled.

Though the allies were still vastly outnumbered, the tide had begun to turn. The imbalance, while still present, had narrowed.

The sky darkened. The sun that had blazed brightly throughout the talismanic ritual was now veiled by clouds as the suffumigation smoke faded, and darkness fell quickly, unnaturally. Day turned into night. A rumble of distant thunder followed, as if the heavens themselves were warning the opposing side to retreat.

Madness broke out on the ships with mixed crews of Satrians, Mavortians, and Saffirans. The Mavortian Salii were seen arming themselves, eager for the bloodshed they had come for. The Saffiran triarii looked grim, realizing it might all come down to them.

An omen the Satrians needed no interpretation for occurred: a bolt of white lightning split the sky, striking far in the distance. Jupiter had made his displeasure known.

The flash lit up the enemy fleet—figures frozen in fear, their faces pale with terror. Many now believed the Ancient Gods had sided with the allied forces. Even the Saffirans, distanced from the Old Religion, knew lightning was not to be ignored.

Thunder boomed, lightning split the sky again, and Saffiran and Mavortian ships erupted into chaos. Captains shouted over one another, arguing. The allied fleets waited, weapons ready, hoping the god's warning would send the enemy fleeing.

Not all fled. A dangerous number of ships still lingered, unmoved. Then lightning cracked again, and one Saffiran ship began to approach Amaury's vessel, closing in fast.

Andrea spun toward Nella. "You and Lyra—below deck. Barricade the doors with whatever you can. NOW."

Lyra didn't move. "No. I'm staying."

Nella looked furious. "Let's go. Please, Lyra!"

Remo had never heard her plead before. Lyra took her hand gently. "You go. I'm staying."

Andrea and Nella looked ready to argue, but a shout rang out from the enemy ship.

"HAUL!"

Grappling hooks flew through the air, latching onto the sides of Amaury's ship. Amaury's men rushed forward, hacking at the lines until Andrea shouted, "Stop! Defensive position only. They're not storming; they want to parley. Let them board. Stay alert."

Remo's brow furrowed. "Then why wouldn't they raise a white flag if they want to surrender?"

Andrea grimaced. "Because my father has never surrendered to anyone or anything in his life."

Remo reached instinctively for the hilt at his side. He told himself he was ready, that Andrea had trained him well, that he could hold his own. But as he watched Saffiran triarii, Mavortians, and a few reluctant

Satrians board the ship, his pulse quickened.

One man, face scarred, raised his arms and called, "Parley," signaling he was unarmed. Behind him came a pale, imposing figure. Without thinking, Remo stepped in front of Lyra and Nella—Amaury did the same.

Andrea stepped forward toward the fearsome man and drawled in a deliberately bored voice, "Hello, Father."

Emperor Varro bore the faded vestiges of Andrea's handsomeness, but none of his warmth. Violence clung to him like a second skin. His armor was similar to that of the Saffiran triarii, though highly decorated.

Varro's expression curdled into open disdain as he looked at Andrea. "I have no son."

Hurt flashed in Andrea's eyes, but only for a second. Then his gaze went cold, drained of its usual spark. He hardened, the way Remo imagined he always did around his father.

Maybe he feared that one day, the armor would never come off. That he'd stay shut tight, even to those who loved him, that he'd become what stood before him.

Varro's eyes dropped to the talisman around Andrea's neck. "When did you learn witchcraft? Was it during your pitiful failure in Satria, where even the lowest men refused your leadership? King Ultor's spies tell me offerings were found in Lunaria's temple. I assume that was your work."

Andrea's face was expressionless, as though he'd extinguished something essential inside himself just to endure this conversation.

Varro turned to Amaury, recognition sharpening his sneer. "So Vecontii has chosen its side. I'm not surprised. Your deity is a whore, and your king is a bitch."

Amaury drew his sword. The emperor's men mirrored him. Nella seized her brother's arm. Andrea raised a hand in a silent command, his eyes locked with Amaury's.

Reluctantly, Amaury sheathed his blade. One by one, Varro's men did the same.

Andrea spoke with no trace of emotion. "Anxur's allies stand united while your forces retreat. Either we negotiate peace now, or you get off our ship, and we allow you to leave alive until another meeting can be arranged."

Varro sneered. "You dare make demands of me? You've already disgraced our name. Disgraced Saffiro. And now you hide behind magic and diplomacy because you've never been man enough to fight."

Remo stepped up beside Andrea. "A monster is measured by how much blood he spills. Not a man."

Varro didn't deign to look at Remo, or at Lyra, or Nella, who had flanked Andrea. They stood with him, ready to fight, just as he had once fought for each of them.

"How touching," Varro said. "Your vermin friends want to die with you. Arrest them all. They're traitors to the empire. Let their executions serve as a lesson."

Varro's men lunged. Amaury's men responded in turn. Swords clashed across the deck, sparks flying as steel met steel. Remo parried the blade of a Knight of Saffiro lunging for him, his training and instinct locking into place.

Amaury disarmed his attacker and searched for Nella. A Knight of Saffiro had thrown her to the deck. Remo rushed to help, but Lyra was faster. Though trembling, she didn't hesitate. She kicked the knight off Nella, seized a fallen sword, and leveled it at his throat.

The knight moved to strike, but Remo intercepted—dodging a near-fatal blow and drawing him away.

Elsewhere, Amaury held off two knights at once. Lyra and Nella stood behind him, guarding his back. Around them, the nearest Vecontiian and Saffiran ships began to close in, each side preparing to send reinforcements onto the ship to shift the tide of battle.

Remo spared a glance across the surrounding ships. Crossbows fired, arrows flew, boarding lines snapped into place. Then came the signal.

Andrea's alchemical devices launched, flashing, popping, and releasing thick smoke and blinding light across enemy decks. Screams rose and frightened soldiers stumbled back, unsure of what they faced.

On their own ship, Varro and Andrea turned toward each other. Varro called off his men. His voice was cold, seething. "I'm going to do what I should have done years ago when you proved what you are: a weak, pathetic excuse for a man. I won't let you disgrace me or Saffiro any longer."

Andrea stood firm, circling. "I offered you and your men a chance to live. Why do you always choose blood?"

Varro studied him, eyes sharp, looking for a break in his stance. "I don't run from battle. I'm the emperor. I'll die a warrior before I ever beg like a coward."

Lightning flashed again. Varro lunged. Andrea met the blade with his own, steel ringing out across the deck.

All around them, allied forces—Vecontiians, Lunarians, Merucians, Anxurians—were subduing what remained of the Saffiran and Mavortian resistance. Many turned to watch as the emperor and exile clashed in the stormlight.

Varro fought with the force of a man possessed, driving Andrea back step by step. His swordsmanship was ruthless, focused entirely on the kill. But Andrea never faltered. He guarded himself with unshakable calm, the golden talisman glinting at his throat.

He didn't strike back; he only defended himself. He didn't feed his father's bloodlust.

"No, Father," Andrea said, blocking another blow. "You're the coward between us. You let your ego dictate your life. You'd rather die than face being wrong. But death is only a temporary escape from pain. You'll face it eventually."

Andrea stepped in, closing distance, matching Varro with fluid precision as the storm raged above.

"Fight me back! Strike, you bastard!" Varro screamed, eyes wild. He looked unhinged, as if Andrea's refusal to meet his rage was unbearable, as if he craved his son's hatred and had no idea how to respond to anything else.

Andrea blocked every blow. When he disarmed Varro, he let him retrieve the sword. All eyes watched in stunned silence as Andrea showed honor to a man who would have shown him none.

"That's twice I've spared your life," Andrea said calmly. "Surrender now, and we can negotiate peace. There's still hope for you, Father. You don't have to keep living the way you were taught. You can choose differently. I forgive you for not knowing what you were never shown."

Varro faltered. He looked shaken, cornered. Andrea's blade was pointed at his chest. Behind him, the ship's edge. Around him, the remains of his army, many now disarmed or surrendered.

Before him, the talisman glinted. And within his son's steady gaze, something he couldn't bear: forgiveness.

The realization hit. He had lost. And worse, he had been bested by his disgraced, exiled son in full view of those who had once feared him.

The narrative he had clung to all his life, passed down from his father before him—the lie that mercy was weakness, that failure was shameful, that being unloved was a reflection of worth—fractured.

He could not accept his son's mercy. To him, it wasn't grace; it was defeat. And he would not let the world record his failure. He would end the story himself. True to his word, Emperor Varro stepped to the ship's edge and plunged his sword into his own heart.

"Father!" Andrea cried, reaching out as their eyes met, and in that final breath, he glimpsed a flicker of something unspoken, a nameless emotion his father had never learned to name, let alone give. Then Varro fell back, swallowed by the indifferent sea.

A wave of shock rippled through the ship. Andrea stood at the edge, tears in his eyes, watching his father's blood disappear into the sea. Above, the storm began to break, its fury finally spent.

Nella was the first to move, hurrying to Andrea's side and pulling him gently away from the ship's edge. Lyra stood frozen, one hand over her mouth in horror. She reached instinctively for Remo's arm, and he covered her hand with his own, anchoring her there.

Andrea clutched the talisman. It was cold now, heavy as dead iron. Whatever power it once carried had given itself wholly; its purpose was finished.

Then Amaury stepped forward. He looked at Andrea as if seeing him for the first time. A few steps closer, then he knelt.

"You've shown strength, fairness, and mercy like Terramundi hasn't seen in over two centuries," he said, voice steady. "Prince Andrea, you have my unwavering loyalty, and my endorsement to become our emperor."

Remo and Lyra stepped apart and lowered to their knees, joining Amaury. Then the others followed reverently. Not in submission, but in belief. In recognition of the man who had shown them what leadership could be. Even the remaining Mavortians and Saffirans fell to their knees, pleading for mercy from the one they now hoped would rule them, should the Senate choose him.

From the neighboring ships, more knelt. Saffirans. Lunarians. Merucians. Vecontiians. Anxurians. Satrians. All bowed to Andrea—the exile restored by the people's will.

# Chapter Thirty

T HE NEXT TWO MONTHS were spent recovering from what many had begun to call The Siege of Saffiro or The Seven Nation Stand-still.

Word of Emperor Varro's death spread quickly. Andrea returned to Saffiro for the first time since his exile, and was narrowly elected by the Senate as the new emperor. His first act was pardoning Cosimo. He traveled to Mavortis himself and invited Cosimo to serve as his Advisor.

Cosimo had only chuckled. "I'm afraid not, my dear boy. I have an Academy to run, if you'll kindly legalize it."

Andrea did exactly that, abolishing the laws that had long banned the practice of arcane arts. While public suspicion of the occult remained, it was a necessary step in undoing the damage done 227 years earlier.

Lyra and Nella returned to Mavortis. Turi waited faithfully, and Lyra fed him berries and seeds, just as she'd promised.

Remo, meanwhile, returned home to Anxur and found his mother and brother well. He learned that Aemilian had been among the Light-Bringers who resisted the Knights of Saffiro. Remo cried at the sight of him, whole and alive. He silently scolded himself for ever thinking Aemilian was simple just because he'd found happiness in a quiet life. He now saw his brother had grasped a truth he hadn't, that happiness is a choice, independent of circumstance.

It was a truth Remo knew he'd need to remind himself of for the rest of his life, that contentment is not granted, but chosen. And those who seek it only through what lies outside themselves are always left searching for what is rarely found: peace.

When Remo embraced his mother, Andrea's words echoed in his mind. *I forgive you for not knowing what you were never shown.* He repeated them inwardly as he let go of old grievances toward his mother and late father.

He climbed the hill that once marked the boundary of his small world. Trota's cottage stood just as he remembered. She opened the wooden door, afternoon sun casting a golden glow over her face as she beamed at him. Remo returned the smile and embraced her warmly.

She welcomed him in. "Now," she said, "tell me everything."

He did. But he had lingering questions for his old mentor. "That message in the bottle... did you know it was Serafina's?"

Trota smiled knowingly. "I suspected. But you wouldn't have appreciated its weight then. Between your Sagittarius Moon and North Node, I knew you wouldn't fulfill your potential in Anxur. And when the eclipse hit your first house, I knew change was coming. That, combined with the reports from the Order of Aquarius and other signs... I had a feeling you'd be part of something bigger. I just didn't realize *how* big. Not to mention," she added with a wink, "my selfish wish to see another healer-astrologer in the world."

He grinned. "Will you read charts openly now?"

She exhaled. "Alas, no. The law may have changed, but people's minds don't shift so easily. I'll still study the stars, but quietly, as I always have, until the day I die."

She eyed him thoughtfully. "So? Did your adventure live up to the stories in your books? Do you still feel the same way you did before you left Anxur?"

He thought a moment. "I've changed. I can't imagine my life if I hadn't taken the risk. I can't imagine never meeting Andrea, or Lyra, or—" He faltered. Trota pretended not to notice.

He shook his head as if to clear it and continued along a different vein. "My friends helped me realize that it wasn't the magical aspects of my books that I truly desired. Magic means nothing without someone to share it with. Being a king in an empty castle... being immortal but alone—that would be a curse. What I really longed for was friendship. And—" his cheeks flushed, "love. And now I know those things are real.

Because I've lived them."

Trota's eyes softened. "If I didn't know better, I'd think you studied Alchemy. Something essential has changed in you. You speak with wisdom now. What will you do next?"

He looked out the same window he'd once stared through, back when the world was still unknown.

"I'm going back to my friends," he said. "To see what our next adventure holds."

Remo was now free to return to Mavortis without fear of imprisonment, thanks to Andrea's swift move to legalize arcane studies.

He reunited with Lyra at The Crooked Cupola, where celebrations erupted nearly every other day. Students from the Academy and members of the Order gathered to mark the hard-won victory that belonged to them all.

Sevo poured them a wine as terrible as it was ancient—"aged since the founding of the Academy," he claimed. "You're a musician, right? How about a song?" he asked Nella during one such revelry.

"No, I'm a physician," she replied flatly. "But I *do* play a mean scalpel."

Sevo left her alone and didn't charge her for the wine.

Andrea lingered in Mavortis longer than he needed to while arranging Cosimo's release. The delay was bittersweet. He knew life would change drastically once he returned to Saffiro as emperor.

On their final morning together, the three friends slipped out of the inn before dawn while students lifted a tipsy Sevo above their heads and paraded him around the tavern. They wandered the familiar path to Andrea's lodgings, where they had shared countless late-night talks, and stood on his balcony, each lost in their thoughts as they watched the sky turn a clear, pale gold.

Andrea broke the silence, his voice unusually hesitant. "I need to ask you both something. I know you each have your own lives, and I can't ask you to come to Saffiro. But if not for the two of you, we'd be living in a very different world. I don't deserve to be emperor by my own merit; I only got this far because of you. So—what I'm asking is—and of course, you can leave whenever you want—but I'd like it if, for a time..."

"Do you think he'll manage to ask us to come with him before the day's over?" Lyra asked Remo with a grin.

Remo smirked. "At this rate? Unlikely." He raised an eyebrow at Andrea. "Honestly, I thought I'd have to ask *you* if I could come. This is a relief." Although he tried to ease Andrea with his words, they were sincere.

Now that the Order had completed its mission, Remo could no longer rely on their payments. He knew he'd need to find work as a healer elsewhere, at least while Acerbi remained in Mavortis. But for once, he didn't fret about the future. He had a vague sense that things would continue to work out.

Andrea relaxed at last, his tension giving way to hope as he looked to Lyra.

She smiled brightly. "I've been following you around like a shadow for years. What makes you think becoming emperor would get rid of me?"

Andrea looked like he might cry, then whooped, shouting his joy across the red rooftops of Mavortis. The three of them laughed, swept up in a perfect, transient moment.

The realization dawned on Remo as gently as the rising sun: magic is elusive. It arrives in fleeting moments, in waves. It comes when you're sitting with your friends, laughing over something ridiculous. And it leaves just as quietly as it came.

The moment you recognize it for what it is and try to hold on, it slips away. But it always returns—unexpected, unannounced—when you're fully present. Let it go when it leaves, and stay open to its return. Magic will always come again, so long as you leave the door open.

It was with them now, surrounding all three friends as they looked toward the rise of a new adventure.

# Epilogue

"T HERE'S MY PRINCESS!" ANDREA bellowed from across the marble entrance hall of the Saffiran palace.

The corner of Nella's mouth tugged into a reluctant smirk. "Call me that again, and I will go directly back to Mavortis."

Andrea ignored her. He crossed the space quickly and swept her into his arms, kissing her passionately, right in front of Remo and Lyra. Remo glanced at Lyra, subtly gauging her reaction. She smiled, but her eyes betrayed something more complicated as she watched the couple embrace.

Nothing escaped the shrewd perception of a Gemini rising; Remo had first noticed Lyra's secret affection for Andrea months ago. He saw it in the way her gaze lingered during serious conversations, in the wistfulness behind her eyes when she watched the two together.

Remo understood it all too well—he, too, longed for someone out of reach. Though betrothed to his enemy, Sabelle still haunted his thoughts and daydreams. The wet sound of parting lips brought Remo's attention back.

"Sorry—my *physician,*" Andrea amended smoothly, voice velvet-soft with a lover's promise.

"Better," Nella allowed, as he set her down. She turned and embraced Lyra tightly.

"Star boy," she added with a nod to Remo, who returned it in kind.

Only Andrea and Lyra ever seemed to soften Nella's famously guarded exterior. Remo didn't mind. Their acquaintanceship was cordial, and he'd always be grateful for what she'd done to save his life.

Some of the sadness in Lyra's eyes faded, replaced by genuine happiness as she reunited with Nella, even if only for a little while. Nella had resumed her physician training in Mavortis and was only visiting.

Remo felt grateful that she had come for Andrea's sake. He knew how deeply Andrea missed her. He wondered if Nella felt that same ache of separation.

A dull pang twisted in his chest as he decided she likely didn't.

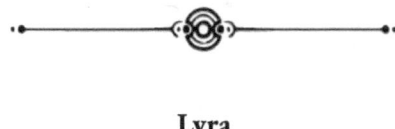

### Lyra

"So, did you like *Sunset in Saffiro* better, or is *Fates of the Fae* still your favorite?" Nella asked over dinner in Andrea's private chambers, where she and Lyra were comparing the latest courtly romance novels.

Lyra pushed vegetables around her plate. "I think *Fates of the Fae* will always be my favorite. I prefer a slower kind of love story."

Nella tore a hunk of bread and groaned in protest. "If there's no indecency by the sixth chapter, I've no reason to read the seventh."

Andrea smirked, his posture too casual to be innocent. One arm was clearly reaching beneath the table toward Nella. "So impatient," he murmured.

Lyra looked toward Remo, whose grey eyes seemed to darken. She suspected he found it just as difficult as she did to be around the couple, especially now that he no longer had a romantic life of his own. She felt for him, knowing how things had ended with Sabelle. He still clearly carried the weight of a broken heart.

"*Sunset in Saffiro,*" Andrea huffed around a bite of roasted fowl. "How come there's no filth written about, oh, I don't know..."—he twirled his fork dramatically—"dark and handsome emperors?"

Lyra arched an eyebrow. "Oh, don't feel too sorry for yourself. There's certainly a rich *oral tradition* on the subject."

Nella winked. She was always telling Lyra stories she didn't want to hear—half-jokes, half-confessions. They only complicated Lyra's private feelings for the man who was both her best friend and entirely off-limits.

Andrea grinned. "I want my legacy in ink and paper. I've already got a working title, *Emperor Andrea's Colossal Co*— "

Nella flicked his head before he could finish. Everyone laughed, and for a moment, it felt like they were all back at The Crooked Cupola on a normal night in Mavortis. But those days were gone, never to return.

Lyra shifted in her seat. She could feel Remo watching her. When she glanced his way, she thought, just for a second, that he looked at her with pity. As if he saw what she didn't want anyone to see: how much it hurt to sit through dessert, pretending not to notice Andrea licking icing off Nella's lips.

Lyra and Remo shared a look of quiet understanding, like he knew every thought running through her mind. She downed her drink, though it did nothing to quench the deeper thirst for partnership, for connection.

Romance novels had helped her reconnect with her body and desire. She had begun to heal by reading about pleasure, imagining it, claiming it again in private moments, rewriting what had once been taken from her.

As if sensing that her energy for the evening was fading, Remo stood. "Thanks for dinner," he said to Andrea. Then he turned to Lyra. "Ready to go?"

Lyra met his gaze and tried to pack gratitude into her smile. "Yes. Thanks for hosting us, Andrea. Goodnight, Nella. See you both tomorrow."

"See you," Nella called as they reached the door. Andrea offered a nod of farewell.

They walked in silence through the vast halls toward Lyra's chambers, not far from Remo's. The palace was so large they still managed to lose their way sometimes. When they reached her door, Remo hesitated, like he wanted to speak but wasn't sure if he should.

"Thanks for walking with me," Lyra murmured. She hoped he heard what she meant beneath it.

Remo studied her, his face lit by the warm glow of candlelight. "Anytime."

She turned, took a few steps toward the door, then stopped when he spoke again.

"You're not alone," he said. "I feel the same. I want someone I can't have."

Despite her suspicions, Lyra was stunned. How long had he known? She took a step closer. "I see. And... have you any advice for what to do with that sort of feeling?"

Remo's expression didn't shift. "No. But at least we can sympathize. Misery loves company."

The corners of Lyra's mouth lifted as she extended her hand and took another step forward. "Nice to meet you, Mr. Misery. I'm Company."

Thank you for stepping into the world of *The Mundane and the Arcane*. Ahead lies a glimpse of the next adventure in *The Sacred and the Profane*.

To explore even further, I'd love to welcome you into the Ninth House, where you'll get updates, bonus lore, and a free Andrea novella delivered straight to your inbox.

Join the Ninth House at https://daniellecerrone.com/contact

If you enjoyed *The Mundane and the Arcane*, please consider leaving a review online. It means so much and helps more readers discover the series!

# Sneak Peek: The Sacred and Profane

## Andrea

A NDREA WAS FLOATING, THE rhythmic motion of the sunlight-dappled sea lulling him into a false sense of security. Nothing disturbed him—until a fly buzzed in his ear.

He swatted it, but it lingered, insistent, almost purposeful. He fought it with both hands, but more flies came, a swarm surrounding him. Panic surged as he looked down and saw a sword buried in his chest. He screamed as they feasted on his rotting flesh.

The buzzing rose, drowning out his cries, as the green waters darkened with blood. Then the sound vanished, leaving a hollow silence in which he realized he felt no pain. He floated above the scene and saw the truth; the body wasn't his, but his father's.

Andrea jolted awake, heart racing as he reached left to an empty bed. The ache of that vacant space slowed his pulse as he remembered Nella had returned to Mavortis two days prior.

Though she had come with him to Saffiro for the first few weeks after his arrival, she couldn't stay indefinitely. He'd always known she wouldn't abandon her studies or her life in Mavortis just because he'd become emperor. Knowing it didn't lessen the sting of her absence.

He stood, wiped the sweat from his brow, and crossed the room. He didn't blame Nella for choosing her own path. He'd never want to burden her with a life she didn't choose.

Still, somewhere in a selfish, needy corner of his heart, he secretly harbored the hope that she might change her mind, that the separation would gnaw at her the way it gnawed at him. But Nella seemed fine, perhaps even relieved by the growing distance.

Their first nights had felt normal. Nothing explicit had happened to cause alarm. He wanted to believe he was just being paranoid—that when she broke eye contact a little too quickly, it meant nothing; that when she changed the subject about her next visit, it was uncertainty, not dread; that she hadn't heard him when he whispered *I love you* in the dark beside her.

Better to pretend it was fine than face a final goodbye. He would let the silence grow until it killed him. At least then he wouldn't have to survive her absence.

He paused as he passed the decanter of wine, temptation tugging at him. For a moment, he considered using it to calm his nerves. But he moved on, choosing his original plan instead. He grabbed a robe and lantern and stepped into the corridor.

On nights like these, Andrea appreciated the luxury of his private wing. Being emperor had its drawbacks—namely, the slow collapse of his relationship and the constant presence of people who hated him—but at least the excessive solitude came with a degree of comfort.

He descended into the alchemy chamber, adjusting his robe across his bare chest as cold stone greeted him. Centuries ago, the chamber had been used by the king's own alchemist for much the same purpose Andrea used it now.

Wide wooden worktables housed pelican flasks, scales, crucibles, and all manner of glass distilling apparatus for spagyrics, the branch of alchemy devoted to herbalism. A broad, empty hearth stood against the far wall, meant for calcination and heat, its mantle engraved with alchemical symbols. Cabinets tucked into alcoves brimmed with jars of ingredients, shelves lined with tinctures and prepared essences.

By lantern light, Andrea searched the shelves. There was no tincture of chamomile, but valerian would do. He dropped it beneath his tongue and waited for the bitter taste to bring him calm.

The room grounded him. It was a remnant of Mavortis, of who he'd been. Though his imperial duties left little time for study, alchemy remained his passion. He carved out moments for it still, for the peace it brought his soul.

Remo and Lyra were his other solace. Without them, he wasn't sure he could bear the weight of the crown. He'd offered them titles, homes—whatever it took to keep them in Saffiro after the Standstill.

They never had to work again; he'd see to that. Yet his friends chose purpose over ease. Even if Andrea didn't feel he deserved it, they stayed to fight for the Order, and for him.

Andrea chuckled as he opened the door and remembered Remo declaring his "official" court titles with mock-serious pride.

*"Ambassador to Shitshow?"* Remo had once offered.

*"Saffiro,"* Andrea corrected dryly.

*"Same difference. How about... Head of Liaisons?"* Remo added, though the innuendo was lost on no one.

Lyra arched a brow and said, *"Court Jester would be more fitting."*

The memory soothed him as he slipped back into bed, drowsiness blooming. The cheerful recollection lingered like a fading ember, its warmth carrying him into a sleep free of dreams, and for now, free of fear.

## Lyra

Lyra slipped into a white gown, the simplest among the lavish rainbow of her armoire. Since Andrea had named her *lady,* life had grown heavier with silk and ceremony.

He'd insisted on dressing her for the part, gifting her tailors, fabrics, and finery. No protest could dissuade him; generosity was his armor, and she'd learned not to fight it. For Lyra, being granted shelter and purpose within his palace had already felt like more than she could ever repay.

She fastened the gown while glancing over her shoulder in the ornate, floor-length mirror. For a moment, Lyra paused, studying her reflection and contemplating how fortunate she was. Once, everything she owned had been Nella's castoffs; now she dressed in silk of her own. The only gift she truly treasured, though, was the pair of brass elven ears Remo and Andrea had given her last Saturnalia, symbols of friendship she wore with pride.

Her mornings began in a sunlit circular room. A half-read romance novel from the palace library rested on her nightstand, while the carved posts of her canopy bed twisted like forest branches and the gold-trimmed trunk at its foot brimmed with more adornments than she'd ever imagined owning.

Beyond the arched window, the palace gardens swayed in the breeze, and she couldn't help but feel a little like royalty herself. All of it delighted her Libran soul. To Lyra, beauty itself was divine, but of all her blessings, none meant more than Remo, Andrea, and Nella.

Life in Saffiro kept her near those she loved, though Nella's visits from Mavortis had grown infrequent. Shamefully, Lyra sometimes welcomed the distance. Though she missed Nella dearly, her absence quieted the guilt that flared whenever Lyra's thoughts strayed toward Andrea in a way she knew they shouldn't.

With a click of the locks, she opened her trunk and searched for her matching satin slippers, hoping the task might distract her from the sorry truth that she had been pining for Andrea ever since he'd rescued her years ago in Satria from a fate she didn't like to recall.

In Lyra's romantic mind, Andrea was her knight in shining armor—the one who had saved her from an actual knight. Outside the pages of her beloved novels, it seemed only the offending kind existed.

After that night in Satria, it had been difficult to meet his eyes. He had witnessed her at one of the darkest points of her life, and that kind of knowing was a strange thing to share with anyone. Through his kindness and generosity, Andrea had slowly proven himself a man she could trust, a safe presence in a world that rarely offered such things.

He never crossed a line, and never so much as made careless contact with her. She knew he was conscientious because he understood, and that care became the lifeline she hadn't known she needed. His restraint, his respect for her boundaries, meant more to her than words could ever express.

For years, she'd feared men—their closeness, their eyes, the threat hidden in their attention. But Andrea's gaze was different: steady, soft, and safe. It made her pulse quicken, but not from fear. And though her heart still raced whenever she looked into his brown eyes, she had learned not to fear the feeling anymore.

But Andrea belonged to Nella. Every time Lyra's thoughts wandered toward him, guilt struck like lightning. She hated herself for noticing the way his muscles flexed while he trained, or how his smile warmed her like he was the sun itself. While reading her novels, she often caught herself imagining him as the dashing hero, and herself as the woman he desired.

Nella was more than a friend; she was a found sister. Lyra loved her deeply, and remorse always followed when she caught herself daydreaming about Andrea. It tore her apart just as much to see him and Nella together, sharing small moments of affection she feared she'd never experience with anyone.

Whenever Andrea and Nella broke up, they both turned to Lyra, asking her to play the role of mediator. Out of love for them both, she always did faithfully, with a smile that hid her ache. But even in their worst quarrels, she knew that even if they ended for good, Andrea would never look at her the way he looked at Nella.

With a deep breath, Lyra gathered her composure and descended the spiral staircase to the main floor of the palace. She made her way toward the library, not for pleasure this time, but for business.

The Order of Aquarius' mission hadn't ended with preventing Saffiro's conquest of Anxur. There was still much work to be done, bridges to rebuild, and trust to mend. Now, through Andrea's position as emperor, they possessed the influence to begin.

Lyra and Remo worked side by side, helping him prepare a summit between every kingdom in Terramundi. Today, Lyra sifted through the empire's endless correspondence, weighing dates, places, and politics. Andrea had named her and Remo his Consuls. They were the only two he trusted completely, regardless of their inexperience.

It was Lyra who'd urged him not to summon the rulers to Saffiro. Let them meet on neutral ground, she'd said; peace begins with humility. Andrea had agreed, and placed the entire arrangement in her capable hands.

Remo, now serving as both Astrological Advisor and Consul to Emperor Andrea, had proposed that the summit be held during Libra season, the sign of peacemaking. Lyra had agreed at once; it felt fitting. She was drafting a letter in reply to the Lunarian Queen's ambassador when

Remo entered the library, joining her at the long oak table.

"Good morning," he greeted, setting down two cups of tea and a pair of cornetti wrapped neatly in cloth.

"Good morning, and thank you," she replied cheerily as she grabbed her steaming cup.

They hadn't revisited their talk from two weeks ago, when he'd revealed that he knew about her feelings for Andrea. She'd been mortified and secretly touched to learn he'd seen through her careful disguise.

Remo had an uncanny gift for reading her moods and seeing past her facades. She appreciated how his gaze lingered thoughtfully on her, while Andrea, by contrast, was always content to take her polite smiles as truth.

"Any progress choosing a location for the meeting?" Remo asked, tearing off a piece of his cornetto, his pale blue shirt rolled at the sleeves. He'd trimmed his dark hair shorter, and the loose strands falling over his forehead gave him an effortlessly charming look. Lyra bit back a smile, remembering how he'd kept a neatly groomed beard ever since she'd complimented him on it months ago.

"None," she admitted with a sigh, taking a sip of her favorite tea spiced with cinnamon and cloves, just the way she liked it. Remo always prepared it perfectly, sweetened to her taste without needing to ask. "And you? How's your draft coming along?"

At Andrea's request, and with his own eager volunteering, Remo had been tasked with drafting an accord between all seven kingdoms, to be signed at the upcoming summit. Andrea's hope was simple but ambitious: to create lasting peace throughout Terramundi, not through fear as his father had done, but through unity.

"It's coming along," Remo replied. "Though of course it'll have to pass through the Senate before it can be presented at the meeting. I imagine they'll have plenty of objections."

Lyra smiled faintly and returned to her letters. The two worked in companionable silence, the scratch of quills and rustle of parchment filling the air. As midday sunlight spilled through the tall windows, they finally set aside their work and agreed to take a stroll through the palace gardens to clear their heads.

# Remo

July blazed over Saffiro, the sun a white coin overhead as Remo and Lyra followed the garden path.

Golden lilies and clematis bloomed in profusion, turning their faces skyward. Remo almost smiled, thinking how these gardens were so unlike the ones in Mavortis; they were wilder here, louder, extravagant in their beauty.

For a moment, he thought of the company he used to keep among Mavortis' courtyards, and the memory of Sabelle tugged at him like a stone in his chest. Before it could settle there, he forced it away with words.

"Do you ever miss singing in those taverns back in Mavortis?" he asked, glancing at her. Lyra was good at distracting him; she made conversation easy.

Lyra tilted her head as she bent to admire a yellow lily speckled with orange. "Not really," she admitted. "I loved singing, but not the stage. I never quite grew comfortable performing. I'd get nervous before every show." A small shudder passed through her before she added more quietly, "I'll always be grateful for the work, though. And to Andrea, for helping me get it in the first place."

He knew her well enough to hear the unspoken debt in her tone. Lyra always spoke of Andrea with a reverence that left no room for anyone else.

"Andrea couldn't have gotten you work if you didn't already have the voice of an angel," Remo said. "If you'd sounded like me, not even an imperial decree could've convinced a tavern to host you for a night."

Lyra giggled, the sound bright and lilting. "Then I have to ask—what *does* your singing voice sound like?"

He fixed her with a serious look, though she was already grinning. "Legend has it that the last time I sang, every dog in the world howled in protest."

"Oh come now, you can't be *that* bad," Lyra teased. "Perhaps we should change our positions and serve as the emperor's official minstrels."

Remo flashed her a wry smile. "Are you trying to make sure Andrea stays wildly unpopular in his own court?"

Lyra's eyes widened as her laughter filled the garden. Then he caught his lip between his teeth, the weight of prohibited words pressing against his tongue, as he debated how to bridge from laughter to the conversation Andrea had expressly forbidden him to start.

He cleared his throat, the soft sound marking a shift in tone. "Do you ever think about going back to Satria? Just for a visit?"

Her laughter stilled instantly. The light in her face dimmed as she turned her gaze toward the marble fountain ahead. "I've written to my grandmother and sister," she said at last. "And now that Andrea's pardoned my father and he's out of prison, I'd like to see him again. But I don't think I can do it... go back there and face those memories."

Remo stayed silent, walking beside her in the hush that followed. When it became clear she wouldn't add more, he said softly, "No one will ever force you to go back there, Lyra. But if you ever did, I think you'd find you're stronger than you know."

She offered him a small, uncertain smile. "Wait... are there plans for a visit to Satria?"

Guilt twisted in Remo's chest as he nodded, confirming her suspicion. "As you know, Andrea wants to strengthen relations between Saffiro and Satria to help rebuild the kingdom as an independent power. But the Satrians are understandably wary of Saffiran influence. Having *you* there, a Satrian close to the emperor, could make a real difference. You're the first Satrian in history to hold a leadership position within the empire. Your presence alone would speak volumes."

The silence that followed stretched too long, and Remo felt the weight of it. He feared he'd gone too far.

"There are other ways to help," he added quickly. "The responsibility doesn't, and will never, fall solely on your shoulders. However involved you want to be is entirely your choice. I'm sorry for bringing it up." He grimaced. "It was my idea. Andrea argued with me for even suggesting it."

The memory of that argument still made Remo wince. He understood Andrea's protectiveness, but he couldn't agree with keeping Lyra in the dark about something that might empower her. She was a member of the Order of Aquarius, someone who had risked her life during the Seven Nation Standstill.

She had already faced danger that would have broken most people. And though part of him shared Andrea's instinct to shield her, another part knew Lyra was no fragile thing. She was a grown woman who had survived pain and loss and still met the world with grace. Shielding her entirely wasn't respect; it was a denial of her strength. She deserved the chance to decide for herself.

Lyra met his gaze. "Don't apologize. It's a really good idea," she said. "I'm the one who should be sorry. I *want* to help, I do. But I'm just... not ready to go back there. Not yet."

Remo shook his head, his expression gentle. "You don't owe me an apology—or anyone, for that matter. It's not your burden to carry. But if you ever did want to visit Satria, you wouldn't have to face it alone. I'd be right there with you."

Her small smile returned, tentative but genuine. "I promise I'll at least give the idea some thought," she said, dipping her chin slightly.

Remo smiled back, still fearing he'd reopened an old wound. But when he searched her eyes, he found resolve there, and the certainty that this moment would not be undone.

# Acknowledgments

I'd like to offer a special thank you to Mary-Grace Fahrun, author of *Italian Folk Magic*, for her insight into *tarocchi*, *malocchio*, and the witchy wisdom woven through the spiritual heritage of my bloodline.

Thank you to Tyler Penor of The School of Living Astrology for his holistic approach to teaching astrology—Cosimo sends his regards.

I wish to honor the diverse spiritual traditions whose wisdom has quietly shaped this book. The philosophies woven through *Awareness* draw inspiration from many lineages, from the contemplative practices of Tibetan Buddhism and Hindu Vedanta to Western mysticism and ancient animist understandings of the living world.

I'm endlessly grateful for the beauty and depth of these teachings. While the spiritual ideas in this story are creative interpretations, not representations of any specific faith or practice, they were written with deep respect and admiration for the cultures and philosophies that inspired them.

I'm also grateful to the voices and visionaries who've shaped my spiritual worldview: Steven Forrest, Dr. Joe Dispenza, Deepak Chopra, Michael A. Singer, Neville Goddard, Michael Newton, Eckhart Tolle, and so many others whose teachings have expanded the way I see the universe.

Thank you to the beautiful souls of the Bibliophiles book club. Your kindness, laughter, and support have meant the world.

Finally, thank you, reader, for opening your heart to a new story and letting this world live, even for a moment, inside your imagination.

# About the Author

**Danielle Cerrone** is a fantasy author and apprentice astrologer. She writes for those who live through books, and her first series begins with *The Mundane and the Arcane*, a blend of spiritual fantasy and slow-burn romance. She draws inspiration from her Italian heritage, history, and the magic hidden in everyday life.

She lives with her husband in Westchester, New York, where she can often be found decorating, giving natal chart readings, or exploring other fantasy worlds.

For updates, sneak peeks, and bonus content, visit daniellecerrone.com